I0741062

Joseph Gardner Swift, Harrison Ellery

# The Memoirs of Gen. Joseph Gardner Swift, LL.D., U.S.A.

first graduate of the United States Military Academy, West Point, Chief Engineer

U.S.A. from 1812-to 1818, 1800-1865 - to which is added a genealogy of the family

of Thomas Swift of Dorchester

Joseph Gardner Swift, Harrison Ellery

**The Memoirs of Gen. Joseph Gardner Swift, LL.D., U.S.A.**
*first graduate of the United States Military Academy, West Point, Chief Engineer U.S.A. from 1812-to 1818, 1800-1865 - to which is added a genealogy of the family of Thomas Swift of Dorchester*

ISBN/EAN: 9783337734114

Printed in Europe, USA, Canada, Australia, Japan

Cover: Foto ©Raphael Reischuk / pixelio.de

More available books at **www.hansebooks.com**

# THE
# MEMOIRS

OF

## Gen. Joseph Gardner Swift, LL. D., U. S. A.,

FIRST GRADUATE OF THE

UNITED STATES MILITARY ACADEMY, WEST POINT,

CHIEF ENGINEER U. S. A. FROM 1812 TO 1818.

1800—1865.

*To which is added a Genealogy of the Family of*

THOMAS SWIFT OF DORCHESTER, MASS., 1634,

BY HARRISON ELLERY,

*Member of the New England Historic Genealogical Society.*

PRIVATELY PRINTED.
1890.

Copyright, 1895,
By Harrison Ellery

# INTRODUCTORY.

The genealogy of the descendants of Thomas Swift of Dorchester, Massachusetts, which is added to these Memoirs, was written a few years ago, during leisure moments, with the intention of confining it to the first four generations of the family, and contributing the same to the pages of the *New England Historical and Genealogical Register.* It was to have been one of a series of genealogies of those families with which I am connected by marriage, and which I hoped from time to time to complete. But the temptation to all who engage in genealogical work to expand has been yielded to, and what was intended to be simply the history of the early generations of the family has become what this book contains.

While corresponding with various members of the family on the subject of its history, I found in possession of the sons of the late General Swift, of the United States Army, his journal. At my solicitation they permitted me to examine it. It proved a very interesting document, and it seemed to me that it would be a valuable contribution to history if printed. I suggested to them that it be embodied in one book with the genealogy, provided I could obtain enough subscribers to warrant it. They expressed their willingness,. and also from their family pictures contributed the illustrations which adorn the book.

General Swift was much interested in his family history, having made considerable effort to collect facts concerning his ancestry; and it seems particularly appropriate that what is herein printed on the subject should appear in connection with his Memoirs.

While the descendants of Thomas Swift who bear the name have been few, those of his contemporary, William Swift of Sandwich, Mass., with whom no relationship has as yet been established, have been very numerous. They may be found in all parts of the United States. But not all who bear the name of Swift in this country are descended from these two primitive settlers, for among the immigrants to this country during the past half-century will be found those who bear this respectable patronymic.

It is but justice to myself to say, that this genealogy was printed before the History of Milton, and that the use of my advance sheets was made by my permission, in writing the article on the Swift family which appears in that work.

HARRISON ELLERY.

# ILLUSTRATIONS.

# MEMOIRS.

---

*FROM THE DIARIES OF J. G. SWIFT.*

---

WEST POINT, July, 1807.

From very early life I have been in the habit of making memoranda of events, and in reference to persons who have in any wise interested me. This habit was induced by the example of my father, who left me often in care of his office, and with permission to peruse his diary. My earliest essays in this imitation were puerile, but they were kindly received by my mother, who taught me early to read, and who, pleased with my essays, encouraged my progress. As may be the case with most young people, a diary of their time, however impressive to them may have been the event when recorded, could afford but little to amuse, and less to interest, grown-up folks. I therefore set me down at my *alma mater* to review the records of my boyhood. A first impression is to obliterate all that precedes my entrance into the army—while indeed there can be but a morsel to glean in the seven years of cadet and subalternship in times of peace. I find myself at this time commandant of a post that had occupied some of the pages of our revolutionary history,—a housekeeper also at the head of a family of a wife and one son—so to amuse my leisure, and may be gratify my son, and may be to gratify a common feeling that " Every man's world is important to himself," I conclude to overhaul my files of diaries and to collate what might seem useful to show the influences that give a cast to a young man's pursuits.

Of the origin of my family : They were husbandmen from England, who migrated to Massachusetts Bay soon after the first colony landed at Plymouth.

Tradition lands them at Squantum, in Boston Bay. They were the family of Thomas Swift (son of Robert) from Rotherham in Yorkshire, which Thomas became a "freeman" 6th May, Anno 1635 ; the year his first son, Thomas, was born. He purchased fourteen hundred acres of land in Milton, then Dorchester, the eastern part of which tract is elevated and overlooks the whole of Boston Harbor, and is situate eight miles from Faneuil Hall, that cradle of American independence. This tract became subdivided among the descendants of the said Thomas. His oldest son, Thomas, my ancestor, was also the ancestor of the Swifts of Sandwich, and of Colonel Hermon Swift of the Revolutionary Army, of Chief Justice Zepheniah Swift, both of Connecticut, and also of the Swifts, Senator Swift of Vermont and Generals John and Philetus, of New York and other States of the Union.* He, the second Thomas, was also the father of Rev. John Swift of Framingham, and of Colonel Samuel Swift, a lawyer of Milton, whose oldest son, Samuel, was my grandfather, Samuel Swift, a graduate of Cambridge College, 1735, and who died in Boston 1775. Colonel Samuel Swift of Milton was also a judge of the court, and a member of the Ancient and Honorable Artillery of Boston, of which company also his son, my grandfather, Samuel, was a member. The oldest son of this Samuel was my father, Foster Swift, who studied medicine in Boston with Dr. Joseph Gardner; in February, 1783, married my mother, Deborah Delano, the daughter of Captain Thomas Delano, at Nantucket, where I was born the last day of the year 1783, during the absence of my father in Virginia. He had gone thither with letters to General Washington from General Lincoln, for the purpose of settling as a physician in the vicinity of his only brother, Jonathan Swift, a merchant of Alexandria. My maternal grandfather was a direct descendant from Philip de la Noye, a Huguenot or Protestant emigrant from Leyden to Plymouth. The variation in spelling the name is of record in the Plymouth annals, omitting the two final letters.

As was usual at Nantucket dwellings, my grandfather had constructed upon his house-top a " walk," with a staff and vane thereon, to indicate the

---

* Note.—General Swift is certainly in error here. Genealogical research does not connect, on this side of the Atlantic, the Swifts of Sandwich, who descend from William, with the Dorchester family.— *H. E.*

course of the wind, and also a mariner's compass and spy glass to observe the vessels going and coming upon whaling voyages. In this lucrative business Captain Delano had an interest. He had been an early and successful voyager to the Brazil Banks, and also a shipmaster in the London trade, which latter had enabled him to educate his sons in England. His daughter Deborah wrote a fair hand, and kept her father's accounts and correspondence. Her father was of a gentle nature and kind to children. He often gratified me with views from the "walk," and gave me ideas of the use of a spy glass and compass. He was also a sportsman, and occasionally took me with him to his farm at "Anaise" [Quaise?] and "Siasconset," near the sea side, from whence he brought returns in the "calash" of shoal duck and sea bass. He was also one of the proprietors of the sheep folds, and with him I have been to the Nantucket sheep washings and shearings, a period of much rejoicing in cakes and ale on that island of "primitive people." I was too young while residing with my grandparents to 1792, to note the peculiarities of the people, but my mother used to say that the simple and free visitings among Nantucket families was very unlike any association of other places of her residence. It was a confiding intimacy and unrestrained hospitality. Their tables were abundant in simple fare. Bread formed by baking green corn and from flour made of parched corn, and soup from the dried green corn, formed characteristic dishes at their unpretending tea drinkings, the prominent hour for sociability at Nantucket. My mother said that dinner gatherings were unusual, although it was not deemed good Nantucket fellowship to evade or decline to participate in a meal that might be suitable to the time of day that found a neighbor at their houses. Those days of simplicity have given place to fashion and less sincerity—and we may say, less happiness.

My father returning in bad health from Virginia, had determined to remove his family to Apponagansett, near New Bedford, and he there practiced medicine. I have a recollection hereabouts in time, 1789, of being tied to the pump on board a packet, to prevent my falling overboard. The occasion was one of a visit to my father's relations in Boston. It was the period of Washington's tour to New England, when, with many other children of larger growth, I was on Boston Common "beholding the hero." I have retained in memory the real or ideal features of Washington, as then seen, to which my mind refers whenever I see his portrait.

Near my father's residence there were mills on the Apponagansett River, and William Russel, the miller, was a "friend of the boys." He once sprang into the river and rescued me. I had fallen in from the bridge and cut my head against a stone in the bed of the stream, the scar from which is visible at this time, 1807. In 1792 my father removed his family to Taunton, a beautiful village on a river of that name, situate half way between Boston and Newport, and Providence, R. I., and New Bedford. Upon the spot where my father built his house was the tomb of Elizabeth Pool, which, with its monumental stone, was removed to the public cemetery. This woman was a bold adventuress from Taunton in England. She had purchased the township of Taunton from the Indians, and the town was incorporated by the General Court in 1630.

I was placed at Mr. Abner Alden's school. He was a good teacher and the author of some useful books. My last teacher had been "Master Hart," for the benefit of whose school I had been placed near him at a friend of my father's, John Smith, Esq., at the head of the Pasquemonset River. While my father was on a visit to me there occurred a scene which remains vivid in my memory. A negro had run away from Rhode Island, 1791. A rumor had reached "the head of the river" that William Anthony had apprehended the negro and would pass "the bridge" that night. The people were anxious to rescue the negro, and the boys of our school were employed in collecting stones at the bridge to intercept Anthony. The crowd of men, women and boys remained up until late in the night, when a horse's step was heard approaching rapidly. In spite of the missiles, Anthony plunged his horse into the crowd, and riding with ability he escaped, leaving the negro at the bridge. This instance is a strong indication of the feeling upon slavery. These people were worthy Quakers.

In the fall of this year, 1792, the small pox being rife in Boston, my father sent me thither to the care of his sister Lovering, and I passed lightly through that disease by the aid of my father's friend, Dr. L. Hayward. In

Boston I enjoyed the friendly attention of John Gardner, Esq., the author of "Helvetius" and other political essays in favor of Jay's treaty with England. He was the nephew and heir of Dr. Joseph Gardner of Boston, with whom my father studied medicine, and who had promised my father a legacy to me, his namesake. The legacy was never received, but Mr. John Gardner was my friend, and much contributed to my enjoyments at the public exhibitions in Boston.

In September of the following year, 1793, Miss Sally Cady, a very well educated and handsome young lady from Plainfield in Connecticut, opened a school on Taunton Green, a beautiful area of sward around which the village was situate. At this school, among other branches of instruction was taught drawing and declamation. I was a pupil, and proprietor of a nice writing desk and chair, a present from my father; it was quite an attractive novelty in the school, and I had the pleasure of having the pretty girls of the school exchanging their usual bench for a seat at my desk; which desk soon set the fashion that was followed by both girls and boys. Miss Cady introduced recitations from Noah Webster's "Third Part," and also dialogues between the girls and boys, taken from the works of Hannah More and other authors.

In the year 1794 I had become useful to my father by transcribing justice's papers. He was of the quorum, and I was also useful in his drug and medicine store, pending his professional rides in the adjacent country. Sometimes I accompanied my father in his rides on horseback. It was in this year that I commenced my boyish journal in imitation of my father's habit, and whose diary I was permitted to read and make extracts from, at his writing table. Among my father's books a Dictionary of Arts attracted my attention; a recipe therein to make fireworks induced me to experiment with gun powder. It took fire from heedlessness and burned me badly, from the effects of which I was unable to use my eyes for several weeks. A near neighbor, Mr. Cobb, hearing the concussion, ran to my father's office, and covered my blistered face with ink. In this plight I was taken to my mother, greatly to her dismay and alarm, in my father's absence; a scene of distress still vivid in my memory.

When my father's family removed from Dartmouth to Taunton, 1792, the Revolution of France was an absorbing theme of discourse, and a song among the boys. The village barber shop, Mr. Sider's, was ornamented with prints of the battle scene and overthrow of the Bastile, and with portraits of warriors and scenes of tumult in Paris. My father's diary had several aspirations against the influence that this revolution was exciting upon the minds of our countrymen, and especially on those who had a share in Shay's Rebellion, with the details of which insurrection he was familiar. He described to me the skirmish at Springfield in which General Shepard had a narrow escape from death by a shot from one of David Shay's followers. My father was also familiar with the scenes of our war of the Revolution, in which his father's family had suffered, and to which his father had fallen a victim, and died under the confinement inflicted upon him, and other prominent citizens of Boston. Among our family friends in Taunton was General David Cobb, who had been an *aid-de-camp* of Washington. I have heard him describe scenes of the war and of suffering at Valley Forge, but particularly of his agency in quelling the rebellion of Shay's, and of his having dispersed a band that had in 1786 assembled on Taunton Green to prevent the session of the courts of law in Bristol County. The band was commanded by one of Shay's lieutenants, one Valentine, of Freetown. General Cobb harangued the rebels, and being a judge also of the court of pleas, he told the rebels that he would that day sit a judge or die a general, and then ordered a field piece to be unlimbered and pointed at the rebels with the match lighted. They became panic-struck, and fled in dismay at the report of the piece that sent a ball over their heads. This Valentine was a noisy babbler to the mechanics and boys who assembled in pleasant evenings upon Taunton Green, to whom myself and others used to listen. His theme was the French Revolution, urging that our country should return the favor of the aid that France had given us in our late war, by joining our force to theirs to dethrone tyrants. This eloquence was popular with the boys until the rumor reached them of Genet's insulting Washington. This touched the patriotic feeling, and affection for the hero. The boys even began to question the propriety of the civic feasts given in

1793 in honor of French liberty. These feastings had become common in the country. When I was nearly ten years of age I was placed on the festive board to sing the translated French songs then common among the boys. I had a fair voice and my love for music was cultivated by a friend of my mother's, Mrs. Olive Leonard, who sang sweetly and played also on the guitar. Perhaps I owed some of my taste to a strolling Portuguese, Emanuel Cuidozo, who habitually visited our village and sung the plaintive airs of his native land, accompanying himself with the lute strung to his shoulder. This was a frequent entertainment in summer evenings on the Green, for which the boys contributed many "a copper." Emanuel had the tact to apply his Portuguese airs to American ballads, describing the battles of St. Clair with the Indians in 1791. A young officer, Lieutenant Cobb, had been killed in one of these battles. He was a Taunton boy and son of the general; the general was also our member in Congress at Philadelphia. He sent my father "Poulson's Daily Advertiser" and documents of Congress. These I used to read to my mother, by which means I had some vague ideas of the Constitution, and plied my mother with many a question about Congress. I remember an expression of force in my father's diary for 1791, that "Rhode Island had escaped damnation by adopting the Constitution." In his diary for 1794 he noted the resignation of Senator Jefferson as a treason to Washington's administration, after having served therein as Secretary of State. My father's diary also commented on the prominent conduct of Albert Gallatin in the Pennsylvania Rebellion, the whiskey boys' treason. He called the movement a leading act to aid in "overthrowing the system and policy of Washington to advance his country's glory and peace," etc.

In the following year, 1795, his diary notices the treachery of Secretary Randolph as an event of sad import to the character of American statesmen —the chief minister in the Cabinet betraying his trust. This notice was soon succeeded by remarks on the vileness of the assault on the integrity of Washington, made by a "Calm Observer" in the "Philadelphia Aurora." Early in the year 1796 his diary commends Jay's treaty with England, and scouts the idea of anti-Federalists who oppose the treaty on an assumption that it was virtually a breach of our alliance with France. My father denounced the assumption a Jacobinic emanation, and deemed the treaty the best that could be obtained while the United States had no navy to sustain its rights on the ocean. He rejoiced, therefore, that the Senate had adopted the treaty.

About these days the French cruisers began to capture our merchant ships. This, and the impressment of our seamen by the British cruisers, placed the country in a double dilemma—our treasury small, our means of defence in no condition to go to war with either power.

These items in my father's diary, and my newspaper readings to my mother, had furnished abundant themes for my comments and patriotic effusions that occupy several pages in my diary. They may as well be omitted here; they would not aid my son's reflections as well as the few extracts from his grandfather's journal.

1796. Very early in the history of Massachusetts, provision was made by law for schools, one to every fifty families. Nay, it was made a penal offence to omit their establishment. The same State at a later period endowed many academies with lands in Maine. Among the number was one incorporated, 1792, in Taunton. The construction of this academy was begun in 1795 and completed in 1796, in July of which year the building was dedicated to the care of Rev. Simeon Dogget, an highly educated graduate of Rhode Island College, and of Miss Sally Cady, whom I have previously mentioned. In this institution I commenced Latin, Greek and Geometry, with the then purpose of entering Harvard University. Among the scholars of the academy of whom I retain friendly and respectful remembrance were John Mason Williams, since a judge on the Massachusetts bench; Francis Baylis, a member of Congress and *Chargé* to Buenos Ayres; Nicholas Tillinghast; Edward Mitchell of South Carolina, a distinguished physician; Thomas Paine, an officer in the U. S. Navy; Charles B. King, an artist of City Washington; Henry and Charles Cobb; Jona. Ingalls; John Presbury; Charles Richmond, a manufacturer of great enterprise and energy; Appolos Cushman; Philo H. Washburn, a distinguished lawyer in Maine, etc. These halcyon days of '96–'97–'98 were of the most delightful character. On one occasion John Presbury was in default in composition. I sold him mine for cakes, and wrote another for myself; he won the prize and of course I was obliged to be mum. On another day my map was not ready, and Presbury put in his own for me. Such intercourse it is that makes the bonds of school-days strong.

In the year 1797 I lost a schoolmate and friend, Joseph Leonard, of the family that had been iron masters from the first days of the colony. His grave was for some time a rendezvous for several of his mates. He possessed fine generous qualities and was an excellent scholar.

In the year 1798 my cousin, William Roberdeau Swift, from Alexandria in Virginia, became a member of my father's family. He introduced the game of fine, at our school recesses, and he had a fine graphic talent.

It was in the same year that political parties became high in their disputes, and the respective sides taken by the parents were visible among their sons, and the boys had their discussion on the merits of Mr. Adams, Mr. Jefferson and Governor Pinkney, and English or French became the appelatives of men and boys. Among the laws of Congress was a "Stamp Act" which disturbed the people, more from the fact that the name recalled to mind one of the causes of the war of 1776 than from any inherent defect in the principle upon which the tax was based. My father was an inspector of the revenue and collector of the tax under this law. Occasionally it became my duty, in my father absence, to deliver these "stamps" for notes, bonds, &c., from which the boys called me an aristocrat.

At this time there resided in Taunton an Eaton scholar, Mr. Charles Leonard, the son of the Chief Justice of the island of Bermuda, and of the same family that I have before mentioned as iron masters in Raynham and Taunton. This gentleman took the fancy to give me lessons in drawing, and also upon the German flute, and he made me the present of a box of Reeves' water colors. To these he was prompted by observing me at work upon a camera obscura, to finish which he had furnished a suitable lens, and by which some sketches of Taunton Green and River were made. Soon after this my mother's brother, Captain Henry Delano, came from England and made us a visit. He had a fine voice, and taught me several of Dibden's sea songs. He brought with him his "freedom suit of clothes," a common perquisite in England, being made of fine scarlet cloth. He gave this suit to me, from which myself, and years after, my brother William and my own sons wore several garments. My uncle Henry was of a cheerful temper, a sailor and ship-master who had seen many vicissitudes. In a cruise to the Levant he had been captured by Algerines, and retained in slavery several years, and finally ransomed by his adopted country, England, where he had been educated and apprenticed to a London merchant. He married a lady of the family of Osborne, and resided near the "Bell in Edmondton." In the ensuing winter of 1798, I had an escape from drowning. While skating upon the river at the margin of my father's garden, in company with my cousin, Wm. R. Swift, and in presence of my parents and uncle Henry, I broke through the ice and disappeared, while my cousin had turned to another direction. Providentially I rose to the surface through the broken ice, and was drawn to the shore by a pole extended to me by Mr. Sherman, a Quaker, who, with several others of his sect, were near the river side "on the prison limits." They were confined by process of law for conscience sake—the Quakers refusing to perform militia duty.

There was at this time residing in Taunton Mr. Benjamin Dearborn, a very ingenious machinist and much respected citizen. He had established in that town a factory of steel-yard balances. His factory was a very interesting place to me, and he not only indulged my visits but he also taught me the use of a theodolite, invented by himself, and aided me in the construction of a wooden circumferentor, with which I made a survey of Taunton Green—the plot and diagram of which is now among my files.

In these days we became familiar with the name of Talleyrand and the French Directory, and of his offering our ambassadors money to form a treaty. These, and the accounts of French cruisers capturing our merchant ships, tended to encourage the building ships of war, the "Constitution," etc. Several of our youths were ripe for becoming midshipmen, and General Cobb had many applications to procure warrants for them. Some of these applicants succeeded. My mother's views were of a peaceful nature. Her family were of the sect of Quakers, or Friends, and her preference was that I should become a physician; my own inclinations were to become a traveler. Readings to my mother had furnished excitement to this purpose. The appointment of General Washington to the command-in-chief of the army had given a serious aspect to the times, and consequently there was an increasing amount of subjects for discussion among men, and by similar consequence the interest spread among the boys. I listened to the conversation between General Cobb and my father on the prospects of anti-Federalism — a party that opposed a war. The building of two frigates was deemed an untimely threat to France, and the Federalists were accused of a purpose to aid England in arresting the march of liberty among our allies. The boys generally were disposed to favor both army and navy, and we began to form companies in the "Manual Exercise," etc.

By the summer of 1799 I was prepared to enter Cambridge College. It was at this period that there marched into town, and encamped on a beautiful site near the margin of Taunton River, the 14th United States regiment of infantry, commanded by Colonel Nathan Rice, composed of two incomplete battalions of the Provisional Army. My father became the temporary surgeon of this regiment, whereby, as his messenger, I became a familiar in the tents of the officers. In a few weeks thereafter Captain Amos Stoddard marched a company of United States Artillerists and Engineers into camp, on its route to garrison Rhode Island Harbor. This officer was an intimate friend of my father's, and had been a student of law in our neighbor, Judge Padelford's office, on Taunton Green. It was very pleasant to me to find that this officer recognized me as an acquaintance. Lieutenants Williams and Steel were his subalterns. In their visits to my father's family they indulged me with accounts of the artillery service, and asked me if I would like to be a cadet in their corps. Here was a charm for a boy. Under its influence I urged my parents to request the aid of General Cobb to procure a cadet's warrant. Mr. John Gardner of Boston, whose country residence was near that of President Adams, interested himself in this matter. He gave Mr. Adams a sketch of Taunton Green, a specimen of my crude pencilling. These gentlemen procured from Mr. Adams the promise that the Secretary of War should send me the warrant in the ensuing spring of 1800.

My whole time was now devoted to reading whatever I could find on military subjects. My preceptor, Mr. Dogget, permitted me the use of his library, and from the encyclopædia I transcribed the articles "Gunnery," "Fortification," "War" and "Pyrotechnics," and copied all the plans, including the implements of Sappers and Miners. Lieutenant Steel had loaned me the military works of Muller, which I found, in several articles, too profound for me.

At the close of this year of 1799, the death of Washington spread dismay throughout the country.

In Taunton, as in most other towns throughout the Union, there was much gathering of the people at the funeral obsequies. The boys of our village were permitted to join the procession, and it was my province to draw devices for the truncheons of the Marshals, and for the banner borne by the scholars of the academy.

Anno 1800. With the anxiety of a boy I waited upon the post office from an early day in the spring of this year, for the result of the promise of President Adams. Late in the month of May my eyes were gladdened by the sight of the frank of Secretary "McHenry," containing my warrant of cadet, dated 12th May, 1800, with orders to report myself for duty with Colonel Lewis Tousard, the commandant of engineers in the harbor of Newport, R. I. My excellent mother soon filled my trunk, and also, giving my schoolmates an evening party for my leave-taking, dispatched me in less than three weeks, so that on 12th June I presented myself to Major Daniel Jackson of the Artillery, at Newport, who commended me to Lieutenant-Colonel Lewis Tousard, the engineer of the harbor. This veteran gentleman received me with courtesy, invited me to dine, and introduced me to Mrs. Tousard, and a handsome Philadelphia lady, Miss Gillespie, who appeared young enough to be the daughter of the colonel. I was attached to the company of Captain Stoddard, at Fort Wolcott, and received as a member of the officers' mess, renewing my acquaintance with Lieutenant Steel, and returning to him the works of Muller previously mentioned. Colonel Tousard had been a Captain in Count Rochambeau's army; was at the battle of Quaker Hill, 1778, where he lost an arm in a very gallant action. This want of a limb, and his fine military aspect gave the veteran an heroic appearance; and although one-armed he was a good draughtsman, and favored me with some lessons in military plan-drawing, and he also bestowed upon me a case of Paris drawing instruments. The colonel sent me, in the capacity of aid, in his barge to look after and bring him account of the works on the forts at the Dumpling Rocks, and at Rose Island, Fort Adams and Fort Wolcott. These works were then closing under the immediate care of Lieutenant Droasy—in fact suspending for want of appropriations—leaving, among other exposed walls, those of an extensive barrack at Fort Hamilton, on Rose Island, in an unfinished condition. Fort Wolcott was one of the designs of Colonel Rochefontaine, a very small redout of a Cross-Moline form, enclosing a stone magazine, upon which is engraved the name of that officer, and Mr. Boss, the United States agent, to commemorate the event of its erection, 1794; and on the key-stone of the gateway arch at Fort Adams, the names of Colonel Tousard and John Adams, the President of the United States, were inscribed, for similar information, 1798. A "South Wing Battery," as it was called, was constructing at Fort Wolcott, and of earth, and it was my duty to superintend the laborers in forming this parapet, upon which were mounted six thirty-two pound cannon; in which operation I received my first lesson in the use of the "French Gin," in proving some brass howitzers that had recently been received from the foundry of Mr. Paul Revere, of Boston.

The change of scene from quiet Taunton Green to military duty upon the fortifications of Rhode Island was a charm, and it was some time before the novelty wore off, and before the reveillé found me in bed. The circles of Newport were rendered fashionable by the summer residence there of several Carolina families, and, though young, I was favored by the attentions of some of them, and by those of the resident families, the Gibb's, Champlain, Auchmety, Hunter, Whitehouse, and Mr. Gold S. Silliman.

The period had arrived for the disbandment of the Provisional Army, a part of which, with its ranks not half filled, was cantoned at Oxford, Massachusetts, including the 14th Regiment before mentioned; the military stores from whence were re-stored in the garrison of Newport Harbor, in the making returns of which I had my share of employment. In this summer arrived General Hamilton, with his suite, Colonel Aaron Ogden and Captain Abraham R. Ellery, to inspect the fortifications and the troops in the harbor. It was my good fortune to be charged with the salute of cannon at Fort Wolcott, and on resuming my position on parade was introduced to the general, who, may be in consideration of my youth, complimented me on the accuracy of time in the salute, and invited me to join the other officers at dinner at "Thomas Townsend's," in town. The deportment of the general was a very easy and pleasant dignity, and I listened with all my ears to his remarks. Among the guests at the general's dinner were Captain Perry, United States Navy, and his son, Oliver H., who had entered the service as midshipman a few months before my becoming a cadet, and with whom a pleasant intimacy was formed, and indulged at my own quarters and in the steerage on board the frigate General Green. Before and after dinner comments were made upon the fact that President Adams had not promoted General Hamilton on the death of Washington—some of them not flattering to the justice of the President—but the pretensions of other generals, and the settlement of prominent difficulties with France, were deemed to be sufficient reasons for the omission.

In the fall of the year I visited my mother at Taunton, and instead of finding her in the new house, had to witness its destruction by fire on the 16th of September, during my father's absence at Nantucket, whither he had gone to receive some aid to pay for this building from the estate of my grandfather, who had died in November, 1799, at the age of 68. This scene was very sad, but my mother bore it with an equanimity that distinguished her among those who knew her best. As is common in house-burnings, suspicions were in this case attached to an incendiary; but it was ludicrous to hear a superstitious cant that the fire was a divine retribution for disturbing the ashes of Elizabeth Pool — before alluded to as the first proprietor of the town, and whose tomb had become the site of my father's house. In the month of October I returned to my post at Fort Wolcott. The company drill had become an old story, but we were amused with some experiments in throwing thirty-two pounder shot, some of which, at a small elevation, reached the Dumpling Rocks. At this place Colonel Tousard had commenced an oval tower, to form a cross-fire with the other forts. Its unfinished caserns were left by Congress exposed to decay in common with other masonry at the three other forts. In our recreations at the mess table politics, as a topic, were not tolerated, although the officers held decided opinions, and were generally Federalists. During the past seasons of 1800 there had been much irritation through the country on the coming elections. President Adams, it was said, had abandoned the Federalists, by whom he had been elected, and his conduct to his Cabinet was said to be disrespectful to the memory of Washington, whose Cabinet Mr. Adams had retained. But Mr. Adams was not quiescent under the insults of France, and this course was deemed by the Jacobins an offence to gratitude. We had letters of marque and some frigates at sea, and the "Insurgent," forty-four, had been captured by Commodore Truxton in the "Constellation," thirty-six, while a third embassy to France had been instituted. This endangered the election of Mr. Adams or General Pinkney, at the same time that the urgency of M. Talleyrand, to come to terms so suddenly after insulting our embassy, was deemed to promote the elevation of Mr. Jefferson. The convention, in the finale, had secured nothing but promises to adjudicate at some undefined period for the spoliations committed on the seas. These were prolific subjects in all societies, and their discussion created much personal animosity. My friend, Captain Stoddard, to whose mind I was wont to defer, said that these relations with France were risking the permanence of Federal measures, while other Federalists held that Mr. Adams' course was wise and peaceful. At any rate, these discrepancies were confusing the action of the Federal party, and advancing the influence of Mr. Jefferson.

There were portions of the work at Fort Adams, upon the magazine and wharf, that were incomplete, and which the artificers of the companies of Stoddard and Henry had been detailed to execute. I was placed on duty there under the direction of Lieutenant Droasy, and attached to the artillery company of Captain Henry, and became messmate of Lieutenant John Knight and Lieutenant John W. Livingston, a native of New York, and a gentleman of prudent and systematic habits. Lieutenant Knight was of a more errant character. He was from the Eastern Shore of Maryland, and married Miss Sally Malbone of Newport, by whose introduction I became acquainted with her brother, Edward Malbone, the artist, and also Mr. Washington Allston, the intimate associate of Mr. Malbone, and a recent graduate of Cambridge College—both of them very interesting gentlemen. I found Captain John Henry an Irishman of many pretensions, but his wife a pleasant acquaintance. She was a daughter of the family of Ruché, or Duché, of Philadelphia. The lady was a Swedenborgian, and she observed some peculiar rites of that sect.

1801. It was not until the lapse of some half dozen of years that the essay of Mr. Adams to commend appropriations for defensive work son the coast and Niagara frontier was revived. The appropriations for the army for the year 1801 were two millions, and for the *fabrication* of *arms*, and for *repairs* of fortifications, six hundred and thirty thousand dollars.

Early in the winter of this year Major William McRea, of the 2d Artillery, had relieved Major Jackson in the command of Newport Harbor. Our new commandant was from Virginia. He had been a captain in the 3d Sub Legion, under Generals Wayne and Wilkinson. He married in Newport a belle, Miss Mary Champlain. The major established his quarters at Fort Adams, and received me into his mess. The winter was very boisterous, and my chief employment was reading.

At this time the change of the national administration to the presidency of Mr. Jefferson had not evinced any material change of measures. Much disturbance was exhibited in the newspapers as proceeding from office-bidders and office-seekers. Mr. Jefferson was, in the opinion of the *latter*, too tardy in displacements, a measure of doubtful utility generally; and as ejecting subordinates, it is undoubtedly a vicious policy, the office being intended for public, and not for personal benefit, save by its incidental effects. The official experience of clerks is a species of national property, and changing them, save for incapacity, vice, or old age, must produce delays and errors in official transactions.

The 4th of July was this year celebrated at the forts in Newport Harbor with a display suitable to the day, and also with some show in town, where William Hunter, Esq., was the orator; a gentleman who had been educated in England—a Federalist. His oration was deemed by our officers to be too florid, but to my apprehension, it was learned and beautiful. Mr. Hunter had a small collection of fine paintings at his residence, the work of Rosa de Tivoli. These pictures had been presented, in Italy, to the father of Mr. Hunter, who had been a surgeon in the British army, and "who had rendered important professional aid to some gentlemen of distinction near Florence," who had bestowed these pictures on the doctor. These specimens of art were placed in the Academy of Fine Arts in the Bowling Green, New York.

In the ensuing month of August I had leave of absence to visit my father's family at Taunton, and was accompanied by my brother cadet, Lewis Lowdais, the brother of Lieutenant Philip of the 1st Artillery. I found that since I had been home a brother had been born, who was named for two of my mother's brothers, William and Henry. While in Taunton I apprehended a deserter from the army, one Seth Robbins, and marched him and myself to Newport — thirty-six miles, in twelve hours — and for which service the Secretary of War, General Dearborn, had directed the reward of ten dollars, to be sent to me by Mr. William Simmons. Robbins made an unsuccessful essay to leave me on the road, which made it needful to bind both his hands.

During this summer of 1801 General Dearborn, the Secretary of War, had given notice to our little army that President Jefferson had directed the establishment of a military school at West Point, for the instruction of cadets, under the law of 1794 and subsequent acts of Congress that authorized the appointment of professors of the arts and sciences, and for the purchase of apparatus and instruments necessary for the instruction of the artillerists and engineers. General Washington had uniformly, and to the close of his life, urged the necessity of this school, and had made an effort in 1794 to open such a school at West Point, but the officers did not relish the discipline of a school — at least it was so said of the younger by several of the older officers of the army.

On the first of October I received a letter from General Dearborn directing me to repair to this school. The order found me in the act of closing a survey of the forts in Newport Harbor, and in making a schedule of the armament, by the order of Major McRea. As soon as this duty was accomplished, to wit, on the 7th October, I took my passage on board a New York packet "up the Sound" and arrived at the city on the 10th. This was my first voyage so far from home. The next morning I took a "Whitehall boat" to Governor's Island and presented my letter of introduction from Lieutenant Knight to Dr. James Scanlan, the surgeon of Fort Jay on that island, who presented me to Captain Cochrane and the other officers of the garrison. The doctor proposed an excursion to the various points in the beautiful bay, and in the garrison barge the following day accompanied me to the old military works on Brooklyn and Gowanus Heights, the scene of the first discomfiture of Washington, Anno 1776. The doctor was a great admirer of military history, and quite familiar with the scenes before us. The courtesy of this gentleman made a strong impression on my memory. He was from the eastern shore of Maryland, and a relation of Lieutenant Knight of Fort Adams. On the 14th October in a Newburg packet I was sailing before a fine breeze up the Hudson. The day was clear and the palisades and precipitous walls were a novelty in height, as they have been to multitudes of other travelers. From failure of wind and tide the vessel came to anchor in Haverstraw Bay, near Stony Point, and the master permitted me the use of his boat and an oarsman to visit the ground where Wayne and Gibbons had won laurels in the storm of that point. The entrance into the highlands was at sunset — an impressive scene to one who had never before seen a mountain like the "Dunderberg." We reached West Point at dusk. The name of this place had raised many pictures to my imagination of Revolutionary history — the treason of Arnold; the fate of André. It was a calm October evening; the only sound was that of the cow bell. This sound at West Point has no doubt left a pleasant remembrance with many a cadet. To this day the sound of the cow bell revives the evening of my first landing at West Point. I reported myself to the commandant, Lieutenant Osborn, and to Professor Baron. Was received by Lieutenant William Wilson and Lieutenant Lewis Howard as a member of their "artillery mess." Professor Baron furnished me with Dr. Hutton's Mathematics, and gave me a specimen of his mode of teaching at the blackboard in the academy. The academic hours were four in each morning, from eight o'clock. There were twelve cadets that formed, as yet, one class. The lesson to be given was accompanied with a lecture from Mr. Baron upon its application. The afternoons of the day were variously occupied in some brief military exercises, but much more in field sports. Our professor, George Baron, was a north of England man from Berwick-on-Tweed, or South Shields. He had been a fellow teacher with Charles Hutton of the military academy at Woolwich. Mr. Baron was of rude manner but he was an able teacher. He deemed Lieutenant Wilson's hospitality to me as too exclusive, and wished me to join a small mess of cadets who were not comfortably lodged; and moreover there was as yet no regular cadet mess at the Point. Soon after my stating this objection to Mr. Baron, he sent his servant with a verbal order to me on this subject of mess. I declined receiving any order from the mouth of a servant. In an hour after Mr. Baron appeared at the fence of the yard called the old artillery quarters, in which I was conversing with Lieutenant Wilson. He said to me, "Do you refuse to obey my orders?" My reply was, "No, sir, but I refuse to receive a verbal order by any servant." Mr. Baron replied, "You are a mutinous young rascal." I sprang over the fence to assault Baron. He fled to the academy, and thither I followed him. He bolted the door in my face, and from the window of the upper story, the "long room," he applied coarse epithets, and to which I retorted. At this time Mr. Bradock Havens, the master of the Butter-Milk Falls packet "Ranger" was passing, and Mr. Baron desired him to witness my language. In less than an hour after Cadet S. Gates called on me with a written order to consider myself in arrest. The whole of these things I faithfully reported to the Secretary of War. By some influence unknown to me General Dearborn condescended to write to me in reply, advising me to make some apology to Mr. Baron and avoid dismissal from the army. To this considerate attention Lieutenant Wilson counseled my rejoinder, stating that the officers of the post deemed Mr. Baron's conduct to me so ungentlemanly and irritating that an apology could not be made to him. At this juncture a circumstance occurred that suspended action against me, and an official report was made to the Secretary of War by the commandant, Lieutenant Osborn, that Mr. Baron had been guilty of a crime. Mr. Baron was placed in arrest in the month of November, therefore the academic course was suspended, and I was at leisure, and my arrest of no further restraint than it held me in readiness for trial. A portion of my leisure was employed in exploring the Point more minutely than I had done and the hills and redouts in the vicinity.

West Point Plain is one hundred and ninety feet above the level of the Hudson, and forms an area of seventy acres bounded by the margin of the plain overlooking the river on the east and north. The buildings which I found on my first arrival at the Point were, at the dock a stone house; on the brow of the hill above the first dwelling is the "White quarters," the residence then of the commandant, Lieutenant Osborn, and his beautiful wife; and then the artillery mess of Lieutenants Wilson and Howard. The academy is situated on the western margin of the plain, near the base of rocks on whose summit, four hundred feet above, stands Fort Putnam. Near the academy was an office on the edge of a small hollow, in which depression were the remains of a mound that had been formed at the close of the Revolution, to celebrate the birth of a Dauphin of France, our great ally in those days. To the south of this relic were the headquarters that had been the residence of General Knox and the scene of many an humble meal partaken by Washington and his companions in arms, at this time the residence of Major George Fleming, the military store-keeper. Farther south the quarters of Lieutenant J. Wilson and A. Macomb, and a small building afterwards used for a laboratory. In front of these was the model yard, containing a miniature fortress in wood, used in the lectures on fortification, the handiwork of Colonel Rochefontaine and Major Rivardi. Around this yard Cadet Armistead and myself planted twelve elm trees. To the south and at the base of Fort Putnam Hill also were Rochefontaine's quarters, now the residence of the family of Lieutenant Colonel Williams; diagonally from the garden gate of these quarters Rochefontaine had constructed a paved foot walk to the barrack on the northeast side of the plain, now the cadet's quarters. They are two hundred and forty feet in length and were constructed by Major Rivardi, whose quarters were in a building at the northern base of the Fort Putnam Hill, by the road leading to the German Flats and Washington's Valley. Below the plain at the northwest, near the river, were the military stores, two long yellow buildings, containing the arms and accoutrements of the army of Burgoyne and also numerous brass ordnance surrendered at Saratoga, and especially a couple of brass "grasshoppers" taken by General Green in South Carolina, and by resolve of Congress presented to that very distinguished commander—all under the care of Major Fleming, who seemed to view them as almost his own property, he having served in the conquest at Berries Heights and Saratoga. To the east of these stores was the armory, and also the residence of Zebina Kingsley, the armorer, and his exemplary wife. To the east was the hospital, under the charge of Dr. Nicholas Jones, our surgeon, and brother of Mrs. Lieutenant Osborn. At the northeast angle of the plain was Fort Clinton, a dilapidated work of Generals Drefortail and Kosciusko, engineers in the Revolutionary War. This work was garnished with four twenty-four-pounder cannon, on sea coast carriages. The fort also enclosed a long stone magazine filled with powder "many years of age." The gloomy portals of these walls might remind one of Dante's Inferno. To the west, overlooking the plain and five hundred feet of elevation, is Fort Putnam, a stone casemated castle, having on its platform a couple of twenty-four-pounder field pieces of artillery. This work was commenced in 1777, and had been repaired at various periods and never completed. The tradition was that Arnold had purposed to admit British troops from the rear of this castle to overawe the plain and works below. A surer plan for the purpose of the traitor could not have been devised. On the eastern margin of the plain and sixty feet below, there are stone steps leading to a small area whose outward edge is of rock, sloping almost vertically to the Hudson. In this area is a small basin in which had played a fountain, the whole having been constructed by Kosciusko, and was his retreat and called after him, "Kosciusko's Garden." Lieutenant Macomb and myself had repaired this garden, and it is a favorite resort.

Some ninety yards south of Rivardi's barracks is a circular depression in the plain, on the west margin of which are the ruins of the "old provost." Nearly a mile northwest of the Point a ravine leads to a cascade over a rock, the water from which winds to the Hudson at the "red house," the occasional resting place of Washington, called Washington's Valley, and is at the termination of the slope of the Crow's Nest, a mountain of fifteen hundred feet in altitude that overlooks the point and river and many miles around. Adjoining the south boundary of the plain a road leads down the bank of the Hudson to Butter-Milk Falls and to Fort Montgomery. The last named is the scene of the defeat of General Clinton, October, 1777. The road previously mentioned passed through the farm of Esquire North, whose house stood near the south boundary of the plain, a tavern that much annoyed the command at West Point by selling rum to the soldiers, because of an illegal act of Captain Stelle of the army, who in 1794 had levelled a field piece at North's house and suffered a severe penalty therefor in a law suit. Mr. North's victory proved him to be a bad citizen, and his success an evidence of the law's supremacy.

In the fall of this year, 1801, Lieutenant-Colonel Tousard had established his family in the Rochefontaine quarters as "inspector of artillery," and on his departure to this duty at various points, Niagara, etc., he requested me to escort Madame Tousard to the city, New York, a very pleasant excursion

—and in the city, with the families of William Denning, Esq., of Beverly, near West Point, and that of his son-in-law, Mr. William Henderson, my time was very agreeably passed. To the family of Mr. Denning I had been introduced by Lieutenant William Wilson, and generally dined there on Sundays. This place, Beverly, was the headquarters of General Arnold and the scene of his first open act of treason, when he escaped in his barge to the Vulture. My lodging room at Beverly had been the chamber of Arnold. It was at Mr. Denning's that I first met Aaron Burr, who was then a guest at Beverly. The place had been the property of Beverly Robinson, who with his family had fled to Nova Scotia in the Revolution, and the property had been confiscated under the laws of New York, and purchased by Mr. Denning.

In December I returned to West Point and reported myself to Major Jonathan Williams, the inspector of fortifications. Mr. Jefferson had required of this gentleman "to repair to West Point and make himself thoroughly acquainted with the military school recently there established, and to assume the superintendence of the same." Major Williams received the cadets at his hospitable board in the "Rivardi quarters," and stated to us the course of instruction that he proposed to pursue. Mr. Baron's case had first to be examined by a board of officers; improprieties were proved, and by order of the President, Mr. Baron was dismissed with unusual marks of disgrace, *i. e.*, his name was set upon the public buildings as a disgraced officer. The court found me "guilty of using disrespectful words to my superior officer," but I was released and ordered to duty.

Mr. Jefferson had now been in office nearly a year, and though it was said that he was opposed to the existence of the army, still there had been in this year, 1801, $230,000 appropriated to repair and keep in order the fortifications that had been commenced in 1794 and 1798, and $400,000 for the fabrication of arms; nevertheless I had left the works of Rhode Island nearly suspended.

Politics were not generally discoursed upon at the Point, although the political opinion of every person there was well known, and newspapers of both parties were taken. My paper was Major Ben Russel's *Columbian Centinel*, of Boston.

In the ensuing spring the new military law of Congress, of 16th March, had remodeled the army, and discharged many a worthy. Among the number was the veteran Tousard and Lieuteant Droasy, my instructors upon the public works in Newport Harbor. The case of Lieutenant-Colonel Tousard occasioned much sorrow at West Point. He was aged, and had been crippled in the service of the country; an industrious officer, well educated at the military school of La Fere in France. By the operation of the law some promotions had been made in the new corps of engineers.

In April the Academy was opened under the Professorate of Captain William Amhurst Barron, formerly a captain of artillerists and engineers, and transferred to the new corps. He had been a tutor in mathematics in the University of Cambridge, of which he was a graduate and classmate of John Quincy Adams. He was the son of a surgeon in the army of England, who belonged to the medical staff of Lord Amhurst in Canada, and for whom Captain Barron was named. He was of a social temper and kind nature, and these qualities did not impair his ability as a teacher; he had a facility in teaching. In a few weeks thereafter Captain Jared Mansfield, of the engineers, became the acting professor of Natural and Experimental Philosophy at the academy. This gentleman had a high reputation for learning, and was the author of an erudite essay on the Motion of Bodies in Free Space. He had been a teacher in Yale College, and was an intimate of Mr. Jefferson's. The course of study was Hutton's Mathematics, Enfield's Philosophy and Vaubau's Fortification, with practical exercies in the field in Surveying.

In the month of May a letter from Major McRea, the commandant at Newport, R. I., requested me to report the survey of the fortifications in Newport Harbor that had been made by me under his orders, to Major Williams, the inspector, and which I did my best to accomplish. This was my first essay, and it was favorably received by the inspector. This report occasioned me to examine what had been done by the government. I found that the inspectorship of fortifications and employment of two engineers had been authorized by Congress in the year 1799, implying a new purpose on the part of the government, to improve upon the system commenced in 1794, and somewhat enlarged in 1798. In the first years of the government under the new Constitution — 1789 and '90 — the whole expenditure of the War Department had been $137,000. In the two following years the Western Indians, instigated by our own rapacity for land, and by the policy of England to retard the progress of the Union, had brought on a war in the North-West Territory that resulted at first in the defeat of General St. Clair, but ultimately in the overthrow of the Indian power by General Wayne, by the battle of the Maumee, in 1796. The expenditures on these wars from 1791 to 1794, including the purchase of arms, had been $923,000. In the year 1794 Congress appropriated $76,000 for maritime fortifications, and $96,000 for armament, and $131,000 for Western defences. This maritime system of defence on the Atlantic border embraced the harbors of Portland, Portsmouth, Gloucester, Salem, Marblehead, Boston, Newport, New London, New York, Philadelphia, Wilmington, Del., Norfolk, Alexandria, Ocracock and Cape Fear, Georgetown, Charleston, Savannah and St. Mary's. In selecting sites for these works, those where defences had been constructed in the Revolutionary War indicated the suitable points. Colonel Rochefontaine, Major Rivardi and other officers of the regiment of artillerists and engineers were employed in the construction of small redouts. None of sufficient area could have been attempted under a fund of $76,000, nor prosecuted usefully in the three following years; during which period $94,000 had been appropriated among these works, including $20,000 for West Point, appropriated in 1796. But early in the year 1798 the aspect of war with France had induced Congress to appropriate $310,000 for fortifying the Atlantic harbors.

In the month of June I became security for the payment of a debt of $119 by Lieutenant Strong of the army, son of Colonel David Strong, 4th Infantry. This affair gave me extreme trouble, my income being meagre. Strong left West Point with promise of early payment, but he got into bad company, became an inebriate, and soon after committed suicide in prison.

In July, by transfer, I became a cadet of engineers. The corps, as organized by the law of 16th of March, 1802, consisted of Lieutenant Colonel Jonathan Williams, a gentleman of much learning and devoted to science. He was born in Boston, and had been brought up in his father's vocation, a merchant. He had been a man of business in London, married the daughter of William Alexander, of the Scottish family of Sterling. Mr. Williams had also been the agent of the United States at Paris and Nantz under the auspices of Dr. Franklin, his kinsman, and who bequeathed to Mr. Williams a part of his library. Mr. Jefferson had said that Mr. Williams resembled Dr. Franklin in character and pursuits of science. It was at the instance of Mr. Jefferson that Colonel Williams was placed at the head of the corps of engineers. The next officer in that corps was Major Decius Wadsworth, a graduate of Yale, a good mathematician. He had been a captain of the artillerists and engineers. Then followed Captain William A. Barron and J. Mansfield, previously mentioned, and Lieutenant James Wilson, a highly educated gentleman, the son of the Judge of the United States Supreme Court, who had distinguished himself in the Constitutional Convention of Pennsylvania, and Lieutenant Alexander Macomb, late a cornet of dragoons and aid-de-camp to General William North, the adjutant-general of the late Provisional Army. Neither Wilson nor Macomb had been cadets. The number of cadets at the academy was twelve. Among them were Simon Magruder Levy, from a respectable Jew family of Baltimore, and formerly a sergeant in Captain Lockwood's company of infantry, and thence promoted to cadet for his merit and mathematic attainments. He was now twenty-five years of age. Walker Keith Armistead, from Virginia, a very amiable young gentleman of eighteen years of age, and to whom I was much attached; Henry B. Jackson, son of the major of artillery, and John Livingston, a merchant of Norfolk, Va.; then Ambrose Porter, a man of six feet height and abounding in story-telling talent; Joseph Proveaux, from Charleston, S. C., a youth of seventeen, of generous spirit but passionate, addicted to duelling and much opposed to study; two brothers, Samuel and William Gates, the sons of Captain Lemuel Gates of the army—the former a good scholar and very taciturn— the latter was the youngest cadet at the Point, very active, a sportsman and a general favorite among the cadets; Hannibal Montresor Allen, a wild youth of seventeen years, the son of Ethan of Ticonderoga memory; Julius Frederick Heileman, a handsome youth of sixteen years, the son of a surgeon in our army at Fort Jay, who had belonged to the corps of Colonel Baum of the Hessian corps of England, at the battle of Bennington.

During the summer I was attached to the company of artillery of Captain George Izard, as acting lieutenant. In some infantry exercises a private soldier, Wm. Goodwin, on the left flank of the company, had lodged several cartridges in his musket before it gave fire. The piece burst, wounded Goodwin severely and prostrated me upon the ground, from which I was confined to the hospital for several days. My captain was the son of Ralph Izard, the United States Senator from South Carolina. Captain Izard had been educated at the Military School of Metz, in France; and at the Experimental School of Metz, he was esteemed to be an accomplished officer. He had a fine collection of books and charts, and very kindly permitted me to look into them. He was at this time suffering from a wound received in a duel with Mr. Pierre of Philadelphia. The cause was the captain's declining to fulfill an engagement with the sister of Mr. Pierre, but without the least injury to the honor of the lady.

During this year there was no new fort commenced in our maritime harbors, and the appropriation of $70,500 was not sufficient to keep the redouts in repair.

Early in this summer of 1802 Lieutenant Macomb and myself repaired the dilapidated garden of Kosciusko, relaid the stone stairway to the dell, and opened the little fountain at the base of " Kosciusko's Rock" in the garden; planted flowers and vines and constructed several seats, which made the spot a pleasant resort for a reading party. In the exercises in the field, Colonel Williams commenced with the cadets a survey of the country about the Point by a series of triangles, to determine the position and altitude of the adjacent mountains. It was found that Crow's Nest summit was one thousand four hundred and eighty feet above West Point Plain; the Break Neck, one thousand five hundred; Anthony's Nose, below the Point, nine hundred; the Sugar Loaf, seven hundred; Fort Putnam, four hundred; and the plain itself one hundred and ninety feet above the Hudson.

On the first of September commenced the first public examination at the
Military Academy, conducted by Colonel Williams and Professors Barron
and Mansfield. The text books were Hutton's Mathematics, Enfield's
Philosophy, Vaubau's Fortification and Scheet's Artillery; using the model
front of a fort that had been long at the Point, constructed, as the tradition
ran, by Rivardi and Rochefontaine.

Cadets J. G. Swift and S. M. Levy were the graduates, and they were
both commissioned to rank in the order just named from 12th October, 1802.
On the 18th of October Colonel Williams invited me to accompany him to
Albany, the object being to identify certain estate documents that were to
be sent to England; and thither we proceeded on board an Albany sloop,
(and found our fellow passengers to be Judge Leonard Gansvoort and his
beautiful niece, Miss Storm of New York). We had a long passage, and
arrived at Albany on *fifth* day. At this time the trial between Gouverneur
and Kemble and a French mercantile house was in progress, and we
listened to the eloquent arguments of Alexander Hamilton and Aaron Burr.
General Hamilton recognized his acquaintance of Newport two years previously, and he invited me to dine with him at his father-in-law's — General
Philip Schuyler's. After dinner, among the subjects of conversation was the
canal and improved navigation of the Mohawk, to connect with Lake
Ontario at Oswego. It was graphically described by General Schuyler,
who, though suffering with gout, was eloquent on this subject. He
regretted that the locks were too small, and the Mohawk unmanageable.
He spoke of the object of the tour of Washington in 1789 to be, among
other enquiries, to learn what improvements could be made to connect the
Hudson and the lakes. He also mentioned Mr. Western, an English
engineer, who had been over the Mohawk route and was deemed a skillful
engineer, etc. The conversation of General Schuyler on the Revolution was
very instructive. General Hamilton spoke of Washington visiting General
Webb at Fort Lee, and that General Webb was not there, at which it was said
that General Washington threw his sword to the earth in a passion at the
absence of Webb, and swore; General Hamilton said it was not so; General
Washington was much displeased, and expressed himself in strong terms

of disapprobation. In the evening an amusing scene occurred at Rannie's Exhibition. He placed a card in the hand of General Hamilton, promising to turn it into a bank bill. The General joined heartily in the general laugh and joke at the failure of the mountebank to redeem his pledge. The following day General Hamilton, Colonel Williams and General Schuyler discussed the subject of the Military Academy, the colonel giving his ideas and purposes to encourage an enlargement of the present plan; General Hamilton approved, and he regretted that the Book of Instruments that had been collected at West Point during the administration of Washington had been lost, by the burning of the "Old Provost" at the Point, in 1794. He said that the fire was by some deemed a design of such officers as had been sent to the Point for instruction in the arts and sciences, as provided for by law. This building had been of stone, and was situate at the edge of a hollow south of the barrack before mentioned; and the story ran, at the Point, that behind the Provost had been the scene of a duel between Colonel Rochefontaine and my friend Lieutenant William Wilson; in fact Wilson said so to me, and that but for an accident in backing the pistol cock it had been a fatal affair to the colonel — Anno 1795. Colonel Williams and myself examined the old octagonal Dutch church, that stood at the junction of Market and State Streets, and the old Hall where, in 1754, a congress had been held, which had been described to him by his friend and relative, Dr. Franklin. After purchasing Neetat's General History and the Works of Hogarth, from Leavenworth and Whiting, the colonel and myself returned to West Point by an Albany sloop; and being becalmed at Newburg, walked over Butter Hill and the Crow's Nest, and arrived at the Point the first of November.

On the 12th of this month a meeting was assembled in the "long room" of the Academy, consisting of Lieutenant-Colonel Williams, Major Wadsworth, Professors Barron and Mansfield, Lieutenants Wilson, Macomb, Swift and Levy, and Cadet Armistead, for the purpose of forming a Military Philosophical Society, to promote military science and history. This society soon embraced as members nearly every distinguished gentleman in the navy and Union, and several in Europe. Its funds were invested in New York city stock.

The academy was closed in December, and I visited my parents in Taunton, and accompanied my mother to visit her mother at New Bedford. This visit had several objects. One of them was to receive from my grandmother something left me by her husband, Thomas Delano, who had ever distinguished me with marked affection, and who had now been three years deceased. I found the estate still unsettled, and returned with hope deferred. Among my mother's friends was an elderly lady, Ma'am Wilbur, the sister of Dr. Gideon Williams, who had the fancy to teach children to read. I had been her pupil. The mode of Mrs. Wilbur was a species of musical cadence, spelling each syllable and sounding the same in time, with open and clear voice, in the due order, until the whole word and sentence was spelled and sounded simultaneously by the whole class—one of the best modes of acquiring distinct pronunciation. We all loved her heartily, and I presume none of her pupils ever visited Taunton during her life without paying their respects to Ma'am Wilbur.

While at New Bedford my grandmother Delano gave me an account of her ancestors, the Swains of Nantucket, who came thither from Newburyport when the island was purchased. Her father married Eleanor Folger, the sister of Abiah, the mother of Dr. Franklin. Her "father was a ship-master, and commanded a whaling vessel in the South Seas."

1803. In the month of January I made a jaunt to Milton Hill and Boston, and, with my cousin John Swift of the former place, visited the graves of our ancestors in the "old burying ground of Milton," and thence to the former residence of Thomas Swift, our immediate ancestor, as before mentioned in this diary; where, suspended over the mantel is an emblazonry of the arms* of the Swifts of Yorkshire, that had been brought over by our ancestor Thomas. In Boston I met my friend Mr. Gardner and Colonel Samuel Bradford. To the latter I had a letter of introduction from his brother-in-law, Colonel Williams. I also met Colonel Joseph May of Boston, who gave me many particulars of the "Mohawk Indians," who had destroyed the tea in Boston Harbor—the precursor of the Revolution. Colonel May had been a friend of my grandfather, Samuel Swift, who he said had been active in promoting that event of destroying the tea.

---

* The same from which the coat-of-arms in this work is taken. — *H. E.*

In the month of February I returned to my father's in Taunton. My sister Nancy was now "in company," and one of the most beautiful women I ever saw; my brother William Henry, an active and noisy boy not yet in jacket and trowsers. My father's house, that had been rebuilt on the ruins of the one lost by fire, was a very commodious and pleasant residence. The acquaintances of my boyhood received me with much kindness, and my father's friends with hospitality. My leave expiring in March, I took a packet from "the Ware," the head of navigation on Taunton River, and by Newport through Long Island Sound, in which we encountered a north-west gale and snow storm, and caught a glimpse of Huntington Light at the moment when the main sail split by the wind and weight of snow, in which plight the packet was driven ashore upon the beach of Long Island. The next day the crew succeeded in floating the vessel and we had a quick run to New York, and arrived at West Point the day after, just in time to answer to my name at the muster roll-call at the close of the month.

In the month of April by order of the Secretary of War, Colonel Williams, as chief engineer, left West Point for Wilmington, North Carolina, and Charleston, South Carolina; Major Wadsworth to New London and Newport. The repairs of the fortifications had heretofore been conducted under the direction of officers of the artillerists and engineers, and this movement of the War Department was to commence the action of the new corps of engineers. Lieutenant James Wilson had orders to repair Forts Mifflin and Norfolk, and Lieutenant Macomb the works in New York Harbor and Portsmouth, New Hampshire. Congress authorized the enlistment of twenty-one men as artificers and aids to the engineer service, and also a teacher of French and drawing was authorized at the Military Academy, and $109,000 appropriated to repair the forts, the arsenals, and the armories of the United States.

The excitement in reference to the cession of Louisiana, and consequent prospects of war with Spain, had caused an appropriation of a million and a half, and also of $80,000 for the calling out of the militia, and $25,000 for western arsenals; looking to Baton Rouge as a point for that purpose in case of trouble at New Orleans.

This spring George Bomford was appointed a cadet. My acquaintance with this young gentleman commenced at a country store opposite to West Point, in Warren's Valley, where I had gone to kill trout, and where Bomford had established himself as a dealer, and from the proximity of the marsh he had taken the ague and fever. I invited him to my quarters at the Point, where he regained his health; and on the strength of my acquaintance with General Dearborn, in the Baron affair, I wrote an application to him for a cadet's warrant for Bomford, and in a short period the warrant was received. Bomford was well informed on many subjects, ingenious and musical. Soon after his appointment he made good progress at his books, and became our principal in the laboratory, in which place Bomford and myself had a narrow escape. A rocket had taken fire while in the mould and driving, the flame from which reached the floor above, upon which, on cartridge paper, was a mass of gun powder. Both of us sprang to the window and became jammed for want of space for both, and there struggled until the rocket was exhausted. Bomford was born on Long Island, the reputed son of a British officer.

In this month of May Captain George Izard marched his company of artillery to Norfolk. There had been some refusal on his part to obey a requisition of Colonel Williams for a detachment from his company. To avoid future collision this order to march had been given. Soon after this event Colonel Williams returned to West Point from North Carolina, accompanied by Cadet William McRee from Wilmington. The colonel informed the corps of engineers that in consequence of a difference between himself and the Secretary of War on the subject of the rights of rank and command, he, the colonel, had resigned his commission. This intelligence was a grief to every one at the Point. The cause of it was the unmilitary and needless obscurity in the terms of the law of 16th March, 1802, in reference to rank and command.

In the month of June Francis De Masson was appointed teacher of the French Language and Topographical Drawing at the academy, and Lieutenant Levy and myself became his pupils in both branches.

At the celebration of Independence this year, while superintending the salute at Fort Clinton, the concussion produced by a twenty-four pounder brought blood from my left ear, and injured permanently my hearing. This was occasioned by negligence in position.

On the 21st of this month of July, the family of our worthy chief left the Point, breaking up our principal social circle, and depriving the cadets of an important source of instruction. Colonel Williams had been the friend and adviser of every one of us.

In the following month I was summoned as a member of a court martial, on the trial of Lieutenant Van Rensselaer of the army, at Fort Jay; at the termination of which, on leave, I visited Colonel Williams at Perth Amboy, where, with Lieutenant A. Macomb, was presented our views of an appeal to Mr. Jefferson to commend to Congress a modification of the law of March, and thus restore the colonel to the corps of engineers. The colonel declined any action, but we wrote a suitable letter to the President and took our leave of our retired chief, and proceeded to Belleville, N. J., the pleasant residence of Macomb's family on the Passaic, and with them made an excursion to the falls of that river. On returning to West Point in September, we found the academic affairs much deranged by the resignation of Professor Mansfield, upon whom Mr. Jefferson had conferred the surveyor-generalship of Ohio, upon which service Mr. Mansfield entered in the fall of this year. His nephew, Cadet J. G. Totten, became an assistant in this service. The departure of this family was a serious loss to our society. Mrs. Mansfield was a very intelligent lady, and her conversation not only agreeable but instructive to the young gentlemen who found a welcome at her residence.

In the month of November a general court martial was convened at Frederick Town, in Maryland, and on the 12th of the month with Lieutenant Charles Wolstoncroft of our army (a native of England, and brother of the notorious Mary Wolstoncroft Godwin,) and Lieutenant W. R. Boot, also a native of England, and Lieutenant R. W. Osborne, a native of St. Croix, and Lieutenant William Hossack (the brother of the doctor of that name) and myself, also under orders to attend this court, took the stage at Paulus Hook, and, passing a day in Philadelphia at Frances' hotel in

Furth street, we arrived in Baltimore at the Indian Queen, and on the
18th found ourselves at the celebrated tavern of Mr. Kimball, in Frederick.

 This court was convened for the trial of Colonel Thomas Butler of the
army, charged with disobedience of the orders of General Wilkinson, which
order was for the army to crop the hair of the head, and the whiskers to be
no lower than the line from the ear to the mouth. The colonel denied the
power of the general so to deprive a citizen of the United States of that
which nature had conferred for use and ornament, and the colonel appeared
at the court with a long queue of hair. The court was also to investigate the
case of Major George Ingersoll, charged with selling milk in the garrison
of Fort Jay while commandant of that post; an accusation made by Lieut.
Wolstoncroft, who was himself charged with shooting the ducks of Major
Ingersoll while in arrest at the said Fort Jay. For such objects — though
connected with points of military discipline — officers were summoned from
the extremities of the Union. While these trials were in progress, and
pending the recesses of the court, the thirteen members and other attending
officers enjoyed the hospitality of the Marylanders, especially those of
Roger B. Taney, Esq., a counsellor of distinction, and John Hanson
Thomas and his father, Dr. Philip Thomas, George Murdock, Capt. William
Campbell of Monocacy, Richard Pitts, Baker Johnson and Col. McPherson,
all gentlemen of note and distinguished Federalists. Such an association
was the occasion of some slander at Washington City. Among the
Democrats there it was said that these officers were too familiar with the
opponents of the Government. The truth was, that every officer in attend-
ance and of the court were Federalists, save Major James Bruff and Lieut.
Wolstoncroft, an English gentleman. The president of the court was
Colonel Henry Burbeck. He had been a pupil of Colonel Gridley, the
engineer of the American army at Boston in 1776, who said that Washington
was his model in politics. Lieutenant Colonel Constant Freeman, an officer
of merit who had been employed on the boundary line between the Spanish
Possessions and the United States, and his brother, Captain N. Freeman, a
man of letters, were members, as also was Colonel Jacob Kingsbury, a
veteran of the Revolutionary War. He had been a sergeant in the Con-

necticut line at the seige of Yorktown — a fine sample of modest integrity and common sense. At our mess table he recounted the scenes before "York." He was at the storming of the redout on the right, under Colonel Hamilton, October, 1781. Colonel Kingsbury remarked, "I was leading my squad through a small gap in the abbatis, and was coming over the parapet when something struck me a blow on the head, and my first consciousness was in finding myself extended upon the platform inside the redout." My former commander, Major William McRea of Virginia, who used to amuse us with accounts of General Knox, the then Secretary of War, his orders and notions for equipping and training the "sub legions" of General Wayne's army; also Captain Stelle of the artillery, formerly commanding at West Point — he was from New Jersey; Captain McClelland from Maryland, and Captain John Saunders, an eccentric gentleman from Virginia; Lieutenant James House from Baltimore, a native of Connecticut, a gentleman of much taste and an artist; also my friend Lieutenant Alexander Macomb, full of frolic and fun, an accomplished gentleman, and Lieutenant E. Beebee of New York. There was also Major Thomas H. Cushing, the adjutant and inspector of the army, a gentleman of high intelligence and who, under the orders of General Wilkinson prosecuted the trial of Colonel Butler. In December the court terminated its proceedings. No other consequence of an historic character has followed this trial save the perpetual knot hole in the coffin that we see in Washington Irving's Knickerbocker's History of New York, through which hole still protrudes the queue of Colonel Tom Butler as he there lays in his shroud. The officers reciprocated the courtesy of Frederick by a ball and supper given at Mrs. Kimball's, arranged with much and peculiar taste by the advice of Lieutenant Macomb.

On 23d December the members of the court and all the other officers proceeded to Georgetown and to the war office in Washington, and paid their respects to General Dearborn, the Secretary of War. The general invited me to dine at his residence in Georgetown, where I thanked him for the trouble he had taken in my affair with Baron at West Point in 1801. The secretary said that no injury had resulted to me, although he could not approve of the disrespect that I had been excited to show to Mr. Baron. On my taking leave, after being presented to Mr. Jefferson, the secretary said that he should require my services in the ensuing spring to repair the fort on Cape Fear, North Carolina, and also said that such work had not been previously given to the graduates (three) of the military academy because of their youthfulness and inexperience.

The subject that had mostly engrossed conversation in the past year, of a public nature, was Mr. Jefferson's purchase of Louisiana. The general idea among thinking men was that the United States, already large enough, would be injured by extension, but the people will hardly be restrained from migrating beyond the Mississippi. It was therefore wise in Mr. Jefferson to settle as far as possible future questions by peaceable purchase, trusting to the country to remedy any constitutional defect in what the Federalists deemed to be a dangerous precedent. The alteration in the Constitution in the mode of electing a President was by the Federalists deemed anything but an improvement, nay, that it was a breach in the unity of that almost sacred instrument, moreover there must ever be more than two men in the country at least equally qualified for the presidential office. The change was deemed a strong measure to sustain the power of party that had already become proscriptive.

1804. By leave from the Secretary of War the remainder of the winter was passed with my father's only brother, Jonathan Swift, at Alexandria, who had there married the daughter Ann of General Daniel Roberdeau of the army of the Revolution and of the Congress of 1778 that formed the Confederation. He related to me incidents of his travels in England and Ireland in the years 1786–7 and of his visit to the country of our ancestors at Rotheram in Yorkshire, and to some distant relatives in Dublin. These friends presented him a portrait of Dean Swift and some relics of that personage. In Alexandria, by the introduction of my uncle, I was received courteously by Mr. William Fitzhugh of Chatham, Mr. William Herbert, Mr. John Potts and his beautiful daughter Sophia, and also by the Rosins of Notley Hall, and Addisons of Oxen Hill in the vicinity. In February my first visit to Congress was made. The prominent topics of discussion were the surplus revenue, as to what could be done with it; and here came up incidentally or accidentally, views of improving the country by roads and canals. The troubles with the Barbary powers had its share in debate, and also a scheme to widen the privileges of naturalization, also the contemplated impeachment of Samuel Chase, a sound judge and honest, though of violent temper, and which was deemed more an assault upon the permanency of the judiciary than from any belief in the malversation of that judge. In exploring the unfinished capitol I found the portraits of Louis XVI. and Marie Antoinette, that had been presented by that king to Congress in 1779. They were fine specimens of art, though not respectfully treated, for they were suspended in a committee-room of the capitol. I made in Washington the acquaintance of my fellow boarder, Luther Martin, Esquire, and heard from him some of the scenes that occurred in the Maryland Convention, of which he was a member at the time of the adoption of the Constitution; and also with General William Eaton, the hero of Derne, in Africa, who gave a recital of his efforts in that useless expedition. With the other gentlemen of our mess we partook in the celebration of the birth of Washington, at Georgetown. Had also the honor to dine with Mr. Jefferson, and to converse with the Secretary of War upon his purpose to send me to North Carolina, as before mentioned. Early in March, in company with Thomas Cadwallader of Philadelphia, proceeded to Frederick Town and passed a day, and thence to Lancaster, in Pennsylvania, where Mr. Cadwallader introduced me to the speaker, and we listened to some debates in the halls of the state, and then we departed for Philadelphia, where we arrived on the 9th. The next day made a jaunt to Germantown to see my father's friend, Isaac Roberdeau, the son of General Roberdeau before mentioned. Found him and his young family at his father-in-law's, Rev. Samuel Blair. Mr. Roberdeau had been employed with Andrew Ellicott in laying out the city of Washington. He mentioned the interest that General Washington took in this work, and of his frequent visits from Mount Vernon on horseback to look at the progress of the work, and also at the plans of Major L'Enfent, who had designed a very extensive elevation for the capitol. It was his purpose to give the building a front of six hundred feet. enclosed in a collonade of the Corinthian order, the columns to be one hundred and ten feet in altitude. On my return to the city with Lieutenant William Wilson, formerly of West Point, paid our respects to the disbanded veteran Tousard, and also to his lady.

From Philadelphia on my way to West Point, at Elizabeth Town on the 14th of March, had the pleasure to visit my friend Colonel Williams, who resided in that place. He introduced me to Count Reimsowitz, the poet, and also the friend of Kosciusko, and found him a very interesting narrator of the wrongs of Poland. I also met here James Ricketts, Esq., a Jamaica planter. His residence here was a very pleasant and hospitable mansion. I also saw Mr. Bellasis (Viscount Bolinbroke,) in retirement from England for some scandalous cause. He seemed a morose man. I was much better pleased with the Rev. Mr. Kellock, to whom the colonel introduced me, and who is an able Presbyterian preacher. From the residence of Colonel Williams, and in company with Lieutenant Macomb, rode to Belleville, and repeated our visit to Passaic Falls, and also to his father, Alexander Macomb, in Broadway, New York. This gentleman had been a very extensive merchant in Detroit. He mentioned seeing the noted Daniel Boone a prisoner in Detroit, captured by some mistake. The governor then was a Colonel Hamilton, who treated Mr. Boone with much kindness, and gave him an order on Mr. Macomb for any merchandise that Mr. Boone chose to take home to his family in Kentucky. Mr. Boone was thankful for the favor, but would only take a *paper* of pins and a *pound* of tea for his wife — a characteristic evidence of the self respect of Boone. The last of the month, with six hundred and ninety-two dollars received from Lieutenant Charles Wolstoncroft, paymaster, to pay the cadets at the academy, arrived at the Point in season to be reported present on the monthly rolls. The academy was opened on the first of April, under the auspices of Professors Barron and Francis De Masson. The latter gentleman was an emigrant from France and St. Domingo; he was of the Royal School, an highly educated man. His father had been president of a provincial parliament; had suffered by the Revolution, and also by the insurrection of the slaves of St. Domingo.

Congress had appropriated one hundred and nine thousand dollars for the reparation of the forts in the current year, including armories and arsenals.

At the close of the month of April I received orders from the War Department to repair to North Carolina and examine the harbor of Cape Fear, and to report a plan of defence therefor, and also to direct the execution of a contract with General Benjamin Smith of Belvidere, to construct a battery at the site of old Fort Johnson, in Smithville, of a material called "tapia." Macomb was sent to Rocky Mount in South Carolina, Levy to Fort Jackson, in Georgia, and W. Amistead to Fort Nelson, at Norfolk.

In taking leave of my *alma mater*, Major Wadsworth being the superintendent, I was much annoyed by my liability for the debt of Lieutenant Strong. The paymaster had been authorized to advance me two months' pay, which, with the sale of books and my watch, enabled me to discharge the debt and relieve my endorser, Major George Fleming — and also to retain enough to defray my expenses to Wilmington. The veteran major had been very kind to stand between the law and myself. He had been an officer of artillery, and was at the surrender of Burgoyne in 1777: at the present, and for a long time he had been the military store-keeper at West Point, and he abounded in reminiscences of the war of '76, and especially of Saratoga and Yorktown — at both of which surrenders he had been present, a conductor of ordnance. He had been selected by General Knoxwhen, Secretary of War, for his present office and station.

Among my associates left at West Point was Cadet William Gates. He was recovering from a wound recently received in the hand by a wooden ramrod discharged from a fowling piece. In the absence of our post surgeon I had in vain rowed to Peekskill to seek the aid of Doctor Strang. He declined the trouble, may be from a fear that he might not easily recover his fee from the United States, or from the slender means of a cadet. By the time of my return Gates' hand had become extremely swollen. He bore well my essay and successful cutting out of numerous splinters, filling the cavity with lint and laudanum from the hospital. The hand was saved, and was considered a fortunate result, though it was disfigured for want of a more judicious and early surgical treatment.

On my route to the South had appointed to visit my former chief, Colonel Williams, to learn what had been his views of the works needed in the harbor of Cape Fear. I found him at his country seat, Mount Pleasant, near Philadelphia, on the Schuylkill, in the month of May. The colonel introduced me to the family of Mr. Clement Biddle, formerly quartermaster-general of Washington's army; the family an intellectual group living in enviable harmony. And I also renewed my acquaintance with Colonel Cadwallader. Colonel Williams gave me letters of introduction to Joshua Grainger Wright, Esq., General Benjamin Smith and Mr. John Lord—gentlemen of Wilmington, North Carolina. The remembrance of the disinterested friendship of Colonel Williams forms one of the brightest reminiscences of my life.

I made a visit on my way south at the Indian Queen, in Baltimore, to pass a little time with my cousin William Roberdeau Swift, son of Jonathan. He was in the counting-house of William Taylor, for whom this cousin, as supercargo of the Orozimbo ("India-man,") made a large amount of money. William and myself revived the bygone days on Taunton Green, and among our schoolmates there. His memory was very minute and redundant. At the Indian Queen I was the fellow boarder of General Arthur St. Clair, who honored me with his acquaintance, and gave me the story of his unfortunate battle with the Indians in Ohio, 1791. An impressive dignity distinguished the deportment of this soldier, and once president of the congress of the United States. I accompanied the veteran to Washington, whither, he went to revive a claim for money expended by him in the war of the Revolution, to meet the now pressing necessities of age and poverty.

The last of May I reported myself to General Dearborn, at the war office in Washington, who again presented me to Mr. Jefferson, and I met at his table the Secretary of State, Mr. Madison, and other public officers. The President is remarkable for his urbanity to young men. An observation of his is that "Young and not old men are the most instructive associates." True, no doubt, in reference to political future purposes. At this (1806) dinner, among the subjects of conversation was that of gun boats. The President complacently gave me an opportunity to express my thoughts thereon, and with, it may be, the vanity and candour of youth, my notions were given adversely to the system. This uncourtly opposition to a favorite project was received by Mr. Jefferson in a kind manner, and he replied: "My young friend, your opinion may be popular, but remember that in time our navy may cause us to become as arrogant upon the ocean as ever Britain has been. True, the commercial necessities of a maritime people make a navy popular, but its success will encourage us to depart from the simplicity of our institutions." Mr. Jefferson jocosely asked me, "To which of the political creeds do you adhere?" My reply was, that as yet I had done no political act, but that my family were Federalists. Mr. Jefferson rejoined: "There are many men of high talent and integrity in that party, but it is not the rising power": a hint that was lost on me, though General Dearborn reminded me of it in a short period thereafter. The style of Mr. Jefferson's dinners is truly tasteful, and the conversation as free as is consistent with the respect due to a chief magistrate.

By leave of General Dearborn I sojourned a few days on my route at Alexandria, where, meeting Mrs. Lewis at Mr. Potts', I was invited by that lady to make a pilgrimage to the tomb of her deceased connection, General Washington. Mrs. Lewis presented me a relic of the general, and gave me many anecdotes of his life, and presented me a button from the coat that he wore in "Braddock's defeat" in 1755. It was embossed yellow metal marked "56th Reg<sup>t</sup>." I long used this as a letter seal. The Mediterranean squadron, consisting of the frigates Congress, Essex, and other vessels, was at this time at anchor in the Potomac opposite Alexandria, under orders to coerce Tripoli to justice. The officers of the squadron enjoyed the hospitable coutesy of the Alexandrians, and at the adjacent seats of Notley Hall and Oxen Hill. On this occasion I made the acquaintance of Mr. Tunis Craven at these parties — a remarkably handsome man. He was an agent in the navy department. I also met here Captain John Heth of Richmond, and of the United States army. On the 12th June proceeded with him to that capital of Virginia.

where he introduced me to his relative, Chief Justice Marshall, commonly called General Marshall in Richmond. His manner is among the most bland, unaffected, and conciliating of any that I have met. Knowing that he had been a captain in the Virginia line at' the battle of Monmouth, I asked him of the conduct of General Charles Lee on that day. General Marshall replied that Lee's conduct on that oppressively hot day was not failing in intrepedity, nor in external personal respect to General Washington. His vanity had led him into error, and he was too proud to acknowledge it. I inquired of the rumor of profane language used on that occasion. General Marshall said the rumor was not true, though severe language was used — not disrespectful. General Marshall said he was an accomplice of Miflin, Gates, Lovel, Rust, Conway and others in the celebrated conspiracy, but was not a secret but open foe. Gates left a record of his infamy which, with Washington's original scathing letter to Gates, I saw in the hands of the worthy John Pintard, secretary of an insurance company in Wall Street, New York — who had a view of all the MSS. left by Gates.

In prosecuting my journey to North Carolina I had the pleasure to accompany General Marshall to Raleigh, where the United States Supreme Court was to hold a session. The chief justice is sometimes an "absent man." As an instance, he came·on this occasion from home in a dark blue silk dress without an overcoat. It gave me pleasure to take from my trunk and lend him a new blue cloth cloak, that my father had given me, the stage ride being on a chilly morning. On our arrival at High Towers Tavern, near the borders of the State, the general made a mint julep for our refreshment, the first of those drams that I ever saw. The jaunt to Raleigh was to me agreeable and instructive, the affability of the general favoring me with many items of the close of Mr. Adams' administration, of whom the general spoke in high personal respect; but he disapproved of the rupture in the Cabinet to which Mr. Adams had assented, debilitating the power of those who had elected him and strengthening the influence of Mr. Jefferson's partisans. In taking leave of this gentleman he gave me a warm invitation to visit him in Richmond, and which I hope to do.

Arriving in the middle of June at Fayetteville, I met there Nicholas Tillinghast of Taunton Green, my schoolmate. He had come from the manufactories in Pawtucket, R. I., as their agent, and we revived the memory of our school days. Proceeding by the right bank of the Cape Fear River to Negro Head Point ferry, opposite Wilmington, I arrived at Mrs. Meek's boarding house in that town on the anniversary of the battle of Bunker Hill, and on that day reported myself by letter to my chief, Major Wadsworth at West Point, using the day and 1775 as the figurative date of my letter by way of friendly memento. After presenting my letter of introduction I took the packet for Fort Johnston, and there paid my respects to the commandant of the post, Lieutenant John Fergus, an uncle of Cadet McRee, and commenced a happy acquaintance with the surgeon of the post, John Lightfoot Griffin, and with whom established our quarters at Mrs. Ann McDonald's. Here I also met General Benjamin Smith, and to the last of the month had conferences with him as to the best mode of executing his contract with the war department in the construction of a battery on the site of the old Fort Johnston, Smithville.

Early in July I employed Mr. Wilson Davis, one of the most intelligent of the pilots, and with his aid I sounded the entrance over the main bar of shifting sand into the harbor of Cape Fear, and also the entrance at the new inlet, and then viewed the capacity of the anchorage within, together with the relative position of the several points of land near the entrances, of which I made a plot, and upon which I based my report of 26th July to the Secretary of War. The substance of this report was that the main objects to be secured were those that had been set forth by my late chief, Colonel Williams, to wit: to cover an anchorage in the harbor and to command its entrance by a small enclosed work on Oak Island, and an enclosed battery at Federal Point, at the new inlet, and also to complete the battery of tapia at the site of old Fort Johnston, the last being contracted for by General B. Smith. Pending the decision of the war department upon this report, much of the summer was a leisure among agreeable families from Wilmington, that passed the warm season in slight frame houses at "The Fort," as the village of Smithville is called. Among these was the family of Captain James Walker, to whose daughter Louisa and her cousin Eliza Younger, I was introduced at a dinner given to Dr. Griffin and myself by Captain Walker. There were the families of Mr. John Lord and of the founder of the place, Mr. John Potts, and of General Benjamin Smith, who was to construct the public work under a contract, and of Captain Callender, the surveyor of the port, who had been an officer of the army in the war of the Revolution, etc. General Smith became the governor of the State. He owned a large extent of property on Cape Fear River, and was of the family of Landgrave Thomas Smith, the colonial governor of South Carolina in the preceding century. He had become security for the collector of the port of Wilmington, who was a defaulter to the government, and it was to discharge this liability that General Smith had contracted to build the "tapia" work at "The Fort." His lady, Mrs. Sarah Dry Smith, was highly accomplished, and was an hospitable friend to Dr. Griffin and myself, and one of the finest characters in the country. She was the daughter and heiress of Colonel William Dry, the former collector in the colonial time, and was also of the king's council. This lady was also a direct descendant from Cromwell's admiral, Robert Blake. There was also residing at "The Fort" the family of Benjamin Blaney. A native he was of Roxbury, near Boston. He had migrated to Carolina as a carpenter, and had by industry acquired a competence to enable him to dispense aid to the sick and needy and other charities, in the performance of which he was an example of usefulness and charity, and unostentation. Most of the families at the fort were Federalists, and though all deplored the event, they were the more sensibly impressed with the news of the death of Alexander Hamilton, who in this month of July had been slain in a duel with Colonel Burr, the account of which had been written to me by Colonel Williams. The whole Union was in a measure moved to grief by this sad event. Colonel Hamilton occupied a large space in the public mind. He had been the able leader of Federalism — a class of men who may in truth be said to have been actuated by far higher motives than those of mere party.

My advices from West Point were that Major Wadsworth, Captain W. A.

Barron and Mr. De Masson formed the academic corps; that Lieutenant Wilson was on duty at Fort Miflin, Lieutenant Macomb in South Carolina, and Lieutenant Armistead in New York.

In my excursions on the waters of Cape Fear I was aided by Captain Walker, Dr. Griffin and Mr. Blaney, who as sportsmen were familiar with the numerous shoals and channels and anchorages thereof, so that the returns were not only in game, but also in giving me knowledge of the capacity of this harbor, situate as it is on one of the most shallow and troublesome coasts to navigators. The anchorage, covered from the ocean by Bald Head, or Smith's Island, extending from the main bar to the new inlet, and upon which island there is a growth of live oak and palmetto, and abounding with fallow deer.

Intimacy with Mr. Walker furnished me with many items of the war in Carolina, with which he was familiar, although not partaking of the battles, for he had been a moderate Tory, adverse to taking arms against the mother country, in which his friend and brother-in-law, Louis De Rosset, had influenced him. Mr. De Rosset was of the king's council. Mr. Walker had been the executor of General James Moor, the planner and director of the American force at the battle of Moor's Creek, fought by Lillington and Shingsley. From the papers of that officer he had gathered many an anecdote of the march of Cornwallis. Mr. Walker had been in the regulating war of 1770, and then commanded a company in the battle of Allamance, in the western part of the state. He was cured of much of his Toryism by the tyrannical conduct of Major J. H. Craig, the British governor at Wilmington, afterwards governor-general of Canada. The conduct of this man had been oppressive and needlessly cruel to the people of Wilmington, and Capt. Walker had been able to influence some relief to those who were in arrest, etc. He with his brother-in-law, John Du Bois, had been appointed commissioners to arrange the cartel of prisoners, and to negotiate for the families who were to leave Wilmington therein when Cornwallis marched to Virginia, thus showing the confidence that both Whig and Tory had reposed in those gentlemen. Mr. Walker's family were of the settlers called "Retainers," coming from Ireland under the auspices of Colonel Sampson, and of his father, Robert Walker. Among the families of these "Retainers" were those of the Holmes, Owens, and Kernans, etc., now become independent planters and distinguished citizens. The father of Capt. Walker, the above Robert, was of the same family with that of the Protestant hero, the Rev. George Walker of Londonderry. The mother of Capt. Walker was Ann, of the family of Montgomery, of Mount Alexander in Ireland, and had made a runaway match with Robert Walker. Capt. James Walker married Magdalen M. Du Bois, the daughter of John Du Bois and Gabriella De Rosset, his wife.

In the month of September, in reply to my report of 26th July, I received orders from the war department to proceed with so much of the work therein contemplated as was embraced by General Smith's contract upon the tapia work at the site of old Fort Johnston, that had been there constructed by the then colonial Governor Johnston from South Carolina, Anno 1740. In clearing away the sand I found much of the tapia walls then erected finer in their whole length, on a front of the ordinary half bastian flanks and curtain of two hundred and forty feet extent, far superior to our contemplated plan for the battery of tapia.

Soon after this the slaves of General Smith commenced the burning of lime in pens, called kilns, formed of sapling pines formed in squares containing from one thousand to one thousand two hundred bushels of oyster shells (alive) collected in scows from the shoals in the harbor—there abundant. These pens were filled with alternate layers of shells and "light wood" from pitch pine, and thus were burned in about one day— very much to the annoyance of the neighborhood by the smoke and vapor of burning shellfish, when the wind was strong enough to spread the fumes of the kilns. In the succeeding month of November I commenced the battery by constructing boxes of the dimensions of the parapet, six feet high by seven in thickness, into which boxes was poured the tapia composition, consisting of equal parts of lime, raw shells and sand, and water sufficient to form a species of paste, or batter, as the negroes term it.

At the close of this month of November a large Spanish ship called the "Bilboa" was cast away on Cape Fear in a storm. It was alleged by the crew, who were brought by pilot Davis to my quarters, that the ship was laden with sugar, and that there was much specie in "the run;" that the captain and mate had died at sea, and that having no navigator on board they had put the ship before the wind and run her on shore near the Cape. There were twenty-one in this crew, a villainous looking set of rascals, that I had no doubt they were. Lieutenant Fergus detained them in the block-house at the fort until the collector sent inspectors to conduct the crew to Charleston, where the ship was known to some merchant. These men all had more or less of dollars in their red woolen sashes tied around their waists. On their arrival in Charleston they were detained some time, but no proof could be found against them, and they went free. The pilots and others were for some time after this exploring the remains of the wreck, but there was no valuable found among the drift save spars and rigging.

In the previous month of September Alexander Calizance Miller was introduced to Mrs. General Smith, Dr. Griffin and myself and others by John Bradley, Esquire, of Wilmington. Mr. Miller was an accomplished gentleman — especially so in music and drawing. He interested us much in his history. He stated to us that he had escaped from France in the year 1797; was a cadet in the family of De la Marche; had been a mere boy in the corps of Condé at the battle of Dusseldorf; made his escape to America from Rotterdam by the aid of the master of the ship, Captain Miller, whose name he bore, and arrived in Philadelphia, where he earned his bread by teaching the piano and violin, and drawing. He is of remark-able personal beauty and elegance of manner, and Dr. Griffin and myself became very intimate with him. This friend of mine, Dr. Griffin, was from Virginia, near Yorktown. His mother was of the Lightfoot family, and his uncle was Cyrus Griffin, the United States district judge. His father and mother both died in his infancy, and his cousin Thomas, a member of Congress, had procured for him the appointment of surgeon in the army, the duties of which office he was now discharging at Fort Johnston.

1805. In January, by order of General Wilkinson, I relieved Lieutenant Fergus in the command of Fort Johnston. There having been a contra-riety in opinion at the war department whether the commander of the army had authority to place an engineer officer in command of a post and troops, except by the especial order of the president. This act of General Wilkinson's was as well a convenience to the service as a test to decide, so far, the question of his authority under the law of March, 1802. To which arrangement the Secretary of War consented, and the function of my command, with a detachment of a company of artillery, remained until the following year, when, by my request I was relieved from that command. A memorial in reference to this question was presented to the President of the United States, and a request to have the opinion settled by law in December, 1804, by the officers of engineers then for the time at West Point, viz.: Major Wadsworth, Captain Barron, Lieutenants Wilson, Macomb and Armistead, of which Macomb sent me a transcript. The question was so far settled in the following year, 1805, and Colonel Williams was rëcommissioned then, and resumed command of the corps of engineers.

This winter I became engaged to Miss Walker. The season ran by charmingly at "The Barn," Mr. Walker's residence in Wilmington, and at Belvidere, the residence of General and Mrs. Smith, and at Fort Johnston. This engagement gave, of course, new prospects of life, and as is usual, my wishes gave them many agreeable hues. I had stated to Mr. and Mrs. Walker that my chief dependence was my profession. Mr. Walker said he could not subdivide his property during his life; that he approved of the marriage, and should do all he could to promote the interests of his children.

In the month of March Colonel Tathem, of Virginia, arrived at the fort, bringing a collection of surveying and levelling instruments, and an highly finished sextant, to commence by determining the longitude of the fort. He presented himself to me, and described his services in Virginia as a partizan officer in the Revolutionary war. His demeanor evinced an erratic mind; I, however, promoted his wishes, and he commenced to establish the elevation of the block-house above the level of tide water, and extended a line of levels toward the ponds near Brunswick. At this juncture Captain Coles and party arrived to prosecute a survey of the coast of North Carolina by order of the United States navy department, and commenced observations to determine the longitude of the light-house on Bald Head. This operation disturbed Colonel Tathem, who "boxed his instruments" and departed. Probably the colonel had learned at Washington City of the purposes of the navy department, and had come to the coast with some vague ambition for precedence of knowledge.

A recent law of Congress having reference to the interdicting the ports on our coast to any vessels that had been sailed with predatory purposes, had awakened some inquiry about the condition of the fortifications. Congress added twenty-four thousand dollars to the previous appropriation of one hundred and nine thousand, and also sixty thousand dollars for Mr. Jefferson's gun boat project. Little, however, was attempted beyond the ordinary duty of "garrison fatigues" to dress the parapets of the decaying works of defense in the harbors along the coast of the Atlantic. On the 20th of March I received a package of books that I had left with Lieutenant Wolstoncroft at Fort Jay, N. Y. They came through J. S. Bee, Esquire, of Charleston, S. C. Wolstoncroft had, however, returned my Works of Hogarth, contrary to my request.

In April the Secretary of War sent me a modified contract that had been proposed to him by General Smith, for his more convenient discharge of the bond of Colonel Reed, to which my reply was that it would delay the construction of the tapia walls, and so it proved, for there was a suspension of the collection of shells and lime-burning, and the workmen departed with their implements, leaving me to await the conclusion of the negotiation between the War Department and the contractor.

On 5th May, to test the capacity of the channel-way into the harbor, I went to sea over the main bar in the Swedish ship "Louisa," Captain Asmus, loaded with ton timber, and drawing eighteen and one-third feet of water; thus establishing the facts set forth in my report of 26th July in the preceding year to the Secretary of War on that subject—returning to the Fort in the revenue cutter that had, at my request, accompanied the ship to sea.

On 3d June Dr. Griffin, Mr. Miller and myself went to Wilmington in the revenue cutter, and on Thursday, 6th June, 1805, Miss Walker and myself were married at her father's residence, "The Barn," by the Hon. John Hill, he using the Episcopal service, and was selected by me for that office because of his friendly relations to my father—they having been class-mates at Master Lovel's school in Boston in 1775. This resort to a magistrate was made in consequence of the low estimate by Mr. Walker of the character of the then Rector of St. James, in Wilmington. The bride's attendants on this occasion were Eliza Younger, Cecilia Osborne, and Maria Swann; mine were Dr. Griffin, Mr. Miller, George Burgwin, in lieu of his brother, John Fanning, accidentally absent.

In the following week Mrs. General Smith gave an entertainment in honor of the marriage, at the town residence of the general. The hilarity of this party was temporarily intercepted by a letter and challenge from Captain Maurice Moor to General Smith, who called me to his office to arrange the affair with the friend of Mr. Moor— Captain Grange. On 22d of the month John Fanning Burgwin, Esquire, gave us a wedding fête at the Hermitage, in a party of about one hundred persons, that continued for two days. On that same day I received my notice of promotion to the rank of first lieutenant of engineers, and also advices from Colonel Williams of the promotion of others of my brother officers, and of the appointment of several cadets at the Military Academy, and that there was some prospect of his return to the corps.

On the anniversary of the battle of Fort Moultrie, in South Carolina, 28th June, the meeting of General Smith and Captain Moor took place in South Carolina, not far from the sea side, where stands the Boundary House of the two states, the line running through the centre of the hall of entrance, where was held a parley with some North Carolina officers sent in pursuit—our party occupying the south side of the line in the hall, and thus beyond their jurisdiction. Captain Moor was attended now by his cousin, Major Duncan Moor; General Smith by myself and Dr. Andrew Scott, the surgeon of both. At the second fire General Smith received his antagonist's ball in his side and fell. The surgeons, Drs. Scott and Griffin, conveyed the general to Smithville by water, while I hastened to Belvidere, and, in a chair conveyed Mrs. Smith in the night to the Fort, through one of those storms of lightning and rain that often rage in Carolina summers. On this occasion the lightning destroyed two trees, one on either side of the road, apparently at one flash, and for a moment blinding us; but the anxiety of the wife was superior to the alarm, and the lady found her husband quite cheerful at the Fort, with the ball lodged near the left shoulder blade. The party proceeded to Wilmington, where the General recovered after a few weeks' confinement. Family rancour between these *cousins* was the cause of the duel.

The 4th of July was celebrated this year at "The Barn" by Mr. Walker's inviting my friends to a dinner given by him for the occasion, and where I formed the acquaintance of William Gaston, Esquire, of Newbern, and John Hayward of Raleigh. In the following week, on 8th, the family moved to the summer residence at the Fort, and renewed our fishing and other sports of the season. On 12th of the month I was summoned to the death-bed of our surgeon, Dr. Griffin, at Wilmington, where he had been attending the wound of General Smith. The doctor died of yellow fever, and in the act of repeating the death scene of Shakspeare's Julius Cæsar. In his lucid moments he pronounced his case mortal, and asked to be buried in Mrs. General Smith's flower garden at Smithville. This lady had been as kindly attentive to both the doctor and myself as if she had been our parent. To Mrs. Smith the doctor bequeathed his portrait that had been drawn by our friend Mr. Miller. Mrs. Smith adopted a daughter of the doctor's, and educated the child until its early death—a daughter named Mary Ann. Her remains were placed beside those of her father in Mrs. Smith's garden at Smithville. The doctor left me his horse, sword, pistols, watch and library. He was a young man of genius and a faithful friend. In a few days after this mournful scene in Wilmington I was assailed by the same type of fever, and by the care of Dr. De Rosset was conveyed to sea air at the Fort, but did not regain my health until the following September, when, by authority of the Secretary of War, I employed Doctor R. Everett as surgeon for the port at Fort Johnston, and by the same authority a hospital was commenced there, which not only served for the garrison but also received many a sailor from the European ships that carried the ton timber of North Carolina to the dock yards of England.

Before leaving West Point in 1804 I had in casual conversation with my brother officers, mentioned my having seen Colonel Burr at Mr. Denning's, at Beverly, in 1803, and of his conversation with Mr. Denning about the American provinces of Spain — Mexico, Florida, etc. — and that probably Mr. Jefferson's purchase of Louisiana might be extended over these provinces. By some means, unknown to me, this occasioned a query to be put to me from Washington, whether Colonel Burr had at any time remarked to me anything in reference to colonizing or other movement to the West. My reply was that he had not; and I said that at my only interview with him at Beverly, in 1803, the only remark made *to me* was of the season and weather. In the current summer and fall it was common to hear speculations about Colonel Burr and his friends having objects in the West — that were known to Mr. Jefferson — reminding me of the foregoing facts.

In November moved from my post quarters to the Bay Street house of Captain Walker — that had been prepared for his family residence at the Fort — for my winter quarters. In December I received a request from the Secretary of War to examine the live oak and other growths on Bald Head Island, to ascertain the expense of delivering the timber to the government by contract. Lieutenant Botts of the revenue cutter and myself explored the whole Island, east and west of "Flora's Bluff," and estimated that there were then standing at least twenty thousand live oak, sixteen thousand cedar and twelve thousand palmetto trees; and we found that the expense for furnishing live oak by contract would be one dollar per cubic foot delivered on board of a United States vessel in Cape Fear River, and reported the same to the Secretary of War: palmetto and cedar at half that price.

1806. This winter, at the Fort, we received much company from Wilmington and Charleston, S. C., by the packet of Captain McYlhenny, a favorite ship-master of that name. We were sometimes obliged to borrow bedding from my friend Benjamin Blaney, and sometimes borrowed sheep-skins from the public stores, for the gentlemen's beds, while venison and wild turkeys were abundant from the woods in the vicinity, and my waiter, Riley, was an expert gatherer of oysters from the shoals, and we had abundance of sweet potatoes and corn bread from the plantations.

As the spring approached I began to conclude that the tapia contract to build the battery would not be fulfilled; indeed I had letters from Washington informing me that General Smith had extended his negotiations with the Secretary of War to the Treasury Department, and to secure the " Reed bond" had mortgaged rice lands on the Cape Fear river. Thus I was left with but slight duty in my small command of troops at the post. I wrote the Secretary of War for such leave as would allow me to look after some domestic affairs up the river a few miles, that might be done consistently with my responsibility as commandant at the post of the fort. The request was granted in a three months' leave under the conditions proposed, and thus I left Sergeant Fowler in charge of the troops and public stores, Dr. Everett in charge of the hospital, and moved my family to Barnard's Creek, on the Cape Fear, four miles below Wilmington, in the month of February, 1806. The one-half of this place, including a tract of pine land of four thousand acres, Mr. Walker had given to Mrs. Swift. My object was to essay in planting and milling. The plan was commenced by widening and deepening a canal from the mill pond to a rice mill, and by constructing a set of conduits at the tail of the mill-race to run the water used on the wheel into the rice field below the mill, extending to the margin of the river—for the water-culture of rice. I also constructed several of Evan's elevators, and brought the rice machine into useful and profitable service.

On 15th May my first child, James Foster, was born at the residence of his grandfather Walker, and in walking to see the mother and son, from the mills, overheated and injured myself. By the middle of June the unhealthy residence at the mills had convinced me that rice planting and milling were not suitable pursuits for me in that climate. My good servant Erickson, a Swede, had died of the fever, and I buried him under the live oaks at the margin of the creek. The honest man gave me his silver sleeve-buttons as a memento of his regard. This exposure to ill health caused me to return to the fort in May, and to move my family thither the last of June, 1806; and with the usual monthly report to the War Department I sent an application to be sent to any northern port that might be deemed proper for me, and was replied to, that such should be done as soon as the good of the service might indicate a station.

Congress had this year remodeled the Articles of War, and in the 63d article provided for the service of engineers in an incongruous and invidious form of comparison. The aspect of our affairs with Spain had caused a law to call out one hundred thousand of the militia in case of need, and appropriated for fortifications one hundred and fifty thousand dollars, and two hundred and eighteen thousand dollars for arsenals, arms, etc. From the commencement of the government the harbor defences had ever been tolerated only by some vague ideas that England—ever hoping for some fatal mistake on our part to give them foothold in some part of the Union—might come suddenly from Halifax or Bermuda and seize on Rhode Island, or some point in Chesapeake Bay, etc., to prevent which, the wisdom of Congress had imagined that some one hundred thousand dollars a year, expended on these harbors, would "keep the foe at bay." This pittance, however, was not found sufficient to afford the nation one single fort in complete order for defence, even on the smallest scale.

On 14th July Lieutenant William Cox, of the United States artillery, arrived at Fort Johnston, to relieve me from that command, but found me too ill of fever to proceed to make up the returns and receipts of and for public property, and so continued until 26th of August, at which time a storm swept all the craft in the harbor into the marshes, save the revenue cutter. On 28th I received the account of the destruction of my rice crop, mill dam and flood gates at Barnard's, from what source I cannot say, but from that day I began to recover my health, and by 8th September was able to travel to Wilmington, and, with my family, to sojourn at Mr. James W. Walker's place at the Sound. On 15th October returned to the fort, and took receipts from Lieutenant Cox for all the public property at the fort, and transmitted the one part of the duplicates to the war department.

First of November proceeded to Raleigh, and passed a few days of my convalescence there in company with the Governor of the State, Evan Alexander, Esq., and the Secretary of State, Mr. John Guion. By 10th of the month had arrived at my uncle Jonathan Swift's, in Alexandria, and on 13th at the War office in Washington, where I received from the Secretary my commission as captain of engineers. Had the honor to dine with President Jefferson. Among the guests were Mr. Madison the Secretary of State, and General Tureau the ambassador from France, who, in the conversation after dinner gave an interesting account of Bonaparte passing the Alps into Italy and overwhelming the Austrians, and was warm in an eulogium of the venerable Wurmsur. The Secretary of War said that arrangements would be made by Colonel Williams (my beloved chief) for giving me a northern station in the ensuing spring. On my return to Carolina I passed a few days among my friends in Alexandria, and was there assailed by ague and fever, and after the kind nursing of my good aunt Swift was enabled to renew my journey on 20th November, and reached my family in Wilmington, North Carolina, on 12th December, resting on my way at the Bowling Green, Richmond, Fayetteville, and by Christmas reported myself to Colonel Williams by letter, that I was fit for duty. During my absence Major Bruff, of the army, had written a sarcastic letter to his connection in Wilmington, upon such a youth as myself having been selected to relieve his brother-in-law, Captain John Fergus, in the command of Fort Johnston. I asked the major to explain this imperti- nence. He apologized for the error that he had committed, as he called it, and we were restored to as much good humor with each other as need be, or, as seemed to me, could be, with his unfortunate temper. He was a fault-finder with everybody and everything not influenced by his com- placency; he was, however, a gentleman of some ability, and esteemed to be a good administrative officer.

1807. The holidays and January were passed among my acquaintances in and near Wilmington and Fort Johnston, and with an association at the head of which was Archibald F. McNeill, Esq., the object of which was to raise means to aid the poor of Wilmington. The mode was by representing some of the plays of Shakspeare and others of the English drama. The price of the tickets was a dollar, and a considerable fund was realized, and Mr. McNeill was esteemed (and in reality was) a good Hamlet. Mr. McNeill was an accomplished gentleman of the same family as Dr. Daniel McNeill of the Scottish emigrants, after the battle of Culloden, among whom was Flora McDonald, the friend of Charles Eduard "the Pretender." Mr. McNeill's mother was a daughter of Sir James Wright, the colonial Governor of Georgia, and he married Miss Quince, an heiress of Wilmington and cousin of Mrs. Swift. Dr. Daniel McNeill is an intimate friend of mine. His wife, the beautiful Miss Martha Kingsley, is one of the most interesting persons of Wilmington. Among my other intimates is our family physician and friend, and cousin of Mrs. Swift, Dr. Armand J. De Rosset. He is of an old Huguenot family expelled from France. The brothers Louis and John had been early settlers in Carolina, and officers of the royal government, and steady supporters of the Episcopal church. Mr. George Hooper was also a friend of mine. His family came from Boston with his brother William, the member of Congress from North Carolina in 1776. Mr. George Hooper settled as a merchant in Wilmington and married the daughter of the distinguished counsellor, Archibald MacLean, and is a gentleman of inborn hospitality and of fine literary taste, and writes well and with facility on various subjects. The Hon. John Hill, whose family came also from Boston. He was among the prosperous rice planters of Cape Fear. His brother William was a member of Congress. The family of Swann (formerly Jones) of Virginia, were among the oldest and most respectable families of the neighborhood of Wilmington. The ancient family of Moor, descended from Governor James Moor of South Carolina, were residing on the banks of the Cape Fear. Alfred, recently a judge in the United States Supreme Court, and his sons Alfred and Captain Maurice, informed me that this family was of that of Drogheda in Ireland, and that the rebel, Roger Moor, celebrated as the defender of Irish independence in the century before the last, was of the same family.* The family of Ashe was also living here. Colonel Samuel, an accomplished

---

*Major Alexander Duncan Moor, the son of the Revolutionary general, James Moor, was of the same family.

gentleman and son of the governor of that name. They had given several officers to the army of the Revolution, such as John Baptist and Captain Samuel.

My groomsmen, John Fanning and George Burgwin, were the sons of an opulent merchant of Wilmington. The family came from Bristol in England, where these sons were educated. They introduced at their residence, the Hermitage, the modern social habits of the English gentry, and which the elder people of Wilmington said was not an improvement upon the days when the Tories (Dr. Robert Tucker, Francis Cobham and Colonel John Fanning) had given the gentry of Cape Fear a sample of English manners, as practiced in New York when that was a British garrison in the Revolution. Be that as it may, the Hermitage was a delightful visiting place. The sister of the Burgwins was a beautiful woman, and had also been educated in England, and had married Dr. Cletherall of South Carolina.

I had now been nearly three years a resident of North Carolina, and had experienced the kindness and hospitality of many of its good citizens, and become attached to them, and had also in a measure become identified with their institutions; was a master of a few slaves, and had a little experience of their ways and knowledge of their condition. The relation of master and slave in that part of North Carolina is of a kindly character in general on the part of the masters. But with my essays to operate with this class of laborers I could not be reconciled to their perpetual retention in a condition forbidding their mental improvement; and as far as my observation extended a sentiment similar to this was entertained by most of the educated gentlemen. That which seemed to me the worst consequence of slavery was its influence upon the minds and habits of the white children. The natural disposition to rule, that is inherent in the human mind, is nourished in the "young master" and mistress. They become impatient and domineering, and vent their angry passions upon the negro children. These passions grow and strengthen with the years of both white and negro child until both approach their "teens." It is of the nature of human qualities that it should be so with both parties.

[Boston Harbor, 1809.  At West Point two years ago I had collated and transcribed from my diary to the period of my approaching departure from North Carolina, and at the present time—as my public works are drawing to a close, and having sent my family by packet to Wilmington under the escort of my friend Benjamin Blaney, who had been visiting his relations at Roxbury, preparatory to my own return to Fort Johnston on official duty—I proceed to occupy leisure moments in a further collation of my journals.]

1807.  In the month of February I received orders from Colonel Williams, who was then at the war office in Washington, to repair to West Point early in the ensuing April, and receive the command of that post from Captain William A. Barron.

I negotiated a loan at the Bank of Cape Fear for four hundred dollars, and received one hundred and fifty dollars from the United States, and on 20th March was on board the packet Venus, Captain Oliver, with Mrs. Swift's mother and niece Margaret as our companions, and, with Mrs. Swift and our son James and servant Nancy, proceeded before a fair wind by the New Inlet to sea, and on 28th arrived at Mrs. Tilford's boarding house in Courtlandt street, city of New York.  The next day gave Mr. George Gibbs two hundred dollars that I had received for him from Carleton Walker, Esq., of Wilmington, and on 6th April arrived by a Newburgh packet at old West Point, and received the command of the same from Captain Barron, who went to the city.  Mrs. Swift, mother, and niece, took the barge and made a visit to her uncle and Aunt Du Bois at Newburgh, where I joined them in a few days thereafter, and found Mr. Du Bois (John) an intelligent old gentleman, full of reminiscences of the scenes of the war of 1781 in Carolina, and of the iron rule of Major Craig, Governor at Wilmington in those days, and familiar with the events of the De Rosset and Du Bois families, then prominent people in North Carolina. The former he described as refugees to Holland after the St. Bartholomew's massacre, and the latter as refugees to the colonies after the revocation of the Edict of Nantes.

On 14th April received orders from Colonel Williams (he then being, with Major Macomb, on duty in Charleston, S. C.,) to serve an arrest on

Captain Barron, who had recently returned from New York, and who with readiness obeyed the order.

The academy was opened under my superintendence, Professor F. R. Hassler being at the head of the mathematical department, and F. De Masson the teacher of French and drawing.

Among the cadets who joined the academy this spring were Sylvanus Thayer and Alpheus Roberts, graduates from Dartmouth College, and Miles Mason and James Gibson, who were among the most prominent in Mr. Hassler's classes.

By the approbation of the Secretary of War, through Colonel Williams, I commenced the formation of a library for the Academy, and employed Samuel Campbell, of New York, to import the books, and sent Lieutenant George Bumford to New York to aid in this business. In June, while in New York, I was enabled to transmit to my friend John Bradley, Esq., of Wilmington, two hundred dollars, the one-half of my debt to the bank at that place. In this month the family of Colonel Williams arrived at the Point, the colonel being employed on the fortifications in New York harbor, while, by order of the War Department he was held responsible for the superintendence of the Academy, and consequently made, in his visits to his family, frequent inspections at the Academy. The colonel had become pleased with the perpendicular system of defence of Montalembert, and was permitted by the President to apply so much thereof as could be in round towers on Governor's Island, etc.

On 13th June Lieutenant E. D. Wood and myself proceeded to Fort Jay as members of a court martial there, for the trial of Professor William A. Barron. The court adjourned on 19th in consequence of the resignation of the major, and Lieutenant Wood and myself returned to West Point on 24th, where I had the pleasure to find my father, who in my absence had arrived on a visit to us. He became amused in walks among the highlands and redouts of the Revolution, and in the public stores where were the trophies of the war, and also the ponderous chain that had been extended from the rocks of the Point to the opposite shore at Constitution Island, to impede the passage of Sir Henry Clinton's expedition. In these explorations I was his companion, and was inquisitive about the early life of my father, and his marriage and travels. Among his details he said that the death of his father had occurred under the tyranny of General Gage when he was in his sixteenth year, and had been prepared at Mother Lovel's school to enter Cambridge College, but being the oldest child it was necessary for him to remain with his mother, sisters and brother. His father had been an active Whig, and his moderate property in Boston had suffered injury while the town was a garrison ; that in returning to Boston with the family after the evacuation by the British troops they found their residence sadly dilapidated, as was also the similar case of many a neighbor; that the residence in town and a small country place on Dorchester Point formed nearly all the means of support to the family, aided by the needles of his mother and sisters; that his brother Jonathan was apprenticed to Mr. May, a merchant, and that himself commenced in 1779 the study of medicine with Doctor Joseph Gardner, after the completion of which he had the appointment of surgeon in the navy, and in the squadron sent in 1781 to Holland, on board the Portsmouth, commanded by that "dare devil" Daniel McNeill, when that sloop of war was captured by the Culloden — seventy-four guns — commanded by Lord Robert Manners of Rodney's fleet; that he had difficulty in dissuading Captain McNeill from firing into the Culloden for, as he said, "the honor of the American flag." They were carried to the Island of St. Lucia as prisoners of war, where, from having been professionally serviceable to Captain Manners he was permitted to practice on shore on parole, and there received fees that enabled him to assist his fellow prisoners, and where he declined the kind offer of Captain Manners to rate him a surgeon in the English navy. Such of his fellow-prisoners as could swim executed a daring project long contemplated, in a night attempt to get silently into the water and swim and capture a brig laying at anchor, and which was effected by twelve of them, expert swimmers, who boarded the brig by the cable, and cutting the same, and fastening down the hatches on the small crew (their number being eight,) they brought that vessel into Chatham Harbor on Cape Cod, with Captain Daniel McNeill as their leader, and sold the brig, and all reached their homes in safety; that from Boston my father went to Nantucket, with an introduction from Dr. Gardner, and then made an essay to establish himself in Virginia, where he received the friendly aid of General Washington, to whom he had carried a package and introduction from General Benjamin Lincoln, and also his business references of General Roberdeau and Colonel Hove of Alexandria, but that health failing him he had abandoned the project and returned to Nantucket, etc.

In this month of June the Secretary of War sent me the appointment of military agent for the post of West Point. On 10th of the following month of July I accompanied my father to the city on his return home to Taunton. While descending the river we witnessed the fish hawk's surrender of his prey to the eagle, in company with John Garnet, Esquire, the distinguished mathematician and philosopher of New Brunswick in New Jersey, who had been to West Point on a visit to the family of Colonel Williams and to Mr. Hassler. The latter gentleman had been sent to West Point by Mr. Jefferson, at the instance of Mr. Hassler's countryman and friend, Mr. Gallatin. Mr. Hassler was established in the former Rivardi quarters. Mr. Hassler had an high repute for scientific attainments, and he had brought to West Point an extensive library. He was from the Canton of Berne in Switzerland, and had been the attorney-general of that canton, and had also been at the head of the great survey of Switzerland. The cause that he stated to me of his coming to the United States was the conduct of his countrymen in submitting to the interference of France in the affairs of Switzerland. He exhibited a curious union of love of science and politics; his standard of excellence in the latter being the republican views that he entertained for the government of his native land. One of the prominent tones of his mind was a hatred of England. He had been unfortunate in his first investments of property in the United States, and therefore the professorate at West Point was convenient to him. He was an excellent teacher.

On the arrival of my father and myself at the City Hotel, in New York, we found there collections of people in excited conversatian about the outrage committed on 22d ultimo on the United States frigate Chesapeake.

Commodore Barron, by the British frigate Leopard, Captain Humphrey; an act that added contemptuous insult to injuries of impressment of our seamen under an arbitrary rule of 1756. This event excited a war feeling, but Mr. Jefferson's wisdom was of a peaceful nature, and he assuaged the public fever. Congress sustained his views, and looked to placing our harbors in a better condition to resist attack. Appropriations of one hundred and fifty thousand dollars for fortifications from Maine to Georgia—not enough for any one of the larger harbors; the law also providing two hundred and eighteen thousand dollars for armament and arsenals, and five hundred thousand dollars to call out volunteers in case of need; also, fifty thousand dollars for the survey of the coast, including the publication of Thomas Cole's and Jonathan Price's survey of the coast of North Carolina; the latter gentleman having published an interesting map of the whole of that State, one of the best specimens of maps yet published in the Union, fully equal to Mr. Madison's map of Virginia, though both have many errors in them.

The general feeling of resentment through the country, that made the prospect of war with England popular, may have been induced to a sedative condition by a double excitement, one of the consequences of the efforts of Mr. Jefferson to bring Colonel Burr to trial for treason. The zeal exhibited in this effort, and the rigor pursued toward two of Colonel Burr's friends—Bollman and Swartwont—began to give a taste of personal and party rancor against Burr. Although the general impression was adverse to Burr, his intriguing character was feared, and perhaps a greater importance was attached to this propensity than it deserved, for, though Colonel Burr may have been full of designs, he executed none of them, save to destroy General Hamilton—and this an accident of the duel. It was the great position occupied by Hamilton that made Burr the object of public odium. The merits of the duel are to be measured by those of giving and accepting a challenge.

I returned to West Point, taking with me by the request of the paymaster, Lieutenant N. Pinckney, three thousand five hundred and fifty-seven dollars due to the officers, etc., at the Point.

On the last evening of July a meeting of the United States Military Philosophical Society was convened at West Point, in the Academy, at which a member, the traveler Lewis Simond, and also Count Mimeenitz were present—visitors of Colonel Williams. They made some pertinent remarks on military biography, the object before the meeting being some MSS. of the life and acts of Kosciusko, Pulaski and De Kalb. Colonel Williams also presented a MS. on the Field Exercises of Artillery, and Professor Hassler read a paper on his views of forming a general map of the United States, and stated some points of his correspondence with Mr. Gallatin on the subject of a survey of the coast of the United States. Mr. Hassler's mind was of a desultory cast, in fact it seemed to be crowded with ideas. At the black-board he would occasionally branch off into notions of extending the use of the lecture then giving to surveys of the mountains of the country, and referring to the map of the United States would point out the geographical form that nature had made of its mountains and valleys, and water courses, in a sort of opposition to the artificial boundaries of the states. In experiments in the field he gave the cadets clear ideas of the use of instruments for measuring angles and lines, and from the summit of the Crow's Nest measured angles of depression of objects on the plain and river bank by the excess above ninety degrees, using a basin of mercury and the *reflected image* of the pupil of the eye, that being the vertex, etc. During the month of September a comet gave him occasion to measure its angular relation to Lyra and others of the stars, to determine the orbit of the comet, while Mr. Garnet, of New Jersey, was making there similar measurements for the same object.

On 26th October I accompanied Mrs. Swift's mother and niece to New York, and saw them well accommodated on board the packet, and under way for Wilmington, N. C. On the last day of the month received from the paymaster, Lieutenant Pinckney, two thousand one hundred and ninety-four dollars, which, with a former amount received from him, I fully disbursed in paying the garrison at West Point, and closed accounts with that officer. I also received from Peter Gainsevort, at Albany, one thousand four hundred and ninety-one dollars, which sum was also fully disbursed in my military agency at the Point, and accounts closed with him.

On 18th of November went with Mr. Hassler over the Highlands on foot to Newburgh in a very dry and boisterous day. On reaching New Windsor we discovered the dwelling of Mr. Thos. Ellison to be on fire, and a remarkable apathy on the part of the people in efforts to extinguish the flames, that were in the roof; the ladies of the family in great dismay, and at work bringing large quantities of plate and other valuables into the street. Mr. Hassler and myself carried water to the roof, and, not without scorching ourselves, succeeded in quenching the fire, and also succeeded in aiding the ladies to secure and restore their valuables to the house without loss to them. The father, Mr. Ellison, seemed an unconcerned spectator of the scene.

On 23d of this month closed the Academy, and on leave embarked my family on board a packet that had come to the dock by appointment, and, with an early acquaintance from Taunton, Mr. Ingalls, proceeded to New York, leaving the command of West Point with Lieutenant E. D. Wood of the engineers. The next day we arrived at the city, and visited our Beverly friends, the Dennings, and those of the family of George Gibbs, Brooklyn Heights. Found that the family of Dr. McNeill had departed for Wilmington, in Carolina. Our packet sailed on 5th December, and passing through Long Island Sound and Newport Harbor we ascended Taunton River, and arrived at my father's house in that town with Louisa and my son James, and our servant. This was the first interview between my father's and my own family. I had not been at home since 20th March, 1803; found a sad vacancy in the family circle which the death of my sister Nancy had made, and with pain observed its effects upon the countenance of my mother, though my sister had been now two years dead; my brother William Henry absent at school.

My father's neighbors, who had known me from boyhood, received my family with kind attentions, and some half dozen of them, with my early friend, Charles Leonard, Esq., and my teacher, the Rev. Simeon Dogget, honored my twenty-fourth birthday at a party given by my father, a very gratifying scene to me, and which was increased by an invitation from

Mr. Doggett to partake in an examination of the pupils of the academy, where he had prepared me to enter Harvard College, and where I had undergone a similar ordeal to that now visited upon the younger brothers of my then class mates.

1808. In the spring of the year past Congress had commenced in earnest to unfold its views, and a general improvement of the means of intercourse between the widespread States of the Union. Members from those parts thereof, which by nature did not admit of many improvements beyond those of the rivers in the interior, took objections to any action by the United States, on the ground that useful action would be unconstitutional, while those members from the more easily improved parts of the Union were as earnestly in favor of entering upon a general system of improvements, under the clause of the constitution that contemplates the promotion of commerce between the States. The Cumberland Road was so palpably of this tendency that its construction by the United States was authorized.

The early assembling of Congress in October was in accordance with the feeling of the country, that had become more and more hostile to the exclusive and arrogant maratime pretensions of England. This feeling was embittered by the gross act of the naval commander of England, in assaulting a national ship, the defenceless condition of which (whether justifiable on our part or not,) was well known to the British commander; the insult, therefore, of "pouring in a broadside" into the Chesapeake frigate, thus circumstanced, was an act of weak policy in England, and also an act of perfidy made while pretending to desire peace, and while enjoying our hospitality. Yet, although the feeling of the country was warlike, and the treasury of the nation overflowing, Mr. Jefferson preferred non-intercourse to war, for France had also become as arrogant as England. The grasping power of Napoleon contemplated to make us subservient to his views, and what with orders in the British council and the decrees of Bonaparte our commerce with Europe was nearly extinguished. Under these pressures, the influence of Mr. Jefferson with Congress was able to induce the interdict by a general embargo, an act that lost sight of the predominant habits of the North, and by consequence putting a stop to the carrying trade from the South. The measure was deemed by Congress to be of a peaceful tendency, while in January that body appropriated a million for fortifying the harbors, and making promotions in the corps of engineers to the extent of the law, in order to construct the requisite works in those harbors; also granting two hundred and eighteen thousand dollars for magazines of ammunition, three hundred thousand dollars for arms, two hundred thousand dollars annually thereafter to arm the militia, and also provided for adding five regiments of infantry, one of riflemen, one of light artillery and one of dragoons, to the existing army.

This winter we received the sad account of the sudden illness and death of Mrs. Swift's father, Captain Walker, in Wilmington, North Carolina, on 18th January, at the age of sixty-six years. He sent me a message through Dr. De Rosset of his hopes that I would approve of his will. I did not, however, see the justice by which his son James received the greater portion of the estate. This will diminished my prospects of settling my family, as was contemplated to be done, near Boston, in accordance with arrangements to be made under the orders of my official chief, with whom I was exchanging thoughts in reference to his purpose to assign me to duty in that quarter. The Secretary of War had directed Colonel Williams to divide the Atlantic coast into departments, and to assign the officers of engineers to the various harbors where defensive works were to be constructed. On 10th March, with my new commission, as major of engineers, came the orders of Colonel Williams that assigned me to the Eastern Department, comprised of the states of Rhode Island, Massachusetts and Maine, with Lieutenants S. Thayer, P. Willard, and J. G. Totten as my assistants, and with orders to correspond directly with the Secretary of War on the subject of plans of forts, etc. Without surveys it seemed to me impracticable to commence the duty assigned to me, beyond repairing the already existing redouts. I knew nothing of the capabilities of Boston Harbor. Of Newport Harbor I had some clear ideas from my services there upon the fortifications in 1801. Upon inquiry at the War Department I learned that there had not been any surveys made by the Department since the projections in General Washington's time, made by Rochefontaine and Rivardi, and in Mr. Adams' time by Tousard, which last embraced repairs upon Castle Williams (thereafter called Fort Independence,) and upon an ill-contrived redout at Fort Constitution at the mouth of the Piscataqua, New Hampshire, and upon the block-houses and magazines at Portland and some minor points, as at Marblehead, etc.

These works had been commenced by Colonel Rochefontaine, of the pontoon train in the Army of France in the Revolution, and at Newport by Colonel Tousard, an officer of distinction in the same army.

The plans of Bureau de Pazzy for the harbors of New York and Boston, that had been devised in President Adams' time, were deemed to be far too extensive, and *expensive*, to be embraced by the appropriations. In this view the main error may have been in omitting to adopt such of the views as were contemplated by those plans that were in fact appropriate to the proper sites, and within our means to accomplish.

It is to be admitted, that whatever may have been the talents of Colonel Rochefontaine, he had occupied many good positions with his narrow redouts, and also that such works were more commensurate with the views of Congress at the time than in accordance with those of the Colonel. My replies from the War Department also informed me that plans for " new positions" were then maturing at Washington, while my idea was that they should be designed on the spot where they were required.

On 16th March, 1808, I proceeded to my duties at Boston, and with boats and other instruments explored the harbor, and reported to the Secretary of War that George's Island and Long Island Head commanded the entrance to the main channels, and that whatever might be determined upon, those points should be embraced by the works of defence for the harbor, knowing that Governor's Island had become the most important point in the estimate of the advisers of the Department at Washington.

In the ensuing month of April made an excursion to the east, and selected Naugus Head at Salem, Black Point on the Merrimack, Kittery opposite Fort Constitution, New Hampshire, Spring Point and House Island at Portland, for new positions for defensive works. I did not proceed further east, being advised by the Secretary of War that Colonel

Moses Porter had been charged with the defenses further east in Maine, Henry A. S. Dearborn, Esq., of Portland, Captain Walbach and D. Langdon of Portsmouth, Mr. Hartshorn of Salem, Mr. Kittredge at Gloucester, Mr. Eustis at Boston, and Captain Lloyd Beale at Newport, R. I., had been appointed the agents of fortifications, to all of whom I gave requisition for materials to be collected at the respective points. It was determined to repair the Rochefontaine work at Marblehead, and at Gloucester Point. On commencing the latter I found the salt marsh sod firm and compact as it had been laid in the parapets in 1775.

On my return to Boston made a flying visit to my father's, in Taunton, where I found a son born 30th March, both his mother and self doing well. I named him Jonathan Williams, in honor of my patron, the chief of the corps of engineers. Early in May moved my family from Taunton to Fort Independence (Castle Williams,) where my aunt Mary Swift joined my family.

On 10th May Lieutenant S. Thayer reported himself for duty at Fort Independence. On the same day I received from the War Department several plans of a species of Star Fort, contrived at Washington, too small for any flank defense, and too complicated for a mere battery, unsuited to the position for which they had been devised. The only resort left to me was to turn these plans on their centre until they might suit the sites as best they might, in Boston, Portland, and other harbors.

I have now (1809) been nearly two years conducting the constructions of these works, and presume these plans to have emanated from some Revolutionary worthy near the War Department—probably Col. Burbeck. Evidently they were adopted in preference to the plans of us young officers who had given our opinion in favor of a more appropriate form and extent. We were indeed very young and inexperienced, save our chief and Major Wadsworth, whose opinion in the matter was avoided in consequence of the Secretary of War not approving the round towers in New York Harbor. It was not unreasonable to doubt the "constructing ability" of young men, though they knew far more of the theory of defense than any of those who were advisers at the War Department; and it seemed to be forgotten that the experience now to be attained by these young men was the only way by which they could be improved.

In the month of June Dr. Eustis, of Boston, was requested by the Secretary of War to counsel with me on the subject of a plan to enforce the embargo law of December last. At the rooms of the doctor I met Mr. Benjamin Austin, and other warm supporters of Mr. Jefferson's views, but it was evident that embargo was a severe test of their party views. I stated to them that there would be no difficulty in planting a battery that would ensure an obedience to the law, and that they would find that political sentiment would have no influence with any officer in the harbor. There had been meetings of the citizens, and much talk of resisting this embargo law, but the battery was constructed under my direction, and vessels were brought to anchor under its guns, and no other disagreeable consequence than an interruption to some social intercourse in Boston. It was not until the middle of the month of June that I was enabled to proceed to New Bedford and Plymouth to apply the "Washington Stars," to suit the commanding points in those harbors. On my return to Boston Governor Sullivan requested me to meet the Council of the State at his rooms, (he was ill and lame,) to consult in reference to any calling out of the militia to occupy, in case of need, the works that were in progress of construction on the coast of the State. This meeting was held on 23d June, and I presented to it the maratime condition of the coast, and found Governor Sullivan full of intelligence on the subject. On 18th of the following month of July the Secretary of War arrived in Boston upon an inspecting tour. He consented to examine Long Island Head and George's Island, in which excursion I gave him my thoughts upon the inutility of expending money upon Governor's Island and the Upper Harbor. His reply was that the appropriations did not allow of any change of plan at this time, and that an impartial distribution of the amount must be made on the whole frontier of the Atlantic. The Secretary directed me to meet him at Portsmouth in September, and also at Portland, to which places he would return from a visit to his farm, and other private concerns at Kennebeck, that had been long neglected.

On 26th July proceeded by Taunton to Newport, to examine the points of defense in that harbor, and recommended to the War Department that an enclosed work on the Dumplin Rocks and at Coasters' Harbor would be a better expenditure of money than to repair the masonry of Forts Wolcott and Adams, and then returned to Boston Harbor to await the decision of the Secretary.

In the first week of August, General Brooks and General David Cobb, Governor Gore and J. C. Jones, George Cabot, H. G. Otis, William Tudor, Josiah Quincy and James Lloyd, Esquires, and Rev. Jno. T. Kirkland made a visit of inspection to the various points in Boston Harbor, by my invitation.   Received them under a marquee on Governor's Island, and on 25th of the same month these gentlemen, and others of my Boston friends, dined with me under the same marquee pitched on the rampart of Fort Independence; the chief object being to witness some experiments in throwing shot and shells, to indicate the range and extent of the fire, etc.

On 8th September met the Secretary of War on the works at Portland, and proceeded thence with him to Portsmouth, and in company with Governor Langdon and Captain J. B. Walbach, agent of fortifications, laid off a battery at Kittery, to coöperate with the fire of Fort Constitution. On 20th September returned with the Secretary to Boston on his way to Washington, and mine to New Bedford, with Lieutenant S. Thayer, to the fort there.

Early in October the Secretary of War, in reply to my report on the subject of occupying Connanicut and Coasters' Harbor in Narragansett Bay, made in July, directed that the repairs on the old works must first be finished, which of course was obeyed, and Captain Lloyd Beale, the commandant of the harbor, the agent of fortifications, was instructed accordingly.

On 10th of this month of October, with a view to arming the new forts, and by orders from the Secretary of War, I proceeded to the furnaces in Taunton, and directed the casting of 24-pounder shot at eighty-two dollars per ton.   My early friend, Benjamin Dearborn, made the gauges at his balance factory in Boston, using a copy of the English tower measure for dimensions. On 1st November, under similar orders established workshops in Boston, for the construction of gun carriages and other military appurtenances for all the forts in my department. These ordnance orders emanated from Colonel Burbeck at Washington, and the gun carriages were the three-wheeled sea coast carriages, using the same standard of measure.

On 19th November made an excursion with Dr. Eustis of Boston, to Portsmouth, on an inspection tour. On our way we discussed a new formation of the army, to include a staff corps instead of detailing company officers to that service, and also an enlargement of the Military Academy, introducing a school of practice by a corps of sappers and miners. The two latter Dr. Eustis did not approve. This gentleman had been a hospital surgeon in the Revolutionary War, and had had much intercourse with all the departments of the army at that period, and at the present time may have had some expectations of going into the War Department under Mr. Madison. The doctor had many reminiscences of the war, and among them of the manner in which the committee was formed at Newburgh that produced the celebrated letters of General Armstrong. It was done by a general meeting of the officers and an open election of three to select a writer. Colonel Timothy Pickering was a member of that committee of three, and they appointed Major John Armstrong to be the composer and writer, etc. In reference to the treason of Arnold, his escape from Beverly, near West Point, was by the energy of the coxswain of his barge, Corporal Levy, who supposed they were going upon an interview with the British; that on their arrival on board the sloop of war Vulture General Arnold offered to make Levy a sergeant-major in the British service, with some remark on the cause of abandoning the American cause. Levy replied that one coat was enough to wear, and said to Dr. Eustis, this reply made Arnold look like a dog with his tail between his legs; that the commander of the Vulture commended Levy for sticking to his country, and treated the barge crew with good fare, and allowed them to return to West Point.

In this fall I commenced, by approval of General Dearborn, a water battery at my request, on the head of Governor's Island, to command, or rather to secure a raking fire in the channel way in two directions, and completed the work by Christmas, using large blocks of Quincy granite, and without mortar.

On 8th of the previous October I accompanied my father's eldest sister, Elizabeth, to Long Meadow on the Connecticut River, to witness her marriage with Colonel Gideon Burt, the service being read by Rev. R. S. B.

On 28th November removed my family from Fort Independence to No. 3 Leveret Street, West Boston, my father and sister Sarah joining us soon after.

1809. On 2d of January commenced an inspection of the shot at the Taunton foundries. Found the work novel to the founders, who had much difficulty in making the moulds to cast a true sphere, and a solid. The shot were improved in a lathe. Also I inspected and proved the carriages, rammers, sponges, etc., at the Boston workshops.

In this month I commenced a well in Fort Warren, on Governor's Island, and on 20th had attained a depth of one hundred and thirty-three feet — a point forty feet below the level of the sea. Stoned the well sides, and in a short time it had forty feet of water in it, by filtration no doubt.

At the request of J. W. Walker and S. R. Jocelyn of Wilmington, N. C., I examined the salt works at Dorchester, and employed Thomas Mayo of Cape Cod to proceed to the Sound, near Wilmington, where he constructed similar vats for evaporation. The plan was very successful.

February 1st attended, as pall bearer, at the funeral of my friend John Gardner's wife, the daughter of Jonathan Jackson, Esq. Mr. Gardner's health failed rapidly after this event, and he declined to death in a few months. He was of a warm heart, and a true friend. He had been a distinguished Federalist and author of "Helvetius" and other arguments in defence of the Washington system of conducting the government.

In the first week of this month I attended, by invitation, several meetings of the Massachusetts Legislative Committee on Roads and Bridges, to consult on the mode of executing their purpose to build an experimental road from Boston to Salem, on the English model.

March 1st the Secretary of War, General Dearborn, resigned, and accepted the collectorship of Boston. This was the commencement of breaking up Mr. Jefferson's administration. The officers of the army near Boston paid their respects to this indefatigable public servant, and also gave him a dinner at the New Exchange.

During the first fortnight in March the condition of the public works permitted my serving as president of a general court martial at the Castle, with officers of the newly organized army, and (save Lieutenant-Colonel James Miller) they gave me more trouble than they did service to the United States. Lieutenant Selleck Osborne Judge-Advocate, a much better poet than soldier, very eccentric, and of utter indifference to discipline.

In March Dr. William Eustis was appointed Secretary of War. He invited me to accompany him to the War Office, which I of course accepted, and on 23d of the month arrived with him at Patrick Jeffry's on Milton Hill, formerly Madam Haley's, thence the next day proceeded to Taunton and lodged at my father's, and there met General David Cobb, the former aid-de-camp of General Washington, and camp companion of Dr. Eustis; thence to Newport, R. I., to inspect the forts in that harbor, and by packet to New York; by stress of weather driven into New London Harbor, and there met Colonel David Humphrey of the Revolutionary Army, and also formerly aid to Washington and an ambassador to Spain. The three dined with George Hallam, Esq.; thence by land to New Haven in company with Colonel Humphrey, who gave us an account of the flocks of Merino sheep in Spain, and of his importation of a number with the hope of spreading the breed in the United States and improving the manufactories of the country. He gave many anecdotes of Washington. At New Haven we met Hon. Pierrepont Edwards, and visited the graves of the regicides Goff, Whalley and Dixwell — amusingly emendated account of them by Dr. Styles.

We arrived in New York on the last day of the month, and took lodgings at Mrs. Loring's, (the friend of Sir William Howe, who is immortalized by Trumbull the poet,) a lady of commanding deportment, who said she recognized me from a likeness to her schoolmate in Boston of fifty years gone by — Ann Foster, my grandmother.

The next day, with Colonel Marinus Willett and others inspected Colonel

Williams' tower on Governor's Island; the colonel absent. Colonel Willet was communicative of the early scenes of the Revolution, and of his own experience; said that in the expedition on the Mohawk he had never met an Indian who could aim and fire a rifle as quick, or run as fast as he could himself. He is a fine specimen of the men of '76. On 2d April the Secretary of War arrived at Philadelphia, and was waited on by Hon. Pierce Butler of South Carolina, on the subject of some military claims. He is a gentleman of as much personal formality as any one of the house of Ormond can be. We also met the celebrated Dr. Logan — quite a contrast in personal deportment. Here Colonel Williams joined the Secretary, and exchanged some opinion on the inutiltiy of star forts, etc., and with Colonel William Duane, an officer of the new army, inspected Fort Miflin. Thence proceeded to Newcastle and to Gadsby's in Baltimore, on 5th April, and dined with General Samuel Smith. Madam Jerome Bonaparte and Miss Nancy Spear, a female politician and very intelligent lady. On 7th arrived at Washington. after inspecting Fort McHenry early in the day. On the following day to the War Office, to meet the officers and subordinates of that Department, and presented Isaac Roberdeau to the Secretary of War, and recommended him to be employed in the engineer department. Dined that day with Mr. Madison and the Secretary of the Navy, when the conversation turned upon the defences of Chesapeake Bay and of River Potomac, which resulted in my examining the site at Warburton, opposite Mt. Vernon, as a point for defensive works. My report was that it was too far up the Potomac unless the mouth of the Patuxent be fortified. The plan of building at Warburton was pursued, however, and Captain George Bumford the engineer thereof.

Visited my uncle Jonathan Swift and other friends in Alexandria, and on my return to the city of Washington dined at Mr. Madison's, and was presented by Mr. Madison to Mr. Erskine, the British minister, and General Stewart of Maryland. Mr. Madison is a very instructive person in conversation, and fond of story telling. He gave us reminiscences of the progress of the government after the peace of 1783. and especially of scenes in convention in forming the Constitution in 1787. On 19th April

I returned to New York, and with my chief, Colonel Williams, examined his towers, and I gave him my views of the inefficiency of the star defenses of the New England coast, allowing them some moral influence as indicating the occupation of many points, and that therefore I should prefer the colonel's towers as serving an equal purpose and superadding safety from surprise; and a capability to resist attack until the militia of the country could be arrayed. Had pleasant meetings of officers at the colonel's quarters at Mrs. Wilkinson's, No. 40 Broadway, and made the acquaintance there of General Jacob Moreton, distinguished for his hospitality and for general intelligence. Thence through the sound to Newport, and to Taunton at my father's, where I renewed my acquaintance with my early and true friend, Charles Leonard, Esq., of Bermuda, and could but regret that so much talent as he possessed should be wasted in a listless life. On 27th April moved my father's family to School Street Court, Boston, my brother William H. having been sent to school in New Hampshire, at Charleston, the residence of my uncles Delano and Fitch.

Early in May reported all the works in my department in good progress, Lieutenant J. G. Totten at Portsmouth soon to come from New Haven, Lieutenant P. Willard in Rhode Island, and Lieutenant S. Thayer at New Bedford; and on 1st June the gun carriages were ready to be placed on the platforms, and the cannon balls were in process of delivery. The appropriations by Congress were, for new works, four hundred and fifty thousand dollars, to finish those commenced, seven hundred and fifty thousand dollars, and two hundred and nineteen thousand dollars for arsenals, magazines and ammunition. While I was in Washington the conversation there upon the non-intercourse indicated the continuance of a warlike feeling against England. Mr. Madison's opinion was that no faith could be placed in the pretensions of either England or France, both of whom desired to involve us in the war with their respective antagonists. Thus the appropriations looked to an early finishing of the coast defenses.

The 4th July was quite a distinguished and marked celebration under a canopy at the base of Bunker Hill in Charlestown. Among the guests were ex-President Adams, Robert Treat Paine, Elbridge Gerry, Charles

Gore, Lieutenant-Governor David Cobb, General H. Dearborn and others, of whom several had been in the battle on the hill over us; where were recounted many of the events of that day in 1775 on the neighboring Breed's Hill, especially from General Dearborn, who commanded a company in that battle, and described the manner in which a private in his company had singled out Major Pitcairn as he rode at the head of his battalion, and "brought the major to the earth over the crupper of his saddle" by an aim and shot from a long duck gun, the man remarking: "I wait until that officer reaches a small mound in front," and then gave fire.

On 5th July an express came before day to me from Captain J. B. Walbach, with an account of an explosion of an ammunition chest on the rampart of Fort Constitution, by which eight persons were killed and others wounded, at the salute on 4th. The concussion had shattered the barrack, old magazine, etc., requiring my directions for repair, etc., and wishing my counsel in other matters. Accordingly I proceeded 7th to Portsmouth, and arrived at Fort Constitution in eight hours from Boston. The repairs were completed by Captain Walbach in a few days thereafter. On examination there was no blame to be attached to any one save the poor corporal who was among the killed, and who had permitted a too close proximity of the chest and the slow match.

Captain A. Eustis, of the army, accompanied me to the east on a visit of inspection of the forts on the 7th, I having attended to witness his marriage on 6th to Rebecca Sprague, a beautiful creature, in the Episcopal church at Dedham.

July 10th at Portsmouth, at Governor Langdon's met Mr. Ogilvie, a remarkable elocutionist and improvisator when under the influence of opium; Shakspeare, Dryden, and Massinger his favorite authors.

On 29th July, with my father and Julius H. Walker, and my brother William H. and some others who were desirous to see the works in the harbor of Boston, went on an inspection of the forts, and the next day they and my mother, sisters and other friends attended the baptism of my son Jonathan Williams by Rev. John Thornton Kirkland, named for my patron, the colonel of that name, and also my father's brother, and The Dean, our cousin of many rumors.

On 5th August the army officers waited on Hon. John Q. Adams, to take leave on his departure on the embassy to St. Petersburg in the ship Horace. He was also saluted by all the forts on his way down the harbor.

August 8th Colonel Burbeck arrived on ordnance duty to inspect the armament of the new forts, especially the three-wheeled carriages that bear his name, and appointed to visit the other works at the East.

Having in contemplation to go to North Carolina after my duties in the eastern department are terminated, Mrs. Swift gave a meeting of leave-taking to our list of friends in Boston, and on 14th of August, with our sons James and Willie, she sailed in brig "Short Staple," Captain Ingersoll, for Wilmington, under the escort of my friend Benjamin Blaney. Accompanied them to George's Island, and there, meeting the frigate Essex, Captain John Smith, coming in, boarded her and sailed up the ship channel by Captain Smith's invitation, to see the bearing that the forts would have to a ship under way, etc.

September 1st, the Secretary of War and Colonel Burbeck on a tour of inspection of the forts in the harbor of Boston; on which occasion I had an opportunity to acknowledge General David Cobb's kindness to me in my early life, by introducing his grandson, David Cobb Hodges to the Secretary of War, and requesting for him an appointment in the army. The Secretary engaged to see that the wishes of his Revolutionary comrade should be accomplished. On this occasion the Secretary handed me a letter to him from the governor of North Carolina, urging that the plan of defense for Oak Island, on Cape Fear River, should be constructed as I had advised in 1804, and I stated to the Secretary that it could be executed for the amount then estimated, seventy-five thousand dollars.

During the summer, in my excusions to the east, and by invitation from Nathaniel Bowditch, Esq., made my resting place at his residence in Salem, at which times I have found him at breakfast time at work upon the translation of La Place's *Méchanique Céleste.* I brought him and Professor F. R.

Hassler to the acquaintance of each other, and interchange of their respective notes and observations.

September 5th, in presence of the Secretary of War and Colonel Burbeck, at the request of the Secretary of the Navy, laid off upon the ground at Charleston Point a magazine for that department, to contain three thousand barrels of gun powder, and gave the masons plans and instructions to construct the same. Arranged with Mr. Penniman to receive my brother-in-law, Julius H. Walker, to complete his preparation to enter Harvard College; have appointed with the president to that effect at the commencement on 30th August, at which time John F. Burgwin and others with me dined with the masters in the old hall—and according to ancient usage.

Cape Fear River, Fort Johnston, North Carolina,<br>
*January, 1812.*

My last dates were at Boston in the month of September, 1809, soon after which time, with the Secretary of War, I went to the eastern part of my department upon a tour of inspection of the closing work upon the new forts on the coast, and making a call upon the Secretary's army companion of the days of '76, Doctor Clement March, at Greenland, we arrived at Portsmouth. I proceeded to Fort Constitution, leaving Dr. Eustis to pursue his suit with Miss Caroline Langdon, the beautiful and accomplished daughter of Woodbury Langdon, which lady the doctor married.

The Secretary made his examination of the fort with Captain Walbach while I repaired to the works at Portland. The following week he returned with me to Boston. On our route the Secretary renewed the conversation about my contemplated departure for Cape Fear, and he mentioned another petition that he had received from North Carolina for the erection of the works that had been planned for Oak Island by me in 1804 as a subject that would be embraced in the estimates for 1810. While the works were drawing to a close in Boston Harbor both the present Secretary and ex-Secretary Dearborn made excursions to view these forts, and the magazines for the Navy Department that were in progress at Charlestown ; and with both of these gentlemen, at General Dearborn's residence at Brinley Place in Roxbury, we had several meetings on the prospects of the country, and with a view to defense of the harbors in case of war. By the 1st of October the works in the eastern department were closed, and on 9th reported my engineer's functions in the department to be also terminated, and placed the works in Boston Harbor under the control of Captain N. Freeman.

On 14th October gave orders to Lieutenant S. Thayer to proceed to West Point for the winter. My brother-in-law, Julius 'H. Walker nearly prepared to enter Cambridge College, and a member of my father's family in School Street Court, in Boston, and in whose charge I left my furniture, when, with my books and baggage on 31st October was on board the brig "Short Staple" at sea on my passage to Carolina, and on 1st November passed near to Nantucket, my native place, not seen before by me in nineteen years. The day was clear and my reflections not easily described. At night we put into Martha's Vineyard, and in the rest of the sail along the coast amused myself by keeping the ship's reckoning, and in observations for time, etc., having with me a circle of Borda's belonging to the United States. On 6th November we were at the New Inlet of Cape Fear, and landed on Federal Point, the proposed site for a work recommended to the War Department in 1804, in my report made at that time. Thence proceeded to Wilmington and found my family in health at "The Sound," and remained there until 10th November, at which time made a temporary residence at Mrs. Swift's mother's, Mrs. Walker, in Wilmington, preparatory to going to Fort Johnston. After an absence of two-and-a-half years find North Carolina but little changed in aspect of country. The best of North Carolina is constituted of warm hearts and an early flowering spring. My intimacy with the people of North Carolina, and some acquaintance with the interests of the State have grown with me, and attached me to both.

In December, 1809, the Legislature of North Carolina re-ceded the site of Fort Johnston to the United States.

On 11th of the month I received orders from the chief engineer constituting me the engineer for the State coast.

1810. In January, previous to my professional excursion to the Harbor of Cape Fear, I renewed, at Judge Wright's, Mr. John Lord's, the Hills and other families my social relations with increased pleasure. At one of these re-unions, a numerous party, Dr. Caldwell, from the University of Chapel Hill, exhibited the declining condition of that college, and the whole company joined in a subscription to improve the condition of that institution, the *alma mater* of several of the younger persons of the party.

In the course of this month I visited Fort Johnston with Joshua Pitts, General Smith and Mr. John Lord, and examined the boundaries of the public land at that place, and the dilapidated condition of the work, and reported on the same to the War Department. Lieutenant Robert Roberts was in this Board of Examination, and was also the commandant of the post. The reply from the department is that no more would be done at that post than occasional repairs and the construction of permanent barracks. With my friend Blaney visited the grave of our departed companion, Dr. Griffin, in the flower garden of Mrs. General Smith.

In February, at a deer hunt with a party at Major Duncan Moore's, in the forks of the north-west and north-east branches of Cape Fear River, got up some sixteen fine deer. On this occasion Major Moore offered me one hundred acres of rice land on terms so liberal, (if I would settle my family in his neighborhood,) that I could not accept them without incurring too deep an obligation, but the liberality is not forgotten.

March 18th, in company with many gentlemen from Wilmington on a search for the son of our friend, Samuel R. Jocelyn, on the second day the body was found in Holly Shelter Swamp, he having wandered thither in a demented state, and was chilled to death lying in some four inches of water. His name, Samuel, and recently married to a daughter of Counsellor Sampson, of the county of that name.

In April I accompanied John R. London and others to the Sound, on an excursion to see its adaptation to salt-making. I gave these gentlemen the plan of the works on Cape Cod that I had received from Mr. Thayer of that place. No doubt that the ocean water in this shallow sound, not being freshened by rivers, and constantly receiving the tide from the sea, must afford a good surface for evaporation.

On 15th of the month I received orders from the War Department to construct permanent barracks at Fort Johnston, with funds to defray the expenses thereof, and also orders to relieve Lieutenant Roberts in the command of that post.

The appropriations for the military service of the United States contemplated two hundred and eighty-three thousand dollars for fortifications. The previous construction of forts had been deemed sufficient to meet any maritime aggression. Little, therefore, was to be done beyond some repairs and the construction of permanent barracks at the various posts in the year 1810.

Whatever might be the ultimatum growing out of the relations with England and France, all were satisfied, save Congress, that it would be wise to prepare for the worst. Due preparation cannot be made by such an amount of money. Parties in and out of Congress are more engaged with small distinctions in the merits of the question of war than by a just estimate of the objects that France and England have in reference to the United States. The former can have no maratime views averse to those of the United States that cannot be successfully opposed on the ocean; while England has a powerful navy, and claims the persumptuous and prescriptive right to rule on the seas, that, the United States can never admit "while the stormy winds do blow."

During the past season I had attended the Masonic Lodge in Wilmington, having been admitted to that fraternity while at West Point in the year 1802. Observing an abuse of the test for admission, and considering the objects of the society, as a secret society, not agreeable to the spirit of our political institutions, I ceased to be a member of any Lodge, though having no doubt that the conduct of the society had ever been respectful of law, and with benevolent purposes.

I am now preparing my family to go to my post at the fort, increased in number by a third son, Alexander Joseph, born in the house of his grandmother Walker, 4th March, 1810; but disappointed in means by the will of Mrs. Swift's father, who, though intending to do justice, had so left his estate that, instead of receiving five thousand dollars, I was glad to compound with the son, James W. Walker, for one thousand two hundred dollars, payable in three years.

April 20th, renewed my official visits to the fort while the commandant is preparing his returns to obey the orders of the War Department; examined at the workshops the gun carriages made on Colonel Burbeck's plans, and condemned them. They are of pitch pine, but not strong enough to resist the concussion of a proof charge of powder. I had reported these facts to the War Department, and also that the works at Beaufort, in my command, required seven cannon and carriages and a barrack magazine, that would call for an expenditure of fifteen thousand dollars.

May 1st, received the command of Fort Johnston from Lieutenant R. Roberts, and gave him receipts for the public stores. The next day, with the collector of the port, examined the beach at Bald Head, and the encroachments of the sea at that place, and advised the placing of facines confined by piles of thirty feet in length, as a protection against the action of the waves.

May 15th, moved my family to the fort, and at housekeeping in the "Blaney Place," near the fort. June 1st, deposited the United States funds in the Bank of Cape Fear, and commenced the collection of materials for barracks, etc.

On 15th June, with the commissioners of the town of Smithville, marked out the lines of the United States land, and set red cedar posts for landmarks.

During this month of June was employed with the collector in arranging to execute the law of the United States in reference to French and English vessels entering our ports. The first armed vessel that came in was the British schooner "Eliza," Captain Bradshaw, who landed his guns at the battery.

June 28th, a riot among the pilots and the sailors of European ships, and was obliged to place some of the most turbulent in the block-house. This occasioned a legal question as to my authority. The necessity was made apparent, and the court sustained my conduct, having a constable with me whom I had accidentally met on the occasion, and invited to my aid.

From the great mobility of the sand on the coast the storms had produced a variety of changes in the form of the large shoal near the entrance of the harbor, called the "Middle Ground." I employed the pilots early, and at several times, in the month of July, to sound out and buoy the Oak Island channel, and found thereby several changes in the course of the channel that had been made since my survey in the year 1804. During these operations the pilots employed, (two of them, Davis and Cope,) left the survey to board a vessel then coming in. They had some dispute, when Cope struck Davis in the bowels with a knife. The citizens of Smithville requested me to confine Cope until the civil authority could take charge of him. He was thereupon confined in the block-house, which, with all the United States works, is situate in the centre, and extending to the water front of the town. This occasioned some disturbance about the interpolation of military authority, and I was "excused" on the ground that I had done the "service due from a citizen."

The 4th of July this year was celebrated with the usual essays, though on a very limited scale. The town honored me with the appointment of orator of the day.

On 3d of August, in the presence of the collector of the port, Robert Cochran, Esq., and General Smith, the proprietor of the island of Bald Head, and others, Mr. S. Spring, the keeper of the light-house, etc., surveyed and marked with a theodolite, ten (10) acres, including the site of the light-house, and having reference to the abrasion of the shore of the sea, as examined last May, I included a wide sea-beach margin on Bald Head.

August 9th, with a theodolite, above mentioned, received from Jones of London, made observations that proved the magnetic variation at Fort Johnston at this time to be fifty-five minutes west from the true meridian.

The August election of State officers came on this year on 9th of the month. I gave the troops a fishing excursion to Oak Island for that day, with a view to prevent any question of "interference of troops at the polls," in reference to which, as an abuse of the franchise, much had been said, but, as far as my experience extended, had never witnessed any such interpolation.

On 12th August the United States brig "Nautilus," Captain Arthur Sinclair, came into port in a storm that had wrecked an English brig on the "Middle Ground" shoal. Received the officers at my quarters.

On 25th September accompanied Captain Sinclair to sea for the purpose of examining the "slew" through the Frying Pan Shoal, which we found, at a distance of thirteen miles south of the lighthouse, a four-fathom channel directly through the Pan, bearing east-by-south. After a cruise of a few days the "Nautilus" returned to anchor off Fort Johnston, and finally resumed the cruise along the coast on 7th October.

During the months of October and November the weather was excellent for labor, and by 1st December had completed the brick barracks and guard-house, and discharged the workmen. Moved the troops into the new barracks, much to their comfort.

December 12th, by order of the Secretary of War, transported the military stores from Wilmington to the block-house at the fort. These appurtenances had been in the use of 12th United States Regiment of Infantry in 1799, and were stored in Wilmington in 1800.

Passed our Christmas at the wedding of our fair cousin, Mary Vance, with Mr. James Orme, and with my friends Alexander C. Miller and General and Mrs. Smith at Belvidere, and at General Brown's seat at Ashwood, on the Cape Fear, and returned to the fort on the last day of 1810.

1811. January 5th, the governor of the State and suite inspected the post of Fort Johnston, and was received with military honors.

Judging from the debates in Congress that a more enlarged plan of defensive works would be constructed on the coast, on 17th of this month, with my reports to the War Department expressed a hope that I should be employed at some other point, as very little could be expected to be done on the Cape Fear, and also wrote my chief, Colonel Williams, and Lieutenant-Colonel Macomb, soon after, on that subject.

In February I employed Dr. Egbert Haywood Bell as surgeon of the post, which was confirmed by the Secretary of War. The doctor is distinguished in his profession. The family of which he is a member are generally noted for talents; they reside in the upper country of North Carolina. During the winter Mrs. Swift's sister Harriet and husband, Colonel Osborne, had been members of our family, and in the spring they moved to Salsbury, when Mrs. Swift's mother joined our family. Mrs. Osborne is not only amiable but has also an highly cultivated mind, that has contributed much to our enjoyment. With Mrs. Osborne we had the pleasure to receive as guests the father and daughter, Colonel John De Bernier. They were from England; and from Edward Jones, Esquire, I learned that this gentleman, with his brother Henry, had (both) been lieutenant-colonels in the army of England, and in command in Canada, where they had been suddenly relieved from command, and chagrined by the order, they had both sold out their commissions, which act was soon succeeded by orders giving both of them more distinguished commands in India. The mortification resulting from those occurrences may be imagined. In the case of Colonel De B. melancholy was marked on his face. Mr. Jones, who gave me this information, is an Irish gentleman, and has filled the office of attorney-general of North Carolina with high repute. The Colonel Osborne before mentioned is the son of Audly Osborne, Esquire, of Iredell County, North Carolina, reputed to be a son of the family of Leeds, in England. The colonel is a lawyer of much ability, and who, with four of his brothers, had received the first honors of Chapel Hill College.

During the months of February and March flocks of pigeons were daily passing over the fort, with a sound resembling a gust of wind. Several of these flocks were more than a mile in extent, and vast numbers of them were destroyed. Their roost was on Bald Head Island, where they found an abundance of acorns, and from whence sportsmen brought many thousands of these birds.

On 12th May while at Wilmington dining with George Hooper, Esquire, was summoned to the bed of his son-in-law, Mr. James Fleming, who had a few moments previous left us at table, and had been thrown against the corner of the brick market house in town by an unruly horse. Mr. Fleming's brains were forced through the ears by the concussion, and I found him breathing with some violence, but he was dead within an hour.

The 4th July was passed at the seat of General Brown at Ashwood, with a purpose to attend the marriage of my friend, Alexander C. Miller, and the general's daughter, Miss Mary Brown. The general asked me of the origin, etc., of Mr. Miller; my reply was that all that I knew of him had been received of him, and to judge from his uniform deportment it left me no reason to doubt that he had been highly educated, etc. Before leaving the fort, Lieutenant Roberts and myself had set our watches together and arranged to have the salute at the fort commenced at noon, and to fire at intervals of fifteen seconds. I placed myself alone at the margin of the Cape Fear River at Ashwood, sixty miles distant from the fort, in due season to listen, and heard the sound of distant cannon, but not at precise intervals. The sound was that of a puffing, continuous sort, and I counted only fourteen of them. My ear was not more than three inches above the surface of the water; the day was quiet, and the air from the south-west; my position in a direction a little west of north from the fort. In the banks of the Cape Fear at this place, some seventy feet below the general surface of the country, I found an abundance of shark's teeth and other organic remains in the earth, washed by every successive rise of the river.

I returned to the fort on 6th, and on 10th July, having received the long expected 24-pounder new cannon, carriages, and six hundred round shot, replaced the old guns by mounting the battery with the eight new ones.

The appropriations this year for fortifications are four hundred and seven thousand dollars. These and preceding preparations may show both France and England that our endurance of their decrees and orders may find a limit. Both nations seem, from our own dissensions, or contempt for us and for our form of government, to consider our ability or purpose to sustain a war as of small importance to them. Both parties in our country greatly mistake their policy; the Democrats in their evasive palliations of the cause of France; the Federalists by their efforts to prove that the decrees and orders are equally insulting and therefore deserving equal resistance.

They lose sight of the hope of England that we may make some error to favor her pretentions, and that her superiority on the ocean gives her power to annoy, and they lose sight of the fact that if we ever are to assert our rights on the seas, we must commence to do it while England is practicing her arrogant power of impressment.

A letter from my mother informs me of the death of my grandmother Delano, at the residence of her son in the State of New Hampshire, at Charlestown, on 31st May, at the age of eighty-three years. The letter also informs of the disposition of her property, and of the end of my expectations of receiving something that had been willed to me by my grandfather Delano.

July 11th received at the fort, Treasurer Haywood and other guests from Raleigh, who came to look at the ocean, and to be informed of what plan of defense might secure the entrance to the most important harbor on the coast of North Carolina, in which the Legislature of the State had taken a deep interest, and here were several of her prominent members to prepare themselves to give that body such account of their observations as they could collect. It was very evident that these gentlemen had no respect for the moderate use of naval power of England in case we should have a war with them.

In my memorandum of my visit to Ashwood I omitted to state that there stands a tree whose bark has been marked, indented in the year 1780, with a figure representing the Revolutionary general, Robert Howe. These marks had been spread by the growth of the tree, and now exhibits a gigantic rude figure of a man in military costume. This is a result of a slight engraving on the bark of any tree, especially the beech, but if the indentation be deep the growth of the bark covers the work and so obliterates the design.

July 15th sent to Mr. F. R. Hassler, then in England, or going thither, to direct the construction of instruments for the United States coast survey, to cause a telescope to be made for me with one eye-piece for astronomical use, with a power of one hundred and seventy-five.

July 20th received orders to repair to Fredericktown, Maryland, as a member of a general court marshal to be there assembled in September, for the trial of General Wilkinson.

August 1st delivered the command of Fort Johnston to Lieutenant Roberts, United States Artillery, and reported the same to Lieutenant-Colonel C. Freeman, commanding at Norfolk, Virginia. On 4th August proceeded to Raleigh and Richmond, and passed some days there with Major Gibbon, the hero of Stony Point, 1776, and kept my appointment with General Marshall in accepting an invitation to visit him while I was the guest of the major, and found at the general's a delightful assemblage of talent in Mr. Wickham, Colonel Gamble, Colonel Mayo and others, that was very tempting to prolong my stay among the hospitalities of Richmond. I soon after arrived at my uncle Jonathan Swift's, in Alexandria, and then to call on the Secretary of War in Washington. In company with Colonel Williams, Lieutenant-Colonel Macomb, T. C. Smith and others, arrived at Fredericktown the last of August.

On first day of September the general court marshal assembled. General Wilkinson came into court with his counsel, Mr. Taney and Mr. Thomas, and with eloquent address said to General Gansevoort : " Mr. President, this sword (unclasping it from his side) has been the untarnished companion of my thigh for forty years, with a resolution never to surrender it dishonorably to an enemy, I am now by the order of the government of my country, ordered to place it in your hands, etc.," and stepping forward, handed the sword to General Gansevoort, who with much simplicity and dignity, and uncommon brevity, replied, "General, I receive your sword. These officers are assembled to try you, and will doubtless do you justice. Are you ready, General?" "I am," said Wilkinson. "Mr. Advocate, General Walter Jones of Virginia, please to proceed with the trial."

The charges against General Wilkinson were numerous, and extended from the year 1789 to 1810 — treason, conspiracy with Colonel Burr, corruption with the Spanish governor of Louisiana, Manuel Gayozo de Lemos and Baron Carondelet, disobedience of orders, neglect of duty, etc. General Wilkinson waived the act of limitation. The court was several days employed in an argument whether the waiver of the accused would justify the court in trying for offences charged beyond the limit, etc. The court continued on this trial nearly four months. The court acquitted General Wilkinson of all the charges. Many very queer transactions of a political and mercantile character were exposed, but neither military offence nor official or personal corruption, nor any act of treason or conspiracy thereto, or with Colonel Burr, were proved. In reference to Colonel Burr, no fact of a treasonable character was established against him in his trial before Chief-Justice Marshall at Richmond in 1807. It was testified before the general court marshal that the expedition of Colonel Burr had for its object the conquest of Mexico, in which no doubt General Wilkinson, General Jackson and many other prominent men of the United States would have been engaged; in fact, the purpose of such a conquest, to proceed from the United States was known to General Hamilton and Colonel Pickering, and to William Pitt and others in England.

During the trial Colonel Williams, Macomb and myself and other officers renewed our pleasant intercourse with the social and hospitable residents of Fredericktown, and in the course of which many ill-natured and silly rumors were circulated of an unbecoming intimacy with the ultra-Federalists of that place, on the part of the officers, and especially was it censured that General Wilkinson should have been invited to the same parties where were found officers who were daily on his trial.

On 16th September Colonel Williams and others observed the comet that was brilliantly seen in the north in this season, which observations were sent to Mr. Garnet in New Jersey, together with others made upon the annular eclipse the next day, 17th. The day was clear and the observations satisfactory.

October 4th, I received from Colonel Williams an account of the barometrical measurement of the height of Catskill Round Top, three thousand five hundred and sixty-six feet, and White Hills in New Hampshire, six thousand two hundred and thirty-four feet, and other minor points, by Captain A. Partridge, United States engineers.

October 10th made a report of the ordnance and of the defences that had been completed in Smithville, Fort Johnston, to Colonel Burbeck, as the chief of artillery, United States.

November 14th. To Harper's Ferry to examine the workshops of the United States arms, and to explore Jefferson's Rock there with Lieutenant-Colonel Macomb, and the next day to measure the barometrical height of the Colocton Mountain; broke our instrument; the view admirable; counted some two hundred and seventeen cultivated fields. These excursions were pending adjournments of the court. Among Macomb's and my excursions we several times visited Monsieur Payer, or Vaneaudier, an emigrant from France, who with his family had erected a chateau, of style similar to such buildings in France. They were living in genteel elegance, but maintained a species of *incognito* that no one was allowed to question — a sort of nonsense that is very striking and romantic to young people.

November 17th, Colonel Williams, Lieutenant-Colonel Macomb, Major Armistead and myself sent our opinion of the bill for the improvement of the corps of engineers to the Secretary of War. It embraced a corps of sappers and miners.

The general court martial brought its proceedings to a close on 24th December, and every member signed the same, and they were sent by an officer to the Secretary of War at Washington. The members of the court soon dispersed, and on 26th December I paid my respects to the Secretary of War, Washington, and found myself not as graciously received as was the wont of that gentleman, who had favored me with his intimacy. I also found in this place of large gossip, especially so in the time of the session of Congress, that the acquittal of General Wilkinson was received with disappointment by the executive, and it was rumored that some charges had been made by an underling of the War Department adverse to the impartiality of some of the older officers on the court, but that Mr. Madison would not consent to any such mode of impugning the right of opinion, and thus the charges were suppressed.

The sentiment among congressmen was of a conflicting nature on what were to be the results of debates upon the orders and decrees of England and France. Receiving from the War Department no especial orders for duty, I returned to my family, then in Wilmington, North Carolina. I still retained my quarters at Fort Johnston, where I found the family of Lieutenant Roberts in deep distress, he having died in the previous month of November. I had written to the Secretary of War to have his accounts settled, in order to pay off his debts and afford some relief to his family, and this was accomplished. On my return to North Carolina from Washington I was informed that the daughters of my friend Major Gibbon, of Richmond, were at their uncle Duvale's, in Washington, and had just received the mournful account of the destruction of the theatre in Richmond on 26th December, in which their brother, Lieutenant Gibbon of the navy, had been one among the seventy burned to death in that fire. I waited on these ladies, and escorted them to their father's in Richmond, and met a scene of distress that cannot easily be described; and early in January reached my family in Wilmington.

WILMINGTON, NORTH CAROLINA, <br> February, 1813. }

1812. At the close of January arrived at the fort with my family, and found there Lieutenant J. Ewing of the United States Artillery, with orders to report to me for duty. Received from him a box of public papers, being the unsettled accounts of Lieutenant Roberts with the United States, with good and imperfect vouchers amounting to fourteen thousand eight hundred dollars. Sent these papers to the account office in Washington, claiming as balance due on them eight hundred and twenty-eight dollars and twenty-seven cents, and one hundred and forty dollars on a recruiting account. The auditor replied that the claim cannot be allowed until further vouchers be found.

February 1st, gave orders to Lieutenant Ewing to detail a party to work daily in the block-house, cleaning the arms, etc., received there in the previous year. This was in pursuance of orders received from the War Department, together with the appointment of myself as military agent for the coast of North Carolina, and was the first intimation in orders of *haste*, in preparation for war!

February 21st, the United States brig "Vixen," commanded by Lieutenant Charles Gadsden, arrived at Fort Johnston on public business with me.

In March I received orders from the Secretary of War that the state of public affairs required an inspection of the fortifications on the coast of Virginia, the two Carolinas and Georgia, and requiring me to make the same as soon as my present duty permitted.

On 1st April proceeded on this inspection in the packet to Charleston, South Carolina, (at the same time escorting the daughter of Colonel De Bernier on a visit to her friends in South Carolina. This lady is the wife of Harper Harper, Esquire, of Wilmington,) leaving the command of Fort Johnston to Lieutenant Ewing. Bad weather delayed my arrival at Charleston to 6th April.

The next day, 7th, inspected Fort Johnson on James Island, and the day following, the Palmetto Fort of 1780, now called, for its brave defender then, "Fort Moultrie," and heard from General Pinckney the story of Sergeant Jasper's heroism in that defense and repulse of Admiral Parker. By invitation, the day after, met the two Generals Pinckney on the subject of the defenseless state of the coast, from the Chesapeake to Tybee. The elder general, C. C. Pinckney, commented on the recent laws appropriating seven hundred and ninety-six thousand dollars for fortifications, and providing for calling out one hundred thousand militia, and the organization of a quartermaster-general's department as convincing to him, though not in the secret of the cabinet, that war was at hand.

On 11th examined Castle Pinckney, and on 13th proceeded to Savannah, and with Captain William McRee, United States engineer, examined Forts Jackson and Tybee on 15th. On 16th returned through the Sound, and on 17th examined Beaufort, South Carolina; arrived on 20th at Charleston; on 24th at Fort Johnston, North Carolina, and found letters with Lieutenant Ewing from the War Department advising my postponing a visit to the fort at Beaufort, North Carolina, until after my inspection at Norfolk, in Virginia. After inspecting Oak Island and the New Inlet with Lieutenant Ewing, I proceeded to Wilmington, on my way to Washington, with A. F. McNeill, Esq., as far as Warrenton, where his daughter Mary was at Mr.

Mordecai's school. Leaving Wilmington on 1st May, on 7th arrived at Petersburg, and viewed the Appomattox River below the town, also the "Punch Bowl of Pocahontas," and by the Isle of Wight county arrived at Norfolk on 10th. The following day, with Colonel Freeman, the commandant of the post, Commodore S. Decatur and L. W. Tazuell, Esquire, examined the harbor of Norfolk, having reference to the expected war with England; wrote to my chief, Colonel Williams, my views of defending this harbor, and by a packet from Norfolk to England wrote F. R. Hassler to procure for me one of Troughton's circles of reflection. The following day, 13th, examined the navy yard and Hospital Point with Lieutenant Thomas R. Swift of the United States marines, and found him to be a far-removed cousin; consulted also with Captain Evans, of the navy, on Norfolk defenses, and found him a very highly informed person, whose opinions I respect.

On 15th proceeded up the bay by packet, to Baltimore, and, after an inspection of Fort McHenry on 20th took the stage for Washington. A fellow-passenger observing me reading a work of Dr. Doddredge expressed his good opinion of the book. He was Hon. James Millman, on his way to Congress from Philadelphia. That has commenced a pleasant acquaintance. Arrived in Washington the same day in season to attend the levee of Mr. Madison, and to arrange joining the mess of the Hon. Samuel Smith of Maryland, Nicholas Gilmore of New Hampshire, and Charles Goldsborough of Maryland, at O'Neal's. At breakfast the following morning the conversation was upon the effect of the embargo law recently passed. A majority of the mess, including John Polk, Esq., of Kentucky, were adverse to war, but in favor of ample preparations, as for instance, the fortifications, the corps of engineers, and the ordnance department.

On 21st made my report to the War Department upon my inspections in Georgia, South and North Carolina, Virginia and Maryland, and dined with the President at a private dinner on 23d, when he expressed the highest respect for the patriotism of General Pinckney, and for his eminent ability. I commended to the President Major Duncan Moore and A. F. McNeill, Esq., as in every way worthy of the attention of the government for military service.  A regiment was at my command if I so desired.  I preferred the prospect in my own corps, and mentioned the chief of my corps as in every point of view worthy an elevated command in the new organization of the army, etc.; with the Secretary of War, and met there the notorious Jacob Lewis, making pretensions to military and naval command combined; a man of many words, and of no consequence.  The Secretary gave me orders to return to South Carolina and report for duty to General Thomas Pinckney *via* Norfolk.  On 26th dined with Hon. William Lowndes and Colonel George Izard, my former captain at West Point, and discussed the probability of a campaign into Canada, and the mode and route.  The Colonel was for Quebec, Mr. Lowndes was for not going into Canada at all, and my idea was to organize a campaign in Lake Champlain and divide the two Canadas, etc.

On 3d June took leave of the mess at O'Neal's, where I left Mr. Curtis and Colonel Lloyd Halsey of Rhode Island, and his daughter, and *via* Baltimore and the Bay arrived at Norfolk on 8th.  There gave Colonel Freeman a requisition on the War Department for the quartermaster-general to supply intrenching tools, etc.  From Fort Nelson I sent orders to Captain William McRee in Savannah, and Captain John Niex at Beaufort, in North Carolina, to prosecute the works at those places with all the means in their control.  Wrote to Major W. H. Armistead at West Point to advise me, through Colonel Williams, of the condition of the Military Academy.  This was done in consequence of letters from the colonel that evinced some disgust at the neglect of the War Department.

On 12th June by Petersburg, and, meeting Mr. Miller at Mr. Mordecai's, in Warrenton, arrived at Fort Johnston, Cape Fear, on 19th, having with me the amount as exhibited on the auditor's statement of differences, and I disbursed the same (one thousand three hundred dollars,) among the creditors of Lieutenant Roberts, saving the amount due to Benjamin Blaney and myself.  Loss of, and imperfect vouchers, and want of books, have deprived Lieutenant Roberts' family of much of his claim.

The day after my arrival at the fort was joined by Captain Dent of the United States navy, and employed in arranging to proceed to South

Carolina. On 26th June, with orders from both Navy and War Department, Captain Dent and myself proceeded to sea in a whale-boat; overtaken by a gale of wind and driven into Little River through the surf on the bar, and thence on horseback to Georgetown, where we met the eccentric Colonel Peter Harney in his cottage, formed after the fashion of a ship's cabin. He was full of patriotic feeling on reading the declaration of war that Captain Dent and myself had received at Fort Johnston, North Carolina, and the colonel expedited our journey to Charleston on 29th. On the 30th June reported myself to General T. Pinckney, as chief engineer of his department of the army.

July 1st, commenced tours of inspection with General Pinckney, in which he associated his brother, C. C. Pinckney, and the governor, Henry Middleton, and at my request Captain William McRee. The subject at first was the association of the militia under Colonel John Rutledge for coast defense, with the Eighteenth Regiment of United States Infantry, Colonel William Drayton, and Lieutenant J. Hamilton, adjutant. Several of these consultations were held at Mrs. Horry's, the sister of the Generals Pinckney; a lady of extensive knowledge with great simplicity of manner; and I observed that both of her brothers paid great respect to that lady's opinion on every public subject discussed in her presence.

At this time a singular occurrence gave the character of some of our newly-appointed officers. By the general's order, I sent an order to Colonel Welborn and Colonel Pickens, then at Salsbury, North Carolina. These gentlemen acknowledged the receipt of the order, but, from some view they had taken, said "they had concluded not to obey the order, and to divide the responsibility between them." They were arrested, but on explaining restored.

The last of the month of July made an excursion to Fort Johnston, North Carolina, and returned to Fort Moultrie 10th August with Lieutenant Ewing, and also my man Jack and my horses. Since 20th July had been performing the combined duties of chief engineer and of aid-de-camp to General Pinckney, having in the same period received my promotion to lieutenant-colonel of engineers, on the promotion of Lieutenant-Colonel

Macomb to the command of a regiment of artillery. I found on my table at headquarters letters from Washington, advising of the resignation of Colonel Williams, but no order signifying my consequent advancement. This resignation of Colonel Williams was induced by the neglect of the War Department in selecting general officers for the new army. A subordinate position of brigadier was mentioned for the colonel — he did not choose to accept. I notified the corps of engineers of the great loss we had sustained in the retirement of our friend and commander, and accompanied the same with my views of a suitable arrangement of the respective officers to various posts of duty, which would be issued in orders as soon as the War Department sent me official notice of the event; which notice was received on 19th August, on which day I notified Captain William McRee to report himself to General Pinckney on 28th of that month, and assume the chief engineership of the southern department, and also orders to Lieutenant-Colonel Armistead to report to me in season to meet me in Washington before the last of October.

Was necessarily detained in General Pinckney's department, to close up the public business in my two departments, until the last of September, when I took my leave of General Pinckney, in whom I had found a wise and discreet commander, a gentleman of moderate and firm mind, and of all those qualities that constitute an accomplished gentleman; and of whom it is also said that in character and manner he resembles General Washington more than any man at this time living. His brother, Coatsworth, a most delightful companion and intimate with Washington, said he was his brother Tom's model. Neither of them credited the story of Washington *swearing* at Lee at Monmouth.

On 4th October arrived at Fort Johnston, North Carolina, on my route to the city of Washington, and there, by appointment, met General Thomas Brown of Ashwood, to arrange with him the mode of calling out the militia of the State, under the order of the governor, to guard the coast on the plan adopted by General Pinckney. Reported the result of this interview to the last-named gentleman; occupied a few days in arranging my official affairs at the fort, and on 10th October left Lieutenant Ewing in command,

and, having arranged for my family to move to Wilmington at the close of the season, proceeded with my man Jack to Fayetteville on the 14th. The next day wrote General Pinckney my views of the mode in which General Thomas Brown would, under the governor of the State, execute his plan (General Pinckney's) to embody the militia at the coast. In the night at nine o'clock proceeded in the stage to the north. At midnight, while crossing the Cape Fear near Averysborough, our heedless driver discovered that the water had risen during the day, and we found the stage floating and the horses swimming. Fortunately the stage wheels caught in the branches of a tree called a planter. I took off my upper garments and succeeded in cutting clear from the harness one of the wheel horses, and with the aid of my man Jack and this horse we saved the passengers and United States mail and part of the baggage, when the stage swung clear of the planter and was swept down the river, drowning the three other horses. The distance from the stage to the bank of the river was about twenty yards. The passengers arrived at Averysborough about daylight, and there dried their clothing and such baggage as had been saved, and thankful to God for deliverance from peril. At this place the succeeding stage from the south brought Langdon Cheeves and John Galliard, Esquires, from South Carolina, on their way to Congress; the former a native of Ireland, came a boy to Pennsylvania, and by his own powers became a very distinguished counsellor, and moved to South Carolina. As a traveling companion, sociable and full of wit, he gave us recitations pathetic and ludicrous, to make the lumbering way short. This meeting commenced a very agreeable acquaintance with him. Mr. Galliard is from an old Huguenot family, not brilliant nor strong but of unassuming good sense, a gentleman of bland and kind deportment. I found him to be a relative of the wife of Professor Hassler of the coast survey. Our party arrived at Washington on 21st October. The War and Navy Departments much employed in reference to the supplies called for by law, the former department especially in procuring the ordnance stores with the one million dollars appropriated therefor, and with a very capable officer at the head—Major D. Wadsworth, aided by Captain Bumford; and also in filling vacancies in the thirteen newly appointed regiments, and fifty thousand volunteers. In my department, estimates for the coming year, in addition to five hundred thousand dollars recently appropriated are needed, to which work I immediately went by examining the reports of my late chief, Colonel Williams, and Lieutenant-Colonel Macomb, and gave the estimate to the Secretary of War amounting to four hundred and ninety-seven thousand dollars, exclusive of any field works which might be called for in any campaign, referable to the quartermaster-general department.

At the request of General W. H. Harrison, sent an order to Captain E. D. Wood to join the general as an aid-de-camp at Cincinnati as well as his engineer. From the time of my leaving West Point in November, 1807, I had been without account of the progress of the Military Academy save the cursory views given in the letters of Colonel Williams and Major Armistead, accordingly I wrote to Captain Partridge for a full report thereof. My name was now before the United States Senate to fill the vacancy of chief engineer. On 10th November General Samuel Smith and Governor Gilman of the Senate informed me that Dr. Eustis was privy to a plan to supercede me in that office, by appointing, under the provisions of the law to promote without regard to rank, and that Robert Fulton, the distinguished civil engineer, was the candidate that he preferred. This sacrifice of the continued intimacy between the doctor and myself may have been just in estimating the relative ability of Mr. Fulton and myself, but it met no support from Mr. Madison, and both General Smith and Governor Gilman state that my nomination passed unanimously 4th December, 1812, and with expressions from senators commending nomination, etc. Whether the disappointment that the acquittal of General Wilkinson produced had any influence in this matter I have not the means of knowing with certainty, but it is certain that from the date of that acquittal the deportment of Dr. Eustis was less friendly than previously. Early in December the doctor resigned the War Department of his administration, for the foregoing causes. I omit remarks upon his official course. The slanders at Washington about an undue partiality on the part of four members of the court that tried General Wilkinson had been traced to Mr. Simmons of the War Department, and referred to parties and feuds in the army that commenced between General Wayne and General Wilkinson. In the consultations of the court such gossip had very properly no influence. At Washington, however, now, in December, 1812, more rational views of the matter had commenced in the cabinet, where all but one said that "if General Wilkinson had been indiscreet, the testimony before the court was not of a character to justify a verdict of guilty." The war was commenced and it was needful to make the best use of our few officers of any experience, and it is observable at Washington that as trouble presses, military men have become more important than previously in the estimation of members of Congress, to judge from their speeches and personal deportment to officers on the floor and in the lobbies of the hall.

In this month of November Commodore Stewart gave a gala on board the frigate Constellation, then lying before Washington. The President and heads of departments and many others witnessed this exhibition of that fine frigate. Many members of Congress had never before seen a " man of war." This is a very sensible piece of tact on the part of Stewart to overcome the influence of Mr. Gallatin, who was of the opinion in the cabinet that our ships should be laid up in safety. Thanks to Stewart, Bainbridge and Mr. Madison, such counsel, however patriotic, was neglected, and Hull captured the Guerrier, and now on 8th December I had the pleasure to be present at a ball given in honor of Hull, where we had a second trophy scene. Lieutenant Hamilton in the name of Commodore Decatur laid the flag of the Macedonian at the feet of Mrs. Madison. With characteristic delicacy this lady said, " raise the flag ; such a humiliation is not due to a conquered foe."

At the close of the month received letters from my family informing of the birth of my son Thomas Delano, at the residence of his grandmother Walker in Wilmington, 23d November, 1812.

November 22d sent to Major Gibbon and General Marshall at Richmond, and to General Pinckney in South Carolina, maps and descriptions of the points of opening war on the lakes, etc., etc.

Wrote to Colonel Williams 18th December of my having orders to return to Carolina for the winter, and enclosed his son's (Alex. I.'s) commission in the army. On 17th December sent orders to Captain Partridge in reference to opening the Military Academy next spring, and with orders to Lieutenant-Colonel Armistead, Major McRee and Major Bumford, Captains Willard, J. G. Totten and S. Babcock, Lieutenants Thayer, De Russy, Cutbush, Lewis and Findley to be ready to take the field early in the spring, and also sent them their commissions. The same evening waited on the President to introduce Colonel Wadsworth and to consult on the services of our respective departments. A very interesting conversation, Mr. Madison being in favor of a total change in military operations for the next campaign.

Received a present from Colonel Gilman of New Hampshire of a silver drinking tube for the wounded.

December 22d wrote Governor Turner of North Carolina on the defenses of Cape Fear, at his request, to be laid before the Legislature of that State, Proceeded to Wilmington and Fort Johnston, North Carolina, and arrived there on 30th December, 1812.

Before leaving Washington I observed that great difference in opinion prevailed among the prominent men there, the President being in favor of a change in our plans of operation upon Canada, while others thought the Detroit system the preferable direction of attack. A species of apathy that it was hoped would be changed for action if General Armstrong accepted the War Department.

Definite orders to the engineer department were deferred for the present, and I pursued my way to my family, stopping in Raleigh, North Carolina, to confer with the military committee of the Legislature in reference to the subject of the coast defences, contained in my late letter to their senator, Governor Turner.


HEADQUARTERS ENGINEER DEPARTMENT, BROOKLYN, N. Y.
*10th March, 1814.*

1813. On my arrival in January at the residence of my family in North Carolina, and by the approbation of the President of the United States, I submitted a memoir to the military committee of the State, through their chairman, General W. W. Jones, embracing views of the defence of the two entrances into Cape Fear Harbor, and a plan of organization of the militia to guard the sea coast against predatory assault from Bermuda, etc. In the middle of the month went to Ashwood to confer with General Thomas Brown upon this plan. I was accompanied by my friend, Dr. Daniel McNeill, who visited my companion, Major Alexander C. Miller, to reduce an imposthume in his thigh, and succeeded in the operation.

In the month of February visited the sound, inlets and Smithville anchorage with Lieutenant T. N. Gautiere, United States navy, in reference to the coöperation of gunboats for the protection of the coast, etc.

On 1st March the expected orders came from the War Department to take charge of the defence of New York Harbor as chief engineer. On 2d, with my man Jack, proceeded to Raleigh and on to Fredericksburg, Va., where Lieutenant-Colonel Armistead joined and accompanied me to the city of Washington, from whence I sent him to conduct the works at Norfolk.

On 12th, consulting with General Armstrong, the successor of Dr. Eustis in the War Department, in reference to my future functions in New York and at the Military Academy, and upon the application of the four hundred and ninety-seven thousand dollars that had been appropriated for fortifications on my estimates made last fall; which, with the twenty new regiments of infantry, two hundred and fifty thousand dollars for barges for harbor protection, two hundred and fifty thousand dollars for hulks to obstruct the harbor channels at points where the defences were insufficient, ten companies of sea fencibles and ten companies of rangers, with also a newly organized staff and a commissariat of purchase and supplies, evinced the influence of our new secretary and promised vigorous operations.

On 24th arrived at Baltimore and consulted with General Samuel Smith upon militia and other defences of the Petapsco, and we inspected Fort McHenry and gave directions for repairs of the same.

On 26th to Philadelphia, and passed a day with my late chief, Colonel Williams, at Mount Pleasant on the Schuylkill, who though retired was deeply interested in plans for protecting the Delaware, in reference to which, and my own views for New York, I remained a few days for the benefit of the counsel of this patriot. April 1st at Mrs. Wilkinson's, No. 40 Broadway, in New York, that had been for years the city quarters of Colonel Williams and other engineer officers.

On 6th April reported myself for duty to General George Izard, the commandant of the department, and by an especial order of the President, received the command of Staten Island with a brigade composed of Colonel Samuel Hawkins and Colonel Alexander Deniston's regiments of infantry, the 32d and 41st, in addition to my duties as engineer, and also such occasional visits to the Military Academy as my duties may permit, and for which purpose I required Captain Partridge at West Point to man the engineer yacht and send the same to me, which was done, and the yacht used for the double purpose of exploring the waters adjacent to New York, and making occasional inspections of the Academy at West Point. April 15th I commenced repairing all the forts in the harbor, and also a system of block houses at Utrecht Bay, west end of Long Island, Princess Bay on Staten Island, at Sandy Hook and Jamaica Bay, to prevent surprise from the English squadron of three "seventy-fours," two frigates and a sloop of war then laying off the Hook. Employed Mr. Cropsy of Utrecht, a very industrious and intelligent mechanic, to construct these buildings, and also Mr. John Tisdale as clerk to the engineer department. He had been similarly employed by Colonel Williams. To aid this protection we had a fleet of gun boats in the Sandy Hook cove. Despatched the yacht with orders to Captain Partridge at West Point to call on Colonel Snowden, the military store-keeper, with my requisition for the wall pieces in the United States stores, which on their receipt were distributed to the several block houses before mentioned, each block-house having a guard formed by detachments made by General John Swartwout from his brigade of militia quartered at Perth Amboy. We had discovered that from the Romilles, seventy-four, a nightly intercourse was maintained with spies in the city. I had arranged with General Swartwout to transport his forces at short notice to the Hook or Long Island, having also an understanding with the commander of the flotilla of gun boats and barges, Captain Jacob Lewis, to furnish barges, relying, however, for efficiency on his second officer, Captain J. B. Cooper, in Armand's corps, and who though never a sailor, had been a cavalry office at the age of seventeen in the War of Independence ; a man of mind and great activity.

On 25th May reported to the Secretary of War that all these temporary defences of New York Harbor were defensible, having cannon mounted in all of them, and supplies, etc., etc. Also reported to the Secretary that I had ordered Major McRee to the northern frontier as chief engineer there and Lieutenant S. Thayer to General Bloomfield for similar duty on the Delaware river and bay. I also sent the Secretary my plans for new buildings at West Point, regretting that the appropriations did not permit architectural taste, space of rooms and despatch in building being essential to the increasing wants of the Academy.

At the close of the month of May the governor of the State and the commandant of the department accompanied me on an inspection of the forts in the harbor and of the temporary works before mentioned. These various employments had postponed my visit to West Point into June, when I went thither in the yacht and inspected the Academy. Among the experiments, found the magnetic variation to be four degrees and fifteen minutes west, and traced on the ground the foundation for the new buildings. Finding some impediment to the execution of my orders at the Academy, arising from my absence and Captain Partridge's idea of his own responsibility in my absence, by the permission of the Secretary of War I remodelled the functions of the Academic staff, assuming to myself the inspectorship of the institution, at the same time providing for the functions of a professor of ethics, history and geography combined with the duty of chaplain, that had long been wanted at the Academy, and for which the Secretary of War permitted me to employ a divine of the Episcopal church. On my return to the city I found my son, James Foster, at No. 40 Broadway, brought from Wilmington, North Carolina, by my friend John Fanning Burgwin, with letters from my wife that the rest of my family would soon come on by land also, under escort of my friend Major Alexander C. Miller.

On the occasion of arranging for the celebration of 4th July on Staten Island, General Izard deemed my views as interfering with his command. In referring him to the orders of the President and the 63d article of war, I also stated that my arrangements were of detail, and that I should adhere to them unless he chose to assume the command by his presence on the Island, or by general orders, and that it offered me an opportunity to gratify any wish he might have in reference to those details, if he would signify the wish. No farther discussion or action on this point of command arose while General Izard was in command of the department.

On 17th July Mrs. Swift and my sons William, Alexander and Thomas, and my servant Nancy, arrived from North Carolina under the care of Mr. Miller, in twenty-one days' travel from Wilmington. They found Julius H. Walker, James Foster Swift and myself at housekeeping in Washington Street, Brooklyn, in quarters fitted by my friend George Gibbs, and by the aid of another friend, Major Fanning C. Tucker, found an excellent school for my sons James and Willy, taught by a Welch scholar, Evan Brynon. Soon after my family was established in Brooklyn, the Society for Manumitting Slaves called (by their deputy, a Quaker gentleman,) in my absence, on Mrs. Swift, and informed her and my servants Jack and Nancy, that the two latter could not be held in bondage. The servants replied that they wished not their interference. I, however, found that the doctrines of these philanthropists had disturbed the quiet of both Jack and Nancy, and I told them that I would give them their freedom as soon as they chose to require it.

The principal object for which I had been on duty in New York Harbor, (to repair the forts, and to construct such temporary works as the time permitted,) having been accomplished, I wrote the Secretary of War that I was ready for duty on the frontier, knowing that an army was to be concentrated at Sackett's Harbor for some movement on the St. Lawrence.

On 9th August I received orders to report myself for duty to General Wilkinson as the chief engineer of the 9th military department. On 14th General Wilkinson arrived in the city, and the same day I had an interview with him, and received instructions in relation to the contemplated campaign.

On 17th I accompanied him and General Armstrong, the Secretary of War, Governor Tompkins and Colonel Gilman of New Hampshire, to Albany, landing my brother, William H. Swift, at West Point, a cadet for the Academy, and giving him letters to Captain Partridge. At Albany I found Major George Bumford industriously and usefully engaged in preparing ordnance stores for the Ontario frontier. The transportation of these ordnance stores and cannon to the lakes had become an exhorbitant expense, frequently in amount exceeding the value. The roads were bad, and the Mohawk at so low a stage of water that flat boats could not be used; all indicating the neglect of preparation for war previously to its declaration, and also the need of those improvements which the growth of the country demanded, and which had been ably presented to Congress six years ago, and which also had become in New York the theme of conversation among such men as Gouverneur Morris, Thomas Eddy, Gideon Hawley, John Swartwout, De Witt Clinton, Elkanah Watson, etc. From the first movement of military stores to the lakes, for naval as well as army purposes, transportation has been the heaviest item of expense.

At Albany were at this time assembled numerous army officers *en route* for Sackett's Harbor. On 25th August the adjutant-general, J. B. Walbach, General L. Covington with other officers, including myself, *en route* for the harbor, and arrived there on 31st, and found the army much distressed by disease from using bad bread; one of the great evils that arise from the contract system in furnishing supplies for an army, especially bread and pork. Renewed my acquaintance with Commodore J. Chauncy, now the naval commander on the lakes, and made the acquaintance of Brigadier Jacob Brown, a self-taught, active, and highly intelligent officer; also found the marquee of Colonel Alexander Macomb, graced by his accomplished and exemplary wife, the only lady in camp, General Brown's family being at Brownville. I had left my own family at Brooklyn, having arranged with my friend John F. Burgwin to supply Mrs. Swift with money in case of interruption in my sending supplies, and commending my family to the courtesies of my friend Fanning C. Tucker and his family, and that of his father-in-law, Joshua Sands, Esq., and also the family of George Gibbs,

Esq., all of Brooklyn, and in the city the family of Captain James Farquhar, whose hospitable lady and daughters made Green Hill (the "Sailors' Snug Harbor" estate left by Captain Randall,) one of the most agreeable circles of domestic happiness that I have ever found.

On 6th September my assistants, Lieutenant James Gadsden and Lieutenant R. E. De Russy arrived, and commenced a reconnoitre of the waters of the bays and the approach to the St. Lawrence.

General Wilkinson's headquarters was the daily point of assembling the staff, and of conference on the duties that were opening the campaign at this time. On 5th September General Armstrong was escorted, as Secretary of War, into the cantonment, the interview at headquarters being too formal for that ease which is desirable for the interchange of opinion among chieftains. I was invited by the Secretary of War to accompany himself and General Brown, mounted, to the battle ground where Colonel Backus fell in the moment of victory, and where General Brown won the commission he now wears by his timely arrival in the action at the head of a band of militia. A line of our troops extending from the block-house at the harbor toward the lake shore, south-east of Horse Island, the point where the British troops landed and made the assault, General Brown's militia arriving through the woods in the rear of Colonel Backus' left flank and thus assailing the enemy on his right flank, which caused the halt and precipitate retreat of the enemy, and thus the winning of the day by Brown.

I was now joined by Brevet-Major Totten as my first assistant engineer, and, with General R. Swartwout, examined the stores of the quartermaster-general's department. At headquarters I observed an inactivity that, as it seemed to me, arose from some doubts as to who was in command, General Armstrong or General Wilkinson. In my occasional excursions with these gentlemen I observed that they did not ride at the same time. In my interviews with General Wilkinson his expressions implied a strong dislike of the interference of the War Department, and in fact the presence of the Secretary did lessen the influence of General Wilkinson. The contemplated junction with Hampton was a subject of discourse, and General

Wilkinson indulged in a too public expression of his dislike to General Hampton, which, on one occasion gave me a fair opportunity of saying to General Wilkinson that his remarks tended to revive the feuds and party feelings of the army that had been described before the court martial at Fredericktown in 1811.

Whatever may have been the influence of General Armstrong's presence there was no increase in the activity of preparation to move the army, which condition of things continued until the 8th October, when a sudden council of war was called and I was questioned as to my opinion of attacking Kingston. My reply was that I would not attack that place at all if the army was ready to move down the St. Lawrence, but if not ready, that Kingston might be surprised and the public stores burned in a couple of days by one thousand men, if my intelligence was to be relied on, as I believed it was.

On the same day I presented Mr. D. B. Douglass with letters from the War Department, informing him that the Secretary of War had acceded to my request to appoint him second lieutenant of engineers, and that he would repair to West Point for duty at the Military Academy, and by him I sent supplies to my family at Brooklyn.

Up to 19th October heard no more of an assault upon Kingston, on which day General Wilkinson directed me, with Brevet-Major Totten, to reconnoitre the St. Lawrence river in the vicinity of Prescott, and plan an attack upon that post, and to sound the river with a view to a rapid passage down the river. On 20th Major Totten and myself were on our way as far as Brownsville, leaving my military cloak in the care of Lieutenant Beverly Randolph, aid-de-camp to General Lewis, and also some books. On 23d, near Oswagatchie, met Colonel Sackett of the United States dragoons at the Bend, and with him arranged to be furnished with escort, and thence we proceeded to Ogdensburg and Morristown, opposite Brockville, in Canada. We here met Arnold Smith, who, with Mr. York of Ogdensburg, gave us much assistance. By 31st October I had procured a plan of Fort Prescott and sounded the channel of the river, and sent my plan of attack to General Wilkinson by express, whose reply was that he should enter the river with his force by 3d November. On 4th instructed Colonel Sackett and Major Woodford to collect the boats that were near Hamilton for the use of the army.

Our reconnoitering was much annoyed by a party of Glengary Fencibles under Ruben Sherwood, a very active and shrewd refugee from Connecticut, so that our movements had to be made at early dawn, and our passage from place to place effected by night. At the close of this day (4th) Major Charles Nourse met me at Ogdensburg with advices from General Wilkinson, then at Grenadier Island, the army on the river. On 5th I met General Wilkinson in his boat on the river near Morristown, and he determined to pass Prescott at night. We were here joined by Colonel W. Scott and Colonel E. P. Gaines as volunteers. On 6th the main body of the army landed to march through Ogdensburg, and at night General Wilkinson directed me to conduct him in his boat past Prescott, which was done, the baggage following, the cannonade from the fort commencing as soon as our boat was under way. Little damage was sustained by the boats owing to the random fire from the fort, and, as I presume, from neglect of ranging their guns by daylight. Many of our officers and men, particularly the aged, were suffering from disordered bowels from the use of bad bread, especially General Wilkinson and General Lewis. The former sought relief in the use of opium, and soon after passing Prescott it was necessary to land, which was done at Sharp's farm, in whose house under the influence of laudanum the general became very merry, and sung and repeated stories, the only evil of which was that it was not of the dignified deportment to be expected from the commander-in-chief. At early dawn on 7th we reached the Indian village on the American shore, followed on the opposite bank of the river by light artillery from Prescott that annoyed our march somewhat. Our force, seven thousand rank and file. General Wilkinson here informed me that he expected soon to meet General Hampton and his four thousand troops. In the evening of 7th we arrived at the Narrows and remained till 9th, sending Colonel Alexander Macomb in advance, and crossing the dragoons from the American shore, our videts informing us that twenty-three boats loaded with troops, protected by two gun boats, commanded by Captain Mulcaster, were following us at a distance of four miles. The evening of 9th we passed the Rapid Platte opposite Hamilton, and put to at Williamsburgh near Chrysler's farm. On the morning of the 11th November detachments were debarked from Boyd's, Swartwout's and Covington's brigades to lighten the boats, and to pass the dangers of the Long Sault. As these detachments were about to move down the margin of the river the enemy was seen advancing in column, their advance guard opening a light fire on us. Orders were given to face about and advance on the enemy in three columns, outflank them, and capture their artillery, each of our columns five hundred men. The enemy retired and formed behind a ravine at Chrysler's farm with their right wing forward, as our movement was to turn the left flank, their force about one thousand six hundred, their right supported by four pieces of artillery aided by eight gun boats in the river, that maintained a constant fire, though ill-directed. Our columns drove the enemy back across a ravine west of the first, and formed line on the brink of the ravine opposite the enemy, our left supported by four pieces of artillery and a reserve of one hundred and fifty dragoons. Both lines opened a fire on each other, and no attempt was made by our generals to charge until Colonel Walbach put the dragoons in motion. They were arrested by the fire of grape from the gun boats, killing some eight men and wounding many at the head of this charge. Both sides ceased firing at the same moment for no apparent cause, as neither side made any forward movement to charge further. Our columns, after having every fifth man killed or wounded, (one hundred and two of the former and two hundred and thirty-eight of the latter,) leaving our dead on the field, marched deliberately to our boats, pushed off and descended the river and the Long Sault, arriving on the morning of 12th at Barnhard's Bay, and were there joined by Colonel Macomb and General Brown of the advance, who had had an affair with the enemy at an adjacent bridge. During the action of the 11th November my duties were two-fold, that of engineer and aid to the commander-in-chief, therefore, being at various points in the field with orders, saw every movement and every neglect of movement that

I have noted. On this same day (12th) Colonel H. Atkinson, General Hampton's inspector-general, arrived at Barnhard's Bay with a letter from his chief declining a junction of his army at St. Regis. This declension put an end to the campaign. Our army left Barnhard's Bay 13th November, crossed the St. Lawrence and ascended the Salmon River six miles, to the French Mills. On 14th we buried with military honors General Leonard Covington, who had been mortally wounded on 11th November at Chrysler's farm. The general died on 12th. He requested me to send his sword to his son, and to give his horses to his servant, both of which were done.

After making proper arrangements in my department I received the following order in a letter from General Wilkinson:

"French Mills, 17th November, 1813.

"Col. Swift: *Sir*,— You will please to proceed to General Hampton with the general order now delivered to you under seal, and having delivered it will communicate to me the result, to which you will be pleased to add freely and confidentially every observation material to the service which you may have made. You will employ an express to bear this communication to this place. You will then proceed to Washington, having leave to call on your family, and deliver to the Secretary of War the letter you have; and should he encourage it give him a detail of the affair of the 11th, and also of all our measures and movements. At Washington you will be able to learn what may be my destiny. Any communication you may make to me on this subject will be gratefully received. I shall also be glad to hear from you on your route through the great towns.

"With unfeigned friendship,

"Your obliged and faithful

"James Wilkinson."

I proceeded to Plattsburgh with caution, having to evade the videts of the enemy, and arrived at General Hampton's headquarters on 19th November, and on 20th I wrote to General Wilkinson by express, as follows:

"PLATTSBURGH, 20th November, 1813.

"*Dear Sir:* I enclose an official report of my progress. I found General Hampton in bed, who said he was ready to obey your orders, with an army out of spirits, not more than one thousand six hundred effectives. I learn from the general that it was not his intention to disobey any order of yours, and that his non-junction was in consequence of the opinion that he was required to act upon your letter of 6th; and from General Armstrong's letter to him, which he showed me, there was no intimation of joining you above Chataugay. General Hampton pledges his sacred honor to me that it was his desire to have formed a junction with you. The last letter of General Armstrong to General Hampton has this expression in it: 'The enemy have been able to overtake General Wilkinson and detain him as high up the river as Cornwall; it is evident that the movement below cannot safely be more than a feint.'

"On passing through Chataugay Four Corners I find all consumed by fire. From General Hampton I learn that all below has been burned by the English. All your supplies, then, must come from this point, Plattsburgh, and unless a force be left here to guard this pass and depôt the enemy can come upon General Hampton's rear and cut off future supply. I therefore think that General Hampton had better remain here. General Hampton is of opinion that the enemy cannot get up to you. He gives me a copy of his order for the march, (enclosed,) and entreats of you to allow a few days' delay. He furnishes relays of express horses to get my letter to you, in order that you may be acquainted with the nature of the country through which the enemy must march to make an attack on you. The roads are so bad on the Chataugay that the English cannot transport their artillery and necessary provisions. Captain McDonough is superior to the enemy on this lake in broad water with a working wind, and inferior under all other circumstances. The enemy could be in this place in twelve hours after General Hampton moves for Chataugay Four Corners. I am fully of the opinion that the government will make the best of our affairs, and I have been thinking of the plan, to wit: Sink all the boats in Salmon River, take sleds and move your army and stores to this place, ordering General

Hampton to build huts for your troops.    Make from this an attack over the ice upon Isle au Noix, carry it and St. Johns, and determine in the spring to transport boats overland fourteen miles and make a descent on Montreal, or wait, with the command of these passes till our army be renovated for an efficient assault.    This plan may be varied.    The main reasons that influence my mind in this are: the necessity of doing something before spring, and of being in the best possible position for action then.    General Hampton has sent his sick and convalescent into quarters at Burlington, Vermont."

The next day I again wrote to General Wilkinson as follows:

"PLATTSBURGH, 21st November, 1813.

"*Dear General:*   Yesterday I wrote you a hasty memorandum, wishing to get off the express without delay.    Though hasty, the more I reflect on the plan of your army moving to this place for winter quarters, and more especially as a new line of operations—the line that, in the end, must be adopted—the more am I impressed with its importance.    From the French Mills the campaign of 1814 will be difficult in operation, and may be, if the enemy manage well with gun boats, defeated; difficult from the distance of army supplies, etc.    Suppose in the spring that our usual tardy supply of recruits prevent any certain operation against the enemy. In such case this position on Lake Champlain would be preferable far to French Mills.    Hold Sackett's Harbor, Fort George, and Plattsburgh with strong garrisons till our army has time to be reformed."

General Wilkinson's letter to the Secretary of War, mentioned in his order to me, is as follows:

"HEADQUARTERS FRENCH MILLS, 17th November, 1813.

To GENERAL ARMSTRONG.    *Dear General:*    This will be delivered to you by Colonel Swift, who took the boldest and most active part in the action of 11th instant of any individual engaged except Adjutant-General Walbach, who is now ill in consequence of his exertions and fatigue.    Colonel

Swift, from his personal observations on the ground, is able to give you many details which I deem improper to commit to paper, and for this purpose I have directed him to wait on you at Washington after he has seen Hampton with the order of which I yesterday transmitted you a copy. Your military system requires thorough revision, and your military establishment great reform, before we can put to the best advantage the natural force and courage of our countrymen. Since the action of 11th, British officers have acknowledged our dauntless courage, but observed we were undisciplined and fought without order, and indeed the scenes of that day justify these observations. Give Colonel Swift your confidence, and I pledge myself to you that he will not abuse it. God bless you my dear general.

" James Wilkinson."

On the day of the date of my letter to General Wilkinson, 21st November, after ordering Major William McRee and Captain S. Thayer of the engineers, then at Plattsburgh, to meet me in New York as soon as General Hampton could spare them, I left Plattsburgh and crossed the lake to Vermont and arrived in Albany on 25th, and by invitation at Governor Tompkins' as his guest, and where I found General Armstrong, Secretary of War, and also General William H. Harrison from our western army. The Secretary of War was in his chamber and on perusing the despatches he enquired into the condition of the forces, etc. I gave him in detail the condition in which I had left them, and of the movements on the St. Lawrence. He attributed the result to the negligence of both the generals. I gave him the substance of my letters to General Wilkinson from Plattsburgh and my reason for changing the course of our error that had been existing from the first year of the war, namely, inviting the enemy to the west instead of keeping him to the east by our operations on the natural line through Lake Champlain, and thereby compelling him to pass to and from Upper Canada by the Ottawa River, etc. These views could not have been novel in such a mind as General Armstrong's, and when at table the conversation was between him and the Governor and General Harrison, and it was jocosely remarked that western war did not occasion John Bull to bring over veterans, as he would do if the war was pressed to the east, the Secretary turned the subject. General Harrison had been a pupil of General Wayne and though not of equal genius or reading with General Armstrong, he had sound military views, and he sustained the point of Governor Tompkins' waggery. The latter never spared a joke because it was true, save when it might injure feeling. There are few of larger generosity of feeling than Governor Tompkins. The power of calling out the militia was also a topic at table after dinner, and United States authority denied, by all, to make the call save through the action of the governor of the State, whose right and duty it would also be to designate the general and other officers until the body joined the army of the United States in the field. As to the causes of failure of the campaign on the St. Lawrence, the sojourn of General Armstrong on the frontier in the autumn had excited the jealousy of General Wilkinson. As the event is, both of the generals and Secretary would gladly attribute the failure to any other cause than their respective errors. The immediate cause of the failure is the delay on the river; overtaking our army by the British on 11th November ended the campaign. My impression is that a junction of Wilkinson and Hampton was not intended, and by consequence an assault on Montreal was not purposed after October, if previously. One of the main causes of delay is bad bread, and its consequent bad health. Our chiefs were old, and from the date of the movement from Sackett's Harbor the two oldest, Wilkinson and Lewis, had not a day of sound health until winter. If the army had been led by General Brown the end had been better than it is.

The evening of 25th, agreeably to his request I wrote to General Wilkinson my idea of his prospects, and mentioned my main views of 20th and 21st on his movements. As I could not with propriety mention the Secretary of War's conversation about himself and Hampton, I briefly said I found him dissatisfied with both.

At the same time I wrote Sheriff T. J. Davies on Black Lake that the Secretary of War had acceded to my request to send his son Charles to West Point as a cadet. I had given the Secretary an account of the zeal that this youth had exhibited in the campaign on the St. Lawrence, and also of the service that the father had rendered to the march of the army between Ogdensburgh and the rapids below, in foraging, etc. The same evening I wrote Mr. Arnold Smith, who had been a very able guide on the St. Lawrence, that the Secretary of War offered him the post of assistant deputy quartermaster-general.

I found in Albany a letter from Professor Mansfield at West Point on the subject of his going to Ohio, and sent him leave to be from the Academy through the vacation of course, and also to 10th April, 1814.

On 26th my faithful and fearless man Jack arrived from Plattsburgh with my horses Scott and Flim Nap; placed them at livery with a cavalry soldier of the Revolutionary War, Mr. Gregory, to await orders for my return to the north, in case that my ideas of a campaign should be adopted.

On 27th November, with General Armstrong and General W. H. Harrison and other officers, taking a steamboat to ourselves and stopping at West Point to make an inspection, and on 28th found my family all in health at Brooklyn, in Washington Street. Thanks be to God!

On 30th November General Dearborn, the commander of the department, and General Harrison, dined and passed the evening at my quarters, and with my cousin, W. R. Swift. General Armstrong could not stay to dinner. The conversation was upon the mode of conducting the campaign of 1814.

We had that morning inspected the forts on Staten Island and west end of Long Island — a British squadron cruising off Sandy Hook.

On 9th December, with Bishop Hobart consulting on the subject of inviting the Rev. Adam Empie to take the chaplaincy of the Military Academy, the Secretary of War having in the previous summer given his consent to offer that appointment to Mr. Empie, and having learned that he (Mr. Empie) had determined to leave Wilmington, North Carolina, I now wrote to Mr. Empie that the Bishop highly approved the plan, and that the selection of an Episcopalian had been made because, aside from my own views, the service of that church was deemed to be the most appropriate to the discipline of a military academy.

December 11, the Secretary of War invited me to accompany him to the War Office at Washington, and on 15th with Mrs. Armstrong and her daughter, Miss Margaret, the journey was commenced. At Princeton, with the general, looked over the battle ground where General Mercer fell in the Revolution, and to whom the Secretary had been an aid-de-camp on that day, the Secretary marking the positions and movements of the American and British forces in that conflict.

We occupied until 24th in looking at the Delaware and Patapsco with military views, and in reaching Washington I found Mrs. Armstrong an amiable lady, and her daughter handsome and intelligent. The general has a fine mind, though personally of very inert habits, abounding in knowledge of the past and strong views of the future operations on the frontier. He spoke of General Washington in highest terms of respect for his integrity and patriotism, but not respectfully of his genius. We discoursed on the " Newburgh Letters." The general said that had he been one year older he would not have written them; that they had been a mill-stone hung about his neck through his life. He corroborated Dr. Eustis' saying that Colonel Pickering was on the committee which appointed him (General Armstrong) to write, and that Dr. Townsend had also been on that committee.

At Washington, on the presentation of my reports and estimates for fortifications and the Academy for 1814. I recommended that the chief engineer should have his office in the city of Washington. The objection was that the station of the corps of engineers was, by law, to be at West Point. My reply to this was that Congress could remedy that by a very brief resolution ; that the necessity was apparent in the fact that the adjutant and paymaster-general's departments were established there for easy communication with the War Office; and that the functions of both of those offices were very simple, while those of the engineer department involved frequent elucidations to the Secretary of War upon expensive plans of construction, etc. There seemed to me to be an impression that having a military staff at Washington would be placing a personal influence there not congenial with our institutions. The wise and worthy President Madison, able to conduct the affairs of the country in times of peace very successfully, found himself oppressed by the disappointments that resulted from the imperfect composition of our army, and of operations concocted by his inexperienced counsellors, which were evinced by failures of campaigns. Neither himself nor his congressional intimates, nor his cabinet, fancied the proximity of a military staff as advisers in a war that had been commenced without preparation, a neglect that had much of its origin in a just though misdirected dread of a standing army; which error had also been accompanied by an omission of competent provision for the construction and keeping in good condition the machinery of war. That is, providing and classifying arms and munitions under the care of competent and responsible officers to conserve the same, and including in said provision a corps of instructed administrative officers with a comparative small number of men as a nucleus upon which may be predicated any force that a war may make needful.

The habits of the nation, for more than a quarter of a century previously to this war, had been that of peaceful commerce; now disturbed by the aggression of foreign powers that had made retaliation necessary, these habits in peace had become so moulded by demagogues that the people were more influenced by personal objects and small party politics than by views for the public good; a course of conduct that had thronged the halls of Congress with representatives, a large majority of whom had but slender mental endowments. In the progress of the war a better state of things was dawning. The pressure of the war had turned quiet and intelligent minds of men at home to reflect gravely on the lack of talent in Congress, and in the cabinet also. The elections began now to return better informed citizens to Congress. The experience of Mr. Madison had been comparatively great, but it had been altogether of a civil character. In appointing military officers, resort was had to those who had survived, and who had held subordinate offices in the great struggle for independence; even these were too aged for prolonged activity in the field. The subject of change in the selection of officers for the army as leaders had become a common topic at Washington, and it was admitted that too much favor to party had been exercised in making army appointments. Such men as General John

Brooks in Massachusetts, and Colonel Jonathan Williams of Philadelphia were now thought of, as of the youngest on the Revolutionary list who were competent to lead.

WEST POINT, December 31st, 1816.

1814. January. On 3d of this month, at the request of Governor Worthington of Ohio, I gave him a plan to form a military academy in that growing State. My view of the use of such institutions in the several States is that it is the best mode to interest militia officers to train no larger body of militia than a battalion; that no larger force of militia could be usefully assembled, and consequently no higher grade of rank should be conferred in the militia than that of major. The duty of a freeman to defend his country could be best initiated at such schools. But by no means to interfere with the Military Academy at West Point.

The appropriations for 1814 were to raise three regiments of riflemen and ten companies of rangers, also five hundred thousand dollars for floating batteries — contemplating the steam frigate plan of Mr. Fulton — and five hundred thousand dollars for fortifications.

In this month of January, at Washington several highly talented gentlemen of Congress, together with some citizens sojourning there, and including some officers of the army, held meeetings to consult upon measures to be recommended to the country through the gazettes and by correspondence with citizens in all the States of the Union, to commend General John Armstrong for the next presidency, under the conviction that to carry on the war with success to attain peace the President should be a military man. Jeremiah Mason of New Hampshire, then in the Senate, was the leader of this plan, and I was myself an humble agent to promote the purpose. The "Newburgh Letters" were the chief obstacle to our essay. But General Armstrong was the strongest mind of the party in power, and it had been useless to have wasted our efforts on General Pinckney; he had the curse of Federalism attached to his most honored name. The subject subsided. It was impracticable from the lowness of motive that had to be addressed to a misguided public. Popularity of a mean species was needed to sustain a fresh candidate. But the essay had one good influence upon the cabinet, to spur it on to make new and suitable appointments, and to adopt a plan of campaign that promised useful success, namely, by concentrating our forces upon Lower Canada.

On 20th January my orders sent Colonel Armistead to inspect and repair the fortifications south of Maryland, and Major William McRee to Sackett's Harbor to construct defences there, taking upon myself the direction of the repairs on the Delaware, and thence eastward to Maine. On 28th January arrived at headquarters at Brooklyn, and until 24th February engaged with General Moses Porter, the officer of ordnance, in commencing the repairs at Fort Mifflin and in New York Harbor. On 24th February my father, Dr. Foster Swift, received the appointment of surgeon in the army, through the efforts of his former schoolmate in Boston, Hon. H. G. Otis.

On 25th February received my commission from Adjutant John B. Walbach, as brevet brigadier-general in the army. Its date, instead of 14th February should have been 11th November, 1813. This omission I have attributed to General Armstrong's dislike of my friendly regard for General Wilkinson.

On 28th February to Philadelphia, to meet the committee of defence there, my former chief, Colonel Williams, its principal counsellor, and by order of the Secretary of War, and with Colonel Williams' advice, formed a plan for the Delaware, and to defend the approaches by land. On the 2d of March proceeded with the committee down the Delaware in the revenue cutter to Fort Mifflin, and to the Pea Patch, accompanied by the veteran Colonel Allen McLean and Commodore Stewart, and selected the Pea Patch and a point opposite on the Delaware as sites for works of defence, to be occupied at once. Commodore Stewart's views are of a true military character, both for land and sea. Reported the result of this examination to the War Department on my return to Philadelphia, where, in consequence of letters from Washington, on 4th March I wrote Mr. Ferdinand R. Hassler, then in London, under cover of Hon. Jonathan Russell, and also through Mr. Gallatin, that his long absence from the

United States was commented upon, and that I hoped he would return to the United States to resume the coast survey as soon as possible. Among the rumors was one that he was dabbling in politics, and corresponding with the enemies of England on the subject of the oppression that his native land (Switzerland) was sustaining. Mr. Hassler was conducting the construction of mathematical instruments for the survey with Mr. Edward Troughton.

On 6th March I went to Germantown to consult with Major Roberdeau on the topography of the Delaware shore, and there met Mr. Stephen H. Long, and examined his successful hydraulic machinery; gave him my aid to enter the corps of engineers as a second lieutenant, and employed him to join me at Brooklyn as an assistant engineer. Returned to Delaware River, and on 9th of March, after consulting with General Bloomfield on the military defences, returned to my family at Brooklyn. On 19th proceeded to West Point to examine the cadets and other matters about the Academy, that employed me there for one week. On 3d April Mrs. Swift and myself were confirmed at St. Ann's by Bishop Hobart, at Brooklyn, L. I.

On 4th April received from Major John J. Abert a letter, enclosing a present from Robert Carey Jennings, of an original letter of three pages, fool's-cap paper, blue, and English make, from General (then Major) Washington to Governor Dinwiddie, dated 3d June, 1754, speaking of an expected battle with Jumonville, and having a remarkable expression in it as coming from *Washington* to a *governor*, to wit: " If Jumonville behave no better than he did last week I shall have little difficulty in driving him to the devil." Which letter may not have been copied by General Washington in his then position, and which therefore may serve to elucidate the slander cast on Washington by the French governor, of cruelty, etc. This letter R. C. Jennings received from his father-in-law, the Rev. Neidler Robinson, living not far from Petersburgh, Va., and who had been a personal friend of Washington's. I, for safety, deposited this letter, by the hands of John Pintard, in the archives of the Historical Society of New York. Of the authenticity of the letter, from the hand-writing, some careless orthography and its whole aspect, not a doubt existed.

April 9th, with my cousin William Roberdeau Swift, and my brother-in-law, Julius H. Walker, proceeded on a tour of inspection to direct the repair of all the fortifications east of New York to Maine.

April 13th we arrived at Boston; met there my father at his post as United States surgeon, the family residing in Sudbury Street; my mother in excellent health. I had not seen my parents for four years and five months. The time had been gentle in its effects on my parents. Examined the works at the Castle and on Governor's Island, and the waters to the lower anchorage.

April 16th, to General Brooks in Medford, to consult about obstructing the channel of Boston Harbor by hulks sunk with care. My cousin W. R. Swift was with me, and after dining with the general we were returning to Boston in our hired chaise, and driving at good speed encountered a country wagon and broke its fore axle, capsized our chaise into a hollow, which instantly killed our horse. The expense of this drive was one hundred and sixty dollars, and we both escaped with very slight contusions.

April 19th, leaving Mr. Swift and Mr. Walker to visit the *alma mater* of the latter at Cambridge, I proceeded with Commodore Hull, United States navy, to Portsmouth, N. H., and on board the frigate Congress there met my cousin John Lovering, a fine scholar, but by dissipation reduced to a clerkship on board this vessel; made arrangements for his discharge, and to return to his excellent mother in Boston. Examined the new seventy-four on the stocks; renewed my acquaintance at the Langdon's and Sheafe's, and with Commodore Hull examined the harbor to plan means of protection against sudden incursion from the British cruisers; gave orders for suitable repairs on Fort Constitution, and a covered battery at Kittery on the Maine shore. The works at Portland being deemed by General M. Porter in as good condition as they could be placed, I went no farther east.

April 21st returned to Boston, and on 23d with General John Brooks, T. H. Cushing and Colonel Sullivan attended an experiment at the navy yard, where one hundred and seventy-five balls of lead, of two ounces weight each, were discharged from seven gun barrels hooped together, each barrel containing twenty-five balls, and the whole discharged at a target two hundred and fifty yards off, the balls penetrating to various depths out of sight into the target. Chamber's repeating gun. Three days after, with Governor Brooks, General Cushing and Colonel Sullivan I inspected the channel-way down the harbor, with a view to planning a system of hulks to obstruct the same. Found Colonel George Sullivan an active and intelligent aid in this matter, giving the subject his whole time.

April 27th, with my mother and sister, Sarah Adams, cousin W. R. Swift and Mr. Adams, on my way to Rhode Island Harbor. Passed a couple of days at Taunton Green, at the academy and other nooks of William R. and my boyhood scenes, meeting Dr. Doggett and the Leonards, and Crockers, and Tillinghasts, Cobbs and other early friends, greatly to the pleasure of my mother, and to all of us. I here finished my plan for so sinking the hulks in Boston Harbor as by aid of pumps to float each vessel at will, and sent the same to Colonel Sullivan to be laid before the gentlemen before mentioned, by the hands of Justice Parker, on the last day of April; the same day saw my mother, etc., off for Boston, and, with W. R. Swift left for Newport, R. I. After examining the forts, gave to Captain Julian F. Heileman directions for the repair thereof, which occupied me to the 3d May, when, with W. R. Swift, proceeded over to Connanicut, and by the ferry and road thence to New London, where, with General H. Burbeck arranged for the best that could there be done to repel any sudden assault of the enemy, then laying off in Gardner's Bay.

Found Colonel Roswell Lee an excellent volunteer officer, abounding in military resources for plans of defence, and an indefatigable and able executor of the field works to enclose old Fort Griswold — the key of the position. To the work done here I have attributed safety from marauding parties, such as succeeded at the mouth of the Connecticut River.

On 7th May, *via* Fort Hale in New Haven Harbor, arrived at my headquarters, Brooklyn, where the Rev. Adam Empie reported himself for duty at the Military Academy. I found on my desk letters from the War Department in reply to my request to be assigned to duty on the lake frontier, which in my opinion could now be done, as every arrangement had been made to repair and arm the fortifications on the seaboard. My request was declined, though General Brown had asked that I might be sent to Niagara; the reason assigned — the need of my services on the seaboard — may be sufficient, they were not so deemed by me. However, General Dearborn proposed examining all the defences of New York Harbor, in which I accompanied him. The spirit of the war of '76, and his experience therein, gave a zest to the reconnoitre, and interest to the opinion of this veteran. We were a week employed in this service, to 17th of May. On 20th of which month I accompanied Rev. Mr. Empie to West Point, and inducted him to his office, that of chaplain and professor of ethics, and also treasurer of the Academy; a novel junction of functions, but rendered needful by the want of officers.

My cousin, William R. Swift, was with me, and with a corps of cadets we ascended to the summit of Crows' Nest Hill, and measured its distance from Fort Clinton by the sound of its cannon, having with us a time chronometer. At one thousand one hundred and forty-two feet the second for the passage of sound, the distance is eight thousand two hundred and seventy-nine feet.

On my return to headquarters, Brooklyn, 29th, was called on by Colonel Nicholas Fish, formerly the adjutant-general of the United States army, who informed me of the apprehension of the citizens of New York, and his wish to consult with me on the mode of communication with the War Department on measures needful to defending the city.

This conference resulted in the appointment of a committee of defence by the city corporation. At this time a British squadron was cruising off the harbor. On 10th I met Governor Tompkins and the mayor, De Witt Clinton. By their advice funds were furnished by the corporation and *spies* were employed by me to visit the squadron off the Hook, who brought me a sketch from the cabins of Sir John B. Warren and Sir Thomas Hardy, which, whether real or speculative, contemplated a descent at some point on the coast between Rhode Island and Chesapeake Bay, and which I reported to General Armstrong at Washington. Upon this I invited the governor and mayor to examine with me the East River to Throg's Point, and the main channel to sea by Sandy Hook, giving them my opinion that the citizens might be invited to construct a line of defence in the rear of Brooklyn, and another from Hallet's Point in Hell Gate across York Island to Mount Alto. These gentlemen approved the idea, and at their instance six thousand dollars were placed at my disposal to commence the plan. I was at this time joined by Lieutenant James Gadsden as my aid-de-camp.

General Morgan Lewis was ordered to relieve General Dearborn in the command of the third department at New York.

On 22d June Robert Fulton, Esq., Commodore Decatur, Hon. Oliver Wolcott, General Lewis and myself witnessed an experiment made by Mr. Fulton at Governor's Island, to show the effect of discharging a cannon under water. Mr. Fulton placed a thirty-two pounder five feet below the surface of the water, and the muzzle five feet from a target composed of oak plank five feet thick, the passage to the vent being secured from dampness and nealed powder packed in a box leading to the vent, the piece charged with twelve pounds of powder and one thirty-two pound shot secured with plenty of wadding. On giving fire no sound was produced, and no violent action of the water. Numerous air bubbles came to the surface. The shot went through the five feet of water and through the target, tearing it in many pieces. In the open air on Governor's Island the same day, a thirty-two pounder cannon was charged with twelve pounds of powder and one shot, and fired at a target of the material and dimensions just mentioned, at two hundred and fifty yards distance. The shot penetrated four and a half feet, and much shattered the frame of the target. This experiment was made to show what could be done by suspending cannon over the side of a ship and running close alongside an enemy's ship.

The last of this month of June my cousin William R. Swift left us to proceed to the South, and I proceeded to West Point to inspect the Academy, and my family accompanied me. We returned 1st July, when, on reporting to the Secretary of War the condition of the Academy, I also stated the incipient measures of the corporation of New York, and received orders from the Secretary to render every aid in my power to such plan of protection as the city might adopt. On 15th sent Lieutenant James Gadsden to commence the works of Hallet's Point, a block-house on Mile

Rock, and a tower in the rear of the Point to cover the right of our line of defence. On the same day the mayor and my late chief, Colonel Jonathan Williams, Major Fairley, General Morton, (an industrious and most useful public officer and patriot,) were, with my father, Dr. Swift and General Stevens, assembled at the Point, and there named the position Fort Stevens in honor of the general, our companion, a patriot of the Revolution, and a prominent officer of artillery at Saratoga in 1777; who gave the party a dinner at Mt. Napoleon, his country seat, in honor of the occasion.

On 17th July commenced the works on Harlem Heights at Mt. Alto on the Hudson, extending thence by McGowan's Pass and the elevated ground that overlooks Harlem Flat to Hell Gate. The trenches were opened by a detachment of volunteers, citizens from the city, under Major Horn, a Revolutionary worthy. This line is taken in preference to an advanced one, because money and men are not yet at command.

On 26th July, with the committee of defence, urging the call upon the citizens to turn out and occupy Brooklyn Heights. A party of one thousand paraded at my quarters on August 6th, and broke ground on Fort Green. By 8th of the month the details became regular of citizen volunteers, each party working one day from sun to sun, yielding a force ranging from one thousand two hundred to two thousand per day, at Brooklyn and Harlem.

On 29th August Governor Tompkins and the mayor (Mr. Clinton,) with the committee of defence, adopted my organization of forces to man the works now constructing; General Armstrong assuring that one thousand six hundred regular troops would be at our command in a few days. We had an encampment of three thousand militia, a gun boat, and sea fencible force of five hundred men; Commodore Decatur had seven hundred sailors at command, General Morton had one thousand five hundred and General Mapes one thousand five hundred enrolled, at one hour's call. The exempts of the city enrolled themselves, one thousand five hundred; two corps under Samuel Swartwout and J. B. Murray, Esquires, were also formed. The steamboats were put in requisition to bring three thousand from Orange and Duchess Counties; General Jeremiah Johnston, of Long

Island, had one thousand men under his very prompt and able command; Newark offered three thousand and lower Jersey three thousand. Thus we had at call twenty thousand three hundred citizen soldiers. They were habitually under arms, and taught the ordinary marching and firing. I had the temporary office of inspector-general, and visited all these corps and examined their arms, flints, and ball cartridges, and established expresses. Addressed the citizens at the city hall, and counselled that no citizen should leave New York but on urgent necessity. In reference to the sick and disabled, caused the "Ten," and other public houses out of the city to be put in order with wards, nurses, stores and surgeons. The mode of defence was thus arranged in case the enemy landed. It was my part to lead to the shore, and Commodore Decatur to cover the flanks. The whole force encamped on Harlem Heights and at Brooklyn at any one time did not exceed twelve thousand rank and file. My functions in the busy scene were various. The committee of defence gave little heed to the regular functions of staff officers, and expected from me not only my own professional statement to them of the progress upon what they termed my lines of defence, but also an account of the progress of the ordnance constructions, the state of the artillery, the quartermaster-general's department and of the hospitals; in accomplishing which the aid of the officers of all departments was freely given, all of them estimating justly the exigency of the times, and waiving the observance of the ordinary routine of accountability to the committee, passed through my hands all the facts that were essential to enable the committee to estimate and acquire from the city corporate authorities the pecuniary means to execute our plan of defence. I had fine health and an excellent saddle horse, to whom the wags gave the name of "Flim Nap," after one of the heroes of the Dean, who carried me at half speed from and to Harlem and Brooklyn with ease, twice, and sometimes three and four times in a day, thus enabling me to forward the working parties of citizens. My principal aid-de-camp was Lieutenant James Gadsden of the United States engineers, who was of efficient and untiring ability. General Jacob Morton and General John Mapes; the comptroller of the city, Thomas R. Mercein, and most especially General Nicholas

Fish, chairman of the committee of defence, and Major Horn were constant aids to my labors, and many others of the citizens of both New York and Brooklyn ; in the latter, Joshua Sands, Esq., was prominent. My extra aids-de-camp were Messrs. James Renwick, John K. Bergwin, William Proctor, and William Kemble — the first and third topographers. Mr. Holland, the artist, volunteered his graphic services to avoid duty in the line of troops, and gave us more than twenty sketches of various parts of the line of works and adjacent scenery. The zeal of the citizens, led on by the most respectable gentlemen of the city in daily labor with the pick and shovel, had in a few weeks accomplished an incredible amount of work upon the lines. To these efforts the eloquence of the city, the patriotic song and thrilling story lent their aid and natural influence. Hawkins' songs, and the apt and facetious sallies of Maxwell were not among the least incentives to labor. The display of valor of our navy, and the heroism of our troops on the frontier gave vigor to the army of youth and age in our trenches, and finally the vandalic folly of Britain in burning the national archives at Washington in the month of September, topped the climax of feeling that kept our citizens with entrenching tools in their hands until the parapets across York and Long Island were bristling with ordnance, that gave token of our readiness for defence. This desirable state of our armament was attained by the close of the month of November, and the lines occupied by the troops from the several encampments of Brooklyn and Harlem.

On 27th December I received orders from the War Department to proceed in the ensuing January to Baltimore, as a member of a military board to revise the present, and form a new system of infantry tactics for the United States army.

In the two years past I have endeavored to promote the interests of the Military Academy by selecting the intellectual sons of my most respectable acquaintance, and inviting them to apply to the Secretary of War for cadet's warrants. Among the number is William McNeill, the son of my friend Dr. Daniel McNeill of Wilmington, N. C.; whom, meeting on my way to West Point, and he on his way to commence theological study with Rev. Mr.

Wyatt of Newtown, L. I., he (William) found my purpose suitable to his propensities, and so took him with me to the Point. He has been there now several months, and gives evidence of being suited to the place.

1815. In pursuance of the orders of 27th ultimo I proceeded from headquarters, Brooklyn, to Baltimore on 5th of January, where on 9th the board to revise, etc., assembled. Its composition was General W. Scott, Brevet-General J. G. Swift, Colonel J. R. Fenwick, Colonel William Cumming and Colonel William Drayton, with Captain John M. Glassell as secretary. This board continued in sessions until the 25th February, when it completed its duties and reported the same to the Secretary of War, by whom I was directed to have the plates executed and engraved, and six thousand copies of the new book printed at New York. While on this duty at Baltimore I received a summons from Judge-Advocate Martin Van Buren, Esq., to appear at the trial of General Wilkinson at Troy, N. Y., as a witness. I wrote the Secretary of War of my receipt of this order, to know whether I was to leave the board in obedience to the summons. No reply was made to my letter, and I pursued my duties at the board. I knew that the trial had no object of a national character in view. I did not feel inclined to recount at that trial the weakness exhibited by Wilkinson at Thorp's House on the margin of the St. Lawrence in November, 1813, because Wilkinson was no more in fault than Hampton for the failure of the campaign, and because Wilkinson had written to General Armstrong a favorable account of my conduct on the field at Chrysler's farm, and because I knew that the campaign was in no wise influenced by the scene at Thorp's, and I had so stated the facts of the day and night to General Armstrong. Mr. Monroe at this time discharged the double duty of minister of war and state. Between himself and General Armstrong there did not exist any amicable relations. The scenes at Bladensburg and Washington in the last year had embittered the feelings of each to the other, and General Armstrong had, by resigning the War Department, given strength to his opponents. On my way to Baltimore I had met him in Philadelphia, and said to him on perusing his memorandum of a letter of resignation, that "in my opinion that letter would place a cudgel in the hands of Mr. Madison."

However, a choice of duties being left to me by the War Department, I preferred the duty on the board at Baltimore. It is true that a summons to a court martial is imperative, and to neglect the mandate may expose one to arrest and trial; but knowing of the animosity subsisting between the parties to this trial at Troy, I had no inclination to appear for or against either as a witness, and heard no more of the summons.

The assembling of the military board at Baltimore had brought thither several prominent officers of the army in addition to the board, and to those who formed the general staff of the military command of the United States district in that city. The probable campaign in the ensuing spring was a general theme of conversation among us, in the midst of which, on 13th of February, came the news of a treaty of peace having been signed at Ghent. On the same day arrived the account of the defeat of the British army before New Orleans by General Jackson. The consequent illumination of the city, combining a double celebration of events, in a calm night when everything was covered with snow, formed a very impressive scene. In the centre of a window in Market Street I observed a brilliant star embracing the whole window, in the centre of which was a quotation from Shakspeare's Henry VI.: "Relieved is Orleans from the British wolves."

On 17th of the month I was called to Washington to consult with the Secretary of War upon a plan to reduce the army to a peace establishment. The board had also been called upon to report its opinion on that subject. On waiting upon the President I found him greatly improved in health, and overjoyed at the conclusion of the war.

The general idea of Congress seemed to be to reduce the army to a standard upon which an army of fifty thousand men might be engrafted, which the provisions of the law fell far below the proper scale to sustain. The old theme of competency of militia became rife, and Congress provided to resume the services of forty thousand thereof in case of need. An appropriation of the sums of four hundred thousand dollars, and two hundred thousand dollars, was made to carry on the fortifications. An extended organization of the Military Academy was proposed, and to that effect I recommended that two of our best officers, to wit, Colonel McRee and Major Thayer, should be sent to Europe to examine the works of France, etc., and on the Rhine and low countries, and to form a library for the Academy.

After sending to the various officers of the engineers orders to inspect the condition of the works on the fortifications, in order to repair throughout the Atlantic ports, I returned on 3d March to my family in Brooklyn, with whom the Rev. Mr. Empie had passed the winter, and where Mrs. Swift had received the account of the death of her only sister, Harriet, Mrs. Osborne, in North Carolina. On my way, at Philadelphia, with my former chief, Colonel Williams, and examined the arrangements made to resist any land attempts that the British might have made, and gave him a description of the works erected around Baltimore for similar purposes; and also gave him a sketch of what had been done on York and Long Islands—positions well known to him—and the plans had his professional approbation.

On 7th of March, at Brooklyn, received from the committee of defence of the city the proceedings of the corporation in reference to my services in the past year. They had requested my portrait, to be executed by the executive John Wesley Jarvis, to be placed in the city hall as a memorial; and they resolved that I was a benefactor to the city. They also sent to Mrs. Swift my half-length portrait, also done by Jarvis, together with forty-three pieces of silver, and also presented me a case of silver drawing instruments, and a very handsome pleasure barge, by which to amuse my family and friends in excursions over the bay of New York.

On 15th of the month I presented to the committee of defence a general view of the system of defence, and the plans of all the works that had been constructed by citizen labor; the whole comprised in a folio atlas, with my report, containing also my acknowledgements of the aid that I had received from Lieutenant James Gadsden, my aid-de-camp. He was of the corps of engineers, and grand-son of the patriot General Christopher Gadsden of South Carolina; and also acknowledging the services of Messrs. Renwick, Proctor, Kemble and others, including the artist Holland. The artist Jarvis, before mentioned, is the grand-son of the great John Wesley, the leader of

Methodism. Mr. Jarvis has many fine qualities as an artist, and great social ability.

On 12th April gave instructions to Colonel McRee and Major Thayer to proceed to France as recommended to the Secretary of War and President in February last, and those gentlemen sailed from Boston on 10th June in the United States frigate "Congress."

On 20th June, returning from an inspecting tour to West Point, I met Captain John M. Glassel, the secretary of the board, and arranged with him to aid me in consulting the printer and engraver to print the work done in Baltimore upon infantry tactics. The work was immediately commenced by Mr. Mercein and others.

On 11th July, in pursuance of orders from the War and Navy Departments, proceeded to Newport, R. I., and met Commodores Bainbridge and O. H. Perry, the three forming a commission with instructions to explore Narragansett Bay and its tributary waters, with a view to the selection of a position for a navy depôt, which order was laboriously executed, including Providence and Taunton Rivers, Fall River and the Watupper Ponds. Our report to the department at Washington agreed in opinion that Newport Harbor was the most important post for navy refuge on the coast of the United States. The report also embraces a system for the defence of the depôt, including the various approaches by land and water, and also commending the closing of the passage between Conanicut Island and the main land by a dyke of large stone, that might afterwards be removed if found desirable to do so. On 24th July the commission returned to my office in Brooklyn, and thence forwarded our report to the War and Navy Departments.

On 15th August I proceeded to an inspection at West Point, and found much difficulty in keeping the place furnished with needful supplies, and was obliged to incur many debts to sustain the Academy. Returned to the city early in September, and in correspondence with the War Department found that funds could not be sent from the treasury. By the authority of the Secretary of War I attempted to negotiate a loan from the banks of the city, which every one of them declined as unsuited to their mode of doing business. In fact they did not like the security — the pledge of the department to pay the loan as soon as Congress supplied the means — a far-off event in the opinion of the banks in the then reduced value of treasury notes. In this dilemma I met Jacob Barker, who liked the security on the condition that I would draw upon him for not more than ten thousand dollars per week, and thus in the course of six weeks I received sixty-five thousand dollars from him in bank paper, and thereby prevented a disbandment of the Military Academy and a suspension of the repairs on the fortifications in New York Harbor. Taking the then condition of "public credit" into view I deem this act of Mr. Barker to be in a high degree patriotic. He is to receive seven per cent. per annum until the loan be paid.

On 5th September invited to a dinner given to Hon. Mr. Clay, Rufus King and Albert Gallatin.

In October sent my views to the Secretary of War for securing the fortifications of the United States from dilapidation pending the scarcity of money, and also in case of relief from the pressure, what new works might be commenced in 1816 if the view given met his approbation, and was sustained by Congress; the whole amount contemplated being eight hundred and thirty-eight thousand dollars.

At the close of the month of October my father and mother came from Boston, to pass the winter in my family in Washington Street, Brooklyn. My sister Sarah and her son Julius also arrived in the month of November, leaving her daughter Louisa at nurse in Boston. My sister was confined at my house with her daughter Delia. My brother-in-law, Mr. Eli W. Adams, and my cousin, William R. Swift, were then establishing themselves in business in Baltimore. I gave them letters to Robert Oliver, Esquire, who aided them with loans. This course of Mr. Oliver was habitual with him toward young men of business. Adams and Swift were much benefitted thereby, and Mr. Oliver, on my thanking him for his volunteer aid in this matter, informed me that Adams and Smith had punctually refunded the loan.

On 21st December Lieutenant Gadsden and myself, accompanied by my sister Sarah and her children, took a private carriage to Philadelphia, where we were joined by Professor F. R. Hassler, and arrived in Baltimore on

28th. Gadsden, my aid-de-camp, and myself proceeded to Washington, and by order of the Secretary of War established the headquarters of the corps of engineers in a part of the house of Mrs. King, the widow of Nicholas King, long a draughtsman to the War Department; and after preparing the reports for commencing the works upon the fortifications I sent Lieutenant Gadsden to General Andrew Jackson, who had written me a request to select a suitable officer to serve as his aid-de-camp. Having entire confidence in the ability and character of Gadsden I thus deprived myself of his services, believing that the measure would promote the interests of a very deserving man, in a field of larger scope than his aidship to me could offer.

1816. In addition to the ordinary duties of my office in Washington I had many communications with the President and Secretary of War during the month of January, upon improvements and extension of the Military Academy, with a view to inviting to that institution some officers from the military schools of France. The question was whether to place these officers as professors at the Academy, or to attach them to the corps of engineers in a bill about to be prepared by the military committee of Congress.

In February I proceeded down the Potomac with Lieutenant Colonel Armistead and Major Roberdeau, to examine Cedar Point as a site for a fort. On our return to Washington in the sloop that had been chartered for this service, the ice cut the bottom of the vessel so that she sunk on a shoal below Alexandria, and we escaped to the shore, with some difficulty, with our instruments and papers.

While in conversation with the President on the subject of this defence of the approach to Washington, he expressed an opinion that Captain Partridge might be detailed on the duty connected with this contemplated work, or on some other duty that would relieve him from West Point. My reply to this was that to displace Captain Partridge suddenly, and without assigning the cause, could not be just to his official rights. The President assented to the correctness of this, but said: Captain Partridge is not deemed by the Secretary of War the most suitable officer of engineers for duty at the Academy. I called immediately on the Secretary of War and stated these circumstances. He said the matter would be considered further, and that though he should not interfere with any order in reference thereto he would prefer that I should send some officer of engineers to relieve Captain Partridge. I then stated to Mr. Crawford that the service of superintending at West Point was not desirable to any officer of the corps. The subject was deferred until I had made my visit of inspection. I then departed for an inspection of Fort McHenry, at Baltimore, where, on my arrival, I took lodgings with my brother-in-law Adams, in St. Paul's Lane, and after visiting Fort McHenry proceeded to Fort Miflin in the Delaware, and thence to my quarters in Brooklyn on the last day of February. Early in March found me at West Point with Captain Partridge, to whom I was not at liberty to communicate what had passed between Mr. Madison, Mr. Crawford and myself. I however said that he had enemies at Washington. I was at this time taken ill with ague, and detained at the hospitable quarters of Mrs. Mansfield, and was relieved by the extraction of my front tooth, and did not reach my family in Brooklyn until early in April; finding there our first daughter, Sarah Delano, born in my absence on 30th March.

On 22d April I was apprised by letter from Lieutenant S. H. Long, that the purpose of the President was to so conform to the new bill before Congress, by introducing a skillful engineer from France into the corps of engineers, and that it was rumored that the plan had received my approbation. By the return mail, on 23d April, I wrote to the Hon. Jeremiah Mason, and to the Hon. William Lowndes, an inquiry what was the actual purpose of the President, for I had received no intimation from the War Department in relation to this matter since the conversation before mentioned in January. Their replies show, that to expedite the passage of the bill before alluded to in January, members of Congress were informed that the bill was in accordance with my opinions. Without delay I wrote to the Secretary of War that the only accordance on my part in this matter was expressed in the conversation that I had with him and the President in January.

On 2d May the Secretary of War wrote me to assign the appropriation, eight hundred and thirty-eight thousand dollars, to the different works in the United States, "to facilitate operations," etc.

On the 8th of that month I returned to the Secretary of War my opinion on the subject of his letter, designating one hundred and seventy thousand dollars for repairs of fortifications and two hundred and three thousand dollars for finishing the works that had been commenced, leaving four hundred and sixty-five thousand dollars for newly projected works. A letter from the Secretary of War was now on its way to me, dated on the same 8th May, stating that at the close of the late session of Congress the President had been authorized to employ General Bernard, or some other " skillful engineer," through the agency of Hon. Albert Gallatin, and that until the arrival of that engineer the commencement of new works would be postponed. (See my files, A.)   On 21st May I replied to the Secretary of War, (see B,) to which he rejoined on 11th June, (as in C,) and to which I replied on 1st July, (as in D,) which documents I requested my friends, Hon. Rufus King and Hon. Oliver Wolcott, to examine and favor me with their opinions.   Mr. King invited Mr. Wolcott and myself to dine with him at Jamaica for the purpose of that examination; both of these gentlemen having been long conversant with governmental affairs, and both of them, by their conduct in the late war, not unduly influenced by party politics. They gave me the opinion that my views, as expressed in D, were sound and just.   To this letter D, Mr. Crawford replied as in E; all of which are of record in the engineer department at the war office at Washington.

Pending these discussions the works on the fortifications of the United States were in no other way progressing than in the ordinary repairs.

In July a large meeting in the city to form the American and Foreign Bible Society; Joshua Sands and J. G. Swift members from Long Island.

The French engineer, selected by the Marquis de La Fayette and Mr. Gallatin, was General Bernard, who this summer arrived in New York, and had his interviews with the Secretary of War and the President, without my being informed of the nature of that intercourse.   The general, however, when he came to the city, was, with his family, received by mine with hospitality, and by myself and the corps at large was treated with every personal respect; and every facility in my power was offered to him, by a view of all our plans and reports, to enable him to acquire a knowledge of the military defences of the country, in order that so skillful an engineer — and one in whom Napoleon had reposed much confidence — might suggest the correction of any error that our young corps of officers might have committed.

This humiliating act of my country made me very unhappy, added to which the War Department made an essay to place me in a position where my sentiments might least influence my brother officers of engineers. Accordingly on 9th September the Secretary of War wrote me that Captain Partridge did not conduct the Military Academy satisfactorily to the President; that it was necessary for me to repair to West Point as soon as my official duties elsewhere would permit, and there to establish the headquarters of the corps of engineers, and to assume in person the superintendence of the Academy, in conformity with the laws that had been in a species of abeyance during and since the war, by reason of my absence in various parts of the Union, on duty. In obedience of which order, on 16th November, I went to West Point, and relieved Captain Partridge, and assumed the superintendence, etc., on 25th of that month.

Soon after this I received from the Secretary of War a letter of 19th November, informing me that a board of engineers had been formed by order of the President, and that General Bernard had been appointed a brigadier-general by brevet, as second in command, and that the general had been ordered to report himself to me at West Point, to receive my views of his functions on said board.

On 2d December, General Bernard reported himself to me at the Point, and became my guest. At my instance we discussed the propriety of introducing foreign officers into the engineer department of any country; General Bernard maintaining that it had been the common practice of France and Russia. On my part it was deemed impolitic, at least, to place in the hands of any foreign nation a knowledge of all our assailable points of defence, and means to occupy them, however high and honorable might be the character of the individuals of any foreign nation so employed. This argument was maintained in mutual good temper. I said to General Bernard that, lest he might misunderstand the principle upon which I acted, or be misinformed by rumor or otherwise, I placed in his hands the correspondence with the Secretary of War, A, B, C, D, E, before mentioned, and advised him to peruse them at his leisure before his return to West Point from Rouse's Point, where he was going to meet Lieutenant Colonel Totten to inspect the work in progress at that place. I gave him a letter of introduction to Lieutenant Colonel Totten, and the general departed on 6th December.

My reflections upon the course of the government in this matter are that my talents as chief engineer are assumed to be inferior to those of General Bernard, which may be a correct opinion, for I have not had the experience of that distinguished man ; in reference to which I had stated to the government that the benefit of that experience could, with some deference to the pride of a corps that had been created at the Military Academy, be secured to the country by placing General Bernard at the head of an engineer professorship at West Point. To be sure the corps of engineers is composed of young men, nevertheless, during the late war they had been found respectable in their vocation, and all of the corps who had been in the field had been honored by brevets. Whether the forts on the Atlantic coast had been judiciously located and constructed, it was a fact that all the principal forts had kept the enemy at bay during the late war. On the whole I come to the conclusion that it is due to my country, and to the corps, that I command, so to coöperate with General Bernard, under the law of 16th February last, as to prove to the country that I am influenced by a sense of duty and not by mere selfishness.

On 21st December I wrote to the Secretary of War what had passed between General Bernard and myself, and also gave him my opinion that in reference to the commission given to General Bernard I doubted the power of the President to confer on him the rank expressed, which commands all inferior in rank to obey him. To this letter I received from the Secretary of War his reply of 30th December, which made it evident that the executive had purposed to place me in a position to make it difficult to interfere with the professional functions of General Bernard as his superior officer. This determined me to adopt a mild and steady course of duty as chief engineer, to avert the tendency of the course of the executive so far as the law would sustain me, and if not successful to resign my commission. My purpose was not to retard or impede the public service, and therefore I sent to every officer of the corps, on fortification duty, my orders to receive and obey any instruction or order for the *progress* of the *works* that might emanate from General Bernard, as if coming direct from myself.

The establishing of my family at West Point, to wit, Mrs. Swift, my sons James and Williams, and my daughter Sarah, had occasioned me much additional expense; leaving my sons Alexander and Julius with my aunt Lucretia Lovering, at housekeeping in my quarters in Washington Street, Brooklyn, and taking the Rev. Leverett Bush into my family at the Point as a teacher to my sons. He also performed the functions of chaplain to the Military Academy, the Rev. Mr. Empie having returned to his former residence in Wilmington, N. C. My son Thomas D. was residing with his grand-father, Dr. Swift, the United States surgeon on Governor's Island. The winter a severe season, the Hudson closed by ice, thus rendering intercourse between the divided portions of my family tedious and very troublesome. The last day of the year, while a party of cadets were dining with me a fire broke out in my quarters, that soon assembled other cadets, who in a few minutes removed the furniture and books from the house, and on extinguishing the fire replaced the same, so that our dinner party enjoyed their feast in the hall where many a social party had assembled in the previous days of our then chief, Colonel Williams. These quarters were known as "The Colonel's Quarters."

1817. The new year was ushered in by a salute of twenty-four, eighteen and twelve-pounder cannon, in which, from the negligence of the gunner in tending the vent, fire was given the cartridge while in the act of "ramming home," which killed cadet Vincent M. Lowe, a promising youth of eighteen years, the only son of a widowed mother. His death was occasioned by concussion, and without any bruise. The funeral procession was one of the most impressive scenes in its march across the plain to the burial ground on the extremity of the German Flat, in a gusty snow storm, which alternately concealed and exposed the party in its route.

On 6th closed contracts with John Forsyth, of Newburgh, to construct several brick quarters at the Point. On my return from Newburgh found "the Hills on fire" by the careless conduct of some boys, my sons James and Williams being the principals in the mischief; and which was extinguished with much delay.

On 7th January Lieutenant-Colonel Totten and General Bernard arrived at West Point from Rouse's Point, on Lake Champlain, to consult upon the further duties of inspection by the board of engineers. General Bernard returned to me the documents before mentioned, and declined any further discussion in reference to their subject; upon which I informed him that no change would be made by me in the course I had determined to pursue, the first act of which would be to attach myself to the board of engineers, unless forcibly prevented by the executive. In the pursuance of which purpose I wrote the Secretary of War that business of importance to the corps of engineers would require my presence in Washington as soon as the examination then in progress was completed at the Academy.

On 10th January General Bernard and Lieutenant-Colonel Totten left West Point to proceed to the Pea Patch in the Delaware River, to discuss a plan for a fortress for that place.

On 13th of the month, with my aid, Lieutenant George Blaney, left West Point, and proceeded by land to the city of New York, and visited my children in Brooklyn, and my parents and son Thomas on Governor's Island, and thence to Washington. Knowing that the administration of Mr. Madison would soon expire, I called on him and made known to him my views in a request that the functions of the board of engineers should be conducted under my orders, and not those of the acting Secretary of War, Mr. Graham, who had given instructions to the board, merely sending me copies thereof for my government. To this, my proposal, Mr. Madison consented, and I was relieved from personal superintendence of the Military Academy, and therefore sent my orders to Captain Partridge to resume his functions as superintendent; and to give attention to the progress of the new Academy and the new brick quarters then constructing, under the appropriation by Congress of one hundred and fifteen thousand dollars. The library was enlarged, for which, and contingencies, Congress had appropriated twenty-two thousand dollars.

On 4th of March, at the accession to the presidency of Colonel Monroe, I went to pay my respects to Mr. and Mrs. Madison, from both of whom I had, for eight years, received kind attentions. Mrs. Madison, from respectable humble life had become not only an ornament to her husband's family, but also a beneficent dispenser of his bounty. This lady has a generous spirit, with bland and courteous manners, rather above the middle size, and very expressive blue eyes. Many an asperity of party, and its threatened personal consequences, have been averted by Mrs. Madison's timely and judicious interposition. Mr. Madison is below the middle stature of man, has a quiet, dignified deportment, and the aspect of one who had been long experienced in public affairs. His manner is easy and his language refined, of social qualities and fond of story-telling. The part he performed in the great constitutional convention, and in the convention of Virginia at the adoption of that instrument, and his papers in the *Federalist*, evince great wisdom. But one act of his life has marred the purity of his character, though that act elevated him to the presidency, namely, his abandonment of Federalism and adopting the utopian democracy of Thomas Jefferson, which has so precipitated democratic influence as to give public measures a stand too far in advance of the intelligence of the people.

Mr. Madison's mind and disposition are averse to military pursuits. During the war he had conceived no plan for its military conduct, evinced little talent in selecting commanders, and was far too exclusive in a party sense in those selections. The only exception among the generals was that of Thomas Pinckney, the force of whose national character could not easily be resisted.

It is, however, due to Mr. Madison to say that on the urgent views of Commodores Stewart and Bainbridge he opposed a major voice in his cabinet, and sent the navy to seek the enemy on the ocean. This was done adversely to the steady advice of Mr. Gallatin not to expose our little fleet to the powerful navy of England.

On 11th March, by appointment with President Monroe, presented my views of a suitable position for General Bernard, namely, at the Military Academy as a professor of engineering. Mr. Monroe replied that under the resolve of 16th February such could not be done until the gentleman had examined our defences, but that he had determined that General Bernard should not exercise command in any case, and that he considered me to be the head of the board of engineers; therefore I gave the board instructions to proceed to the Gulf of Mexico, and there be joined by Captain Gadsden, the engineer in that department. On the return of this board to my office in Washington I exercised my function of supervision, and preferred Captain Gadsden's system of defence of the main passes into Louisiana. But the Secretary of War, Mr. Calhoun, who could know but little of the science of the subject, rejected Gadsden's plans, which then and now are justly suited to the localities for which they are planned, and Mr. Calhoun adopted General Bernard's pentagons, that have since been found to be inappropriate in a military sense. In fact this error of Mr. Calhoun aided to infect members of Congress with an idea that General Bernard had a transcendent genius, and therefore he must be consulted upon all public works; as if he had been possessed of intuitive knowledge of a subject that could only be acquired by actual residence in our country a suitable period of time.

March 15th, by direction from the President, I surveyed the ruins in the capitol — the vandalic ruin of 1814. In this duty Colonel Bomford and myself formed a board. The question to be decided was whether the capitol should be rebuilt entire, or the existing walls retained and the interior repaired. We commended the latter, and on receiving from Mr. Latrobe the requisite plans and elevations for the senate chamber, I took them with me to New York, and employed Francis Kain to complete the marble colonade and other parts of that chamber, and shipped the same to Colonel Lane, the superintendent at Washington.

On 25th March, Bomford and myself accompanied the President to explore the Bresica Quarries on the Potomac, and it was therefore decided to use the same for the colonade of the house of representatives. This excursion was made on horseback, and on the way back to the city the President informed me that he purposed making a tour of inspection of the fortifications and navy yards in the Union, and that he should require my services to aid him in that excursion. I am of course gratified by such an evidence of the President's purpose. But I on this occasion, and on several others, stated to him that my official relations had been much invaded by the resolution of 16th February, and that it would better comport with my own wishes and the interests of my family to seek civil life, if the President could place me in a suitable office with that view. His reply was kind. He said he hoped I would not leave the army, and that at any rate I would be patient and await events. I stated to him that I had already made some incipient arrangements to improve my fortune, with Gouverneur Kemble, to establish a foundry on the Hudson.

On 4th April arranged with the President to join him in Baltimore early in June, to proceed there and elsewhere on his contemplated tour, and after making all official dispositions of orders to the officers of the corps for the few works, as at Rouse's Point, etc., and small repairs upon the existing works pending the action and duty of the board, I proceeded to Philadelphia on 9th and arranged with an old friend of the President, James Gard, Esquire, to secure as quiet a sojourn in that city as his official station could permit, and on 14th April joined my family at Brooklyn, where Mrs. Swift, James, Willy and Sally had two days previously rejoined my aunt Lovering and my sons Alexander and Julius in Washington Street, having been separated all the winter by the closing of the Hudson. My son Thomas still with his grand-father on Governor's Island, in New York Harbor.

April 21st to West Point, and examined the Academy; thence with Gouverneur Kemble to Captain Philipse, who resided on the opposite bank of the river, and proposed to this worthy gentleman (the proprietor of the once manor of his name, and whose honor this gentleman maintained with steady hospitality,) that he should unite with us in establishing a foundry, and to which end we proposed to take about two hundred of his acres on

Margaret Brook as so much of his share of stock, and to which he assented, and agreed that I should survey and plot the tract. Accordingly, with my compass, I paced around a tract enclosing full two hundred acres, and to which hasty survey Captain Philipse agreed, and set to his hand and seal. Mr. Kemble and myself had formed a conditional agreement with the War and Navy Departments of the United States to supply the government with one-third of their ordnance castings; and subsequently he and myself visited the large iron works of Mr. Coleman in Pennsylvania, and the Salisbury works in Connecticut, to inform ourselves in iron making; and I imported from England through Mr. Hassler, a standard of measure, and from Paris the best works on iron and steel making.

On 24th April I laid out on the ground the new north and south stone barrack that had been planned by Professor C. Crozet, and contracted with T. J. Woodruff and John Morse, of the city of New York, to construct that building, and returned to Brooklyn early in May.

On 24th of which month went to Governor's Island, and thence with my mother and sister Mary departed for Baltimore; the latter on a visit to my sister, Mrs. Adams and cousin W. R. Swift, in St. Paul's Lane.

On 1st June the President arrived in Baltimore with his suite, to commence a tour of inspection.

# TOUR OF PRESIDENT MONROE

## IN THE NORTHERN UNITED STATES, IN THE YEAR 1817,

IN WHICH HE WAS ACCOMPANIED BY THE WRITER OF THIS DIARY,

## J. G. SWIFT.

I was in Washington in March and April of this year in company with Colonel George Bomford of the ordnance, examining the ruins of the capitol in order to its repair, in which we were assisted by Mr. Latrobe, the architect. This capitol, and other public and private edifices had been destroyed by the British army under command of General Ross and Admiral Cockburn in 1814.

President Monroe invited me to accompany him in an horseback excursion to the Bresica Quarries on the Potomac, from which it had been proposed to take materials to repair and ornament the hall of representatives and senate chamber of the capitol. This visit had decided the matter, and the material was used for those purposes. During this excursion Mr. Monroe mentioned his intention to make the tour of the Union, to examine its defences, navy yards, etc., and to see the people. He wished me to so arrange my official affairs as to accompany him in the examination, in order to do which I proceeded to New York to direct the continuance of the fortifications in that harbor, and visited West Point to direct the operations of the Military Academy for an inspection of the President, and returning to Baltimore on 1st June, met Mr. Monroe there, accompanied by a son of General Mason, of Georgetown, and Mr. Monroe and suite called to see Charles Carrol of Carrolton, the venerable patriot. He and Mr.

Monroe exchanged several remarks on the scenes of the Revolution. Then, with General Samuel Smith and N. G. Harper, etc., visited the battle ground of North Point, where, in September, 1814, General Ross lost his life by an accidental rifle shot. From the account given by General Striker to Mr. Monroe one would suppose both parties had been surprised. Returning, we viewed the misplaced lines of Baltimore, that should have occupied the passes of North Point, etc. The President passed on to review the militia, and to examine Fort McHenry with General Samuel Steritt — (very gentlemanly and accomplished in manner) — and also with Colonel Paul Bentalon, an officer of the army of Rochambeau, his aspect that of the old French *politesse* of 1780; full of memory of the scenes of Yorktown.

On 3d June the President went to Head of Elk by steamer, and was there received by the Philadelphia and Delaware delegations, and especially by Colonel Allen McLean, full of anecdotes of the movements of Washington to beleaguer Cornwallis. The colonel had been a distinguished and most useful officer, having still the fire of youth in his manner. Also General Moses Porter, whose giant person still wore a fresh aspect. He had been distinguished as an artillery officer in the discomfiture of Lord Sterling on Long Island, August, '76, and who had by merit and long service risen from a sergeant. Here also we met Commodores Murray and Stewart of the navy, and General Thomas Cadwallader, of Philadelphia — the thorough gentleman. At Newcastle we found Captain Babcock, of my corps, with all things ready to take barge to the Pea Patch, down the Delaware; a site which the Hon. Mr. Rodney informed the President had been taken up by Chief Justice Booth of Delaware in 1780. A useful position to defend the double channels of the river. Thence the President ascended the Delaware to the Brandywine, and with Colonel Allen McLean rode over the grounds where Washington incurred the censure of some congressmen for "extending his wing." Colonel McLean pointed out the ground and the need of that extension, a just military movement.

The party visited Du Pont's powder mills, and General Cadwallader and myself tested the drying rooms for four minutes at a temperature of one hundred and forty-five degrees Farenheit. We were here joined by the venerable Mr. Logan, of Pennsylvania, and passing the rich meadows of the Delaware, came by boats to Fort Mifflin, that had been well defended by Colonel Samuel Smith in the Revolution. From Fort Mifflin the party proceeded in barges to the mouth of the Schuylkill, at Gray's Ferry, and with a large militia escort, and the city committee, to the mansion house of Mr. James Head, there meeting the Society of Cincinnati, with addresses and reply and entertainment. The next morning — 6th June — made an excursion to Red Bank, where the farmers met the President, some of whom were of the assailing party against Count Donop ; and they mentioned that the timber felled at that time (in August) had endured many years, proving that to be a better felling season than the winter. The next day took a horseback ride with several prominent citizens to Germantown and Chew House, where General Howe should have conquered our army, and cut off their retreat. The interchange of courtesy of the President and the country people was very pleasant. He found the arsenal and navy yard in as good order as expected ; aided by General C. Irvine and Commodore Stewart in the examination.

At the instance of the President I called on Messrs. Dachkoff, Ten Cate, Redemker, Peduson and other foreign officers, to say that it would be more convenient to receive them when he was not engaged with his fellow citizens. Mr. Monroe observed that for less causes he had been denied access to foreign courts when he was minister to England, France, and Spain.

Hon. Pierce Butler, General Cadwallader, Secretary Long, Commodore Stewart, Ingersoll, Bache and Todd dined with the President. One would have imagined the "blood of the Ormonds" had concentrated in Mr. Butler.

On 7th June the party was received at the Bridge at Trenton by the New Jersey delegation, congratulating Colonel Monroe "on the ground where Washington achieved an important turn in our affairs in the winter of '76 ; where Mr. Munroe, the second officer of the vanguard, and Captain William Washington, were both wounded in the shoulder." Mr. Monroe replied: "I feel sensibly this attention in this place from the citizens of Trenton ; on the spot where the hopes of the country were revived by a prompt expedition planned by Washington." The press of time prevented the President from visiting Commodore Stewart at his farm. Mr. Monroe remarking to say to the Commodore: "The country owed him much for encouraging Mr. Madison to send our ships to sea in the war with England in 1812, against the advice of Mr. Gallatin to keep them in safe harbor. The country owed both him and Bainbridge much for their zealous counsel before the cabinet on that momentous occasion." I bore this nice message to Stewart and dined with him.

The party made a call on Joseph Bonaparte *en route* to lunch. Joseph seemed an unpretending common sense gentleman, thoughtful face, and like his brother's busts. The President and Joseph were old acquaintances. Return to Trenton and Princeton, where Mr. Monroe was inducted to the Cliosophia, and from my relations to Mr. Monroe I was also inducted, after examining the Halls of Nassau. There with Governor Williamson and ex-Governor Aaron Ogden to Elizabethtown on the 9th June, and met the widow of Neursewitz, the friend of Kosciusko. The lady is the daughter of Governor William Livingston, and sister of Mrs. John Gay. At the Point took steam to Staten Island, and became the guests of Vice-President Tompkins for a part of two days, to rest, and on 11th landed at the Battery, meeting General Scott, General Morton, and the city authorities; then explored the lines of Brooklyn, refreshing with Mrs. Swift, who had Joshua Sands, Major Tucker and Mr. March to meet the President; and then to the city to encounter numerous entertainments. One at the Philosophical Society, when Hon. De Witt Clinton made an eloquent address, occupying 13th and 14th. The following day the party at West Point, and Mr. Monroe met the officials in the garden of Kosciusko, and there he related the following story of that Pole: When Kosciusko came from Europe wounded he seemed unable to move when applying to Congress, and received a grant of land. It was said lameness was assumed to excite sympathy among cool-blooded members. Mr. Monroe said it was not feigned, but to impress a Russian spy that he was no longer able to wield a sword, who was so impressed; and Kosciusko resumed his health lost in a Russian prison. Mr. Monroe said Kosciusko had been a faithful friend to the American cause, and that he had recently remitted him several hundred dollars to sustain him in his retreat in Switzerland. This sojourn at West Point, and the examination of the cadets, was very refreshing after city fatigues. It was at this visit determined that Captain Partridge should be brought before a court martial in reference to his disagreement with the professors. My opinion of the captain was more favorable than Mr. Monroe's, but the Chief Magistrate was to be obeyed, and I accordingly proposed a substitute in Major Thayer, who was the officer named to me by Mr. Monroe; and I gave Captain Partridge choice of any duty or leave until the court could be convened. He preferred leave, and the matter rested for the present.

On 17th June the party returned to the city to inspect fortifications, navy yard, and the steamer "Fulton." At the west end of Long Island Mr. Monroe met Hon. Rufus King, and they witnessed the experiments of elongated shell at a target four hundred yards distant, on Robert L. Stevens's place. The shells penetrated the target but did not explode. On 20th June to Hell Gate and the entrance of the Sound, in reference to the location of a navy depôt at Barr Island; then by steam to New Haven. Visited the colleges and the "Groves of the Judges." Mr. Monroe was taken by surprise by a sermon from Rev. Dr. Taylor, an extreme Calvinist, much to the chagrin of the Rev. Horace Holly, a high Unitarian. One of the most interesting scenes we met at Hartford in the exhibition of the deaf and dumb, by Le Clerc and Gallaudet. Mr. Monroe had seen a similar exhibition in France. At Middletown the address of the citizens was emphatic, and national in every sense. A delegation from Massachusetts waited on the President at Hartford to escort him to Springfield, where, on arriving 24th June, an exhibition of five hundred school children met the President on the parade as a token of their respect for the Chief Magistrate, and evidence of adhesion to the Puritan law in favor of town schools. Thence Colonel Roswell Lee led the way to the well-arranged armory of the United States, of which he was superintendent, and had been my assistant engineer in fortifying New London when the British fleet were anchored in Gardner's Bay. Thence retracing his steps the President descended the left bank of the Connecticut River to New London, at the residence of General Jedediah Huntington, of Revolutionary times, who addressed the President in touching allusion to " the war in their youth, and the happy results we were enjoying after surviving a second contest with the power of England." Here the party was joined by Commodores O. H. Perry and Bainbridge, and my father, the surgeon of the post at Fort Trumbull. Taking the revenue cutters at the fort the President visited the Sound and Gardner's Bay, where the navy officers explained to the President the importance of an armed vessel at Gardner's Bay by a view from the headland of the island. Returned up the Thames, and landed at the foot of Fort Griswold. At the old fort the President met Mr. Avery and others who had been among the defenders of that post when assailed by the British under then Major, now General Bloomfield, and explaining the scene that occurred when Colonel Ledyard surrendered his sword, and Bloomfield turned it and thrust it through Colonel Ledyard's body — a dastardly act — after all resistance had ceased ; followed by the cruelty of trundling the wounded down the hill in carts, inflicting torture. Mr. Avery had lost an eye in the contest ; the remaining one twinkled with rage as he described the scene. Here the celebrated Mrs. Baily came forward and recounted her well-remembered exploits, vouched for by the surrounding veterans, and of her disrobing her flannel to furnish cartridge to the artillery men.

On the following day the United States brig " Enterprise," attended by the cutters, (among them the aged Captain Cahoon, of privateer heroism in the Revolution,) took on board the President and suite, and by Gardner's Bay on 27th June crossed the Sound to Stonington, which the President especially visited to compliment the brave Captain Palmer for his townsmen — led by himself — in repelling the assault of the " Ramillies," seventy-four, Sir Thomas Hardy. My own interview with Mr. Palmer was interesting. I had succeeded in sending him some cannon and ammunition in 1814 from New York, by a cunning master of a sloop, which succeeded in escaping the enemy. The captain had ornamented the front of his house with a thirteen-inch shell from the " Ramillies," which had fallen through his roof to the cellar, fortunately without exploding, though it had shattered much in its descent. On the following day the little squadron entered Newport Harbor, where most hearty feeling was shown without a shade of party. The President had a charming evening with the venerable William Ellery at the age of ninety. He remarked: "Ah, Mr. Monroe, we all had prospects of the death of rebels, especially such as myself, who had little of this world's goods to lose, but Hancock and Charles Carroll had launched both character and large estates in the cause." The patriot was reading Horace when Mr. Monroe called. He took a seat by Mr. Monroe in an excursion to the scene of Quaker Hill in Sullivan's campaign, and seemed familiar with the events of the day.

On 30th we proceeded to Fall River and the Watupper Lakes, as a source to serve machinery for a navy depot, and thence crossed Taunton River to Mount Hope Bay, refreshing and lodging with Lieutenant-Governor Collins and Mr. De Wolf, and thence onward to Providence. Here, Hon. H. G. Otis, Colonel Gray, General Blake, Colonel Sumner, Messrs. Thorndike and Oliver, (the colonel as aid of Governor Brooks,) came to lead the escort. Mr. Otis, in an eloquent address, alluded and compared the visit with its only precedent, that of Washington; accompanying the President to Brown University, and on 1st July to the manufactories of Pawtucket; meeting there General Dearborn and Justice Story—a rival committee of welcome coming expressly from the Democracy, giving me some trouble— but all that was said: "Gentlemen, be pleased to fall in and form a part of the cortége," which arrived at Dedham, and took lodgings opposite the residence of the great Fisher Ames. The next day ceremonial consulta- tions as to the two committees at an old redout on Roxbury Neck, both committees desiring to take charge of the President. I took on myself to say to both: "Gentlemen, the care and conduct of this movement has been given to me, and I cannot surrender it without the President's order." Pending this interchange the salute opened from the old redout and the Boston mar- shals, and the committee, without further delay, moved on with the cavalcade to Boston Common, and the President was received by four thousand boys and girls and their instructors; a scene of courtesy well conducted, that the children will remember, and which served to occupy committees and all until joined by ex-President Adams, Governor Brooks, Lieutenant-Governor David Cobb, Governor Phillips and General James Miller (the modest hero,) Rev. Dr. Kirkland, Daniel Webster, Isaac P. Davis and Rev. Dr. Freeman. The Governor opened with a word in his peculiar graceful style, followed by the address of the authorities in the area of the Exchange, which was followed by one of Boston's sumptuous entertainments in rooms ornamented with the works of Boston artists and citizens. The next day the President and Governor Brooks, etc., visited the fortifications of the harbor. The President was highly gratified by his reception in several families of Boston, and especially at Governor Brooks' in Medford, and his neighbor cousin. They rode over the scenes of Washington in his early command of the army, when Brooks was his youthful attendant. The ensuing day was Independence, commencing with a fine breakfast of some hundreds at Commodore Bainbridge's, in Roxbury, in this abundant season of strawberries and cream. Thence a sojourn to the gardens of Colonel T. H. Perkins; to Waltham, on a visit to Governor Gore; to the United States arsenal, and in the evening a pleasant meeting with the Society of Cincinnati. But the distinctive character of the Democracy revived, and the committee called for a reply to the separate address. Mr. Monroe calmly said: "Gentlemen, I will reply amply to your address, and in writing, at my earliest leisure." This was said while the procession was moving to the Old South with the Cincinnati, to hear the eloquence of Dr. Channing—a happy allusion to the visit of the President, not to a party, but to the whole people. Now came on a general meeting at the State House, where the influence of fruit and champaigne seemed to quiet for a time the ground swell of party. This indicated a fear lest the Chief Magistrate should compromise his Democratic duty. Hence to the "Cradle of Liberty," Faneuil Hall, and a display of arms. The next day to the navy yard and "Independence," seventy-four; entertained by the commandant, the gallant Hull, and thence to Bunker's Hill, where Governor Brooks explained with simple clearness the progress of the day and Warren's fall, that lighted a flame through all the colonies. In this scene several veterans of the Revolution were received and welcomed by the

President, and with him enjoyed the tasty light dinner and fruits of Governor Brooks, with ex-President Adams and Dr. Osgood. Monday, 7th, an early ride on horseback with Mr. Monroe to a sitting to the artist, Gilbert Stewart, who exhibited his original head of Washington. Thence to Harvard, where President Kirkland conferred the honor of LL. D. on Mr. Monroe, and then to a review of two thousand militia on Boston Common.

On 8th the President visited the venerable John Adams at Quincy. The ex-President said to Mr. Monroe: " Sir, I am happy to welcome you and your friends, and to acknowledge my high appreciation of the distinction which you propose to confer on my son as Secretary of State." But the gust of feeling that naturally flowed from the mother was thrilling. It overpowered Mr. Monroe, and every one present. His reply was simple: " I have but performed an act of justice to high ability and merit." Mr. Adams at first mistook me for the son of his brother lawyer, Samuel Swift, and poured out his commendation, saying: " I have written to Mr. Wirt my opinion of the merits of that Whig, who fell a martyr to the fury of Gage." I replied: " It was my grandfather, and you gave me my cadet's warrant eighteen years ago," upon which he was pleased to subjoin some civil commendation. The conversation naturally attracted the attention of the whole dinner party; and it was a scene of deep interest to hear the old man scan the days of his life in Congress, when he nominated Washington, etc. This closed the Boston reception — one of sleepless fatigue to me, in hearing and arranging with delegations and committees.

On the route east the President stopped to rest at Salem until the 10th, occupied in correspondence with the departments at Washington. The aged Timothy Pickering, and the mathematician, Nathaniel Bowditch, were among those who addressed Mr. Monroe, and much display of arches and festoons, with throngs of fine children, on whom such pageantry makes a long-lasting impression. Here the reply in writing was made to the Democratic committee of Boston, in substance saying that it was the President's design by this tour to avoid all party distinctions. With similar displays of good feeling at Newburyport and Portsmouth, Mr. Monroe was met by the authorities at the latter place by Jeremiah Mason, in a powerful address of national sentiment, and on the following Monday (14th,) in barges to visit the navy yard and forts at the entrance of the harbor, accompanied by the patriot John Langdon, who had built the "America," seventy-four, that was a gift to France. The next day the octogenarian, Sewell, of York, in Maine, received Mr. Monroe in a fine address of reminiscences of their mutual services and anxieties of the war of '76; and so on to the bridge of Strandwater, Portland, across which was extended twenty arches, as insignia of our States, the centre for Louisiana crowned by a living eagle, and lined on either wayside by some one thousand five hundred school children with wreaths and scrolls—"Welcome to the chief of our choice"—about the most impressive display seen by the President. Here, after a sail in the harbor and a visit to the fortifications, the President concluded his eastern tour, and determined to cross the country through Vermont, of which I had only notified Colonel Totten at Rouse's Point to meet Mr. Monroe at Burlington. Before separating from Mr. Munroe he expressed his gratification with my services, and certainly no man can be easier to associate with in a similar capacity than Colonel Monroe. Here it was determined by the President that Commodores Bainbridge, O. H. Perry and Evans, with Colonel McRee of the engineers, and myself, should proceed to Penobscot Bay with the "Lynx," Lieutenant Stone, and "Enterprise," Lieutenant Kearney, and "Prometheus," Wadsworth, which was commenced on 17th June for the purpose of examining for a site to locate a navy depôt. We paid our respects and took leave of the Chief Magistrate.

During various evening conversations with Mr. Monroe I received from him, and noted down at the time, the subjoined facts of his origin and life:

His progenitors were from Scotland. His immediate ancestor was Captain Andrew Monroe, an officer in the army of Charles I., at whose overthrow he fled to America, anno 1650, and purchased a tract of land in Westmoreland, Virginia, of Lord Barclay, situate on Monroe Creek. The Colonel is the fifth in direct descent from Captain Andrew aforesaid. The Colonel was born 1759, and educated at William and Mary College. In 1776 he joined Colonel Weeden's regiment in the Virginia line, as a lieutenant. At the battle of Trenton he seconded Captain William Washington in carrying the artillery of the enemy at the head of the street leading to the bridge, in which conflict both were wounded in the shoulder. On recovering from his wound in Trenton he entered the family of Lord Stirling as aid-de-camp, and in that capacity, and that of major, served in the battles of Brandywine, Germantown and Monmouth. General Washington advised him to apply to the legislature of Virginia for authority to raise a regiment, but failing in his effort to do this, he resigned his colonelcy in 1780, and became a student at law in the office of Thomas Jefferson. In the following year sold his paternal seven hundred acres in Westmoreland, and with the proceeds purchased his estate in Albemarle called " Atamusquee," or The Lilly, and in company with his uncle Jones bought the London farm at Oak Hill, to which, on the death of that uncle he became heir, and commenced the practice of law in Fredericksburg. He was then elected to the Virginia legislature, and became a member of the council. In 1783 he was elected to Congress at Annapolis, and was at the session in New York when he and Rufus King were married. Mr. King married Miss Alsop and he married Miss Kortright. Soon after he made the tour of Lake Champlain, River St. Lawrence and Lake Ontario, Big Sodus Bay and Niagara, purposing to go to Detroit, but his guide being killed by the Indians, he, from advice of Colonel De Peyster, abandoned the journey and returned south to Virginia, until the adoption of the Federal Constitution, which he opposed.

Soon after the establishment of the government, General Washington nominated him to the embassy to France, from whence he was recalled, as it was alleged he exhibited too strong favor to French politics. Mr. Monroe stated that the slander commenced thus: Some letters of General Washington had been wrecked on the coast of France; these letters indicated Washington's dislike of the French revolution, and Mr. Monroe was accused to Washington as having referred unfavorably to those letters. In the pending time Mr. Monroe was searching for the letters, and succeeded in learning their fate. This fact he immediately wrote to General Washington, but before his letter reached the General, an impression had been made on Washington's mind that Monroe had misused his letters, and his recall was forwarded before his letter to Washington was received. Indignant at the injustice, he did not call on Washington on his return home. When Washington had read Monroe's letters he said he was convinced Mr. Monroe had done his duty. But Mr. Monroe's dislike of Mr. Jay's treaty with Spain about the navigation of the Mississippi seemed to sustain a coolness on the part of Washington. Mr. Monroe said his treaty with Mr. Fox for reciprocal commerce was interfered with, by Mr. Jefferson's sending William Pinckney of Maryland, which suspended the treaty; and that the treaty then made, was revoked by the omission of Jefferson to send the treaty to the Senate. This implication of Mr. Monroe was a sort of second presidential frown, and it caused Mr. Monroe to again set forth a defense of his embassy. His fellow citizens set their opinion upon his treatment by electing him governor of Virginia, which prevented Mr. Monroe from competing the presidency with Mr. Madison. "So far from that," said Mr. Monroe, "I publicly declined the competition, and also the Department of State." But these events in no way disturbed his friendly intimacy with Jefferson. Mr. Monroe said that during the presidency of Congress of N. Gorham, that gentleman wrote Prince Henry, of Prussia, his fears that America could not sustain her independence, and asked the prince if he could be induced to accept regal power on the failure of our free institutions. The prince replied that he regretted deeply the probability of the failure, and that he would do no act to promote such failure, and was too old to commence new labors in life. The residue of Colonel Monroe's life is in the history of his country. In stature Mr. Monroe is above the ordinary height, well formed, though his shoulders are somewhat high, fleshy, but in no wise corpulent, his complexion without muddiness, his demeanor grave, his eye blue, rather dull unless excited, his features strong, high cheek bone of Scotland, nose straight, lip rather thick, his gait quick and erect, deportment gentle and affable, his temper high but good, his judgment sound though slow and not quick of perception. Such are my observations of Colonel Monroe in an intimacy uninterrupted for ten years.

The little squadron before mentioned, arrived in Penobscot Bay on 18th July, at dark, and made a harbor at Owl's Head, and the next morning commenced an examination of the shore, inlets and landings made, having our rallying point at Castine. Here I was entertained by Job Nelson and Mason Shaw, Esquires, who had known me a boy on Taunton Green ; and they were intimate friends of my father. They received me with a warm welcome, and recurred to scenes of 1796, etc.

At the military post here, I found Captain Luther Leonard, of the artillery, in command. He had been a distinguished officer in the war of 1812 in the battle of Plattsburgh. Also met my protégé, Lieutenant Bonneville, on duty at the fort, to whom the celebrated Thomas Paine had bequeathed some estate. From the fort we received barges to explore the river and narrows to Bucksport. It was soon ascertained that the several anchorages were very deep, and from the openness of the bay would require extensive fortifications to protect them, and a depôt, and that the bay was, as yet, too remote from artisans and material for a depôt, etc.

Our party returned to Portland on a similar survey, and then proceeded to Portsmouth. Of the Lieutenant Bonneville above mentioned, I had, in 1814, procured for him a cadet's warrant, and sent him to the Military Academy at West Point. The commission found the Piscataqua a very rapid tidal river, with many easily defensible localities, and water for any machinery easily drawn from Lake Winnepiseogee, but concluded the post not to be suitable for a depôt, and the same result, from different causes, of Salem and Marblehead. In the survey of these two last, we had the company and counsel of Nathaniel Bowditch, Esq., who had made minute surveys of both harbors, and had often sailed into and out of them when he was a ship-master. We found him continuing his scientific translation of the great work of La Place, which few ever read and fewer comprehend. A gentleman of the most simple habits and most unaffected deportment, and very cheerful as a companion is Mr. Bowditch.

Our squadron proceeded to inspect Boston Harbor, and concluded that the present navy yard would be a valuable adjunct for repairs, but not for a principal depôt. We observed that the seaward side of all the islands in this harbor had been long sustaining an abrasion from the action of storms and water. The time when these islands had a complete form corresponding to the slopes of the existing land and pastures, must have been very remote.

Governor Brooks and the Bostonians were very hospitably attentive to this commission. Among the amusements of the day, and which the President had also enjoyed, was the reading of Voltaire, and revelations by an admirable artist — M. Artiguenave.

The commission proceeded to Rhode Island, where I was to join them over a route of my own by Taunton Green, where, accompanied by my aunt Lucretia, we were received with great civility. An invitation to a public dinner, which, however flattering, I declined, in consequence of the illness of my early instructress, Miss Sally Cady.

My friend Marcus Morton, who had married my schoolmate, Miss Charlotte Hodges, conveyed me in his carriage to the commission, then assembling at Fall River on 8th August, and a survey was made of the Watuppa Ponds and their outlet, and fall, into Taunton River; an ample source to drive any desirable extent of depôt machinery. Thence we made an exploration of Mount Hope Bay. At Newport the commission divided, one part to complete the survey of Gardner's Bay, while Colonel McRee and myself explored the waters east from Sakonnet to Buzzard's Bay. Arriving at the river Pasquemonsett, McRee was astonished to see a miller run into the assemblage at the bridge, and in his mealy clothes clasp me in his arms, covering my military dress with meal, and excusing his joy to see me, whose life he had saved from drowning under the bridge on which we stood; I having fallen in and cut my head on a rock at the bottom, the scar of which remained for the twenty-six years that had intervened. There were present also the Tuckers and Macombs, friends of my father at that period. Hence McRee and I proceeded to Clark's Cove and the Acushnet River, and Elizabeth Islands, and rejoined the board at New London, exploring the Thames. These surveys had reference to the law of Congress on the subject of depôts, and we agreed to meet at my quarters in Brooklyn to complete a report to the Navy Department. On 26th August I found my family in health at Brooklyn. Thanks to God.

----

On 31st August, 1817, Colonel McRee reported to me that Captain Partridge had returned to West Point, and in defiance of my orders, had assumed the command over Major Thayer, the alleged purpose being to recover the quarters he had occupied, and which Major Thayer declined to assign to him. The next day I sent my aid, Lieutenant Blaney, to West Point with an order to Captain Partridge to deliver the command of that post to Major Thayer without delay, and to consider himself in arrest for disobedience. A few days previously to this, on 28th August, Captain Partridge had called and breakfasted with me in Brooklyn, and requested my authority to extend his leave so as to allow him to visit West Point for study. I declined any such consent, and said to him that such a movement would not only contravene the order of the President of the United States to me, but would also injure and defeat at once any purpose he might contemplate of restoration hereafter. The conversation dropped there, and I had not a thought that Captain Partridge would act in opposition to such purpose on my part.

On 2d September, Colonel McRee, Professor Mansfield and myself went to West Point, where, on meeting Partridge, I said to him that he had placed himself beyond the pale of my long-tried friendship to him. At his request I extended his arrest to New York, to allow him every facility to prepare for trial. I reported the case to the Secretary of War and returned to Brooklyn, to meet at my office navy officers on the subject of depôts. From 20th September to 6th October I was confined to my bedroom with fever. While thus confined General Benjamin Smith of Wilmington, North Carolina, called on me, and awaited my convalescence. My brother-in-law, Julius H. Walker, being my amanuensis, I dictated a letter of introduction of General Smith to the Secretary of the Navy, and recommended the purchase of Bald Head, North Carolina, because of the extensive growth there of live oak and cedar, and thus to enable General Smith to liquidate the old bond of Colonel Read, late collector, for whom General Smith had become security.

October 13th Mrs. Swift, with her mother and brother Julius, and my son Julius and daughter Sarah left me, and by packet sailed for Wilmington; Mrs. John London and children occupying my house in Washington Street, and in lieu of rent boarded my sons Williams and Alexander, and my servant and slave Nancy until the ensuing spring. My worthy aunt Lovering having returned to Boston, and my son Thomas remaining with his grandfather, the United States surgeon on Governor's Island.

October 20th, the general court martial of thirteen members, General W. Scott, president, assembled at West Point for the trial of Captain Partridge. I went thither on 24th, with my aid, Lieutenant Blaney, and my son James. Hither Commodores Evans and Perry joined me to consult upon and report in reference to depôts and defences that we had explored from New York to Casco Bay inclusive, and we returned together to New York, and there met Commodore Bainbridge and Colonel W. McRee, and from thence on 30th sent our report to the Secretary of both the Navy and War Departments.

November 1st I returned to West Point, and on 11th the court martial terminated its proceedings. The court sentenced Captain Partridge to be dismissed from the army. On 14th November I returned to my office in Brooklyn, and commenced to remove the headquarters of the corps to the City of Washington. On 17th, my aid, Lieutenant Blaney, proceeded to that place with the books, plans, papers and instruments. I followed him on 20th, leaving my son James with Rev. Mr. Rudd at Elizabethtown school. I arrived at Washington on 25th November, and established the office in Pennsylvania Avenue and Eighteenth Street, east side. I called on the President in reference to the subject of Captain Partridge, and advised a remission of the sentence of the court, provided Captain Partridge would resign. The remission was noted in the gazettes. This case of Partridge is an incident in the history of the Academy at West Point, in which my official conduct was deemed to be a species of favoritism toward the captain. From the day I took command of the corps in 1812, to the spring of 1813 I had had no opportunity to meet Captain Partridge. I then found him at the Academy, where he had been placed by Colonel Williams; an appointment that every officer in the corps would be disposed to respect, from respect to their chief. I made no hesitation to sustain him, and returned to my especial command of Staten Island by order of the President, at that time garrisoned by the 32d and 41st Regiments of infantry, when the harbor was blockaded by the enemy. In the month of August the Secretary of War sent me to the frontier as chief engineer to the army of General Wilkinson, and from thence to Washington. The following year, 1814, I was engaged in the defences of Long and York Islands. The year 1815 much engaged on the board for depôts. So that until 1816 it was not in my power to be much at West Point; and it was early in this year, as elsewhere noted, that the first intimation was made to me by the President that it would be satisfactory to have Captain Partridge super-ceded. I had no idea of doing that; and if I had purposed any such measure, there was not an officer in the corps of engineers competent to be superintendent who did not dislike that service, and none more than the gentleman who so ably succeeded Captain Partridge.

As soon as I knew that the captain had become unacceptable to the executive, it was my duty to seek the first opportunity to place him upon other duty; and this was done, as my journal with the President evinces. Ultimately I was forced to a conviction that I had misplaced my confidence in reference to Partridge, and finally his insane act of disobedience made it my duty to arrest him. The sentence of the court caused the captain to forget the long-tried confidence that I had reposed in him; he turned his pen against me and others, and one of his first acts was to accuse me of waste and peculation in the erection of the public buildings at West Point. These accusations the President and the Secretary of War deemed to be malicious and false, and all proceedings in reference thereto was denied. The vouchers, however, of the disbursements at West Point are among my files, and they were deemed by the accounting officers of the government to be just. I have received them from those officers, and have placed them on my files in case any one might be disposed to examine them — and this unusual displacement of vouchers was made by the permission of the President. The circumstance that induced the Secretary of War to desire a superceding of Captain Partridge, was not his want of ability, for he was a good teacher of mathematics, and a good infantry and artillery drill officer; it was because his aspect was uncouth, a want of what is called genteel carriage, and awkwardness of manner that gave a repulsive first impression. But Captain Partridge had good qualities as well as good sense. He was said to be a graduate of Dartmouth College, and was there deemed a good scholar; and it cannot be denied that many of the youthful officers of the army in the war of 1812 owed much of their success in the field, to the patient training which they received from " Old Pewter " — Captain Partridge's soubriquet among the cadets.

December 6th, the President and the Secretary of War commended to Congress, then in session, the raising a corps of sappers and miners for the corps of engineers. On the same day was discussed and settled to establish a bureau of every department of the army at Washington.

December 7th, Colonel W. McRee joined me at Washington to consult on the duties of the board. We agreed in opinion that it was too late to explore northern positions.

On 19th we two proceeded to Baltimore to explore the harbor, and we selected Soller's Point for the site of the main work. Our board was here joined by Lieutenant-Colonel Armistead, Majors Roberdeau and Kearney, and my aid, Lieutenant Blaney. On 26th December we proceeded to reconnoitre Annapolis Harbor, and on 29th we went to Norfolk, to meet Captains Warrington and Elliot, of the navy, in reference to exploring the James and other rivers of the bay, for a depôt for the navy, and on 30th commenced the survey of Old Point Comfort, and the bay towards Lynhaven.

1818. January 12th, the board of engineers, at the instance of the Secretary of War, postponed the examination of the Chesapeake waters until 1st May, for the purpose of then having the assistance of General Bernard, then employed on the Mexico Gulf reconnoitre. The board having thus far agreed to commend the occupancy of Old Point, and the

Rip Rap shoal opposite thereto. On 26th January the board met at Norfolk, and I reported this result to the War, and Captain Warrington did the same to the Navy Department.

Being thus released from pressing duty, I sent my aid to the office at Washington, and, by leave of the Secretary of War, made an excursion to North Carolina, with a view to meeting commissioners at Edenton, and to inspect the harbor of Cape Fear, and at the same time renew a long-suspended intercourse with friends at Wilmington. On 30th January I commenced my journey with a pair of horses, and at Edenton, North Carolina, met Messrs. Little and Treadwell, the State commissioners, on the subject of improving the navigation of the sound. Compared the maps of Morley's date, 1733, with that of Wimble's of 1738, with the recent surveys of Cole, etc., and appointed to examine the Old Roanoke Inlet in the coming spring, with a view to opening a channel from the Sound to the Atlantic. At a dinner given on this occasion I met my neighbor, Captain Henry Waring, of Brooklyn, whom I found to be a popular intimate of the gentility of Edenton, and who entertained the company with a history of his entering the United States navy in '98 as a lieutenant, and compeer of the now Commodore Chauncy, whom he then "outranked;" but finding that his "trade with North Carolina" was more profitable than his navy commission, he resigned its honors to his friend Chauncy, and contented himself with accumulating money as a merchant.

On 5th February crossed the Albemarle Sound to Plymouth, where the citizens received me under a salute of cannon, and which I acknowledged in a brief speech; and at Mr. Armistead's met the great farmer of that part ·of the State, Mr. Collins, who gave me a minute account of the culture of the "Scuppernong grape," so famous for its wine. This grape is described by Lawson, in his history of Carolina, early in the last century.

On 7th I proceeded to Newbern, where I met William Gaston, Esquire, whose very agreeable acquaintance I had made in the family of my father-in-law in Wilmington, 1806, when Gaston practiced in the courts there. At dinner I also met my friend John Guion, Esquire, and William Graham, and Mr. Donnel, and passed a few hours with John Stanly, Esq., one of the brightest minds of the State. On 9th February arrived at Wilmington, finding Mrs. Swift and my son and daughter in health. Thanks be to God.

On 21st February the citizens of Wilmington gave me a dinner—a flattering token of the remembrance of earlier days. I attempted no speech in response to a complimentary remark, and gave this toast:—

"North Carolina and her liberal spirit, as evinced in her *carte blanche* order to Canova for a sculpture of Washington, at an expense limited only by the artist's decision."

February 26th, to Fort Johnson, Oak Island and Bald Head, and reported from Smithville my views to the War Department. Visited the grave of my friend John Lightfoot Griffin, in the garden that had been the care of its owner in 1805, Mrs. Sarah Dry Smith. I could find no stone in the public graveyard to mark the resting place of my early friend Benjamin Blaney, the friend also of the poor, and that especially of the sick sailor and stranger.

February 28th to Orton, the plantation of General Smith on the banks of the Cape Fear, and passed a day with Mrs. S. D. Smith and himself. The pleasures of our reminiscences of that spot, and of Belvidere, were clouded by the aspect of the failing fortunes of the general. Mrs. Smith presented us at the board, a bottle of the nearly consumed stock of old sherry, with which, and blue perch from the adjacent pond, we were used to regale in more prosperous days; Mrs. Smith evincing a well-balanced serenity, to cheer the gloom of her husband. On 1st of March returned to Wilmington, and found it a fruitless essay to liquidate the large claims of the general's creditors.

Mrs. Swift and myself renewed our associations with the Lords, Mrs. Vance, Mr. Miller and the Browns, Wrights, Toomers, Londons, Hoopers, and other of the friends of our more early days. On 7th visited my correspondent, Alfred Moore, Esq., at Buchoi, and enjoyed a retrospect of our deer hunts with Duncan Moore, now laid low, and the Swanns, Hills and Burgwins, Richard Eagle, etc.

The recurrence among friends to the scenes of early life, when visiting, form some of the finest enjoyments of mind that can be recounted, and probably one among the best of this world's good.

On 11th March, I purchased carriage and horses, and, with my wife, son and daughter, and maid Peggy, commenced a jaunt to Norfolk, leaving of our family in Wilmington, Mr. J. W. Walker and Julius, and their mother, Mrs. Walker — an exemplary parent, and true lady of the old school — and her sister, Mrs. Ann Quince, of equal virtues, and our *semper eadem* friend and cousin, and family physician, Dr. A. J. De Rosset. Mrs. Vance and daughters Mary and Jane took the road to Newbern by the Sound to Sage's, and to Colonel Shine's by Holly Shelter and Trenton. Detained some days by storm in Newbern, entertained by friends there already named, and by the Edwards; employed the rainy hours in reading to Mrs. Swift, whose piety enjoyed the " Rise and Progress of Religion in the Soul of Man," by Doddridge, more than her less pious husband, who, however, found it among the best books he ever perused — thanks be to God. We arrived at the hospitable mansion of John Armistead, Esquire, in Plymouth, on 22d, thence sent my horses and carriage back to Wilmington to be sold, and crossed the Sound to Edenton in company with a very enlightened gentleman, Dr. Norcomb, whose knowledge of the Roanoke country, and its liberal planters, gave Mrs. Swift and myself cause to be thankful for his conversation in a long row in a barge that landed us at Edenton, from whence we took an extra Stage to Norfolk, arriving there on 25th, and by packet thence to Baltimore. On 30th at my sister's, Mrs. Adams, and on the 1st April I to my office in Washington City, accompanied by my father. Found good quarters by renting a house in Colonel Cox's row, in Georgetown, where on 26th my aid, Lieutenant Blaney, arrived with my son James, wounded in the head by a blow received from his inconsiderate teacher, Dr. Rudd, in Elizabethtown ; also my sons William, Alexander and Thomas, and with Mrs. Swift, Julius and Sally, and maid Peggy, and my faithful man Jack, whose bravery and care in the St. Lawrence campaign of 1813 deserves my remembrance, and whose features Jarvis has preserved in the portrait that the corporation placed in the City Hall in commemoration of the Long Island and Harlem scenes of 1814. My man Jack brought with him my well-kept horses "Fox," "Ned," and "Yorick." On 28th my friend, Captain John L. Smith, welcomed the family to our new quarters in Georgetown. Early in May my brother-in-law Adams and myself, with some of my brother officers, commenced to purchase military land warrants, with a view on my part to form some future settlement for my sons in Illinois, on some fine tracts, and to re-sell the balance.

On 26th May, with the engineer of that department, Lieutenant-Colonel Armistead, proceeded to Fort McHenry, Baltimore, and laid off a sea wall to protect the site from the waves of the bay that had been some time abrading the shore; Armistead commenced the work. The next day General Bernard, and Captain Elliot of the navy and myself proceeded to Old Point Comfort, and recommenced our examinations that had been commenced last winter at Gosport. Colonel Armistead joined the board, and we extended our explorations to York River, and from thence despatched Lieutenant Smoot of the navy, in the schooner, to meet President Monroe up the bay, and to signal the meeting by five discharges of cannon. The President and Secretaries of War and Navy having determined to see the several positions that the board had surveyed with reference to a navy depôt and the defence of Chesapeake Bay. *Ad interim* the board proceeded to explore the vicinity of Norfolk and Lynhaven Bay, Elizabeth River, etc. At a place called Cormick, on Trading Point, and also the settlement of Captain John Smith, of Pocahontas memory, we found moss-covered grave stones, one inscribed "Gookings, 1657," another "Hodges, 1687." Detailed Major James Kearney and Captain William T. Poussin to form a topographical map of these regions, by a compass reconnoitre.

On 30th May the board proceeded by a navy schooner and barges to the clay banks on York River; a point commended to examination for a depôt.

On 2d June we went in several boats up Queen's Creek to Williamsburgh, and thence explored Archer's Hope to James River. We visited William and Mary, and viewed the fine marble statue of Norbon, Lord Botetout, in the college land. Also a couple of large live oak trees standing in the corner of the land, the most northerly growth of this tree that I have seen. Returned to Yorktown, and traversed the old lines of October, 1781. On passing the redout stormed by St. Simon and Viomenil, General Bernard, with quite an imposing air, took off his hat and made a profound reverence. While at the redout carried by Colonel Hamilton, we laughed at the fact that it was conquered by the loss of half a dozen lives in a very rapid movement, while Viomenil, more formal in his march, but with success, mastered his redout, leaving some sixty men dead in the trenches. We also looked at the old stone church of York, and found the tomb of Thomas Nelson, son of Hugo, of Penrith, inscribed "*Vitæ bene gestæ finem implevit.*" The stone of the church and the old mill of limestone taken from the banks of York River.

On 5th June the approach of the President was signaled by Lieutenant Smoot, who, with the Secretary of War, Mr. Calhoun, and of the Navy, Mr. Crowninshield, and private secretary, Mr. Samuel L. Gouverneur, joined the board at Yorktown, and visited the site of the marquees of Washington and Rochambeau on the field of 1781, and the next day looked over the positions that the board had surveyed near York, and on 7th sailed to Old Point Comfort, and the next day the President and suite made a ceremonial entrance at Norfolk, as the commencement of the President's southern tour of inspection. He examined the navy yard and forts, and on 9th, with the board as part of his suite, took barges to Drummond's Lake *via* the Dismal Swamp Canal; in which excursion Captain Elliot of the navy amused himself and Gouverneur by upsetting the barge of the board in the outlet, sending Bernard and McRee to the bottom for a moment. The freak was, of course, taken in good part, and we hastened to Farages, on the canal, to dry our garments, and to partake of the fine cane-fed beef of the swamp, and to mix our brandy with the light juniper-colored water of the outlet — deemed especially wholesome.

On 10th the President, etc., visited Elizabeth City on the Pasquotank, and also became guests of Mr. Sawyer in the vicinity, whose accomplished daughter entertained the party with music on the harp. On 12th the President and suite returned to a public dinner given at Norfolk in honor of Mr. Monroe.

On 13th to Hampton and Old Point, examining the topographical maps and plans of the board, from whence, a further extension of the tour being postponed for a season, (Secretary Calhoun having gone to South Carolina,) the President, on receiving despatches from Washington, returned at once with the Secretary of the Navy and Mr. Gouverneur to that city.

On 18th the board proceeded to St. Mary's River on Potomac, where McRee and myself relieved the subalterns, and made in one day a triangulation of that estuary called a river, and extended the same to the banks of the Patuxent at Point Sewell.

On 21st the board examined the Patuxent, where Bernard met, for the first time in his life, the American black snake, a bold fellow of full six feet in length, that raised himself over a bush, and, with his brilliant eye, shook his forked tongue at the general.

On 21st the board arrived in Annapolis, and proceeded to examine that harbor and the Round Bay. From thence sent orders (24th) to Major J. J. Abert and Captain J. Le Conte, to make a topographical survey of Throg's Neck and Hell Gate, with a view to the action of the board.

On 27th we proceeded to Baltimore, and held our meetings at the Indian Queen, in Market Street. The whole board in favor of York River as a navy depôt except Captain L. Warrington, who preferred the present site, Gosport, in case that the Horse Shoe Channel should be found by the engineers to be defensible; but if the line of defence had to fall back to Old Point Comfort, then the whole board would probably select a site for the depôt on Burrell's Bay, or some other point on James River. The board here adjourned, to meet in Washington on 30th September next.

On my arrival in Baltimore I found my sister Sarah and my brother William arrived from New York. I had written Major Thayer to send my brother to me, that I might direct him as to his future pursuits. His fondness for sport had made him popular among the young cadets at West Point, and of course such a standing was accompanied by a low grade in the merit roll, which annoyed his father and myself, and gave the superintendent of the Academy trouble. It had become habitual at the Point in all doubtful cases of mischief, to attribute it to my brother, who, among other freaks had commenced "messing by himself," as he termed his retiring to a lone room with a box of pies that he had purchased of one of the servants at that post.

On 30th June I took William with me to Georgetown, where, after a few days I advised him to return to West Point and apply himself to a better course, and by study to get ready to meet me there on my next visit of inspection; which he promised to do, and then returned to Governor's Island and to the Point. He has no lack of capacity, and will succeed if he apply himself to his books.

The months of July and August were busy days in the office on Pennsylvania Avenue, about one hundred yards west of the war office, in making contracts for the new works on the Gulf of Mexico and Atlantic frontiers. We had a multitude of proposals from Messrs. Farrar, Goldsborough, Mix and others.

During the time I made official arrangements to place the engineer department in the hands of a successor, for I had made up my mind to seek civil service. I also, early in September, made a visit of inspection to West Point, and consulted my friend Thayer in reference to my brother William, who I found would not so pursue his studies as to secure him the proper grade as graduate, and determined to detach him on some duty that would promise improvement, and secure, if practicable, his commission in the artillery; for which object I had been also consulting the Secretary of War, in reference to examining the western rivers, recently commenced by my protégé, Captain S. H. Long, who had made a very interesting map of the Illinois and its tributaries.

In this visit to West Point I was accompanied by General John Mason, the proprietor of the Georgetown iron works, who came on to see Mr. Gouv. Kemble and our rising establishment opposite the Point at Margaret Brook. This was on 17th of the month. From thence to the city, where I met Mrs. Swift's cousin, Mrs. Mary Orme, who returned with me on 26th to my family in Georgetown; finding there my old friend General B. Smith, from Belvidere, on his way to Kentucky, to examine his lands near Henderson. My brother-in-law, James W. Walker, from Wilmington, had been sojourning in my family on his way to seek a new residence on the Limestone River in Alabama, and to examine some lands in West Tennessee to which his father had claims for military service.

On 30th September the board of engineer and navy officers met at the department to finish the plans for Chesapeake Bay, that they might be rëdrawn by the officers engaged in the surveys.

The President returned to Washington on 11th October from his residence at Oak Hill, in Loudon, Virginia. On 15th October met him and the Secretaries of War and Treasury to consult upon my retiring from the army to civil service. I presenteded them my views in reference to General Bernard, and said that under the resolution of Congress, 16th February, I did not see how the executive could remedy the case. It was concluded to confer upon me the surveyorship of New York, the only place that would be vacant, and on 23d October Mr. Crawford informed me that I might take charge of that office as soon as I had made up my mind to leave the corps of engineers. Mr. Secretary of State J. Q. Adams gave his approval to this measure of my appointment.

Our friend Mrs. Orme returned home to Wilmington under the escort of Mr. ———. I wrote by her to Julius H. Walker, advising him of all the facts that had come to me from Lawyer Shight of Newburg, and from uncle John Du Bois of the same town, to wit: That all the children of John Du Bois (Mrs. Swift's grandfather,) were entitled to the said grandfather's rights in the " Minnesink land," and that under the will of Mrs. Swift's mother, Julius H. and Louisa M. Walker (my wife) were entitled to all the said lands that had belonged to Isaac Du Bois, the brother of the said grandfather John ; which land had descended to the only child (Margaret) of the said Isaac and wife of the aforesaid John Du Bois of Newburgh, to whom was born one son, Isaac, who, dying before his father and after his mother, the said father, John, had conveyed by his will all the rights of said Isaac, his father-in-law, to his sister, the aforesaid M. M. Walker, mother of said Julius H. and Louisa M. : *i. e.*, all said Dr. Isaac Du Bois' rights in the patent of land called the "Minnesink Patent" aforesaid, which said Dr. Du Bois died in October, 1745, and was then seized with his brother, the aforesaid grandfather John, (who died December, 1767,) of all the Du Bois right to the said "Minnesink lands," they, two brothers, being the only heirs and sons of the Rev. Gualthemus Du Bois, deceased in October, 1751. See *family Bible* of the aforesaid Louisa M. Swift, where these deaths are recorded.

I employed the latter days of October in removing my family from Georgetown to Mrs. Marvin's, number sixty-one in Broadway, where we had a comfortable suite of rooms, and in placing my sons James and Williams with Mr. Craig at Erasmus Hall in Flatbush, and depositing my funds of one thousand five hundred dollars in the United States Bank.

Early in November, on the 2d, I returned to Baltimore to meet General Bernard and Colonel McRee, to pursue the board duty; thence we three proceeded to Old Point in the schooner "Hornet," Lieutenant Ramage, United States navy, and also to Barnwell's Bay on James River, and Pargan Creek in continuance of our former incomplete surveys for a navy depôt, returning *via* Baltimore to Georgetown on 11th November, on which day I resigned my colonelcy of engineers, reserving all the rights of my brevet brigadiership, by understanding with Colonel Monroe (the President) that in case of war he would restore me to the line, as one of the rights of the brevet rank conferred by the United States.

In reference to my resignation it was said that I should have apprised my brother officers, that such of them as may have agreed in opinion with me might have united with me in leaving the corps. I avoided this to prevent the aspect of concert to interfere with the public service. It may also be noted that up to the day of my resignation General Bernard had not in a single instance objected to the selection of any site for defensive works, that had been occupied by any officer of engineers. He did deem all the works too small, and though they had thus far served the purposes for which they had been constructed, he was generally correct in that opinion. The chief merit of a military engineer is, first, selecting the proper position; next in order is the adopting a suitable plan to the position ; and next, the ability to direct workmen to make the enduring walls.

On 13th November I notified the Secretary of the Treasury of my acceptance of the surveyorship, it having been required by the Secretary of

War that I should complete in the ensuing winter, the duty that had been assigned me on the board of engineer and navy officers.

The next day I proceeded to New York and appointed a very worthy man (Samuel Terry) my deputy, and on 19th of the month commenced my new official duty.

On 30th December, having arranged with the collector for my deputy to perform all the functions of office in my absence, proceeded to join the board of engineers at Washington; to Philadelphia in company with the Vice-President, Tompkins, and Commodore Chauncey, where I passed my birthday in company with the son-in-law of my former chief, and others of the families of Biddle and Cadwallader.

1819.    Early in January arrived at Washington, and arranged an office for the engineer board at Hysonimon's in Georgetown, where were assembled General Bernard, Colonels McRee and Armistead, (my successor in the engineer department,) and Captain Elliot of the navy, and closed our work on 24th February, and laid the plans before the Secretary of War. On this board McRee and myself found Bernard rather shy in giving his reasons for the preference of any part of the plan that was his own; a glaring case was that of Saller's Point, below Baltimore, where Bernard preferred a front of much more exposure to enfilade fire than McRee and myself had commended.   His uniform reply was "Gentlemen, your plan is very good, *mais*, I prefer my idea."   We both said we had a right to his reasons in the spirit of his employment.   McRee and myself also preferred a smaller emicute to the work at Old Point.   I had so stated to Mr. Secretary Calhoun, bu twe deferred to Bernard's preference and popularity, and yet we did not receive his reason for so large an enclosure.   The service on this board at Georgetown left an impression on the minds of McRee and myself that Bernard was not the genius he had been reputed, and that he was not candid or frank in his exchange of thought with us.   I suppose he remembered my letters of objection to his service; but McRee was not as liberal in his views of that gentleman's course on the board.   My opinion of Bernard is that he is an excellent bureau officer, a cold-hearted man ; not in any sense a man of genius.

The 27th February I returned to my duties at the Custom House, New York, where the facetious Major Noah said in his *Advocate* that I had transferred my name from the army register to a hogshead of rum. He did not estimate the causes that drove me out of the army.

I passed the winter, or rather March, in applying myself to becoming acquainted with the theory of commerce and its relations to my vocations; purchased the six musty 8-vos. of Anderson, and read on revenue laws.

On 1st April commenced housekeeping at two hundred and thirteen in Duane Street, and made an agreeable associate in my neighbor, Henry Cruger, Esq., who had formerly been a member from Bristol in Parliament. He gave me a corrected reading of the story of his being on the hustings with Edmund Burke, whose declamation so dumbfounded his mercantile ideas that he did not presume to follow the speech of that great man by any effusions of his own, and said to the audience: "Your Mayor can do no more than say ditto to Mr. Burke." Mr. Cruger appeared to be a very highly informed person, and a thorough gentleman.

On 15th April my son McRee was born, and named for my friend Colonel McRee; and which son and the daughter Louisa of my friend Thomas March, and the son John Ireland of my friend Fanning C. Tucker, were baptized at my house in Duane Street, by Rev. H. G. Feltus, on 28th day of the following month of June. In the month of May Colonel McRee visited me, and to see his namesake, and on 15th of that month he left us to seek a farm in Indiana, having resigned his commission in the engineers in consequence of the course pursued by the executive, in giving General Bernard rank and employment not by any means contemplated by the resolution of 16th February. In the month of May I visited the West Point foundry, and witnessed the first delivery of ordnance castings to the United States agent. On my return 10th May placed James, Willy, Alexander and Tom at Mr. Pickett's school. In the month of April my brother William at Pittsburgh with Major Long, on Yellow Stone expedition. In the following month of June, by invitation of the Secretary of War, John Garnet of New Jersey, James Renwick of New York, Richard Patterson of Pennsylvania, Colonel Fenwick, Colonel Totten, Colonel

Archer and myself formed the board of visitors at the Military Academy, and made our report on 19th June.

The 4th of July was celebrated this year with much *éclat* by the Society of Cincinnati in New York, to which my father and myself were invited, and on which occasion it was agreed that my father had a just claim to a membership of that society, by reason of his naval services as surgeon on board the "Portsmouth" ship of war that was captured by the "Culloden," seventy-four, of Rodney's fleet, 1781.

On 19th of July the Rev. Thomas C. Brownwell went with me to my father's quarters on Governor's Island, and baptized my sister Sarah Adams' two daughters, Deborah Delano and Mary Harper, both born there in my father's house.

July 29th, the families of my friends Fanning C. Tucker, Thomas March and my own, twenty-six in all, on board the revenue cutter, Captain Cahoon, to Oyster Bay, and with Captain George Rogers we passed some pleasant weeks at this watering place; where my son James encountered a hornet's nest, and after much battling, with the aid of Captain Rogers, the nest was conquered after receiving several severe stings.

August 2d, on a visit to Captain James Farquhar at Green Hill — "Sailor's Snug Harbor." I used his telescope to observe the balloon ascent of M. Guilles, and his descent in a parachute to Bushwick on Long Island, landing near Newtown. I estimated the height ascended in a brief space of time at six thousand feet. The whole time occupied in ascent and descent was about three-fourths of one hour.

Although my functions in the army had ceased, I could not become indifferent to the action of the government in reference to fortifying our harbors, and other national improvements, and was glad to find that half a million of dollars had been appropriated for harbor defence for the current year.

From Oyster Bay I had placed my family to board with Mrs. Ross of Jamaica. She is the daughter of the former friend of Colonel Williams and myself, Mrs. Wilkinson, at number forty, Broadway — the headquarters of our engineers in the city. At Jamaica I was within easy ride of my city duties, and early in September established my family on Brooklyn Heights at the house of a friend, George Gibbs, Esq., and placed my sons James, Williams and Alexander at Mr. Armour's school; my son Thomas with his grandfather, the surgeon at Governor's Island.

On 4th September the mayor of the city, Mr. Colden, invited me to aid the corporation in examining sources of a supply of water for the city. Accordingly on this day, accompanied by Dr. Samuel L. Mitchell and Robert Macomb, Esq., we proceeded to the Rye Ponds, and by the usual mode I determined the flow of water from the upper pond to be two thousand one hundred and twenty-eight gallons per minute into the lower pond, and thence into the Broux two thousand four hundred and eighty-four gallons per minute were discharged. I gave Mr. Colden a report of a plan to convey this water to the Harlem River, and across the same to a reservoir of deposit on the Heights, deeming them to be far below the point where the acqueduct should cross the Broux not far below the pond; and that as the season was ordinary in its character, calculated that three millions of gallons of water might be daily received into said reservoir of deposit, at an expense of about two millions of dollars. The amount of the estimate was deemed to be too large by the wise men of the corporation, and the report soon went to sleep in the pigeon-holes of the mayor's office. I neither charged nor received any fee for this service.

Early in October John and Robert Swartwout, two enterprising gentlemen of the city, consulted me on a plan to bank and ditch the Newark meadows, and we explored them, and the meadows near Hackensack bridge and Hoboken. Those gentlemen offered me an interest in these low lands, and I went with them to Philadelphia to consult Langdon Cheeves, Pierce Butler, Thomas Cadwallader, Thomas Biddle and Stephen Girard to form a company to complete this work, and thereby supply the market of New York with beef and a dairy. Those gentlemen were not prepared for the enterprise, but took time to consider the matter, and I proceeded no further, and thus one of the best plans for public and private utility was suspended on 7th October, 1819.

On 14th of this month I purchased from George Gibbs the place where I was living with him on the Heights, for ten thousand dollars—sixteen lots, forming a square overlooking the East River and the city harbor—and on 1st November took possession, and commenced housekeeping there with my family, and commenced trimming a large grape vine that Mrs. Gibbs had transplanted from General Smith's garden in Smithville, North Carolina, and I gave the cuttings of the vine to William Prince, the florist and gardener at Flushing, who wished to name the grape "The Louisa," for my wife, but both she and myself deemed Mrs. Isabella Gibbs entitled thereto, and accordingly the vine was named "The Isabella," and I gave the cuttings to many of my neighbors in Brooklyn. Thus originated the Isabella Grape, 1824.

November 5th wrote the Secretary of War, J. C. Calhoun, Esq., that Robert Tillotson and Colonel Samuel Hawkins had purchased of Roswell Hopkins the contract to build forts at Mobile Point, that had been contracted for while I was chief engineer; and that I had agreed to furnish professional advice to execute these works on condition of receiving one-fourth of the net profits.

November 13th my aunt, Lucretia Lovering, became a member of my family at Brooklyn. She is of Boston, and my father's favorite sister.

December 14th, wrote Colonel McRee at Natchez that five hundred dollars had been deposited for him in the Bank of New York, and that eight hundred dollars had been sent to him from the War Department, the proceeds of the sale of his library.

During the months of November and December much of my time had been employed in comparing the weights and measures, and in the Revenue Department. My report thereon in my files, and in Congressional Document.

In 1820 eight hundred thousand dollars appropriated for United States fortifications.

1820. January, Charles Snowden of Philadelphia proposed to sell to me a large tract of Schuylkill coal lands, and with Professor Hassler and his large carriage, and Mr. Charles Loss, a miner, Mr. Snowden and myself, proceeded on 8th January to Orwicksburgh in Schuylkill County, Pennsylvania, and found the mines very promising, and in presence of Mr. Hassler and Mr. Loss, Mr. Snowden sold me twenty thousand acres of coal land for twenty thousand dollars. We returned by Philadelphia, and there met Samuel Mifflin and Cadwallader Evans, Esq., and consulted on a mode of transporting this coal to market by improving the canal; and on our arrival at Elizabethtown, New Jersey, met Governor Williamson, who agreed to present to the legislature of New Jersey my plan of a canal from the Delaware River to New York Harbor, to transport anthracite. On arriving in New York, the first fire in that city made of this coal was made in my office. The next day Snowden declined to execute the sale he had made to me, and made a bargain with a new association at two dollars the acre, owing me two hundred and sixty dollars, cash lent to him 17th January.

February 1st, Alexander Macomb, Esq., father of the general, mentioned to me that while he was a merchant in Detroit in 1778, Captain Bard of the 8th British infantry captured Daniel Boon of Kentucky, and marched him to Detroit, where the governor (Hamilton) treated Boon kindly, and gave him liberty to return to his family, and to aid him gave an order on Mr. Macomb's store for such supplies as he might require on his march. Boon said: "I cannot accept more than is absolutely necessary, and will take but twelve shillings for myself, and a pound of tea for my wife." What moderation and self respect!

In this year, Mr. March, Major Tucker and myself employed Mr. Samuel Seabury to teach our boys. He is a well informed young man, the son of a clergyman and grand-son of Bishop Seabury. I gave him the range of my library, and found him an interesting companion. He was spoken of as a suitable assistant in the newly projected theological seminary advocated by Bishop Hobart, O. B. Ogden and others, and in which I was a trustee, but opposed to the location of such an institution in such associations as the city of New York must yield to youth.

February 6th, an interesting meeting with many, including Captain E. Trenchard, United States navy, on the subject of the colonization of free colored people in Africa. The captain was on the eve of sailing in the United States ship "Cyane" for Africa with the ship "Elizabeth," having the first gang of such people set free to commence this great project.

February 8th. In reply to an enquiry from Hon. John C. Calhoun on the subject of our relations with Spain, having reference to the island of Cuba, I wrote as may be seen in the Appendix.

March 7th, attended a large political meeting at Flatbush, Long Island, with Lefferts Lefferts, Jeremiah Johnston, Jehiel Jaggar, etc., and addressed the meeting on the inexpediency of moving in the presidential question that had been commenced by Mr. Crawford's friends in Washington, where the Radicals had assailed Mr. Calhoun, charging the war department with malversation on the part of Mr. Calhoun and General Swift in reference to contracts with Elijah Mix, which contracts had been made by me before leaving the army, and approved by Mr. Calhoun.

On 22d April I proceeded to Washington, and notified the committee of Congress of my readiness to show that the engineer department had done its duty in reference to that contract. The committee did not report, and I returned to New York, escorting Mrs. Grace Magruder and ·Miss Mary E. Roberdeau to Brooklyn as guests of Mrs. Swift, and found there my worthy mother-in-law, Mrs. M. M. Walker, and my aunts Lucretia and Philomela, sisters of my father, on a visit; the former from Wilmington, North Carolina, the two latter from Boston.

May 12th. By direction of the Secretary of the Treasury, commenced a chemical examination of the sugars from Cuba and the teas from China, to decide on their respective qualities to regulate the duty, and the qualities and proper names of all the wines imported, and made my report on the same to the treasury department.

June 7th, as president of the Handel and Haydn Society, with F. C. Tucker, Dr. Oakey, B. Armitage and S. Taylor, got up the first oratorio in the United States at St. Paul's Church, and raised eleven thousand dollars for the Orphan Asylum and rebuilding Zion Church. This was a great improvement to the musical taste of our country.

June 8th. Nathaniel Prime and myself were appointed by the legislature of New Jersey to superintend the plan to open the Morris Canal improvement. This was delayed.

June 10th to 28th, at West Point by invitation of Mr. Secretary Calhoun, with Generals Brown and Jessup, Dr. S. L. Mitchell, James Renwick and Captain Le Compte, to examine the Military Academy.

July 18th, Rev. Dr. Ireland, Colonel Totten, Mr. March, Major Tucker and myself had a fine excursion to the Fire Place, on Long Island, where a trout, or more probably a salmon, came up to the mill race of the river, and was captured, weighing thirteen pounds.

August 20th, reported to the Secretary of the Treasury on a plan to modify the tariff on wines, sugars and teas; that a reduction of duty would tend to increase the quantum of importation, and consequently the revenue; and that in reference to spirits, the proof should be high to insure a good quality, and to injure less the public health. It was at this time that Major Noah published a diatribe on my " transferring my name from the army register to hogsheads of rum and boxes of champagne," in allusion to my custom house functions, and in *ignorance of the causes* that had induced me to leave the army, but in reality to assail me as a political friend of Mr. Calhoun.

October 7th, received from the United States Comptroller a deed of trust of Bald Head, Mallory and Blue Banks lands on Cape Fear River, North Carolina — several thousands of acres — with the directions to have the same acknowledged before the mayor of the city, and which was done as agent of the United States Treasury, to aid in suing a debt of General B. Smith as security for Colonel Read a defaulter, and late collector of the port of Wilmington, North Carolina.

This matter involved many difficulties, and final loss by false records.

October 17th, my venerable mother-in-law, Mrs. Walker, returned to Wilmington to live with her son, Julius H. Walker.

November 1st, commenced our Brooklyn meetings of a Social Club: Commodore Evans and Captain Rogers, United States navy, Colonel Totten, F. C. Tucker, Thomas March, Thomas J. Chew, J. Jaggar, G. S. Wise. My brother William returned on Long's expedition to the Mississippi, and laid up the steam engine at the mouth of the Cumberland.

1821. January 23d, my sister, Mary Roberdeau, married to Lieutenant G.

W. Whistler, United States army, by Rev. Dr. J. B. Romeyn, giving my father great uneasiness, as they were without adequate means of housekeeping. However, my mother and myself had a favorable estimate of the worth and ability of Mr. Whistler.

In the previous December, and in this month, a political accusation was made on the part of Governor De Witt Clinton, charging me, as surveyor of New York, with action under the influence of the general government, especially Mr. Monroe, to "oppose State authorities in the elections." This was termed the "Green Bag Essay," and was signally defeated by the oath of every officer of the department under my official control, as the documents of the State at Albany may evince to any reader. In fact Governor Clinton admitted to me that the whole had been the result of misrepresentation to him, and of which Colonel Ferris Pell was too conversant; and I was glad of this explanation at a dinner party given by Consul Bogoot, restoring a pleasant personal relation between Governor Clinton and his less important friend; for friend I had in reality been during the canvass, as also had my deputy, Samuel Terry, Esq.

February 27th, my brother William arrived in Philadelphia on horseback from mouth of Cumberland.

March 21st, William McRee passed some days with me discussing the cause which had driven both of us from the army; the very improper relation that the government had established between a foreign officer, General Bernard, and the corps of engineers. The government made him (McRee) surveyor-general of Missouri, and which office he found he could not hold consistently with his ideas of propriety and the habits of land speculation then prevailing in Missouri. I had a profound respect for Colonel McRee; he had a superior military mind; I named a son for him.

During this spring a general inspection of the revenue service was made by Mr. Edward Jones of the United States treasury; a gentleman of high honor and ability. He found, as had been represented by the three branches of the revenue in the United States custom house, that higher moral qualities were needed in the subordinate officers, to secure the revenue.

Three hundred and two thousand dollars appropriated for United States fortifications for 1821.

In the month of June, by invitation of the Secretary of War, I attended as a member of the board of visitors the examination of the Military Academy, and found great improvement made by the judicious administration of Major Thayer, but not coinciding in views with a majority of the visitors I made a separate report to the War Department, as the United States documents exhibit, and my own files contain. Brother William mapping in Philadelphia till June, then to my father's at New London.

In this month I wrote the Hon. Henry Clay my views of the tendency of the importation of a foreign officer, and interpolating him into the corps of engineers, as may be seen in the Appendix.

In this summer I became interested in some of the stocks of Wall Street, and with Henry Eckford, Esq., the distinguished navy architect, applied to the legislature to incorporate a Life and Fire Insurance Company, to be connected with the coal speculations in Pennsylvania that had caused Prof. Hassler and the miner, Mr. Loss, to explore the anthracite region in the year 1820.

September, brother William to Maine with Major Abert, surveying.

1822. In the spring of this year with the Rev. Dr. Ireland, Colonel Totten, Mr. March and Colonel J. T. Jones, had a successful trouting excursion at the Fire Place on Long Island, and for the first time used Limerick hooks from Dublin, furnished by Colonel Jones. Totten and myself, while busily engaged at the sport, our boat "sprung a leak" and sunk from under us, and we were drenched, though our sport was not spoiled. Remember Martin Kelly, Sackville Street, Dublin, for Limerick hooks.

The last of April I was summoned to Washington on a revival of the allegation of the Radicals of Mr. Calhoun's alleged malversation in the (now become celebrated) Rip Rap contracts with Mix, accusing the minister and the chief engineer, Swift, of partaking. See the congressional documents respecting this infamous calumny, and also my files.

An attempt was made this season by the economists of the Radicals in Congress to reduce the expenses of the government by the diminution of the personal force of the custom house, in New York especially. It was found on inspection that the only change which true economy would justify was to substitute inspectors of ability, and who would not spend their time in porter-house politics.

In this summer I took my family to New London, where my father had been some time stationed as surgeon in the army after leaving Fort Columbus. With him and Captain Rogers of the navy, Captain Way, formerly of the army, and Hon. Lyman and Captain Richard Law, made an excursion to the Rocks in Long Island Sound under the lead of General William North, formerly adjutant-general United States army; and where the aboriginal mode of cooking blackfish, called "totogue," (taken then in large quantities,) between heated flat stones, which made a very acceptable feast.

The legislature of New York had, in the April past, made a law to regulate the streets and drainage of the city of New York east of the Bowery and north of North Street, appointing Professor Adrain of Columbia College, James Renwick, Esq., and myself the commissioners for this purpose; and our essay was to accomplish the same by a minimum of expense to the owners of lots consistently with a thorough attainment of a healthful result—all of which was spoiled by speculating aldermen.

James Renwick, Esq., and George McCullock of New Jersey and myself explored the country to decide on a route for a canal from Easton, on the Delaware River, to New York by the Hopatcong Lake and Rockaway River, and the Muconeetcong River, and deemed the same suitable for canal and inclined planes. This service was performed while the yellow fever had driven the whole population of the lower city to Greenwich, and the custom house to rooms in the State's prison.

While in New Jersey I met Miles Smith, Esq., of New Brunswick, to whom I had given an Isabella grape vine, and visited his residence at Ross Hall to witness its great growth. Upon his farm I found the ruins of an old fort of Revolutionary times, an outpost of the British army, and at the site of Colonel B. Tarleton's marquee, at a grotto of tree roots, found a barrel set in a fine spring of water that had supplied the troops with water, still flowing in abundance and purity.

In the month of July, with General Scott, visited Sunswick, the seat of Colonel George Gibbs on Long Island, to compare his Tokay grapes with Isabellas that had been furnished in roots from my garden. Both growing luxuriantly. Concluded it well to engraft the hardy Isabella on the delicate Tokay. We returned to my house at Brooklyn, and found my father and aunt Lucretia, and my brother William arrived. The latter had become a grave, experienced traveller, from Long's expedition among the Pawnee and other Indians, and an expert horseman and rifle shot, having sustained Colonel Long's party some weeks with buffalo and venison by his rifle. My brother had command of the military guard of the party.

In December met at Mr. Renwick's Captain Sabine of the English engineers, and Captain Chauncy of the navy, and witnessed experiments on magnetic intensity, and on the vibrations of Captain Kater's pendulum-point of suspension and oscillation, practically, as they are in theory, convertible points, and gave them the result of my examination of the weights and measures as existing in our revenue offices.

As a member of St. Ann's in my parish in Brooklyn, gave an estimate to rebuild that church for twelve thousand dollars. Twelve of us loaned each five hundred dollars for the object. One hundred and two pews and seventy in the gallery. On the completion and sale every expense was covered by the price paid for the pews, and leaving the church free from debt.

Three hundred and seventy thousand dollars appropriated for fortifications in the United States in 1822.

1823. On the death of my neighbor, Rev. John Ireland, myself and Robert Bach became his executors, and sold his personal estate for five hundred and eighty-two dollars. Sent his library to his step-son, Major Tucker, the plate to the children, and the gold watch of Mr. Ireland to his namesake, John Ireland Tucker. His real estate were lots near the navy yard. With this accomplished gentleman I had enjoyed a very agreeable and friendly intercourse for ten years.

During this winter the Handel and Haydn Society, *i. e.*, a portion thereof, to wit: Daniel Oaky, F. C. Tucker, Benjamin Armitage, Clement Moor,

Rev. J. M. Wainwright, John Delafield, Walter Phelps, John Chesterman, C. W. Taylor, with a new list of subscribers, formed the Philharmonic Society of the city: Dr. Post, president; J. G. Swift, vice-president; John Delafield, secretary and treasurer. At the opening of its meetings the president and vice-president made each an address. This society did much to improve the public taste in music.

In June my mother-in-law and grand-daughter Mary Ann, and cousin Mary Orme, John Q. McNeill and Mrs. S.'s brother-in-law, Edwin Gay Osborne, returned to North Carolina. Mr. Osborne, a gentleman of fine mind, attempted, by aid of my friend Cadwallader Colden, Esq., to establish himself in the city as a counsellor of law, but did not succeed.

On 10th July I went to Washington to confer with Mr. Calhoun and Virgil Maxey, Esq.; carried with me for him, and set out in his garden, the first Isabella grape of Washington; the next was W. W. Seaton's. The plant flourished there exceeding well, and grew forty feet the first year.

Here it was agreed that I should collect materials and publish a pamphlet to promote the election of John C. Calhoun to the presidency, and which was publshed by me under the title of "Principles, not Men." Returned to New York after having arranged to correspond with Samuel L. Southard, New Jersey, George M. Dallas, Pennsylvania, Judge Gibson, John Conrad and William Fitzhugh of Virginia, Benjamin Howard of Baltimore, John Devereux, William Gaston and William R. Swift of North Carolina, George McDuffie of South Carolina, and James Hamilton, Colonel Hayne, William R. King and Governor Pickings of Alabama, Henry Le Trevor of Louisiana, John H. Eaton of Tennessee, G. M. Bibb Kent and Governor Edwards of Missouri, R. B. Taney and General Winder of Maryland.

Made an excursion to West Point with General Scott and lady, W. W. Seaton and lady, Thomas Marsh and lady, Mary Roberdeau and my own family.

September 16th, my son Jonathan Williams Swift was appointed a midshipman in the navy.

To Morristown to meet Colonel Totten, General Bernard and James Renwick, to consult on the interest the United States may have in the construction of the Morris Canal with inclined planes, to overcome the rise and fall of nine hundred feet. Thence proceeded to examine the copper mines at Somerville, as a source of supply to the United States mint; thence returned to the route of the canal at Pompton and Passaic Falls. At the old hotel of General Goodwin found an album containing a record, and some lines on the scene by General (then lieutenant) Macomb and family, with Walker Armistead and J. G. Swift, 13th August, 1803.

November 2d. Died at Wilmington, North Carolina, my friend Archibald Fotheringham McNeill, late Lieutenant-Colonel United States Dragoons, and father-in-law of Julius H. Walker. He died in the home where I was married, at "The Barn."

In the month of December I made an inspection of the works on the Morris Canal, with my brother commissioner, John Scott, and our engineer, Captain Beach; the company having decided to increase the number of working hands to unite the Hudson and Delaware.

Five hundred and eight thousand dollars appropriated for fortifications in the year 1823.

1824. February 24th, my son J. W. Swift sailed in the United States frigate Cyane for the Mediterranean, with Captain John Orde Creighton.

In March I purchased from Daniel Griswold one-half the stock of the Williamsburgh ferry, and also the one-half of the Jackson Street ferry, Brooklyn; and sold out the latter to J. B. Clark at a good profit—some one thousand two hundred dollars.

Went to Albany with Samuel L. Gouverneur and Thomas L. Smith to obtain a charter for the Sun Fire Insurance Company, and succeeded. In this month also, of April, the legislature appointed Edmund Smith, Thomas Hyatt and myself, commissioners to subscribe for the Richmond Turnpike stock; the object being to aid Governor Tompkins to settle his confused accounts. My knowledge of his heedless mode of business had been, that he had in the late war advanced money to me for the United States to prosecute the public works, and to sustain the Military Academy. Of the integrity of Governor Tompkins I had not a shadow of doubt.

In this month Mr. Jefferson wrote me of his wish to complete the cupola of the University of Virginia, and requested me to loan him my *De Lorme* on such architecture, and I sent the work to him by Colonel B. Peyton; and it was duly returned to my library.

On 3d June died my dear mother, in fine health. With my father she was on a visit to me. She had gone to the city to her sister Elizabeth Howland and niece Nancy (the wife of Captain Bennet), and was seized with laryngitis, which Dr. Mott and Dr. Bull pronounced fatal, though an essay was made by an incision into the throat below the glottis to permit breathing. My father and brother William were present with the Rev. Dr. Feltus. She became easy and died calmly, in full trust in the mercy of her Saviour.

My father's heartfelt prayer at the foot of my mother's bed was for mercy, and her safety in this world, or acceptance in a better, and was a most impressive scene. They had lived in undisturbed harmony and love together forty-one years.

The funeral was from my house, and the interment in the cemetery of St. Ann's at Brooklyn. Dr. William Swift, United States navy (our cousin,) Dr. Prime (another cousin,) Colonel Trumbull, General Gaines, Joshua Sands, F. C. Tucker, Thomas March, Samuel L. Gouverneur, Daniel Okey, my father and brother, and myself. Rev. Dr. Onderdonk officiating.

In this month, at the earnest request of his brother James, I took my son Alexander to West Point, where, by permission of the Secretary of War, and by the kind attention of Colonel Thayer, Alexander was to receive tuition from Mr. Davies and Mr. Ross, my two friends. It was the period of the examination, to which, General Jarvis, the patroon Van Renssellaer, General W. H. Sumner and the Romish Priest Levens, (a very able man), and myself, constituted the board of visitors.

In honor of "independence" this July, the notorious William Cobbet gave a dinner to Governor Tompkins at Tammany Hall. Mr. Cobbet's toast was disrespectful of his sovereign. I declined drinking the toast; Mr. Cobbet asked my reason. I told him not that I had any especial respect for his sovereign, but that I did not approve a subject or citizen's offering a mark of disrespect to the chief magistrate of his native land in so public a form. The appeal was made to the governor, who said I had uttered his own sentiment. The party became uncomfortable and soon separated. I never met Mr. Cobbet afterwards.

In this summer much effort was made to promote the cause of the oppressed modern Greeks. The remembrance of the glory of the ancients caused many meetings. I was elected to preside at a meeting in their favor on Long Island, and liberal gifts were bestowed, and Mr. Clay and Mr. Webster made stirring speeches. The signal of their cause was erected on the Heights, in my garden, by William Wood, Esq., in the name of the ladies of Brooklyn, and several orations were pronounced to aid in gathering funds to send a frigate to the aid of Greece as against the Turk. A frigate was built by Mr. Eckford called the " Hellenese," etc.

As a member of a committee of the American Bible Society, of which I had been a manager from its institution in 1816, the functions of the secretary were presented as deserving remuneration. The person was the Rev. Dr. Woodhull, and until further consideration I urged that one hundred dollars be presented to the doctor for past services, and the same was adopted.

In August the Marquis La Fayette arrived in the " Cadmus," Captain Frank Allen. At the reception he mistook me for his comrade, Colonel Fish, who had not yet arrived. On explaining he said: " The opportunity is happy for me to regret my not seeing your son at the Grange with his letter." I had given Willy a letter to the Marquis on his going out in the " Cyane" with our minister, Mr. Brown. He then asked me to accompany him to call on Mrs. Lewis, " Nelly Custis" when he saw her last at Mount Vernon with General Washington. The meeting was quite a scene. The interview between La Fayette and Van Buskirk was touching. La Fayette had met the father in the trenches of Yorktown, and given him a sword for his gallantry. This son was a stout Jersey farmer. He held the sword in his hand, and with tears in his eyes said: " My father is dead ; he left me this sword, and I am come to see you, and to show it to you, and to tell you that we all love you!" There was not a dry eye in the room.

The next day we had an excursion to the fort of his name at the

Narrows. The work had been built while I was chief engineer, and I had requested the President to name it for La Fayette. While walking the gallery he said: "Do you think the cannon at Monmouth were heard in the Narrows?" looking over to the Monmouth shore. "O, it was a very hot day." I asked him of the conduct of Lee on that day. He said: "General Lee was a brave man, but of bad management on that day." Early in September La Fayette went to West Point, and invited me to accompany him. I was glad to do so, and took with me my son Thomas. On the way up the Hudson he told me Bernard had said to him I had treated him and his family with much kindness, though he knew I was not satisfied with his connection with the corps of engineers. La Fayette mentioned his own and Mr. Gallatin's agency in selecting Bernard, and said: "Your country did not object to my services." My reply was: "O no, general, we are all grateful for your devotion to our cause, but the case is very different, and our necessities also." I craved his pardon for not agreeing with him on this matter. He took my hand in a gracious manner, and hoped I would again enter the army. The meeting at West Point was a burst of boyish and natural feeling. It entirely overcame La Fayette; he wept, but ate a hearty dinner, and drank Madeira by the tumbler, and a good piece of beef, saying: "If I had not had a good stomach the Austrian jail would have killed me;" and so we drank to the health of Huger and Bollman.

On my return to Brooklyn I met my brother-in-law, Julius Walker, and his very nice wife, Mary Ann Smith of Beaufort, South Carolina, a very excellent lady. Julius was ill, and they returned to Carolina early in September on horseback, through upper Virginia and North Carolina, into Pendleton in South Carolina.

In this fall, by correspondence with the members of the United States Military Philosophical Society, the funds of that society were given, by my advice, to the New York Lyceum of Natural History; a large majority consenting, though a few (Colonel Thayer among the number,) thought a better use could have been made of the fund — about two thousand dollars.

In the month of October Mr. Whistler, who had, by my recommendation to General Porter, been attached as draughtsman to the north-west boundary commission, wrote me of the troubles of determining the line, and Major Joseph Delafield consulted me with the maps, and I pointed to what he and myself deemed the true point in the Lake of the Woods.

In November the Schuylkill Coal Company alloted me an interest at par in that company, in some consideration of my services in 1820 in bringing that coal into notice. I sold the stock, and after paying the company the par value had some one thousand four hundred dollars; which is all the benefit I had from an enterprise which, if Charles Snowden had been true to his bargain, had made my family opulent.

This fall Joshua Sands was elected to Congress. Remembrance of my services in King's County during the war, and on Staten Island, and through my friend Mr. Pierson, the iron-master of Rockland, Mr. Sands, an old Federalist, received the major vote at my poll in that democratic district. Mr. Sands told President Adams that but for my exertions he could not have been elected. This was a result of actual personal exertion, with a few influential friends in each district.

At the county court in Flatbush in October, commenced by the grand jury, the first important movement in the improvement of Brooklyn streets. As foreman of the jury I was requested to furnish surveys, which resulted in the opening of Firman Street, the initial act of street opening that led the way to considerable improvement in that place, and market, etc.

In November my father and his old friend and school-mate, General Mattoon, once Adjutant-General of Massachusetts. His object was to get his son Dwight Foster sent to West Point. I made an earnest appeal to that effect to the Secretary of War. From an early day I had advocated sending the sons of the most talented men in the country to that institution, as a better plan than selection by congressional districts, that was beginning to have sway at Washington.

In the same month there was submitted to Governor De Witt Clinton the plan of the Morris Canal. That gentleman consented to go before the New Jersey legislature to give that body his views of the mutual benefit thereof to both States, and by his invitation, and at the expense of the company, I accompanied Mr. Clinton with my plans, etc. Mr. Clinton urged the benefit of extending banking privileges to the canal, and his views were adopted by the legislature.

Seven hundred and six thousand dollars for United States fortifications appropriated in 1824.

1825. In April, as an agent of the Water Company of the city of New York, (of which, by the charter of March I was a commissioner,) an exploration of the Broux was made, and also of the Croton Rivers for a supply of water. The result in reference to the Broux sustained the gauges made by me in 1819, and of the Croton there remained not a doubt of its abundance; but the corporation declined acting upon those data.

In the summer I placed my son Julius at the school of Mr. Clark at Cow Neck, on Long Island, the school in Brooklyn not suiting my views in consequence of improper associates, and the peculiar disposition to avoid study which Julius evinced, though a boy of fine temper and most generous disposition.

Took my family, with Major Tucker, to West Point, where, with General Brown and Colonel Thayer an examination of the Academy was made, and found to have progressed very usefully under the colonel's care. The general and myself returned to New York with our families and Major Tucker's, and were launched in the Ohio, seventy-four, at the navy yard. This fine ship had been drafted and constructed by our friend Henry Eckford.

In September my wife accompanied me over the route of the Morris Canal to Hopatcong Lake; and witnessed the forging of iron from the loup under the hammer, conducted by John Scott and Fay, men of six feet, and of great strength and dexterity, wielding the tongs and loup with graceful ease.

At this place, by appointment, I met the other commissioner, Colonel Scott, and our engineer, Captain Beach, and arranged with them the location of an inclined plane and acqueduct at Dover, near the Tamarack Swamp, and returned to Brooklyn by Passaic Falls.

Had a meeting of the Morris Canal Company, in which I held a large interest, and became a director of the Fulton Bank.

This fall Mr. Eckford purchased, through the negotiation of Mr. Rathbone, the *National Advocate*, and engaged me to superintend the conducting of the same, and for which I employed Mr. Snowden and Mr. Casey. It was Mr. Eckford's purpose to advocate the election of John Quincy Adams to the presidency. Mr. Eckford recommended me for vice-president of the Life and Fire Insurance Company, and thus I became interested in the stocks, and induced my father and my brother William to invest funds in the Life and Fire. My brother William was married this fall to Miss Mary Stuart, the daughter of the British consul at New London.

I purchased the property on the Seventh Avenue between Thirty-first and Thirty-third Streets, (about one hundred lots,) for seven thousand and odd dollars; borrowed the amount from the Life and Fire Insurance Company, and mortgaged the property to that company as security, and commenced a house and garden thereon.

This winter my sons James and Williams went to the city of Washington, the first to procure from President Adams a restoration to West Point, from whence he had been dismissed for absence for six hours without leave, and for declining to answer a query that would have implicated his class-mate. Mr. O. B. Ogden and Mr. Daniel Webster had presented the case, with their opinion of its severity of punishment, and Mr. Adams called on Mr. Barbour, the Secretary of War, to know why this youth should not be restored. Mr. Barbour said that the son of one who had been at the head of the Academy was a proper example for discipline. In my opinion the stronger cause was that the father was the political friend of Mr. Calhoun. Mr. Adams acquiesced in Mr. Barbour's view, but directed that James should be employed in the civil engineer department, under William Howard, Esq., of Baltimore. My son William was at Washington to be examined for his naval position.

In the spring of this year I had been reëlected to the common council of Brooklyn, and had presented several plans for the improvement of the village.

My friends Isaac Pierson, S. L. Gouverneur, and Mr. N. Prime called on me to caution me, in the month of May, in relation to the extent of Mr.

Eckford's ship building liabilities, and that too much use was made of bonds of the Life and Fire Insurance Company in purchases for the Brazilian frigates building by Mr. Eckford. Without using names I mentioned these rumors to Mr. Eckford. He stated to me that all such rumors were groundless, and I had an implicit faith in him and his ability. In July a note from Mr. Eckford astonished me with an announcement that the Life and Fire Insurance Company could not meet the demands for cash on the bonds becoming due. The next day I was served with a notice from the district attorney, Hugh Maxwell, Esq., that the whole company of the Life and Fire Insurance were indicted for a conspiracy to defraud the State. The trials progressed; the great question was whether a company issuing bonds, failing to redeem on demand, could be deemed guilty of a conspiracy or fraud. The court decided that my trial should be separated from that of others, the testimony was brief, and I made all the defence that was made in my case by simply addressing the court and jury in these words: "I know myself not to have been guilty of any fraud, or of any design to defraud, and if this jury can find me guilty on the evidence I shall silently submit as a punishment for my credulity." The jury in a few minutes returned with a verdict of "not guilty — but *persecuted*." The last the judge refused. When the verdict of "not guilty" was alone rendered a cry of approbation rang through a crowded audience, and Peter A. Jay, of counsel adverse to me, came up to me with tears in his eyes, saying: "General, this is a righteous verdict, and I am thankful for your acquittal." But the blows of accusation and trial were of course mortifying, and injurious to my influence as a man of business; a severe comment on a poor gentleman's essay to become rich in Wall Street. The validity of these indictments came before the supreme court, and the whole proceeding, the attorney, Maxwell, pronounced illegal. But beyond all doubt the failure of the Life and Fire had been occasioned by the losses in the ship-building business of Mr. Eckford, and in his speculations in real estate. My confidence in Mr. Eckford was high; I had frequently large sums of money at command of his in bank, but I never borrowed a dollar from him. The only charge found on his books was the purchase money of the *National Advocate*, which had passed through my hands. On my trial it was proven that I was not indebted to the Life and Fire Company. I had placed in Mr. Eckford's hands my city property, in trust to secure the purchase money of that property. Pending these trials President Adams had assured Joshua Sands, Esq., and George Sullivan, Esq., that if my trial acquitted me he should rënominate me for the office in the customs held by me; but Mr. Clay's friends wanted place, and Mr. Stagg was nominated on the expiration of my second four years. Probably the President's interest in me had been somewhat blighted by an accidental omission of mine while presiding at the "Ayacucho dinner" at the City Hotel. The toast of President Adams had been misplaced without my privity. I, however, do not intend to say that he purposed me any injustice. He is a man of strong antipathies, and of no strong friendship, and, indeed, I never pretended to enjoy his favor.

In the summer of the current year the Secretary of War had addressed to several officers in and out of the army—General Cadwallader and General Sumner among the latter, and myself also. My views were given on the subject of the secretary's address—the militia, of its classification— and that no higher militia grade should be conferred than that of chief of battalion, and that commissions should be conferred only upon examination of the candidate. My letters on these subjects, and others, may be seen in the *Congressional Reports* of '26 and '27.

$735,000 appropriated for fortifications.

53,000 wall Boston Harbor.

100,000 for arsenals.

------

$888,000 for 1825.

Seven hundred and nineteen thousand dollars for fortifications in 1826.

In this year was made the first appropriation for constructing and improving rivers and harbors.     .

1827. The commencement of this year found me with a large family and very limited means to support them. I had, by a loan from my brother-in-law, Whistler, the fee he had received for services on the boundary commission; invested the amount in the purchase of a small estate in Flatbush, and commenced cultivation. But it was not adequate to our support, and I turned it over to Mr. Whistler, and he sold it for the full amount of the loan, to wit: one thousand five hundred dollars.

I thought of civil engineering in the West. The estate of Mrs. Swift's father was in the hands of her brother James, and by him assumed as a debt of over five thousand dollars; said brother James held his father's lands in West Tennessee. I concluded to make a home for my family upon Louisa's portion of these lands. In the midst of my purpose our children were attacked by measles, and one, a daughter Harriet, had died, and was interred in the grave of my mother. Going so far was by some friends deemed doubtful — most movements are so — but I could not find success in a city whose archives recorded me "its benefactor" in the late war. My misfortunes had produced the usual effect, loss of prosperity, loss of influence. I had, however, many instances of confidence among my army associates, especially Colonel Thayer, Captain J. L. Smith, General Scott, etc.; among the merchants of the city, Fanning Cobham Tucker and Daniel Okey, and a touching one from the negroes, who, during my trial prayed regularly for my "safe deliverance from the great uncertainties of the law."

Immediate commencement of my journey to Tennessee was delayed by a summons to Washington before a committee of Congress, on a revival of the assault upon John C. Calhoun, now vice-president, and who had vacated the chair pending the investigation of the Rip Rap contract, while Mr. Calhoun was Secretary of War and myself chief engineer. The details of this political struggle, and its failure, are in the documents of Congress, and on my files.

In February I returned to Brooklyn, and sent my baggage, library, and farming tools to my friend, Gilbert Russell of New Orleans, to be shipped to Memphis. Early in March my wife, Thomas, Sally, Julius, McRee, Josephine and Charlotte, and boy Bill proceeded to Barnum's in Baltimore, and thence by private carriage over the Allegheny mountains to Wheeling, and down the Ohio (passing our son James in an ascending boat,) to Cincinnati, and thence down the river to the Mississippi, to Memphis, and purchased a ton of bacon and six barrels of flour, and with baggage in wagons to Haywood County in Tennessee; meeting with the Misses Wright at Narhota, and at Boliver in the Big Hatchie, thence to the hospitable log cabin of Mrs. Swift's nephew, Henry Walker, who allowed me the use of a portion of his people until his father settled accounts with his aunt Louisa. I placed four hands to felling a tulip tree seven feet in diameter, and sixty-six feet to the forks, yielding three cuts of twenty feet each. That gave boards for a large log cabin of one room that served for bedrooms, library and dining room. But as to the land, I found that I could get no secure title, nevertheless planted corn, potatoes and cotton, with plenty of stock in the woods feeding on cane grass and the sweet pea vine.

The course of the season developed ill health for my children, though Mrs. Swift and myself were well; and she, with good courage and affection, encountered our privations, never dreamed of in earlier days.

My son James, then civil engineer of the United States on the Hiwassee, came to us leading a fine Pacolet colt for my riding.

I opened a correspondence with General Jackson, at the "Hermitage," on the improvements of the rivers of the State, and explored the country on horseback to Alabama. On my return the ill health of my children determined me to retrace my steps, and seek civil engineering on the Atlantic.

In November, after the crops were in, I sold my movables, and with my family reembarked at Randolph, and by New Orleans (where I met my friend Russell, who furnished us with the after cabin of the packet "Frances," Captain Ryder,) we returned to New York in thirty days from New Orleans, arriving the last of the year. Here we met the intelligence of the death of the venerable mother of my wife, and of my brother-in-law, Julius H. Walker, and of my own sister Mary, the beautiful wife of Lieutenant George W. Whistler. Her remains were placed by me alongside those of my mother in Brooklyn.

In my absence had also died the patriot Rufus King, in 1827. I sought his and Mr. Wolcott's advice in reference to my letter to the Secretary of

War adversely to the interpolation of General Bernard into the corps of engineers. That letter received the hearty approbation of both Mr. King and Mr. Wolcott, at Mr. King's, in Jamaica, Long Island.

Four hundred and twenty-five thousand dollars appropriated for fortifications in 1827.

1828. After a few days' rest from a sea voyage with our friends Tucker and March at Brooklyn, in January, my family was placed at board with Captain Chapman, near my father's, in New London; my sons Tom and Jule at the select school, Sally with Miss Allen, myself to New York, the guest of my friend S. L. Gouverneur, and opened a correspondence on the subject of civil engineering with various parts of the Union. I returned to New London in March, and caused grave-stones to be inscribed to the memory of my father and mother-in-law, James and M. M. Walker, and sent them to our friend Dr. A. J. De Rosset, Wilmington, North Carolina, who saw them placed at their respective graves in the cemetery of St. James.

Through my brother-in-law Whistler, and my protegé, W. G. McNeill, I was introduced to George Winchester, the president of the Baltimore and Susquehanna Railroad Company, and was employed as chief engineer of that company, and soon located the route of the road to the Pennsylvania line, consulting with that eminent manager, F. Thomas, and S. H. Long, also with Whistler and McNeill (all of the United States army), who were engineers of the Baltimore and Ohio railroad. Mr. Long I had met in Germantown, Pennsylvania, at Major Roberdeau's, and engaged him as my extra aid in the year 1814, and from his merit placed him as instructor of mathematics in the Military Academy at West Point — a gentleman of large mechanical ingenuity. In the month of July, at the instance of the Baltimore and Susquehanna Company, I examined the only railroad then existing in the United States, at Quincy, Mass., *via* New London, taking Mrs. Swift with me to see our good aunt Lucretia, of Boston. We proceeded thence to the railroad and measured all its parts minutely, thence we called on my cousin Fanny Swift, on Milton Hill, and visited the graves of our ancestors in the old Milton cemetery.

On my return to Baltimore I rented the house of Bishop Eccleston in St. Paul's Lane, and moved my family thither in October, and they were kindly cared for by my friend Robert Barry in my railroad absences; my son Thomas teaching his younger brothers and sisters at home. He had been well instructed by his friend and uncle, G. W. Whistler.

Seven hundred and seventeen thousand five hundred dollars appropriated for fortifications in 1828.

1829. On 15th January died my friend Colonel Isaac Roberdeau, U. S. T. E.

In the winter of this year Mr. Winchester and myself before the legislature of Pennsylvania, to extend the charter of the Baltimore and Susquehanna to the river; but the cloudy minds of the legislature deemed a road of much greater length, to Philadelphia, more patriotic as State policy — one of the absurdities of the influence of artificial boundary lines.

In March with my son Thomas to see President Jackson inaugurated, and to offer my services as a civil engineer through my friend Charles Gratiot, and General Eaton, the Secretary of War. The general said " President Jackson had confidence in my ability," and so gave me charge of the construction of harbors on Lake Ontario. Mr. Monroe had asked General Jackson to rëappoint me to the surveyorship of New York, but that place was claimed for party, in which I had no claim. While in Washington I had prepared an essay on supplying the city of New York with water from the Broux and Croton Rivers, and sent the same to the corporation through George Sullivan, Esq., and referred them to my survey of the Broux and Rye Ponds made in 1819.

In April I returned to the Baltimore and Susquehanna railroad, and from thence with my friend John L. Smith, United States engineer, to Philadelphia, and gave Thomas Sully sittings for a portrait for the corps of engineers at their request — see files; thence to West Point, and met my friend Major Thayer and my son Alexander J. Swift, a cadet. So on to Genessee River, and we examined its entrance into Lake Ontario. Major Smith proceeded to Ohio to select a site for an armory, taking my brother-in-law Whistler as his assistant, much depressed by the loss of his wife my beautiful sister, Mary.

In May I surveyed Big Sodus Bay also, and reported the requisite works for both harbors to the engineer department, and fixed my residence at Geneva by the advice of my friend Major Rees of that place. Returned to Baltimore and closed my relations to and with the Baltimore and Susquehanna railroad, and removed my family to Geneva, arriving on 6th June, and taking lodgingsi n Mr. Hemminway's hotel, and then a house on the square, belonging to Colonel Bogert, commencing with iron spoons, for we had been robbed of all our plate, and many gold and silver remembrances. My father came to visit us. My daughter Sally commenced school with Miss Jones, José with Miss Stone, and Jule and McRee with Mr. Davis. Major Rees had purchased the Clark farm of one hundred and forty acres for me of R. C. Nicholas, who made some difficulty about the title, but took the farm himself. Explored the country about Genessee River and Big Sodus Bay for timber and stone for the harbors, and by the last of June had commenced the work at Genessee River (Mr. Wilder my assistant there), and on 4th of July commenced the piers at Big Sodus Bay (C. W. Rees my assistant there), and with John Greig, Esq., Alexander Duncan and Captain Wickham we celebrated our "independence," assisted by Edwards and Dr. Lummis.

In August my sons James and Alexander were with us at Geneva, and my brother William and his wife and son Charles, a year old. My son Thomas suddenly ill; Dr. Cutbush deems the danger to be unequal action of the heart and circulation. He died 2d September, the third day after the birth of a son whom, for him, we named Thomas.

In October my son Williams returned from a three years' cruise in the Pacific, in the "Brandywine," Commodore Jacob Jones. Willy reached home with me in November. I had been summoned to the city in a case between S. L. Gouverneur and the Fulton Bank.

The corporation of Petersburgh, Virginia, invited me to be their engineer on a railroad there, but my other prospects prevented acceptance; being in that month of November in treaty with Martin Hoffman of New Orleans to become the engineer of the Ponchartrain railroad. He had been referred to me by Whistler and McNeill. On the suspension of the Lake works the Secretary of War consented to my sojourn in New Orleans provided I became responsible for the safe-keeping of the United States property at Genessee and Sodus.

On the last of November my son James, having previously taken leave of us, proceeded with Dr. Howard to the Wisconsin River. I left Geneva *via* Niagara Falls, Erie, Ohio and Mississippi Rivers to New Orleans, arriving 20th December, and soon explored a route through a red cypress swamp, (sinking to my saddle girths, but had sand at bottom,) and gave the company a design for their road. While they were cogitating it, and for means to execute, I was invited to the legislature of Louisiana to consult on a plan to improve a system of leveeing the great river to avoid the evil of elevating its bed, as had been long done on the Po, in Italy. Gave them my ideas — see the document in my files. Returned to New Orleans, and made an agreement with the railroad company to return to New Orleans in the following November with mechanics to construct the road. This occupied me the months of January and February.

Seven hundred and sixty-five thousand dollars appropriated for fortifications in 1829.

1830. I had much social intercourse in New Orleans, and very pleasant dinner parties at George Eustis', Mr. Linton's, Mr. Henderson's, Isaac Preston's, etc., where Hon. H. Clay, the patroon of New York, and some foreigners (one who interested me at first, a lineal descendant of Montezuma, a Spanish count, but was disappointed on close view,) were present. The domestic life in New Orleans is charming among the ladies, but the young men are sadly degenerate.

Leaving the railroad under the care of Lieutenant G. W. Long, "on leave" from the army, I left New Orleans, taking my passage in the month of February in the Helen McGregor. Accident detained me till the next boat and we found the McGregor a wreck at Memphis, and her burnt passengers in the hospital there — twenty killed and forty wounded. By Wheeling I arrived at Baltimore on 20th March, at Barnum's, and on entering the reading-room found the death of my first-born (James) recorded. He had been married to Maria Jephson, the charming granddaughter of my friend Captain Farquhar, not three months; had recently returned from civil engineer duty with Dr. William Howard on the river Wisconsin; had fallen through the ice, but kept at his duty, from which a cold settled on his lungs.

His brother Willy and his aunt Mary Swift did all they could, and my brother William also, who was there on duty in the general post office.

I returned home to the distressed mother at Geneva with my son Willy, from his examination as midshipman, early in April. We changed the name of my son, substituting James for Delano.

During my absence the War Department had been furnished with accusations that more material had been paid for at Genessee River than had been furnished. The department ordered Major Maurice to examine into this accusation. He reported to the department that he found no truth whatever in the accusation. The department ordered me to proceed with the works; and he also examined the same subject at Sodus Bay, and reported the same result. In June my father came to see us from New London, his military station as surgeon, and in July Alexander came with his widowed sister, Maria Jephson Swift. In August I surveyed Oak Orchard Creek for a harbor at its entrance into Lake Ontario. At the ensuing session of Congress the committee reported a bill in favor of my plan, and Congress appropriated the means.

In this month I employed George Barclay and William Sentell, and carpenters and hewers to go with me in November to construct the Pontchartrain railroad.

I purchased this month the residence of Christopher Campbell and a seven acre lot south of the village, for two thousand one hundred dollars, and moved into the house on 10th September, after recovering from a bilious fever taken at Oak Orchard, and was probably, under Providence, saved from death by the skill of Dr. Cutbush.

The United States funds being exhausted on the Lake works, I closed them for the season 20th September, and then (leaving Alexander with his mother) Willy and I went to West Point and Cold Spring, and to New York, where, with my workmen, we embarked for New Orleans, and by the

"Hole in the Wall" and Tortugas, arrived at New Orleans, on 1st November. Found the city gloomy from yellow fever.

This fall, Alexander commenced his engineering at Oak Island, in Cape Fear, where I had commenced mine twenty-six years previously. Alexander had commenced his first duty, after graduating at West Point, at Newport, R. I., under Colonel Totten, where I had commenced my first duty thirty years previously.

Established my quarters at the Darcoutel Convent and also those of my workmen, and commenced the construction of the Pontchartrain Railroad. Willy returned home in December, my daughter Sally being with Mrs. Chew in Brooklyn, to attend Mr. Van Doren's Seminary in that place. In the progress of the Ponchartrain Railroad I found that dead shells formed a good foundation and hard track. From Tangepaho we transported by steam some millions of bushels across the lake for sill foundation and horse track. This success gave to New Orleans a fine, hard cover to their streets, at my suggestion.

In the excavation of the vast shell mound of Tangepaho we met the skeleton of a human being of large dimensions, and by comparative anatomy our surgeon and myself measured the bones; they must have been of a being at least nine feet high. I boxed them for the Natural Historical Society of New York. Red cypress from the swamp was used for cross-sills and stringers. Upon the latter was laid the first T rail used in the United States.

Eight hundred and forty-one thousand dollars for fortifications for the year 1830.

1831. Early in March, Hon. Henry and Mrs. Clay, of Ashland, breakfasted with me at Darcoutel. To amuse Mrs. Clay I bloomed the buds of the magnolia G. F. by placing the stems in claret bottles of hot water on the breakfast table — a process of from twenty to thirty minutes.

We gave our guests their first ride on a railroad, using a baggage car, and by aid of six men, whom I had drilled for the purpose, with iron-pointed poles, attained a speed of ten miles the hour for a couple of miles.

In April we opened the road from the Lake to the Mississippi, with the governor of the State and General Wade Hampton and other magnates for guests, who gave due commendation to President Martin Hoffman for the original design, and to my master workmen, George Barclay and William Sentell, for the excellent workmanship. The last of April I went to Mobile to escort our niece, Julia Osborne, to visit Mrs. Capt. Spatts in New Orleans — Julia's school-mate at Mrs. Clitherall's, in Smithville, North Carolina.

In the month of May, designed a harbor for the lake end of the railroad, and after visiting the battle-ground of Gen. Jackson, Julia and myself ascended the Mississippi in the Convoy, Capt. Rudee, passing the cut-off of Red River Island, that had been a peninsula when I was there in December, 1829. Delayed by breaking a shaft in straining through this ·cut, arriving at Laneville 28th May; lost four days; by Wheeling, Wellsburgh, Ashtabula, on Lake Erie, to Buffalo, and arriving at home in Geneva on 8th June, finding all well, thanks to God. In the past spring, my son Willy had re-commenced for me the United States harbors at Genesee and Sodus, and had also added to my house five rooms.

Find my United States affairs under good way at the lakes, and, with Major Cook, took a horse-back view of Dr. William Campbell's route of a canal from Cayuga Lake to Sodus Bay by the Montezuma Marshes; concluded it would be better to commence that canal at Clyde, and cut through the Sandy Ridge to the north to the Bay.

Seven hundred and sixteen thousand dollars for fortifications for the year 1831.

In the month of July (20th) Gen. Simon Bernard wrote me a farewell letter on his retiring from the service of the United States, and returning to that of France with much knowledge of every means of defence possessed by my country. He acknowledged my uniform courtesy to him personally, to which I replied as became my position, as may be seen in my files. The correspondence between the Secretary of War and myself on the policy of interpolating into· our engineer service any foreigner; and see also the records of the engineer department at Washington, 1816, '17, '18.

The last of July my son Willy left, ordered to the Mediterranean; my friend Thomas J. Chew and I to the head of Seneca Lake, he from his visit returning home to Brooklyn.

In August, at the commencement of Geneva College, the faculty and board of trustees conferred on me the professorate of "Engineering and Statistics,"—an empty honor, as also was the membership of the Paris Society of Statistics, for which courtesy I returned my thanks to President Moreau, of Paris, through General H. A. S. Dearborn, of Boston. See the document on file.

In September, by request of John Greig, Esq., I explored a new route for a canal from Clyde to Sodus Bay, with General Adams, Major Cook and C. W. Rees as surveyors. Proceeded to New York with my documents and printed my report; sent copies to many; October.

On 23d October, at New York, General Wm. North and myself and many others, attended the funeral of our friend Capt. James Farquhar, at the age of eighty-nine.

In November, G. W. Whistler, W. G. McNeill, Claude Crozet and myself examining the Marsh near Berg's Ridge, N. J., and the Trap Ridge at Hoboken for a tunnel.

On my return to Geneva, at a public meeting of the citizens in November, appointed several citizens, including myself, to lay before the State legislature a plan for a railroad from Ithaca to Geneva. I explored a route and reported to the Secretary of State my opinion in favor of the plan, but it remained unacted upon.

December, I visited Major Van Deventer, at Lindwood; and at Batavia I purchased of David E. Evans, Esq., a farm adjoining Lindwood of two hundred and thirty acres, for two thousand five hundred dollars. Before returning home, G. W. Whistler and Anna McNeill were married at her brother William's, in Bond Street, on 3d November.

For the want of funds, the works of the United States on the lake harbors had gone into some ruin from storms,—a miserable, short-sighted policy, so to commence and so to neglect such works.

1832. In the month of February I visited Colonel W. Fitzhugh, at Hampton, and read the correspondence between General Washington and the

Colonel's father, Colonel William Fitzhugh, of Rowsley Hall, Maryland, in 1777, '78, '79, '80 and '81, on several subjects, and the Revolution. My daughter-in-law, that was to be, consented to copy for me all these letters, which was done, and they are among my papers, and possess interest in reference to our financial policy, etc., in those days.

The last of this month, Dr. Lummis and myself went to New York, through immense drifts of snow, through the Beech Woods route to Jersey, to explain to capitalists the objects of the Sodus Canal from Cayuga to Lake Ontario, using the counting-room of my friend Peter Burtsell, corner Wall and Broad Streets, to exhibit the plans, etc. In the following month of March, to wit.: 8th, Lieut. J. R. Sands, United States Navy, and myself examined the route for a canal to unite the Wallabout and Gowanus Cove, New York Harbor. This idea had originated with his father, Joshua Sands, Esq. I commended the plan to the board of trustees of Brooklyn. In March, resumed correspondence with the North Carolina Railroad Co., of Raleigh and Beaufort, through General Montfort Stokes, to become their engineer.

From the conflict of parties in Congress on internal improvements and its uncertain results, I visited my friend Col. Totten, at Newport, to consult as to my prospects. Returning, visited my father in New London, and met Lyman Law and examined the Groton monument that I had designed, but it was improved by my nephew, Julius W. Adams. With Mr. Law, visited the grave of Uncas, the Mohican Chief. An aged squaw said to us: "Take care of the good land you took from my fathers; it is a good land."

On my return to New York in April, the Harlem Railroad Co. invited me to accompany their board and to examine the rock cuttings on the route of the Harlem Railroad, *i. e.*, 4th Avenue, which I did, and gave the board my thoughts thereon, as to expense, etc.

I then went to Washington to consult the Secretary of War on the subject of going to North Carolina pending the action of Congress on harbors, etc. He advised to wait awhile, and this suspended my accepting Mr. Mhoon's invitation from North Carolina.

In May, on my way home, at Philadelphia, met my friends, the widow and daughters of Colonel Roberdeau, pleasantly settled in their own house, the result of my efforts, with those of Judge Chase, of Washington, to reclaim from one Pierce, who had married Frances Blair, the sister of Mrs. Roberdeau, the life-rent leases inherited from their grandfather, Dr. Shippen, in that city.

On arriving in New York, I accepted the chief-engineership of the Harlem Railroad at four thousand four hundred dollars per annum, and in a few days had the whole line of work under contract and the rock blasting successfully going on.

In the middle of June, G. W. Whistler and myself went to Little Falls, of the Mohawk, and devised a plan for the town and manufactories of that place for the " Little Falls Co."

In July the cholera appeared, and in a few days nearly depopulated the city, *i. e.*, drove the people to the country. The disease soon spread among the workmen on the Harlem Railroad, and the work was accordingly suspended.

Congress, in this July, appropriated for the lake harbors too late for the commencement of any important work. I, however, got them under way, and in August, at Rochester, was seized by cholera and sunk to a collapse. My cousin, James Watts, hastened to Geneva and brought my dear wife to my bed-side. My escape, as the physicians said, was the consequence of deep blood-letting that reduced me to an extreme debility.

In September I was able to travel to New York to recommence the Harlem road; found the rooms beset with pretenders to engineering among its members. Informed the board that I could not submit to such superficial nonsense and delay without compromiting the trust they had reposed in me, and resigned my office, and returned to the lake harbors, and by the end of October the chill of the season closed all the lake works.

In December, to New York in consultation with Mr. Radcliffe to proceed to the Gulf of Mexico and explore a canal route by the Atrato to the Pacific; the plan suspended. Before leaving home, Julia Osborne and A. M. Frink were married at my house.

This month of December, my son Willy arrived at Portsmouth, N. H., from a cruise in the Mediterranean, and my son Alexander arrived from Rhode Island. They came with my daughter Sally, who had been on a visit to Mrs. Wm. Kimble in St. John's Square; leaving me in the city, they went to Geneva over the "Beech Woods" route. In this month an association of twelve hundred young men in the city appointed me their chief to offer service to General Jackson, to march in case of any breach of the Constitution, to sustain the laws under his command — having allusion to Southern nullification, — for which I received the thanks of the President.

Six hundred and fifty-four thousand dollars for fortifications in 1832.

1833. In consequence of the illness of the wife of my friend, F. C. Tucker, I had delayed my return home. On this New Year's Day, this beloved lady died. The interment the second day after was in the cemetery of St. Ann's, among her father's family, Joshua Sands, Esq.

The next day I returned to Geneva, passing by Newburgh. The softness of the roads made my travel tedious, and I did not reach Geneva until too late to reach the wedding of my son Willy and Belle at her father's, where Mrs. Swift, Sally and the boys had gone; they soon after joined us at Geneva, i. e., the last of January. Soon after, placed José with Mrs. Record — in April — and sent my son Julius to my farm at Newstead, under the auspices of Major and Mrs. Van Deventer, and with some purpose, myself, to sell out at Geneva and become a farmer in Erie County.

On 11th May attended the funeral, as pall bearer, of Geo. Gallagher, Esq., whose sudden death had left a large family of children in Geneva.

Congress had appropriated this year funds for the harbors, and by the end of April had all the lake works well under way.

In May, Wm. Bayard wrote me that, in examining the records of mortgages in the city, he found one from me to Henry Eckford of my estate on 7th Avenue, and, on calling on the assignees of the Life and Fire Insurance Company, found that my debt thereto had not been paid by Mr. Eckford, as had been declared at the conspiracy trials. Now, I had mortgaged and conveyed this property to Henry Eckford for the express purpose of paying that debt. John B. Thorp wrote me to the same purpose. This information determined me to commence suit for the equitable decision of this matter, and regain my just rights.

On 6th June I sent to the editors of the *National Intelligencer* an obituary of the late Colonel William McRee, who had died of cholera at St. Louis. (See my files.) Messrs. Gales and Seaton inserted the same.

I was in this month in correspondence with my friends, Rev. J. M. Wainwright and John Delafield, on a plan for a seminary in the city—a university,—and upon the comparative merits of modern systems of instruction, and as to how much of the West Point usage could be introduced into such a university.

My father was with us this summer, and he visited Colonel Fitzhugh and attended an ecclesiastical trial of Rev. Mr. Croes, who was convicted but deemed to be demented. I did not like the aspect of the bishop's influence in the trial.

In July, Colonel Totten inspected the harbors of Lake Ontario, on complaints of waste, injustice and an intimation that *some other* engineer would be acceptable to the public. Colonel Totten reported that the works were properly constructed and at reasonable prices, and that there was no just cause of complaint. My farm at Newstead had been progressing with my purchase of teams and implements, and I began to think of selling out at Geneva and becoming an active farmer. My friend J. L. Smith dissuaded me from this. But I purchased one hundred and twenty acres more land of my adjoining neighbor, John Russell, for one thousand three hundred dollars. I had taken Mrs. Swift and my son Jim Tom to see our friends the Van Deventers this summer, and returned by way of Hampton; the next month of August, Sally and the Carrols from Washington city; and Belle and Willy to Niagara Falls. I left them there and went to Buffalo to consult with Mr. Isaac Smith, an ingenious gentleman, on the construction of a light-house for Buffalo, and other piers to secure the harbor.

Early in September I was in the city with Willis Hall about my chancery suit with the Eckford heirs, and purchased the bonds of the Life and Fire Company to liquidate my debt and to make the assignees co-operators in that suit. This purchase of bonds J. B. Thorpe made for three hundred and fifteen dollars.

Returning to Geneva and to Rochester to explore a route for a railroad to Batavia and Attica.

In October, died my cousin, William Roberdeau Swift, at Gen. Blount's, in Washington, North Carolina, my last remaining male relation of my family, save my brother and his son, and my own sons.

In October, General Gratiot, the chief engineer, and myself visited Col. Totten and my son Alexander. Alexander and I, in crossing Narragansett Bay, were run down by a sloop, carrying away the mast, boom and bowsprit of our ferry-boat, breaking the shafts of our carriage, and wounding our horse. The sloop towed us to Newport. Repaired and re-crossed, and went to see my father at New London.

In November I returned to the city of New York, and Mr. Gouverneur, Mr. Bibby and myself, *the only* attendants upon a notice of removing the remains of the late President Monroe (who had died 4th July previously), to the new cemetery—a negligence and indifference of the city, in striking contrast to the pomp and sycophancy there exhibited in 1817.

In this month of November died the daughter of Colonel Isaac Roberdeau, Mary E., and also Maria, the daughter of Gen. Winfield Scott. I was with them at this sad scene. Of Mary Roberdeau's death, Elizabeth Morris wrote me an impressive account. She was accomplished and amiable, and an entirely natural character, beloved generally, and by the family of John Quincy Adams especially. (See my files.)

In my absence from Geneva was born there my son Foster on 31st of October.

In December, Mr. Charles Hoyt, of Brooklyn, proposed my return to Brooklyn as a residence, and joining him in purchase of lots there. I agreed to consider his proposal, and returned to Geneva, where the agreeable family of R. A. Tucker, formerly chief justice of Newfoundland, had taken residence for the winter. Before leaving Brooklyn I had, on 12th and 13th November, at 4 A. M., observed a host of meteoric stars, covering the whole space of air, and continuing a long while. It was said to be in the constellation of Leo.

Seven hundred and seventy-seven thousand dollars appropriated for fortifications in the year 1833.

1834. January. The Rochester and Batavia Railroad, not liking my terms, employed another engineer, and had commenced that work without preparing the sill foundations. They soon found their road in swells and vales and inequalities of surface, the result of a bad economy to save the price of a fair salary in order to have safe advice to follow. A comment of similar nature will apply to many States, and especially to Pennsylvania — losing vast sums by incompetent engineering.

I sent my son McRee to Batavia to be prepared for college in Rev. Mr. Ernst's seminary.

At Lyons, with General Adams, preparing a petition to the legislature to remodel the Sodus Canal charter, and to induce a more useful subscription and support to that important work.

In reply to a request of Governor Marcy, wrote him a plan for a normal school in each senatorial district, and gave a comparative view of ours and the Prussian school discipline.

Early in February observed the defect in vision in my son Willy's eye. The doctor deemed it amaurosis, from too much use at sea, and prescribed the usual remedy. The course was followed by debility and a depression of mental power, unfitting him for full sea-naval service.

I observed in this month of February that the magnetic variation at Geneva was 3° 49' to the West. In this month, at Newstead, planning buildings for my farm, and in March took a deed at Buffalo from Russell for the one hundred and twenty acres, and at Batavia a deed from D. E. Evans for the two hundred and thirty acres. To Black Rock to see General Peter B. Porter, to consult about farming. In March, at Geneva, Willy became able to do duty and was ordered to the Brandywine at the navy-yard, Brooklyn. When on a visit to Mr. Thomas March he relapsed, and the Secretary of the Navy excused the Pacific cruise, and, with his brother

Alexander, we four returned to Geneva, advising Colonel Fitzhugh of Willy's case in April.

George W. Whistler asks my advice about accepting the direction of the machine factory for steam at Lowell. I reply, "accept, certainly, as a good step to improving that machinery for railroads." He did so.

By the end of April I had the harbors on Lake Ontario under way, though on a limited scale, suiting the meagre supply by Congress, and thus much delay in these works.

In May, Colonel Fitzhugh and Elizabeth visited us, and he had heard from Dr. Backus that Willy's case was a stroke of the sun in the first cruise of the Brandywine in the Pacific, from exposure on duty at the sea-side, watering the ship.

My family and Williamson's and Judge Tucker's—twenty in all—on a jaunt to Bluff Point, of Crooked Lake, and to Jemima Wilkinson's farm, where Rachel Malen—Jemima's successor—was chief of the fanatical, though inoffensive society, save their bad example of pretended spiritual rule. My son Alexander returned to duty at Rhode Island in May, and Willy and Belle to Hampton—his health improving, though his nervous system was shattered in June. In July, my son McRee returned from Batavia to enter Geneva College. My father's health failing, and my brother William with him at New London, he wrote me, and I replied on the most important of all subjects, the future life.

Independence this year at Geneva was respectably celebrated by an oration, feast and fire-works. I presided.

In August I commenced a survey of Rochester, with Mr. Stoddard and Mr. Wallace, my surveyors for drainage. At home, commenced a vestibule to the front of my house. In September, Mrs. Swift's niece, Mary Ann Walker, of North Carolina, with us, and a nice party to Sodus Bay.

In October I explained to the Rochester council my system for a double drainage—the upper for surface water and waste; the under for sinks and other offensive impurities; both to be scoured out periodically by a glut from a spring-head south of the town,—the whole to empty at the falls.

They adopted my plan, and then ruined it by diminishing the mains so as to prevent a man's passage to repair.

In November, recommended my friend Rev. Adam Empie, the President of William and Mary, in Virginia, for the presidency of Columbia College, South Carolina. Escorted M. A. Walker, on her way to North Carolina, to Brooklyn, and José to Mrs. North's school in New London, where I saw for the last time our niece, Julia Osborne Frink, on the eve of going to Florida to seek relief.

The last of November I went to West Hills, on Long Island, with F. R. Hassler, my brother William, J. Ferguson and Mr. Dahlgren, on the coast survey, to observe the great eclipse, giving Mr. Hassler a statement of my observation on the meteoric appearance at Major Tucker's, in Brooklyn, on the morning of the 13th November in the east, near the sign Leo. I received, 1st December, from James Prentiss, an invitation to go to Texas, as he reported, by request of Governor Houston, to become a member of the executive cabinet, but did not acceed. I introduced Mrs. O'Sullivan and her son John, to Mr. Calhoun and Mr. Robbins of the United States Senate, to promote a claim for relief for losses of her husband, who was lost in South America, on the coast of Brazil. William Bayard afterward told me this claim was unfounded in justice. (See my files.)

Mr. Charles Hoyt renewed his offer to unite in business in Brooklyn, he guaranteeing me $3,000 a year for three years. This 10th December, 1834, I accepted the terms and commenced operations with George Winchester to purchase Bolton, and with J. U. Cole to buy the flats at Hoboken with Samuel L. Gouverneur; the matter deferred.

My co-executor in the estate of Rev. John Ireland informed me of the sale of the navy-yard lots of Mr. Ireland for eight thousand dollars — approved by the heirs and also by me.

December 26th, Captain Cunningham gave me a stone image from ruins of a temple fifty miles up the river above Tampico, in Mexico, an Aztec God. I deposited the same in the Historical Society of New York by my cousin, Dr. Wm. Swift, United States Navy. I wrote to Jared Sparks of an original letter of Washington's to Governor Dinwiddie, of date 3d June.

1754, just before the death of Jumonville, that would go far to explain the unjust rumor of harsh and cruel treatment by Washington — a sort of gap in the Washington biography. This letter I had deposited with John Pintard, Secretary of the New York Historical Society, and it was received by me from Needler Robinson by the hands of his son-in-law, R. C. Jennings, of Norfolk, Va.

Eight hundred and seventy thousand five hundred dollars for fortifications for the year 1834.

1835. Returned to Geneva in January *via* New Milford, Onego and Ithaca. Advised General Adams of George Winchester's wish to have the Sodus Company's authority to apply to the Legislatures of Pennsylvania and Maryland to promote the Susquehanna navigation to Cayuga Lake and Lake Ontario.

February 20th, Sally and I to Albany, laying plan before the Legislature to improve the ferries at Brooklyn, in co-operation with Mr. Charles Hoyt.

In March, at the invitation of Colonel Worth, examined the ordnance preparations at the Watervliet Arsenal on prospects of war with France — liking to keep up my regard for military affairs.

To Geneva, and purchased the 50-acre lot there of the Cook estate for three thousand five hundred and fifty dollars.

In April, to Brooklyn with Mr. Hoyt, and took his house on Hicks and Remsen Streets, and my daughter Sally commenced furnishing the same.

Returned to Albany and with Charles Humphrey prepared a memorial to the Legislature on the presenting of a sword to Colonel Worth for war honors in 1812.

Returned to New York and employed Richard Morgan to survey Harlem River, to further my plan of a navy dock. (See files.)

In May, received orders and funds from the War Department U. S., to recommence the work of harbors at Genesee River and Sodus Bay, and to commence beacon lights at both places. On my arrival at Geneva, found Willy packing my furniture for a move. Major Rees takes charge of my Geneva property, and on 30th May shipped all things with horses on a canal-boat at the Brewery, and with my family of ten by canal to Albany and a tow down the river to Brooklyn, and at house-keeping the 6th June, my wedding day. Soon after my wife and I went to see my sick father in New London, and José also sick at Dr. North's. We returned to Brooklyn with my brother.

To Baltimore to examine the dredging at that harbor; to see if the machinery would suit the lake harbors. My son Willy, 1st July, to Coney Island with Belle. In this month of July I agreed with the board of Brooklyn to run out and mark a water front of that city. The last of the month Willy with Dr. McDonald.

August 18th, died at New London my venerable father. I could not be there in consequence of Willy and my son Foster's illness. Colonel Fitzhugh and Elizabeth came to see Willy, and returned to Hampton with Belle. My son Julius had gone to China in the ship Sabina. In September my wife and Foster and my brother William went to New London, where William and I qualified as our father's executors.

Found Holmes' dredging machine at New London — a simple and efficient structure — and sent Holmes to Sodus Bay to construct a machine there.

In October, General Gratiot and myself to Rochester to inspect the works, of which the Secretary of War gave me his favorable opinion, maugre the Democratic essays to supercede me in office.

September 30th, had died the friend of many years, Miss Charlotte Farquhar, at Green Hill, in the city.

In October, revised my water line at Brooklyn and attended the American Institute on a committee of inspection of mechanical products.

November 1st, with Major McNeill and Mr. Kirkwood, examining the route of the Long Island Railroad. My son McRee, bit with the desire to be a civil engineer rather than finish his course at college, became an assistant to Mr. Kirkwood. On 5th November the Brooklyn board adopted my water line plans.

November 11th, at Utica as vice-president of a convention on internal improvements and manufactures; Samuel Beardsley, president. Adjourned to meet again, in Albany, in January.

December 16th and 17th, a great fire in the city, when, by request of the mayor, I took charge of blowing up buildings to arrest the fire, and succeeded in thus saving millions of property without injury of any adjacent buildings, in every instance lifting the structure so as to fall into ruin in itself, *i. e.*, a fair "globe of compression." I was aided well by James A. Hamilton and Charles King, Lieut. John Nicholas, United States Navy, and Samuel Swartwont. For similar service at Quebec, an English officer was rewarded with a pension; I was thanked by the authorities of a city which had in 1814 recorded me as her benefactor.

No appropriation for fortifications in 1835.

1836. In January I addressed a memoir to the government on the prospects of war and upon organizing a corps of naval engineers; and on 15th of that month accepted the command of a brigade of Sea Fencibles, formed by young men of the city, and made a contingent offer of service to the President of the United States, and received from the Secretary of War, Lewis Cass, the President's thanks.  (See files.)

The last of January, by Hartford, Ct., to Albany, before a committee of the Legislature, to explain the nature and purposes of a water front for Brooklyn, based on the least obstruction of the tide-way. In February, Belle joined her sister and brother Genet Smith coming from Hampton, and with Major Tucker and myself to Brooklyn and found Willy greatly recovered in health.

March 7th, sent a memoir to the chief engineer on a new organization of our army in reference to the reciprocal rights and duties of the government and the army, and on promotion by seniority as the only safe rule—first established by Charles V. of Spain and Germany, as his civil author, Azalon, lays it down in his treatise, The Precursor of Grotius.

On March 12th I presented the city of New York a plan to rebuild the burnt district with fire-proof buildings only.

On March 16th, in reply to a letter from General Armstrong, formerly Secretary of War, upon his comments on the war of 1812–14, and subsequently upon McRee's advice to Miller about the redoubt carried at

Niagara, with an account of the council of war at Barnhard's, on the St. Lawrence, in November, 1817, that lost Montreal.

On March 18th I proposed to Thomas Biddle, of Philadelphia, that the United States Bank could enable the Sodus Canal to extend the navigation of the Susquehanna to the lakes, taking the stock for its security.

On March 24th, gave Mr. Richmond a plan, on the survey of McRee, for a harbor at the entrance of Sandy Creek, into Lake Ontario.

Corresponded with Senator Livingston and others upon the tunneling of the Hudson at Albany to facilitate the railroading from the east and south.

April, examined Stewart's system to "Surmount Friction of Wheels" for railroad cars. The plan is fair, but too nice to be applied to the rough machinery and imperfect construction of railroads in their several parallelisms, horizontal and vertical.

On the 19th of April to Albany, where, on the 26th, the law was passed by the Legislature amending the charter of the Sodus Canal, upon which Mr. Hoyt agreed to furnish twenty-five thousand dollars and his and my quota on the work and the town lots. Major John L. Smith, Alexander and myself, on 27th April, examined the major's farm of Sandy Pinery, on the road eight miles west of Albany.

On the 16th of May the lake harbor works were in good progress, Holmes' dredging machine making a fine channel into Sodus Bay of fifteen feet of water.

The last of May, at Mr. Fellows', in Geneva, examining White Springs and Castle Brook, to unite them for water power for the village, and gave the plans and estimates therefor without charge for professional services.

To Ithaca, to consult Charles Humphrey on the improvements south of that town to the river Susquehanna; and thence, on the 10th June, he and Mr. H. and myself to Brooklyn, *via* Erie Canal. At the Montezuma Lock I rescued a boy from drowning.

June 23d, at Brooklyn my Baltimore friend, Robert Barry, called on me with a request from Bishop England to consult on a plan of the Rev. E. M. Johnson and myself to remedy the vagrancy of Irish children in Brooklyn, that had become very annoying, by promoting Roman Catholic schools.

The bishop was very earnest in his school commendation, and was *en route* to Rome to report to the Pope on his Nuncio's acts in benighted St. Domingo.

July 1st, reported to the War Department the successful operation of the dredging machine of Mr. Holmes, of New London, in deepening the channel at Big Sodus Bay; and also that, in all other respects, the progress of the harbors on Lake Ontario were very slow because of the lack of appropriations.

On July 7th, to New York, and, with Major McNeill, to consult with Chas. H. Hall upon the progress of the New York and Albany Railroad — the major as chief engineer, Mr. Allen, the surveyor, as resident engineer, and myself as consulting engineer, by occasional visits, etc.

July 12, Belle, Sally and Willy to Geneva and Hampton; Mr. Hoyt and myself with them as far as Canandaigua, where, at Mr. Grig's office, a meeting of the Sodus Canal Association was held; from whence, on the 16th, the association proceeded to the town plot, at the proposed outlet of the canal, and there confirmed the route of the canal.

In reference to which, I purchased a farm at Clyde of William S. De Zeng, who, failing in title which he could not execute, lost me two thousand five hundred dollars, which sum in justice he is bound to repay to me, I having paid him that amount in cash.

July 19th, from the piers at Genesee river took an open boat and coasted to the mouth of Oak Orchard Creek and there made a survey and planned a United States harbor for that outlet, and sent the same to the War Department.

July 28th, General Adams and myself descended the Clyde River to Cayuga Marshes and Lake, and slept at Colonel Stanley's on the Marsh Island, to explore for any improvement in our plan for crossing the Erie Canal at Clyde, under the Erie, and found no better route.

August 6th, at Geneva, opened the Sodus Canal books for subscriptions to the stock. Half was at once subscribed.

August 8th, to Rochester and arranged with Daniel Ball for my son Julius' interest in the Shiawassee lands in Michigan, and mills. This essay was an entire failure under the sanguine Mr. Ball, to the loss on our part of one thousand dollars, a great part of which was a gift of Alexander to his brother Julius.

From Geneva Sally and myself to Ithaca, with Mr. and Mrs. Charles Humphrey; from whence to Brooklyn, having for a companion, Colonel John W. Livingston, my superior officer in Rhode Island thirty-six years ago. At Ithaca I designed a plan for Alexander Duncan, Esq., to dam the Canandaigua Lake in the outlet for mill-seats, and sent it to him. My daughter Charlotte, with Mrs. M. P. Lomax, Newport, R. I., at school.

The month of September, exploring Harlem River in reference to the navy depot plan, and for an outfitting and repairing station, both on the Hudson and near Hell Gate, by which to render it imperative in war that our enemy should support two blockading squadrons. Thus by opening Harlem River by a few yards of cutting into the Hudson, and by a canal through Randall's Island, at Little Hell Gate, maintain a choice of passage to sea by either Sandy Hook or the Sound.

September 17th, to Lake Ontario and Lake Orchard to complete my plans for a United States harbor at that place. Thence to Rose Valley in Wayne Co. through the swamp to Clyde, and ran a line on good ground for a canal — the severest labor in the field I ever experienced, from Cayuga Marshes to Clyde, with Major Cook, a very capital surveyor, and Mr. C. W. Rees.

By the last of October returned to my family in Brooklyn, and re-commenced the Hell Gate survey, and Barn Island — a strong position for every species of magazines and for defence against an enemy, and especially in case of mobs in the city of New York.

In November, George W. Whistler came to consult on improvements, and he returned to Lowell, Mass., taking my daughter to visit Anna.

In December, at a meeting at Mr. Wm. Bard's, presented a plan of Chas. Butler, Esq., as head of the American Land Company, to establish a town at the outlet of Lake Huron, and a canal from Black Creek to that lake, and sent William Hopkins to make the surveys, while I should visit the Governor of Canada to consult with him on establishing a railroad from

Toronto to the proposed site for a town, and in reference to other Lake Ontario harbors, etc.

December 20th, received from Colonel Justus Post one thousand one hundred and eighty-four dollars, as my share on sales of some lands on Coal River, in which he had interested F. R. Hassler and myself. At a meeting last December of the Sodus Canal Company, at Clyde, the plan of crossing under the Erie Canal there was discussed, and thus to make our first lock at the town plot at Sodus Bay. Sodus is an Indian word of the Seneca dialect, and signifies a creek with a wide mouth — very graphic of Sodus Bay.

One million seven hundred and seventy thousand dollars for fortifications for 1836.

1837. Between the 1st and 15th of January, the canal commissioners at Albany debated the subject of crossing the Erie Canal by the Sodus Canal, and on the 15th made decision in favor of crossing under the canal at Clyde.

Immediately wrote instructions to Major Cook and Mr. C. W. Rees to bore deep in the north side of the Erie at Clyde, to determine the nature of the bed on which to construct the culvert.

18th. Met Fennimore Cooper, and we jaunted to Stockbridge, in Massachusetts, thence through New Haven to the city of New York, as our easiest route thither from Albany.

20th. With Commodore Ridgely, United States Navy, upon a process to lay before the Navy Department the claims of Captain Samuel Augus to a pension, he having been stricken from the navy list by President Adams. Query: the constitutional power of the President to dismiss any commissioned officer whose dismission is not provided for by law in such way.

26th. Sent my declination as engineer to the Pensacola Railroad Company, by reason of engagements with the Sodus Canal Company, and reported the same to President Greig.

In February the speculations in city lots of Brooklyn by others than Charles Hoyt convinced me that he could not fulfill his engagements with me, and on his agreeing to pay me the balance then due me of two thousand dollars when in his power, I concluded to remove my family to Geneva. In this month we had the first information of a lung attack on my brother William's wife, and as he was deeply engaged on duty, I offered to escort Mary to the mild air of Florida, but it was not agreeable to her to leave home.

March 7th I was called to Washington to consult on the progress of the work on lake harbors. Met there the minister from Texas, Newman Hunt, at a dinner party given by him to John C. Calhoun, William C. Preston, General Gaines, etc., including myself. The topic was the adoption of Texas into the Union as a State.

The inauguration of Mr. Van Buren had been attended by Mr. John Greig, Alexander Duncan, Chas. A. Williamson and myself, and William G. McNeill. We had a very pleasant club at O'Neil's. On our return we examined the inclined plane of the Morris Canal at Newark, having reference to its probable use on the Sodus Canal, which had now begun to lag from want of funds, the speculations in land having exhausted large capitals and made money very scarce.

The harbor work under way on the lakes early in April, on the 28th of which month I placed my family and furniture on board a canal boat at Brooklyn and thence towed by steam to Albany, meeting an accident at the overslaugh that had nearly sunk our boat in the night. We escaped narrowly, and on May 1st entered the Erie Canal, and on 6th arrived at the foot of the road near my house at Geneva, on the lake shore.

On May 23d summoned to the circuit court at Lyons to testify professionally to the influence and effects of the Clyde mill-dam, nine miles below, in producing what is vulgarly called "piling of water"—*i. e.*, the surface of the water above the dam becomes a curve of large radius, and so elevates the water far up the stream. My experiment to satisfy the jury had been, by taking away the slash boards from the Clyde dam after the water had run out. I placed graduated stakes at several points on the margin of the river, and then replacing the slash boards, noted the surface of the water on the stakes after the pond had filled, which marks on the stakes indicated ordinates in the canal of the back water, etc. The jury, on the exhibition of my diagram, gave verdict against the owners of the dam for surplus overflowage up the river to a point near Lyons — *i. e.*, a line of eight miles.

In June the United States War Department determined that officers of engineers should superintend the construction of harbors when they were not on military duty — a very proper decision — under which the harbors of Lake Ontario were placed under Lieutenant W. D. Smith (Fraser). Retaining my agency at Big Sodus Bay until other officers could be spared. The dredging at Sodus had opened a channel of fifteen feet, where, in 1829, there had been only eight feet of water.

Independence was celebrated at Sodus this year by the canal company in the Shaker building, the town plot for the new city.

July 19th, wrote Gerrit Smith, Esq., my plan for the abolition of slavery: 1st, to obtain the consent of the slave States to sell all the children born of slaves at birth, and so to be born free; 2d, Congress to make a sinking fund by consent of three-fourths of the States of five million dollars a year, which would buy all the children of slaves, born in one year; 3d, to colonize these children when from ten to twelve years old, under the auspices of emancipated competent blacks, west of the Rocky Mountains.

Aug. 4th. To my farm at Newstead to save what the shark Shipherd had left, Van Deventer having made him our common tenant. I found no crop, and took away my horses and wagon and a harrow, all that was left of many things. Met Alanson Palmer at the farm, to whom Van Deventer in his ill state of health had sold his farm — a sharper — made some settlement with him in Van's name, and advised to retain the land and avoid Palmer.

In September to Eighteen Mile Creek, below Lockport, on Lake Ontario, by order of War Department, to project a harbor for that place, which was done, and the plan sanctioned by the Government.

Thence to Niagara and Toronto, to confer with Governor Sir Francis Head upon a plan of the American Company and the Sodus Canal Company to establish a railroad from the West end of Lake Ontario to Sarnia, opposite Fort Gratiot, at the outlet of Lake Huron, and from thence west to the mouth of Grand River at Lake Michigan. The Governor agreed to promote the operation by his influence in Canada. On my return at Buffalo in company with Henry McLean, the cousin of Mrs. Swift, who introduced me to Mr. Bates, sold him my farm at Newstead for eight thousand dollars, under mortgage, but he failed to make payment.

October 8th. From Geneva to Sodus, and found the isthmus that unites Point Charles to the main land nearly cut through by storms. Closed up the breach with cribs of stone.

At the request of Major McNeill I went to Alleghany County, taking Louisa and Foster to Hampton with my gray horses, and, leaving them there, went to Angelica to examine the Alleghany County records, and found them very imperfect and much exposed to fire. Thence to Captain Philip S. Church, Belvidere, from whence I wrote McNeill advice how to proceed to save his pine lands, and also to Samuel Glover, his attorney, to prevent attempted frauds through the records.

Early in November, Henry Dwight, Esq., and myself to Albany, and there met the obituary of my brother William's wife, from rapid consumption. She was a fine woman, the daughter of James Stewart of New London, the British Consul, leaving my brother with a son and daughter at the very age when they most required a mother's care.

From Albany to the Waverly in New York, and there delivered the books of the Tioga Coal Company to John B. Thorp, having received them from Joseph Fellows, Esq., at Geneva.

December 1st, visited Major John L. Smith at Governor's Island, and met there General Scott, Colonel Thayer, Delafield, McNeill and Whistler, and my brother William. Thence William and I went to Hempstead Harbor to see F. R. Hassler, who was in trouble from the calls of the Secretary of the United States Treasury to vary his plan of conducting the coast survey, greatly retarding the progress of that work, and gave my advice to Hassler to remain quiet and not write long letters to the Secretary, who probably did not comprehend Mr. Hassler's scientific mode of conducting the work.

December 19th, by appointment made at Governor's Island, G. W. Whistler and myself proceeded to Stonington to meet the Stonington & Providence Railroad Company on plans for improvement thereof, and the next day to Providence with the company and others to remedy the causes of delay. The following day the company returned to Stonington, and on our way cut off the head of a horse by the force of the locomotive as the horse was standing at night with his head over the rail. On my return to New York, stopped at Fort Schuyler to examine that place with Major J. L. Smith, and met here William Cutbush, formerly Captain of United States engineers, and employed as surveyor.

No appropriation for forts this year.

1838. January 20th. Delayed at Brooklyn by the common council, who thought my charge for making a water front to their city too high. My demand was eighteen hundred dollars, including my visits to Albany to explain the matter to the legislative committee. The common council sent me a check for twelve hundred dollars, and remained in my debt six hundred dollars.

On January 22d, to Harlem with Major McNeill and Philemon Dickinson, Esq., of New Jersey, and with Charles H. Hall it was agreed that to promote the navy dock I should draw up a report on the project of the Hudson and Harlem River and Little Hell Gate for docks, yards, etc. Took my quarters at the Astor House, and finished the report. It was laid before the common council of the city, and produced the adoption of the High Bridge of the Croton acqueduct to permit the passage of ships-of-the-line, etc. (See files.)

On February 3d, a meeting of American Land Company at William Bard's. I gave them an account of my sojourn at Toronto and interview with Governor Head, together with my plan for a harbor at the Gratiot outlet of Huron, which they adopted, to wit: Messrs. Bard, McBride, Beers, Willet, Charles Butler, and Arnault; R. K. Delafield, Secretary.

The next day, by aid of Mr. O'Connor, succeeded in settling the affairs between the daughters of my late friend, Peter Birdsell, and their brother John, by which the girls have the income of rent at the old stand, corner of Wall and Broad Streets.

Febuary 7th. Reported to the United States Navy Commissioner and to the United States Chief Engineer my views of the importance of the Barn Island and Little Hell Gate passage, and Harlem and Hudson River sites for United States navy docks and yards, and its offering space and security and two passages to the ocean, thereby obliging an enemy to use two guns to our one by the necessary blockade off the Hook and Montauk, our two passages to sea.

February 17th. With General Scott and Charles King, Esquire, at the Astor, consulting on the necessity of the general's speedy movement in return to the frontier to check the secret movements of the sympathizing traitors. The general departed that evening with Captain Keys. Quite a scene between the captain's wife, Colonel Monroe and myself on the lady's objections against her husband's duty.

February 19th. At John L. Graham's with Long Island Railroad Company to treat about my taking charge of that road. The meeting adjourned, etc.

February 23d. The exchange of lands between Dr. Fitzhugh and the Shakers of Sodus delayed by the difficulty in raising funds. John Greig and Charles Hoyt, Esq., at my room at the Astor to devise security to Dr. Fitzhugh. A meeting of the Sodus Canal Company called for early in March. The cold very intense on the 24th, when Mr. Greig and I took stage for Albany, Major John L. Smith meeting us with a noble pair of blankets, his present to Mrs. Swift, that made us comfortable all the way home.

On March 1st citizens of Geneva appoint General Whiting, myself and others a committee to locate the proper entrance of the Rochester & Auburn Railroad into our village.

March 8th to Canandaigua at the meeting of the Sodus Canal Company at President Greig's. "The pecuniary difficulties of the times" suspend the whole work, a severe blow to my prospects ; but shall make further essays to revive the work.

In April summoned to New York to testify on the subject of my blowing up houses with gunpowder in the great fire of December, 1835. The owners succeed in recovering from the city in whose cause the blasting was done.

Last of April my brother William and myself to see the first of the great steamers, the Western, Captain Judkins, a grand movement to promote the intercourse and the peace of nations.

May 1st. The agents of the Illinois Canal called on me, McLaren and Hardy, on the subject of connecting a railroad therewith, and we visit the Long Island Railroad to show them the process, etc. They propose to me to unite with them. I deemed it something of an interference with my brother's affairs, and had no more to say to the gentlemen.

On May 3d I was with General Waddy Thompson, who, as a friend of John C. Calhoun invited me to write to Mr. Calhoun on the subject of nullification. As an intimate friend I did so, embracing my views of the whole subject, and urged on him the settling the matter, as I deemed him to hold great influence with the North. But Mr. Calhoun had gone too far to attempt such a purpose. With his great mind he could have done much, and no doubt did assuage the violence of his compeers.

This spring I continued the small work doing at Sodus Bay Harbor, and finished repairing the breach in the Isthmus of Point Charles.

On August 15th Captain Samuel Swift, my cousin, of Geneva, and family, moved to the vicinity of Princeton, Bureau County, Illinois, to a farm he had there purchased, and left his Geneva property in the care of James H. Woods, Esq.

On the 18th my son Alexander made us a few weeks' visit from Cape Fear, North Carolina. This fall great confusion upon our frontier among the sympathizers on both sides of the line of boundary.

General Adams trying to keep alive the Sodus Canal by a current of water washing out the sandy loam from the Clyde north to the head of Sodus Bay. He is an indefatigably industrious man, and will accomplish as much as he has means to use therefor. I went to look at the successful essay in the month of October, and on my return on November 1st to Geneva, I found Major John L. Smith, United States Engineer, at my house, with instructions from Secretary of War, Mr. Poinsett, for the major and myself to examine the condition of the people in the country on the shores of Lakes Ontario and Erie, in reference to secret operations of " Sympathizers" and the like, to disturb our relations with Canada. At Buffalo we conferred with Colonels Bankhead and Crane, United States Army, and thence to Erie, in Pennsylvania, and Cleveland, in Ohio.

Detected several plans that were urged on by misguided men, and by the close of November returned to Geneva, and the major made his report to the Government, of a confidential nature of course.

One million eleven thousand dollars for forts in 1838.

1839. In January Captain W. D. Smith (Fraser) by order of the War Department commenced to examine into the disbursements upon the United States Harbor at Big Sodus Bay, from the commencement of the work in 1829 to the close of 1838, under secret charges from William Edwards, one of the contractors, of fraud and waste. This occupied Captain Smith eight days from January 15th, and on the 23d he left for other duty. A copy of his report was sent to me by order of the Secretary of War. The report states that not a single fact sustained any charges — that they were totally unfounded. There has been for these ten years a series of essays to oust me from office by good Democrats of Wayne and Monroe Counties.

The last of January to Albany with General Adams to call on Governor Seward on the subject of State improvements, and especially the revival of the Sodus Canal, which the governor approved, and said he would further its progress as chief magistrate. A meeting of stockholders was called at Brooklyn, at Mr. Hoyt's, March 9th, when it was agreed that I should go to Philadelphia to consult with Thomas Biddle and Mr. Dunlap, of the United States Bank, which I accordingly did on March 27th, and left my explanation with them, after a thorough conversation, while I should be absent in Washington. When the Secretary of War expressed his satisfaction with Captain Smith's examination into the Sodus Bay expenditures, the Secretary informed me it had been determined to give me the general supervision of the harbor, and on Lake Ontario, and so far modify the order to employ only the engineer officers; accordingly on April 4th Colonel Abert, topographical engineer, appointed Captain Canfield to aid me in an inspection of all the harbors on Lake Ontario.

April 5th Colonel Abert and myself to see an old friend, Phineas Lacy, at Alexandria. I ride out to see Bruce Walker at the theological seminary, and in Alexandria my cousin Mary Harper Swift, Mrs. Summers — Sophia

Potts that was — my early friend in Alexandria thirty odd years ago, at Notty Hall, etc.

April 9th President Van Buren entertains the pacificator. General Scott, in allusion to his services in nullifying days in South Carolina, border troubles at Navy Island, Niagara, and with Sir John Harvey in Maine. The party consisted of the heads of departments, foreign ambassadors, and three of Scott's friends — Generals Towson, Gibson and myself. On the 10th the general and myself to Philadelphia, at Nicholas Biddle's, etc. I met Thomas Biddle, who informs me the United States Bank cannot co-operate with the Sodus Canal Company on the subject deputed to me. To New York, and on April 15th with Belle, Willy and Louisa march to Geneva. On the 28th to a Sodus meeting at Mr. Greig's, Canandaigua, and report the failure of negotiations with the United States Bank.

May 2d. At Rochester piers, and by steam to Oswego, and meet Captain Canfield, and commence our inspection, as a board, of all the harbors of Lake Ontario, and on the 11th I return to Geneva and send instructions to the agent, Judson, at Oswego, to commence the permanent piers there with Beton, and to Mr. Peters at Mexico Bay, Salmon River, to go on with the piers, and the same to Mr. Rees at Genesee River.

July 4th. Celebrate the day at Geneva. Hon. Gideon Lee recently settled among us, with his excellent wife. He presides on that day.

On the 20th our friends the Marchs, of Brooklyn, come to see us, and we take my grays to Hampton and the Wadsworth's, Miss Elizabeth the heroine of the valley. We get back to Geneva on August 1st.

On August 13th Colonel Abert arrives at Geneva, and invites me to a survey of both lakes with him. The next day we proceed to Oswego, and by steamer to Buffalo, and thence to Erie, Pennsylvania, and return from inspection of Presque Isle to Buffalo, and meet the Secretary of War and Mr. Gouverneur Kemble, at the Falls, and so on to Geneva, the colonel being suddenly summoned to Washington on public affairs. On the 26th to Clyde to see General Adams about his scouring process on the Sodus Canal, and thence by canal to Syracuse and Oswego, from whence on the 28th

Colonel Worth and myself to Sacketts Harbor, and explored our scenes there of 1813, and awaited the arrival of President Van Buren and Secretary Poinsett, on 29th, and proceed to review and inspection of the troops ; and thence to the mouth of Black River and Brownsville, and dined with Mrs. General Brown and Major Kirby, and on to Watertown, where Mr. Fairbanks gave the President an account of his extorting a large amount of money from Paymaster Edmonson, by threats of drowning him in the lake. The money was concealed in a bed, and, on ripping up the same, Mrs. Edmonson committed suicide.

August 30th, to Oswego, where the President in his address, reprimanded his political friends who had been sympathizers, a severe and deserved and well administered castigation.

On 31st President inspected the new Beton Harbor work, and Mr. Poinsett pronounced it good, etc.

On September 1st I went to Sodus Bay with Smith, Van Buren to Alexander Duncan, a farmer living on the Shaker tract. Mr. Van Buren and Poinsett went direct to Genesee River, where the Secretary, with Captain Loud of United States Artillery, inspected the decaying wood work of the piers, and saw the effect of the negligence of Congress in delay of appropriations. The President then went to Geneva to have a few quiet days with his early friend, Judge Sutherland, and to see William K. Strong's fine farm, the old Robin Rose farm on the lake shore, and then returned to Albany and Washington. I accompanied him and the Secretary to Waterloo, and he thanked me for the "acceptable service rendered him in the harbors and by my personal attentions."

November 2d. The vestry of Trinity Church at Geneva sent me a delegate to the Episcopal convention at Rochester.

On December 24th I hurried to Hampton to see the last of Colonel William Fitzhugh. He died on the 29th, at the age of seventy-nine, a worthy and consistent Christian gentleman. I wrote his obituary. He had been a cornet of dragoons in the Maryland line, and aid-de-camp to General Gist in the Revolution. He had reared a family of twelve children, and left them all the means of comfort in this world, and an excellent example.

Three hundred and thirty thousand dollars for forts in 1839.

1840. Alexander left us on 2d January for Washington, to receive his instructions from the War Department to proceed to France to prepare to instruct a corps of sappers and miners, and he sailed from New York for Havre de Grace on February 12th.

During the month of February prominent Democrats of Monroe and Wayne counties wrote the War Department that I was interfering adversely to the interests of the Van Buren party, and requested that some good Democrat should be placed in my office. A silly accusation, but without any foundation in fact, for during my United States agency I had refrained from all political meetings and political action, excepting my free and open vote.

In the spring an effort was made to keep the Sodus Canal project before the public, and General Adams (June 1st) and myself went from Clyde to Geneva to negotiate with the Shakers for securing their payments for the Sodus tract, but without success. Our operations had become impeded by the stringency in the money market, and our own wealthy stockholders could not see the policy of finishing the work for less than a fourth of a million, a work that would open intercourse between Chesapeake Bay and Lake Ontario, and yield to the United States Government every means of transport of military supplies to protect the country and its lake commerce in plaster, salt, iron, coal and lumber. The finishing of the work had become simple and cheap. But our capitalist stockholders did not revive the work, and the land reverted to Messrs. Greig, Duncan, Butler and Fellows. General Adams, however, with respectable perseverance adhered to the plan of scouring out the easy sandy loam from Clyde to the head of Sodus Bay, and exhausted his private means in the essay. I have devoted much time and labor and my means to this work, but shall reap no other benefit than the gratification of knowing it will be revived for the benefit of others and the country at large.

In June I went to New York to advance my chancery suit against the Eckford estate. My counsel, Messrs. Foote and Davies.

June 17th consulting with Mr. Canon of Troy upon employment upon the Schenectady Railroad, and agreed to return to Troy with my brother William on this subject. On 19th Major McNeill and I to Stonington and Providence on that railroad business, and thence to Boston to consult with Patrick Jackson. On 21st William and I via Worcester to view the well conducted asylum there, and thence by Norwich and New York, and with the Troy and Schenectady Railroad agent, Mr. Canon, and not liking his terms I returned to New York, and William to Springfield.

June 28th to Elizabethtown, New Jersey, to consult General Scott in reference to a reply to Thaddeus Phelps, who, at a Democratic meeting had nominated me for the chief magistracy of New York. General Scott said that although the nomination was based upon my official relations formerly with Jefferson, Madison and Monroe, and my never having been a prominent political actor, he thought it would not be consistent with my federal principles to consent to any further proceedings, and by no means suitable to my limited pecuniary means, in all which I agreed with him, and wrote Mr. Phelps in accordance therewith.

July 2d Mr. Foot accompanied me to Mr. W. P. Rathbone's, in Hackensack, New Jersey, and learned from him that my city property on Seventh Avenue he knew had been conveyed to Henry Eckford, solely to secure J. G. Swift's debt to the Life and Fire, and for no other purpose. Accordingly at the next meeting on my case, before Master in Chancery Lansing, the testimony of Mr. Rathbone, S. L. Gouverneur, Mr. Hoxie and General Bogardus, taken and recorded, and these meetings continued at periods until the end of the year, detaining me at my friend Tucker's through the illness and to the death of my child in Geneva. Charlotte died there on December 31st, at the age of fifteen.

Seven hundred and eighty thousand dollars for forts in 1840.

1841. February 8th. At the request of Leffert Lefferts, Esq., at the expected disturbance of the United States with France, I gave him my views on paper on the means of defending New York, with a plan for raising volunteers to occupy the fortifications of the harbor in co-operation with troops of the United States. At the instance of General Scott I examined "Mr. Carter's ball propeller." It had excited much attention in the city. I drew up an argument to show that no centrifugal force created by manual strength and applied to cranks and hollow spokes of wheels, would propel even a small cannon ball with sufficient velocity to accomplish military purposes.

On February 19th the last examination before Master Lansing. The Eckford counsel presented a mortgage of my Seventh Avenue property. It was deemed a bar to further action until I could initiate a new case, because this mortgage is only part and parcel of the one and same transaction, namely, to give Henry Eckford a trust of my property to pay my debt. He never had given a cent in consideration for this property, and I had never been indebted to him for any amount whatever. I am tired of this litigation, and shall leave the pursuit of justice to my heirs.

March 10th. To Washington on a visit to Colonel Totten. The officers of the army at Washington had united in a petition to General Harrison to reinstate me in office, an extremely pleasant evidence of the regard of my military associates. (See the document on my files.) With General Macomb I waited on President Harrison, who said he had something for me to do. This referred to the proposal of Colonel Abert to send me upon a visit of inquiry to Canada, having reference to border difficulties. General Harrison and General Macomb concurred on the necessity of further information of the views of the British Government, and the President requested the Secretary of War, Mr. Bell, to arrange with me for this expedition, my compensation to be that of Brigadier General commanding, and all traveling expenses.

On March 27th to New York, and on April 3d to Geneva, the first meeting with my family since the death of my daughter Charlotte.

On April 16th to New York, and with Major McNeill to Boston. Here I consulted with an early friend, Jeremiah Mason, who gave me letters to Sir John Caldwell in Canada. With Patrick and Dr. Charles Jackson, and my companion of the days of fortifying Boston, and other eastern harbors in 1800, etc. — Henry A. S. Dearborn — who had excellent views of our relations with Canada, and of our means of purchasing the whole province. We passed several days together in examining Colonel Thayer's newly commenced fort at Georges' Island, and visited Mount Auburn.

May 1st, on board the steamer Columbia, and in forty hours over a heavy swell arrived at Halifax, and found rooms at the Masonic Hall Tavern, and passed a week in examining docks, forts, and the canal of Shubenacadie. Sir John Harvey invited me to the review of two thousand troops. I estimated them at twelve hundred. He introduced me to Lord Falkland, the Governor, who invited both to dinner, and had a pleasant discussion on the relations of our respective governments. I gave them my ideas, that they required our timber and we their trade, and both upon equal terms. I met Colonel Smelt of Eighth Foot, who presented me to his lady, a daughter of Beverly Robinson. The lady exhibited much American feeling and courtesy. The colonel is the reputed son of George III, and is much like the portraits of that king. He had been sick.

He had been wounded severely on the Niagara frontier in 1814. He spoke kindly of his treatment by the Americans. Lady Harvey, a plain person, and well-informed, the daughter of Lord Lake, of East India celebrity. Lady Falkland is very pretty, of a sad countenance, as if she were thinking of her mother, Mrs. Jordan, and her father, William the Fourth. Sir John Caldwell was one of the guests. I had a letter to him. We dined at the mess of the Eighth, Thirty-Seventh and Sixty-Fourth regiments, in a room designed by the Duke of Kent, not much of architectural taste. Sir John Harvey sent warm messages to his friend, General Scott. They had been able pacificators between New Brunswick and Maine. On 11th I took the coach, and by that beautiful harbor above Halifax, of an extent sufficient to moor a fleet of one hundred sail; came to the margin of a trout torrent near the dividing ridge, and descending the road, thence to Windsor, through a rough, stunted growth of pine, alder and birch, to the river of Windsor. Examined its plaster beds and the bridge across to Falmouth, the rise and fall of the tide at its piers varying from forty-five to sixty-five feet. I found several of the descendants of the refugees from the United

States in the war of 1776. Judge Halliburton, whom I had been introduced to in Washington by General Scott, the Sam Slick of the romance, and some army and navy officers, all very courteous.

On 14th on the appropriately named steamer, the Maid of the Mist, through much fog in the Basin of Mines, out to clear weather after rounding Cape Blowmedon, to St. John, N. B. Our captain, an officer of the navy, honored me with a salute, which made my entrance to the city more public than I had expected. On our passage I observed very strong cross currents and whirls, and the steering very difficult, arising from the power of the tide and the great volume of water that had to pass and repass twice a day between headlands on both sides of the Bay of Fundy.

At St. John I met Charles, son of the consul, James Stewart, Esq., of New London, now in England; Mr. Jewett, whom I used to know, a ship carpenter at Smithville, North Carolina, thirty years ago. He was in affluence, and he treated me with much civility. Also Mrs. Campbell, the sister of "Tom Moore, the Consul," and Mrs. Joshua Sands of Brooklyn. At high tide over the falls by steam to Frederickton, on the St. Johns, where I was courteously treated by the governor, Sir William Colebrook, and by the officers of the Thirty-Seventh Foot. On May 22d I returned to Boston by the North America, by the Saint Croix and Campo Bello to Tremont House, from whence I made my report to the Government at Washington. (See my files.)

On May 24th with P. T. Jackson, Esq., to examine the water power and steam machinery at Lowell, over the best railroad as yet constructed in the United States. The next day with General H. A. S. Dearborn, discussing the views of the policy of acquiring Canada by purchase, showing England first the inevitable event of our becoming one government; as we were descending the harbor to see our mutual friend, Colonel S. Thayer, and his accurate fort of masonry on George's Island.

26th. Met General Wool at the Tremont, and had some Canadian talk; also G. W. Whistler. We two went to his house in Springfield, and then by Worcester, Norwich and New London, to New York.

June 1st. Arrived at home in Geneva, and found all well, thanks to God.

On 3d to Buffalo and Niagara, inquiring into the purpose of the great assemblage of negroes on the Canada side, as they said, by English authority. Saw many fugitives from the South, and much excitement and threats of revenge for ills inflicted by slavery, etc.

15th. To Saratoga over the grounds of the battles of Gates and Burgoyne. Met James Stevenson of Albany. Thence to Whitehall, on Lake Champlain, to Ticonderoga and Crown Point, and received on board the steamer, Mrs. Colonel Churchill of United States Army. To Burlington. Bishop Hopkins has a beautiful seat here. The scenery of the distant Adirondacks and Green Mountains admirable on one of the clearest days of June.

To St. Johns, passing Isle au Croix, and thence by railroad to Lachine, and through the rapids that had half a dozen stout men at the helm, better than a wheel, because more controllable; and on 17th had nice rooms at Rosco's, in Montreal. Called on Lady Selby, who presented me to several of her Canadian friends. That lady is a daughter of the House of Longueville. On the following day, invited to a review on the race grounds, and had a sham battle of Waterloo. I had a fine horse of Colonel Oldfield's. At dinner Madame Selby addressed me very audibly: " General, I hope when you take Montreal that you will give my house a safe-guard." This badinage drew upon me the eyes of many strangers and army officers. My reply was that my hope was that all my visits to Canada might meet the gentility and hospitality of peace, such as then surrounded me. My time was agreeably filled till 19th, when I went to Quebec and met Sir James McDonnell, the hero of Waterloo. He told me the merit of closing the gates at Hoguemont was more due to Sergeant ———— than himself. General Scott introduced me to Sir James. In reviewing the troops the fine looking men of the Coldstream Guards were conspicuously handsome.

Cape Drummond and General Wolfe's route and monument, where he fell and united with Montcalm in the city, had my respects.

On 21st to the Falls of Montmorenci, stopping at Beauport to see the French, still of the aspect of Louis XIV. At the falls I gathered a bouquet of wild flowers and gave them to a pretty girl in a garden at Beauport.

The people thronged about me and invited me to their church. Quite a scene.

To Point Levy and the navy slips. The whole scene at and from Quebec one of the grandest type in nature.

On 23d ascended the St. Lawrence through the remarkable black rocky gorge of Richelieu, and in Lake St. Peters could only see the tree tops on either shore. Made a halt at William Henry, the outlet of the Sorel, and at Montreal rejoined Colonel Oldfield of the engineers, and Lieutenant Bainbridge, Colonel Campbell, etc., of the army, and again reviewed the troops with General Jackson.

To the mountain, one of the noblest river and forest views probably on the globe.

Examined the Cathedral, and then on 26th up the St. Lawrence to the battle ground of November 11th, 1813, Chrysler's Field.

To Prescott and Ogdensburg, and by the Thousand Isles to Kingston with Mr. Herbert, son of Lord Clive, and met my Genesco friend, R. A. Tucker, and reviewed the troops and looked at the forts, and passed on to Oswego, and met Mr. Henry Fitzhugh, and so home to Geneva, after hearing Sir Allan McNab in the Parliament House, Kingston.

July 19th made my second official report to the government. (See my files).

July 26th to Niagara and Canada, taking Hortense and José to General P. B. Porter's, and with General Porter to his battle ground of Chippewa, 1814. On 31st to Buffalo with Hortense and José to Mrs. Van Deventer's. To Cleveland, Ohio, and Detroit, Lake St. Clair and Canada.

On August 8th to Buffalo; 10th, destruction of steamer Erie. I returned to Geneva and waited till 19th for Anselm K. Terry, to whom I sold my Newstead farm for seven thousand three hundred and fifty dollars.

On 31st at old Fort Niagara with Captain W. D. Fraser, United States engineers.

September 1st to old Fort George and Messisauga in Canada, and on board the steamer Transit to Toronto; my fellow passenger Doctor Edward Mitchell of South Carolina, my schoolmate at the academy in Taunton, forty-two years ago; our first meeting since those days; he had been a lover of my sister Nancy, and much beloved by all of us. We recognized each other on the deck of the steamer simultaneously. I had the pleasure of promoting the enjoyment of the doctor and his family and Mr. Chew of the State Department at Washington, through the civility of General Clitherow, at the reviews of the English troops, Ninety-third especially, in which Captain Neil Buchanan furnished me a fine cavalry horse for the reviews. In Toronto was entertained by the family of R. A. Tucker of Geneseo memory, Captain B., etc.

September 5th to Niagara Falls, Buffalo and Geneva.

On 20th to New York on my way to Washington. At Newark measured the machinery and planes of the Morris canal, and sent the results to Captain Bainbridge, English engineer, at Montreal, for him and Colonel Oldfield.

On October 7th to Philadelphia, Baltimore and Washington, and from the topographical bureau sent the new map of the United States to Colonel Oldfield of the English engineers, with my thanks for the information about Canada that he had furnished me at Montreal.

With General Scott to call on the President to converse on the subject of my embassy. Mr. Tyler renewed an acquaintance that had commenced at Richmond many years previously, when no one dreamed of his attaining the chief magistracy. I found him so full of joy at having brought Mr. John C. Spencer into the War Department, that Mr. Tyler could give little heed to the subject of buying Canada on General Dearborn's plan, which I was endeavoring to explain to him. In fact I was reminded of the remark of Colonel Monroe at the door of General Harrison in the previous spring: "Harrison will die, and the luckiest man in Virginia will occupy his chair." The levity of Mr. Tyler's manner does his sense no justice. Judge Baldwin was with us, and was impressed as I was when Mr. Tyler remarked on Mr. Clay that he was vastly inferior to Patrick Henry—an uncalled for and very unsuitable remark, even if true. We agreed that Mr. Spencer was a man of high attainments and experience in politics, for he had been prominent in every party of the Union, etc. To Mr. Spencer, Mr. Tyler referred me to commune on my Canadian excursion.

October 11th attended as member of a meeting of the National Institute, where my son Alexander's memoir on the moving sands of the south Atlantic shore of France, called the Downs, which he had examined, and the mode of arresting their progress by planting willows and grasses, with a view of employing similar means on the coast of Carolina.

October 17th conversed with Mr. John Bell, late Secretary of War, on the purchase of Canada, and of the purpose of General Harrison in my Canadian expedition. Mr. Bell approved of my views, as also did Secretary Spencer and General Scott and Colonel Abert.

Mr. Spencer addressed a note of approbation on the termination of my service. (See document on my files).

On November 5th General Scott, Major McNeill and myself to Baltimore. At Mr. Sehly's, Baltimore, conversing on the Canadian affairs. Met here my friend Doctor Wyatt, with Bishop Chase and Mr. Whitingham.

On 19th to Brooklyn.

Four hundred and fifty-five thousand dollars for forts in 1841.

1842. This winter had much correspondence with Colonel Abert on national affairs, and especially upon internal improvements and of my conviction that the democratic party had ever opposed them. The next day replied to Mr. Germain's proposal to experiment on some eastern road with his railroad car having a parallel motion to adapt itself to any curvature. On 12th to Springfield to arrange for this experiment with Whistler, *ad interim* to New York to bring José to Springfield, where Whistler had just received letters that invited him to Russia. We went to Boston to consult with Patrick T. Jackson, and the last of April I escorted Whistler's men to Providence and Kingston, R. I. On my return to Providence met Alexander Duncan, Esq., and aided him in conveying valuables to Boston to avoid the threatening aspect of affairs in the Dorr rebellion, meeting there Colonel Thayer and Julius W. Adams.

On May 3d I returned to Springfield to see Whistler on his Russian plan.

On the same day met Mr. Germain with his car from Catskill, and made an experiment on the sixty-feet plane with his car and one of Mr. Winans' eight-wheeled cars. By their spontaneous descent on that inclined plane both cars accumulating velocity by their descent, ran through the depot track. Winans' crossed the bridge; Germain's did not reach the bridge. Equal loads in both, proving that a too easy movement of the parallel, to adapt the wheels to the curve, had caused them to move from side to side too readily, *i. e.*, such an arrangement of motion requires a more perfect construction of railway than has yet been accomplished; also that the spring of the long car of Winans is better suited to the curves of our roads than Mr. Germain's. The last may be improved, but thus far Winans' is best. I was present in 1828 at Baltimore when Winans first proposed his car. The great fact about facile motion is that the car gear and the rail track must correspond in accuracy and nicety of construction.

May 4th Whistler and Debo, José and myself to Albany. McRee went to Geneva with José, and Debo, Whistler and myself to Washington, where we arrived on the 7th, meeting Major Bautatz of the Russian service, and General Tallmadge, who gave Whistler some points in the character of the Emperor Nicholas, in reference to his industry and desire to improve public works, that may be useful to Whistler.

On 8th met the Russian ambassador, Mr. Bodisco, and arranged for Whistler's service at twelve thousand dollars a year. Had with Mr. Bodisco an interesting conversation on the difficulties of a Russian campaign across the Indus and the sands to India, and of its inutility, while England had the supremacy of naval power.

May 10th with Mr. Tyler and Major McNeill to converse upon my plans for a navy dock on the Harlem and Hudson Rivers. (See my report of January, 1838, on my files.) The President too much engrossed in politics to be much interested in our subject. General Tallmadge gave the President some strong remarks on his leaving the measures of the Whigs, who had elevated him. The President replied that the Whigs had left him, and that he had therefore "chumped" Congress, alluding to a waggoner's mode of retarding his wheels.

On May 15th Whistler and myself to Albany, he to Boston for England and Russia, and I home to my family in Geneva.

June 29th Major Tucker and family with us. Examining the new Trinity church, now up to the floor.

At the celebration of Independence our families witnessed a sad scene of negligence at the fireworks, by which several people were killed and wounded by the rockets.

July 19th to Rochester, and by the steamer to Niagara with Major Delafield and family to the Falls. Returning home the last of the month, and found our son Alexander, who had arrived from Washington; his first visit home after his return from France. (See his journals.) Also met at our house the artist, Daniel Huntington, and the artist Verbryck, a very interesting person, as also is his brother Huntington.

September 8th to New York to attend the wedding, on the 15th instant, of my son McRee and Hortense, the daughter of my friend, Thomas I. Chew, at 94 Willow Street, Brooklyn, married by Reverend Doctor Cutler of St. Ann's. Guests, Colonels Totten and J. Smith, A. J. DeRosset, Mr. Dickinson and my son Alexander. On 23d I went to see Alexander and Mr. Davies at the Point, and the worthy widow of Colonel Mansfield said to me, "You may expect most of your worldly joys in the decline of your days."

While in New York on September 16th my brother William and I called on Life and Fire Insurance Company receivers, Mr. Hoffman and J. T. Lawrence, about the notice of July 6th, 1842, in the papers, of a dividend on the stock of that company. I held four hundred and seventy-seven shares of it, four hundred of which had been transferred to me by Henry Eckford while on his trial in 1826, and which four hundred shares after the trial Mr. Eckford had required me to re-transfer to him, and which by advice of my counsel, George Sullivan, I declined doing. These acts of Mr. Eckford I have never understood. I owed him nothing. My mortgage and deed to him of my Seventh Avenue property was to secure my debt to the Life and Fire Company. He never paid that debt, and went to Turkey and died there, and his executors never paid it, but on the above receivers declining to pay me any dividend, I employed John B. Thorp to buy Life and Fire bonds for me to balance the debt therewith, and this he did to enable the receivers to join me in my chancery suit against the Eckford estate. September 22d Reverend Dr. Hawks showed me the memorial of the Episcopal Church of St. James, New Hanover, North Carolina, October 1st, 1759, signed by Lewis John De Rosset, planter and member of His Majesty's Counsel and Receiver-General; William Walker (brother of James), Sheriff N. H. John DuBois (uncle), merchant and justice of peace, and Moses John De Rosset, M. D.

One million, three hundred and sixty-six thousand dollars for forts in 1842.

1843. This winter I employed myself lecturing to the Young Men's Association, and in preparing papers for my files.

The spring opened early. Busied myself with new fences and gardening, having no professional employ.

On June 22d Peter Richards, Junior, and my daughter Josephine were married by Rev. P. P. Irving, Mr. George Richards attending, and Bishop DeLancy and Major Rees, and Mrs. J. W. Woods. Our joy was in some degree diminished by the death of our friend and neighbor, Doctor Edward Cutbush. The wedding party dispersed, some to the Falls, others to New York, etc.

On 26th Judge Brown Whiting, Mr. DeLeng and myself to the head of the lake and to crossing on the Chemung, and thence by railroad to Bloss-burgh to examine the coal and iron mines at that place, in reference to forming a company to transport these to Geneva and to Lake Ontario at Sodus Bay.

August 15th R. C. Nicholas and myself to the Episcopal convention at Auburn, as delegates from Trinity at Geneva. Here was commenced the first conventional action of the laity adverse to the theological influence of the Oxford tracts, and to their influence in the theological seminary in New York. Mr. Nicholas and myself were appointed a committee to see Bishop DeLancey, and to say that if the *Gospel Messenger* published any extracts from the Bishop's address in favor of that seminary, the lay members of the convention would deny their accuracy. The Bishop said *no* extract should be published, and none was. Those of the laity opposed to the ultra church views at this convention, made an essay to sustain their views in a new paper to be published in New York.

September 4th John Delafield came to buy a farm. I aided him to find the three hundred and fifty acres on the Rose tract, opposite Geneva. He moved his family to it in the middle of October, and soon gave that farm the best aspect of any in Western New York.

October 19th, forwarded to Willy at Buffalo orders from Secretary of the Navy for him to join the Ohio, seventy-four, at Boston.

November 2d, Sally and myself to West Point, to see Alexander, and thence to Brooklyn. Met Willy on his way home from the Ohio, he having been there " surveyed " by a board of surgeons and found unseaworthy by reason of the injury received on board the Brandywine.

December 21st a meeting with some quiet Whig friends at General Tallmadge's, where it was agreed that I should proceed to Washington to present to Mr. Tyler the views of those gentlemen in reference to the contemplated annexation of Texas, and upon the purpose of abandoning protective measures. I found at Washington that Mr. Secretary Upshur favored our views in these matters, and with him laid the thoughts before Mr. Tyler, having reference to the wishes of the men who had nominated him at Harrisburg. But Mr. Tyler deemed these views "anti-democratic," an open admission of his abandonment of the Whigs.

Five hundred and eighty-eight thousand dollars for forts in 1843-44.

1844. I continued in Washington the month of January, and early in February visited cousin Mary H., the widow of William R. Swift, and found her at her needle between his and my portraits, by J. W. Jarvis, and the old family tankard on the table. These Mary intends for my family. At Washington I quartered with General Scott and family. The daughter Virginia ill, and had entered the nunnery at Georgetown, where the General and myself visited her, finding there also, as Lady Abbess, Wilhelmina Jones, the daughter of Commander Jacob Jones. The daughter Virginia died in this nunnery.

February 20th, Honorable N. G. Walker, Washington Hunt, Colonel Albert and self and others on board the steamer Princeton, by invitation from Captain Stockton, to go below Mount Vernon to experiment with his immense gun, throwing a ball of two hundred and twenty pounds, with some percussion, two miles at a target. The concussion very sharp and acute in sound, that was injuriously stunning.

February 22d. The anniversary of the great namesake for whom the city was called, rather insipid, and so, unbecoming.

My friends in Washington offer me a place in the War Department, the chief clerkship, but it did not suit me, and, with thanks, I declined any further movement, and on February 27th left for home. In my route was overtaken by an express giving the dreadful news of the bursting of the gun on board the Princeton, killing Secretary of State, Secretary of War, Mr. Maxy and Doctor Gardiner, etc. Colonel Abert and myself had been invited to that experiment, and escaped by my hurrying from the office purposes of my friends.

On March 1st, with my wife and family, left Brooklyn by steam to Bridgeport on the Sound. Saw large flocks of wild geese resting in their northern flight, and by the Housatonic to Albany and Geneva.

On Easter Monday the church elected me again to their vestry. On 11th I gave a lecture to the Young Men's Association on the durability of the Union. (See my files.)

On May 8th Cousin Henry Walker and Mr. Chatham on a short visit from Baltimore, where he from Arkansas, and James W. Osborne from North Carolina, had both been vice-presidents in the Clay convention.

July 19th Colonel Abert came to see me to converse on the probability of re-commencing the lake harbors, and on 21st he returned to West Point.

On 25th had a visit from Mr. Audubon, the naturalist. He gave me the history of the Campinola that corrected the extravagant story of Waterton as to the loudness of the tones of the bell bird. I gave Mr. Audubon letters to promote the sale of his great work.

August 8th an interview between the Bishop and Wardens Nicholas and Rees, in reference to the notions of church furniture, not otherwise import- ant than as indicative of more important purposes in the Oxford party. I confess I do not understand Bishop DeLancy's views, though he returns to ancient usage. At the next meeting of our vestry a motion was lost to print Bishop Onderdonk's last sermon in Geneva, where the movement in Pennsylvania was mentioned in reference to Henry Onderdonk, which influenced the vote in some degree.

On October 16th Colonel and Mrs. Totten came to see us, he to inspect the harbor of Sodus Bay, with Commodore Morris, and in reference to naval purposes.

November 11th I sprained my ankle, and laid up and examined the English and American accounts of the various battles of 1812–14.

Five hundred and eight thousand dollars for forts in 1844–45.

1845. On 12th February went to Brooklyn, and met my son Alexander.

February 25th Alexander and myself went to Washington, and I took my quarters with my brother William H., at the junction of F and Twentieth streets, west. Visited the venerable Daniel Carroll and daughters at Duddington. Mr. Carroll gave me many anecdotes of Washington, with whom he had a close intimacy. The last of the month my friend John L. Smith arrived in Washington from an exploration of the Tortugas in the Gulf of Mexico.

March 1st Governor Marcy and myself called on Postmaster-General to secure the office of postmaster of Geneva to Major James Rees.

March 4th attended, with General Scott, the inauguration of Mr. Polk as President.

March 12th with Colonel Abert on the formation of a board of engineers consisting of Colonel Kearny, Major Trumbull and myself, to repair to Buffalo to form a plan of a harbor and break-water. The last of the month returned on my way to this duty to my residence in Geneva, and on April 7th the board met at Buffalo. (See report in War Department). On May 21st returned to Geneva.

On 27th to Brooklyn, where I wrote Major Whistler a caution not to write me too plainly of the misdoings of Klein Michel, lest his letters should be overhauled and he sent to Siberia.

On June 3d left Brooklyn and went to my brother William in Washington, to remain with his family at F and Twentieth streets, during his absence in

Illinois on the business of the Barings of London as to the canal and lands. The middle of the month with S. J. Gouverneur and daughter Lizzie on horseback to Oak Hill in Loudon County, and explored the Blue Ridge and valley. Surpassingly beautiful.

June 27th the obsequies of the late General Jackson celebrated at Washington. General Scott and myself had a carriage assigned for us, and at the Capitol Mr. Bancroft gave an eloquent eulogy.

July 4th celebrated at Washington, killing three inexperienced gunners.

July 5th Mr. Secretary of War Marcy arrived, and I had a long interview with him explanatory of the works at Buffalo, and closing my agency therein.

July 20th Mr. Harbeck called on me with a report of a fire in Broad and Exchange Streets, New York, destroying among the many the store of my son-in-law, 54 Exchange Place. The insurance nearly covered the loss.

On August 2d my brother, W. H. Swift and daughter, returned from Illinois, and the next day accompanied General Scott and myself to New York.

On 9th to West Point on a visit to my son Alexander, then superintending the military academy *pro tem*, and there met General Scott, who read to me his political paper on the presidency; my opinion given to him was, it was best for him to command the army. We examined Delafield's fine improvements and road through the cedars, etc., round the Point. They do Delafield much credit.

At the close of this month the government at last sent Commodore Morris, United States Navy, and Colonel Totten, Chief United States engineers, to examine Big Sodus Bay. I sent them my views, long since formed, on this subject.

September 8th Mrs. Swift's cousin, Francis B. DuBois, of Tortola, visited us. His account of the evils of British emancipation of West India slaves, though a good object, was made unwisely, and was promotive of laziness and other vices.

This fall I had much corrspondence with Reverend P. P. Irving on the petition of the ladies of Trinity for him to return. Our vestry divided on this high and low subject. I had recently had a grave conversation with

Bishop DeLancy on the bad influence of the decision of the ecclesiastic trial of Washington Van Zant.

At the close of this month Mr. DuBois cammenced a suit to recover the Minnisink lands that belonged to Dominic Gualthemus DuBois, Mrs. Swift's great-grandfather, and I gave Mr. DuBois an order on the consistory of the Dutch church in the city to deliver the portrait of said Reverend Walter to him as next male heir.

Eight hundred thousand dollars for forts in 1845–46.

1846. January. At the last meeting of the vestry of Trinity in Geneva a majority of voices elected Reverend ——————— our pastor, and advised him that the call was unanimous. I informed him on his arrival that the information was incorrect. He then declined.

February 2d the vestry elected Reverend John H. Hobart. I voted for him and was requested to correspond with him. When he arrived he informed me that his church views were higher than Mr. Williams'. I sent Mr. Hobart a drawing of our parsonage, and he preached his first sermon April 19th.

May 3d my brother William from his Baring agency at Chicago. Conversed with him on the war coming with Mexico, and tendered my services to the President, but was not called to serve.

May 22d my son McRee became engineer and superintendent of Weldon and Wilmington, North Carolina, Railroad.

On 12th Mr. Cady and other commissioners examined the vicinity of Geneva for a site for an hospital. They fixed on Rochester. I accompanied them in the Geneva examination.

May 26th General W. H. Adams on Sodus Canal at my house. That had been sleeping a long while.

July 8th my friend, Benjamin Armitage of the musical club of New York and Brooklyn, visited me at Geneva, and revived memoirs of F. C. Tucker, Daniel Okey, Reverend J. M. Wainwright, John Delafield, Joseph Chesterman, Ab Taylor, Walter Phelps, etc.

On July 21st died my friend Thomas J. Chew, at Brooklyn, at the age of seventy years, father of Hortense, wife of McRee.

August 16th Colonel Totten's daughter and her intellectual husband, Telford, and son, visited us.

On 19th declined the membership of our Episcopal convention because I disapproved our church adopting any of the peculiarities of the Oxford school.

September 5th my son Alexander visited us to take leave and march with the "sappers and miners" that he had organized to assault Vera Cruz.

In October I explored Seneca County with John Delafield. He commences to lecture on agricultural chemistry to the farmers, and, as Mr. John Johnson told me, with very great and useful success.

October 3d Colonel and Mrs. Totten made us a short visit, the colonel on an inspecting tour.

November 10th at Newburg, where my son McRee was engineer of the New York and Erie branch. Lodged at the old tavern, where I had lodged when I was a cadet, forty-five years ago.

November 19th I visited our friend Major John L. Smith at Governor's Island. Examined Vanderlyn's Columbus, and Brown's bust of Ambrose Spencer, a good Vespasian.

November 26th conversed with General Scott and Major J. L. Smith on the proposed campaign to Vera Cruz. My age assumed to be the cause of my services not being accepted. I suspect my being a New Englander to be a stronger influence. At the General's request I promised my attentions to his family in his absence, and escorted them to Elizabethtown, December 1st.

On 5th we had our first advices of Alexander's arrival with sappers and miners and pontooneers at Rio Grande.

Consultation with United States officers as to a gun-boat system to occupy the shoals in the lower harbor of New York, laying up the gun-boats, etc.

December 15th I wrote a memoir of Colonel Jonathan Williams, for Doctor Williams of Deerfield, Massachusetts, who is collating facts of that numerous family.

The last of December visit Mrs. General Scott at Elizabethtown, and arranged to accompany Mrs. Scott and family to Philadelphia, in Washington Square, and made a plan to enlarge the Hampton House at Elizabeth-town, and made a contract with Mr. Thompson to execute the plan.

1847. I passed my New Year's day with a friend of long endurance, Thomas Cadwallader, of Philadelphia, who married Miss Biddle; met James Monroe, and conversed upon our prospects in the erroneous war with Mexico, and met General Sam. Houston and Mr. Rusk of Texas on the same subject, and with Monroe and Colonel George Bomford, (United States ordnance) and J. Eakin, Esquire, returned to Brooklyn, stopping at Elizabethtown to give directions to Mr. Thompson in reference to extending the Hampton House for Mrs. General Scott.

Wrote a plan for a camp of instruction on Hempstead Plain for a rifle brigade, to meet the Mexicans in their defiles. Mr. Poinsett says the Mexicans are excellent elements to form an army, from their nomadic life and very simple diet, and recklessness of life. Mr. Poinsett was our minister in Mexico, an observing and accurate gentleman. I wrote and sent to the topographical bureau my ideas of occupying the Huas-a-hualeos Pass and Tehuantepec, and constructing a railroad to the Pacific on that pass.

February 15th resigned my membership of the vestry of Trinity Church, Geneva.

February 16th, Major F. C. Tucker and myself, as guardians of Julia, the daughter of Commodore Samuel Evans (United States navy), closed our relations in that matter — the beautiful Julia having married Mr. Gettings of Baltimore.

March 23d, Major Tucker, Mr. March and myself (three of Judge Leffert Lefferts' intimates) went uninvited to the funeral of the judge at Bedford. He was seventy-three years of age.

April 3d Mr. Richards, Mr. D. Huntington and myself selected a lot in Greenwood — in Twilight Dell — for Mr. Richards' and my family. Deed on my files. On same day my friend Gouverneur Kemble informed me that the books and Bird's scale given to me by Professor Hassler (left by me at the West Point foundry) had been remounted, and had now become worth one thousand dollars; a delicate acknowledgment of my services in establishing West Point foundry, and for which Mr. Kemble sent me his bond at seven per cent. interest. My original investment in West Point foundry I lost by endorsing for Thomas Shields.

April 6th, Louisa and myself sat to Mr. Huntington for our portraits in one cabinet size. We dined that day with the Kembles, and next day with Major M. T. Leslie, United States army.

April 13th, I disinterred the remains of my mother and sister Mary, and my child Harriet, and reinterred them in Twilight Dell in Greenwood; the coffins in good condition, the silver plate on Mary's very bright.

On 18th wrote General Brooks, United States army, New Orleans, of my son Alexander's sickness, there arrived from Vera Cruz with the Mexican bowel disease.

On 19th wrote General James Gadsden, my former aid-de-camp, on my nephew G. W. Whistler's establishing a steam machine manufactory at Charleston, South Carolina.

On 19th, McRee to Brooklyn; met Dr. Wood, United States army, who informed us of Alexander's being very ill at New Orleans. I reported the same to Generals Scott and Worth.

On 29th Mr. Wilson placed stone pillars to sustain my mother's grave stone. On the same day I removed the remains of my friend Thomas John Chew, Chew's son Lawrence and his cousin Samuel to Mrs. Chew's lot in Greenwood. McRee's calls professionally compelled his absence.

On 30th I examined the record at Major Tucker's, and found that the corner stone of St. Ann's, Brooklyn, (which church twelve of us commenced by loan of five hundred dollars each,) was laid March 31, 1824, consecrated July 30th, 1825, fifty-seven pews sold for eighteen thousand three hundred dollars.

On 3d May the dreaded intelligence came through Dudley March of the death of my son Alexander at New Orleans 24th April, 1847. The next day came Colonel Totten's authentic notice thereof. I wrote Captain J. G. Bernard, who paid every attention to the temporary interment at New Orleans, and to send the remains to my son-in-law, P. Richards, Esq., who had that day handed me Alexander's will and stock documents.

May 14th, McRee and self to West Point, where Professor Weir and self went to prove the will before Surrogate Borland, at Montgomery, Orange County.

June 10th, sent my record of my wife's claim for seven thousand dollars on the estate of her father to James Henry, son of James, the executor.

June 11th, Willy and I to New York to meet the remains of Alexander coming from New Orleans; met William Murphy, who came on, Alexander's servant, and who reported the death of Alexander as peaceful; that he read much Wilson's *Sacra Privita* given him by his mother. Placed the remains in the receiving vault at Greenwood, and on 16th interred the remains in Twilight Dell. Funeral service had been performed at New Orleans, as Colonel Bankhead and Captain Barnard informed me.

On 23d to West Point and met Colonel Totten, Professor Mahan and Captain F. A. Smith, who each accepted a silver cup from me in memory of their friend Alexander.

July 4th Alexander's goods arrived. Willy has Mr. Weir's portrait of me, after Sulley's at West Point, for Alexander.

July 17th. Extract from Rev. Francis Hawks' manuscripts, of Hanover County, North Carolina: "Cape Fear, 1st Oct., 1759. Lewis John De Rosset, planter and of the king's counsel, and Receiver-General revenue; Wm. Walker, Sheriff N. Hanover, John Du Bois, Esq., Moses John De Rosset, M. D., the uncles of Louisa, and her grandfather, etc."

July 25th wrote to W. W. Seaton *(National Intelligencer,)* to commend to the Secretary of the Navy to cause navy officers to gather potato seed in the gorges of the Cordilleras, coast of South America, where Pizarro's army had fed on that succulent, as Prescott says.

August 5th visited Judge Ambrose Spencer at Lyons, and took to him some of Mrs. Gideon Lee's fine old port. The Judge was not in good health.

. August 12th Dr. David Drake of Cincinnati visited us. He gave me his thoughts on the Mississippi valley, and of deepening the channel at the mouths of that river. They are all on record in his report to the United States government.

*Memo.*—Of the grave stones sent by me from New London in the year

1828 to Dr. De Rosset, who had them placed at the graves of Captain James Walker, ob. 18th January 1808, æ. sixty-six, and Mrs. M. M. Walker, æ. seventy-two, ob. November 1827. My son's, James Foster, at Washington city, was set up by my brother W. H. Swift, March, 1830, where James died 18th March, æ. twenty-four years.

August 26th, the first regatta on Seneca Lake — seventeen boats.

September 13th, wrote General H. A. S. Dearborn on potato rot. I had observed its approach, and advised the Secretary of the Navy to collect new seed in South America.

October 4th, Townsend Harris, Esq., called on me to enquire as to Professor Webster of Geneva College and the Free Academy. I gave him my opinion of Mr. Webster. I gave my earnest advice to Mr. Harris not to lose Mr. Webster as superintendent of that new institution in the city.

November 15th, my brother, W. H. Swift, arrived from his tour to the Illinois Canal. He informed me that he deemed his vocations forbad his remaining in the United States Topographical Engineers, and that he should resign next spring. Conversed on my becoming a commissioner of light-houses, and which office I expected to receive.

December 6th, wrote Geo. W. Whistler at St. Petersburg, on his son's idea of a steam machine shop at Charleston, South Carolina — to move Ross Winans in its favor.

December 25th, Dr. Fitzhugh, Mrs. Tallman, and Mrs. Whitney, Bell and Willy at our family Christmas. The year closes with all of us in fair health. Thanks to God, through Jesus Christ, our Saviour.

1848. The new year commences very mildly, but by 10th January the thermometer gets down to four above zero.

January 13th, sent to Mr. Rose in Congress, evidence of Mrs. Augu's just claim to her pension.

January 14th, commenced a plan to turn my twenty-one acre lot into a cemetery at Geneva. It will give one thousand five hundred lots, and abundant alley way.

On 15th accepted cousin Samuel Swift's offer of his sixteen-acre lot, opposite my twenty-one acre lot, for one thousand six hundred dollars.

February 5th, attended John Delafield's lectures on agricultural chemistry, to the farmers of Seneca County.

On 23d applied to the Navy Department for a midshipman's warrant for Clarence Delafield.

On 25th to Rochester with Ellen Williams; and met at James Watts' my aunt Elizabeth Delano, who informed me that Zachr. Macy and my grandfather, Thomas Delano, owned the Quaise and Polpi's farms on Nantucket.

March 9th sent rambo apple cuttings to James H. Watts.

May 1st, McRee and I to Greenwood, and selected a plan for Mr. West to execute for Alexander in Twilight Dell.

May 6th, Thomas March and I to Spring Brook, L. I., trouting. He and I and Willy, on 9th, examine steamer "America."

May 18th, closed my executorship on estate of Rev. John Ireland, with Major Tucker. On 19th, with Belle, Willy and Jim Tom to High Bridge, and on 22d home to Geneva, leaving me in the city, where, with Mrs. General Scott I met Governor Marcy at the City Bank.

May 25th, General Scott's reception in the city, arriving from his Mexican campaign.

June 1st, McRee and myself in the steamer "Thomas Powell" to Newburg, and to examine his railroad route, and went to see the old Nicholl place, (Du Bois,) below New Windsor.

June 5th, to West Point foundry, and on 6th my marriage anniversary. Examined, in McRee's possession, Mr. P. P. Hunn's map of the Minnisink patent lands, in which Louisa, my wife, has of the Du Bois lands two shares.

June 7th, home to Geneva; all well, thanks to God.

June 8th, met Charles A. Williamson and Mr. Fraser from Scotland, of the House of Lovat, and with J. H. Woods to Sodus Bay, and explained to them the plan of Sodus Canal.

June 20th, gave Mrs. Ellet the meeting of General Scott with Honorable Lady Johnson, at Bath, G. B. She was a Franks of Philadelphia, and a reformed tory. Also the story of Mrs. Bailey's (of Groton, Ct.) noble conduct before Fort Griswold in the war of the Revolution, and of her interview with President Monroe in 1817.

July 8th, wrote general Scott on the opposition of Mr. Polk and Governor Marcy to his, the general's, prospects for the presidency.

July 19th, Dudley March on a visit to Willy, on his, Dudley March's, way to his western lands. He took two hundred and twenty perch out of the lake at Geneva in four hours.

August 1st, my son Foster entered Geneva College.

August 7th, Mr. J. H. Woods introduced me to J. H. Wilton, an English sprig of nobility. I went with him to visit Mr. John Greig at Canandaigua. He is a very accomplished man, but a rascal of uncommon ability, and has been often rescued by his family in England from degradation and want.

August 11th, Mr. Irving and I to a meeting of the Evangelical Knowledge Society, much disapproved of by Bishop De Lancy.

August 22d, wrote Dr. R. H. Wood at Baltimore on General Taylor's reputed letter, advising in reference to the presidency that the general should not write anything. On 4th September his reply, that he had sent my letter to the general.

September 8th, Timothy Tounay cleaned out my well, and found two small streams of water flowing in at the bottom, one of ordinary, the other of sulphur water. I have a slightly charged sulphur spring in my dell.

September 9th, the first balloon ascension at Geneva. It floated gently through the air up the lake, and came down near Ovid, some fourteen miles "as the crow flies."

September 14th, Sally and I to Rochester, where was a meeting of the Evangelical Knowledge Society. I advised a published reply to Bishop De Lancy's objections.

October 2d, Chas. A. Williamson returned from an exploration of the coast of Lake Superior, and presented me a map of the same.

Fraser of Lovat has his home in Inverness, Scotland, at "Greysachen," *i. e.*, Glass Water. He deems himself heir to the barony.

November 7th, all my family who vote gave theirs for General Taylor's electors.

November 25th, wrote to General Taylor, and recommended to his notice

General Gadsden of South Carolina, formerly my aid-de-camp, who will meet the general in Washington.

December 2d, Mr. Benjamin, president of the Chemung Railroad, called on me to subscribe for shares; and took five hundred dollars of them.

December 21st, sent to General Gadsden my publications in the Rochester paper in his favor as a member of General Taylor's cabinet, and sent them also to my friend Seaton of the *National Intelligencer*.

1849. February 6th, Mr. Williamson and myself to see Mr. Greig, on the wishes of the former to explore the country to California, and agreed to promote it with our government. On my return home found Colonel E. R. Cook at my house, and gave him an introduction to the Chemung Railroad Company, as an able and trustworthy contractor.

February 26th, Mr. John Greig and myself to Albany, at Congress Hall. We visited Dr. Romeyn Beck to examine the presents of Pio Nono to the academy; thence by Housatonic Railroad to the city. Recommended General W. G. McNeill to the President, and Mr. W. R. Thompson, son of the revolutionary captain of artillery for the office of United States store-keeper in New York. Met General Scott, and conversed on his relations to and with General Taylor on Mexican affairs, and I advised peaceable relations. Met Mr. S. B. Ruggles, and Messrs. Greig and Duncan on the subject of reviving the Sodus Canal to the new administration, as a route from Chesapeake Bay to Lake Ontario.

March 9th, with C. H. Hall exploring Harlem River with Mr. John Randall, one of the best surveyors the country had, and with reference to removing the navy yard at Brooklyn to Harlem.

March 10th, wrote Chas. A. Williamson that the government would give him escort across the country to California with Colonel Sumner. Gave John R. Johnson a free right to build the "Ben Loder" steamer on the shore of my sixteen-acre lot, south of my house.

March 12th, died my friend Thomas Morris, son of Robert, the revolutionary financier. He and Mr. Greig were fellow students of law.

March 20th, Judge Ogden Edwards, in presence of C. H. Hall and Henry Weston, declared in their presence, and said it was his purpose to put on record that on the "Life and Fire trials, 1826," his conviction was as judge that my honor as a man was not impugned by the testimony given in that court. See on my files Judge Edwards' letter to that purpose.

March 26th, wrote to Susan Shipherd and Isabella Croysdale, 115 Suffolk street, city of New York, about Arthur Pinnel's wife and child, kidnapped on their arrival in the city of New York from London.

April 1st, Major Brown, J. P. Kirkwood and myself on the New York and Erie Railroad to Binghampton, at Julius Adams', and next day examined viaduct, Cascade Bridge and Susquehanna Bridge, and returned to the city on 4th.

April 5th, before a Master-in-Chancery, Mr. Melville, overhauling my memory of Governor Tompkins' affairs, in settling of which, under the law of the State, making me a commissioner with Edmund Smith and Thomas Hyatt in 1824 and 1825. The master found my memory accurate.

May 6th, Brother William's wife and I go to Jones in Philadelphia, and there meet my brother. In the evening I call on Mr. Helm, an Englishman, who corroborates the accuracy of my memory in the Tompkins matter. He was a creditor of the governor. Met Hartman Bache, and with brother William and wife on to Washington. Sent Charles Williamson his papers to move to California with Colonel Sumner. Made an essay to get Markoe, of the State Department, a chargé at some European court.

April 13th, with General Taylor, and had an intimate conversation with him on his mode of administration, especially on his mode of appointing officers, and, at his request went to see Mr. Clayton, Secretary of State, in reference to the consequences of the exercise of the appointing power. I urged that it should not be merged in the functions of any minister; that such a procedure was unconstitutional, which held the President responsible. The President had said that he would be glad to have me in Washington, and asked me how the patent office would suit me. I replied that, with the extensive acquaintance I had, there was no office in Washington that could enable me to support my family there; that although I had some income well managed by a prudent and sensible wife, I could not expose her to a perpetual necessity of saving, and there that subject ended for the time, and I did not revive it.

April 20th, my brother William and myself dined with the President, and after dinner I conversed much with the general on the subject of his relations with General Scott, and counselled peace between them. I requested the President to have my nephew, Julius Adams, employed as an engineer, but nothing resulted therefrom. I saw that the power of appointing to office had fallen from the President's hands. I left the city to return to my home on 22d, and on my arrival at Baltimore found my friend Barry's family in distress by the death of his son-in-law, Dr. Julius Ducatel. On my arrival in New York 27th April met General Scott, and advised him of my conversation with General Taylor in reference to their affairs, and my belief that he was desirous of peace between them.

April 30th, examined the Free Academy with my friend Professor Webster, its president. Saw evident results of his good management of that institution.

May 2d on my way home, at McRee's, in Newburg, examined his work on that branch of the New York and Erie Railroad. In the cemetery of Newburg I found a red sandstone at the grave of Louisa's worthy aunt, Margaret Du Bois, who died in Newburg 21st March, 1813, æ. sixty-seven years eleven months and twenty-nine days. Her husband, uncle John Du Bois' grave was alongside, without any memorial stone. They were an exemplary pair, of conjugal life, of affection and piety.

May 4th, left my son McRee, and, on board the steamer "Alida" met the daughter of General Armstrong, Margaret, the wife of Mr. W. B. Astor, and her son-in-law, Mr. Delano, (a far-off cousin of mine whose mother was named for mine, Deborah), also Mr. Robert Tillotson, but could not accept their invitation to visit them at that time as they landed at Tivoli. Arrived at home finding my family in health, thanks to God.

May 11th came the painful intelligence of the death of George W. Whistler at St. Petersburg, Russia, on 7th April, in the service of the Emperor Nicholas.

May 21st, sent to Richard Derby a biography of his father-in-law, Colonel

George Bomford, United States Ordnance, whom I had brought into the army in 1803 — a very valuable officer.

May 24th, received accounts of the death, by cholera, of my friend General Worth on 7th May in Texas, and also of the death by cholera of my former friend and neighbor Charles A. Williamson, in Missouri, on way to California, on 14th May, and on 29th came the account of the death of his wife in Edinburgh, Scotland, on 9th May.

June 1st, my son James with us, and a family party to Clifton Springs. These waters had relieved my son Willy from severe tetanus.

July 2d, invited to examine the Chemung Railroad with its board of directors, and met my friend Benjamin Armitage at Jefferson, and commended him for treasurer of their board.

August 2d, met Colonel John Livingston of Newport memory, 1800, and at Ithaca Charles Humphrey, whom I had known in Albany as the excellent speaker of the State assembly. He had served well in the war of 1812 as captain in the Forty-first Infantry.

August 4th, with Major Thompson S. Brown, who had accepted the office of engineer to succeed G. W. Whistler in Russia.

August 22d, letter from McRee on his first son's birth, and another from Mr. Richards of his third son's birth.

On 22d a call on me to aid to pay the debt of Trinity at Geneva. I replied that when those of the congregation who had not subscribed to build the church had done their part I would do mine.

August 25th, in the name of the citizens of Geneva I advised Dr. Wood, at Niagara, that they would be happy to welcome President Taylor on his route to the East. I offered the President the use of my retired house. He accepted it, but was lying ill at the Falls.

September 1st, wrote Williamina Williamson that I had some very interesting papers of her grandfather, Colonel Charles W————, and his journal of a travel in Turkey, and of his original offer to the Hopes of Amsterdam to purchase the soil of the territory of Ohio, etc., and that those papers were subject to her disposal.

September 6th, Dr. Woods writes of the increasing illness of the

President, and of the need of going east at once by steam and lake, and of abandoning any further meetings with his fellow citizens.

The past summer, as president of the board of health of Geneva, we had kept the village pretty clean, and had generally good health.

September 14th, sent McRee my ideas of an inscription for a cenotaph in memory of George W. Whistler in Greenwood, on Julius Adams' design, now in Twilight Dell.

October 2d, sent to Colonel Abert my views of constructing a railroad from the Mississippi to the Pacific, through Texas and the River Gila, and to San Francisco.

October 14th, Louisa's birthday; Colonel Totten came to see her, and to talk about Alexander.

October 17th, my former deputy surveyor of the customs, Samuel Terry, came to see me and urged his restoration to the custom house, and also that of John Morris; two of the most efficient and honest men in that service of the United States. Joseph Grime and Joseph Hoxie joined me in this effort — not successful — and got Terry the place of assessor in Brooklyn; and Morris became a merchant.

November 2d, Sally, James and I to West Point foundry, and to the former residence of Captain Phillipse.

November 14th, closing meeting of the board of health of Geneva, and all accounts settled.

November 16th, for the fourth timed essayed to have a bridge across the ravine at the south boundary of Geneva, to extend in a direct line the main street. Failed.

1850. My thoughts on this New Year in reference to my vocation, that has become null by the omission of Congress to continue the experimental construction of harbors on the lakes, and by which those that remain unfinished are rapidly falling to decay. So I must turn to some other employment, and accordingly, on the 4th January I went to Lyons to see General Adams about the revival of the Sodus Canal charter. I commenced also to write a History of the Rise and Progress of Internal Improvements in the United States, aided by the suggestions of S. B.

Ruggles, Esq., and commenced thereon with my son McRee, who, and family, were with us that day.

January 18th. The "Ben Loder" steamer commenced operation on our lake at Geneva, to the head of the lake; a very good progress in internal commerce.

February 2d, my son McRee commenced to organize his division of the New York and Erie Railroad—Almond to Olean. On 5th he left us, after seeing his brother Julius, who had just arrived ill with a typhoid, taken in the service of the New York and Erie Railroad at Piermont. He died on the 6th—one of the most unselfish of beings. His remains rest beside his brother Thomas and sister Charlotte. His bearers his shipmates, and Dr. Covin Gray, who was with him at his death; a kind and benevolent man.

February 28th, had collected petitions from many towns to revive the charter of the Sodus Canal, and sent them to General Adams.

March 21st, to Albany to aid in the revival of the Sodus Canal charter, and before the canal commissioners heard the objections to that canal from Henry Fitzhugh, while so many were petitioning to have that canal route opened to the Susquehanna River. The charter was renewed.

On 30th March, McRee telegraphed me of the sudden death of my friend Thomas March, at Brooklyn. Hastened to Brooklyn.

April 1st the funeral; F. C. Tucker and Joshua Sands the chief mourners. His two brothers, Charles and Frank were there.

April 2d, at General W. G. McNeill's, at the marriage of his daughter to Mr. Rhodewald.

April 8th, Messrs. Wainwright, Tucker, Oakey (Wm.,) renewed our old club.

April 27th, employed in gardening and improving my south lots—about forty acres.

Received advices from Samuel Gouverneur of the death of his wife Maria, the daughter of President Monroe. Governor Cales called to see me, and revived the days of Mr. Jefferson and Mr. Madison at Washington.

August 22d, Foster and myself to Danville, and met McRee, and in his carriage on to Almond and Belvidere, and revived old times with Captain

Phillip Church, and on to McRee's residence at Friendship, on the New York and Erie Railroad. Examined McRee's bridge at Phillipsburg; to Cuba and Olean, and on 2d September to Sonyea at Dr. Dan. Fitzhugh's, and so on to Rochester, and home.

October 8th, Clarence Delafield arrived from McRee's with the distressing account of Henry Clark's death, by the accidental discharge of his fowling piece.

October 21st, arrived Rev. Dr. Wyatt from Baltimore.

Measured my lot, one hundred and fifty-one feet front and three hundred feet to the lake; about an acre and one-eighth.

November 2d, a law and order meeting at Geneva, self president, Major Rees and John Delafield vice-presidents, to sustain the "Compromise" against the wild purposes of anti-slavery. The evils of slavery not to be reached unconstitutionally.

*Memo.* My orders as chief engineer, 1814, to Lieutenant D. B. Douglass and Lieutenant Horace Story, to report to Major E. D. Wood on the Niagara frontier.

November 13th, to Brooklyn.

November 15th, the family went to see and hear Jenny Lind at Terpsicore Hall. Mr. Daniel Webster and Jenny exchanged salutes.

We also attended Mitchell's astronomical lectures in Brooklyn.

November 25th, gave Malcolm Douglass the resolutions of the Greenwood Association, to appropriate two lots to remove the monument to D. B. Douglass, who had recently died at Geneva.

December 14th, wrote the Secretary of State commending Francis B. Du Bois for United States consul at St. Thomas.

December 24th, called with Colonel Murray on Hon. Daniel Webster, at the Governor's Room, City Hall, and went with Mr. Webster to his room at the Astor House, and had a short conversation with him on the irritable state of the southern mind. I said to him that I hoped to see him President. His reply was: "General, my first wish is to spread a desire to have the laws obeyed, and as to the rest, the country will decide," etc.

December 28th, met Mr. Holford, the wealthy Englishman who had made a large loan to Arkansas, at Colonel Murray's. I told Mr. Holford that his meeting with Henry Walker in Arkansas was intended to support his (Mr. Holford's) claim, and not to promote the evil of repudiation.

The last day of the year, in a snow storm attended the funeral of Maria, the wife of my protegé William G. McNeill, on my sixty-seventh birth-day. She was an excellent wife, mother and friend.

1851. February 10th, had an explanation with Mr. Samuel Swartwont about what he deemed a loan to me of five hundred dollars. I considered it as a fee for my services in promoting the improvement of the marshes at Hoboken. I repaid him the amount at his request, he being in many pecuniary difficulties.

February 27th, Louisa, Sally and myself to Philadelphia at my brother William H. Swift's, and through Mr. Fisher, had a pleasant meeting of my old friends Biddle, Cadwallader and others, at the rooms of the Philadelphia, Baltimore and Wilmington Railroad Company. We examined the college of Girard and Laurel Hill, and the grave of my friend Ferdinand Rudolph Hassler, and his profile in marble on the stone. At the mint Mr. Dale placed in the hands of Mrs. Swift an ingot of gold — six thousand dollars — about twenty-five pounds.

The middle of March we returned to Brooklyn, after having made a run to Baltimore, and meeting Richard Rush, Esq., Governor Patterson, Thomas Biddle and Governor Edward Cales (at Willy's friend Ingersoll's, of the navy,) at dinner.

March 18th, wrote an obituary of Major James Rees; of the meeting of Washington and Robert Morris on the square, head of Market Street, Philadelphia, *en route* with his army for Yorktown, 1781.

March 25th, to Newark and Belleville to see my grandsons Fitzhugh and Joseph G. at Mr. Welles' school; a man of education and talent, but deficient in the common sense of life as it exists. The scenes at Belleville reminded me of Alexander Macomb and myself there in 1803 — shooting and other amusements, visiting Passaic Falls, etc.

March 26th, with James Whistler, a cadet, son of George by his second wife, to West Point foundry, at Gouverneur Kemble's, and next day to

West Point, and introduced him to my friends there, all of whom, for the sake of his father, took an interest in James' success. Had an explanation from Captain Brewerton, the superintendent, that the omission of the name of Colonel Jonathan Williams on Captain Cullum's register, would be remedied in the next edition by an ample record of facts, etc. Returned to Brooklyn.

On 1st May I received instructions from the Topographical Bureau at Washington, to commence to examine the position and condition of light-houses on Lakes Ontario, Erie, Huron and Michigan.

May 9th, to New Haven to see my nephew, George W. Whistler, an engineer on the New York and New Haven Railroad. Was much gratified by my reception by his wife, the daughter of Dr. Ducatel.

May 10th, returned to Brooklyn, and with Louisa to Twilight Dell in Greenwood the next day. We had an interesting view of the British steamer "Pacific" going down the bay for Liverpool.

On 20th May, Louisa and I returned to Geneva, and thence on 26th May I proceeded to Sodus Bay on Lake Ontario, in the execution of my instructions, and so on to Buffalo, up the lakes and among the islands and light-houses, and so on from Detroit through Lakes St. Clair and Huron to Saginaw Bay, and to Mackinaw and Sheboyagow in Wisconsin Lake, Michigan, and thus employed until August, when I returned to Geneva, and sent from thence my report and plans to the Topographical Bureau at Washington.

My son McRee visited me at Geneva to converse on what had occupied our previous thoughts, a sojourn in Europe, and we determined to make the voyage, etc. [See my journal of that journey of McRee's and myself, so omit record here until our return in May, 1852.]

1852. May 9th, my family at church and returned; thanks for the reunion in health and safety.

May 10th, I wrote Bishop Hawks of Missouri a request to interest himself for the discharge of an English youth, Thomas Parr, who had left his friends and enlisted in the United States army, one of whom came fellow passenger with me from England to seek the boy.

May 11th to Rose Valley and Clyde, in Wayne County, with General W.

H. Adams, to examine as to what might be done to continue the general's "washings" to extend the canal from Clyde to the head of Sodus Bay. Did not find any difficulty in the route of the canal, and it seemed strange to me that capital should be wanting to complete so easy and cheap a work to unite Lake Ontario and Chesapeake Bay, and open up the vast resources in that whole line. The mere exchange of gypsum, flour, and fish, for coal, iron and lumber, would sustain a fair profit to stockholders.

Returned to Lyons by a farm owned by an escaped slave from the South, and considered what was my duty, under the constitution, in reference to breaking up this slave's farm, and concluded to be silent.

May 30th, with Mr. Greig on Sodus Canal affairs, he holding large interests in Wayne County. He was averse from again entering into that project. We conversed about his friend Mr. Watson, whom I had seen in Edinburgh, Scotland, in reference to the Williamsons' interests in the United States, and also upon what both of us had seen on the continent of Europe.

June —, corresponded with the Secretary of War, General Totten, and Major W. H. Chase, on the error of introducing a foreign officer of engineers into our own corps — General Bernard — who had served several years, and became Secretary of War to Louis Philippe of France.

June 19th, my friend Colonel Thayer arrived and passed a few days with us, and then traveled West.

July 6th, the remains of Henry Clay arrived in the cars from the East, *en route* for Kentucky, escorted by Governor Cass, General Sam Houston, etc. Introduced Dr. Fitzhugh to them, and had a brief conversation with General Cass in reference to the claims of Colonel Abert to the action of Congress, to place him on a par with other useful officers in rank.

July 14th, I wrote my distant cousin, Edmund L. Swift, of the Tower of London, on the prospects in the United States for his wife, a McGregor, and an highly educated lady, to establish an extensive seminary in the United States, as he was about declining his office of conservator of the crown jewels, etc.

July 15th, wrote to Barrister Guest of the Temple, whom I had met in

England, and gave him all I could collect of what had been done in the United States in reference to codification. He soon after became master of laws at Cambridge.

July 26th, with my son James and nephew Charles Swift to Niagara, to celebrate General Scott's honors there. Met Mr. John King and Washington Hunt, and Mr. Greeley, the distinguished editor. The celebration was a failure. Also met Colonel Andrews of Boston.

From 29th September to 22d October attending, as witness, the trial of Mayor Lawrence and the Pentz, and others, at Newark, New Jersey, in reference to the houses that had been blown up by me at the order of the mayor at the great fire, December, 1835.

General Scott, Samuel L. Gouverneur, who had married Miss Lee of Petersville, Maryland, in Newark.

In November I wrote, for Counsellor Davies, a statement of the gun powder blasts, and what I deemed unjust to the owners of that property, so destroyed, in a strict legal sense, and also stated what I deemed a neglect of my services and exposure at that fire of 16th December, 1835, while England had knighted a young engineer officer for similar services at Quebec, in Canada, on a much smaller scale. To determine how much powder would shake a house down and not damage neighboring houses, was of importance as a service. That had been accomplished at every house so blown up at the great fire of 16th December, 1835.

I returned home to my family in Geneva, where we had assembled at Christmas, eight of my family, and two days after McRee escorted his mother to Mr. Richards', Brooklyn.

1853. On New Year's day I arrived at Mr. Richards', Brooklyn, to where my wife had preceded me.

January 3d, Mr. John C. Adams called on me by previous appointment, and I agreed to go to Boston with him to explain to the capitalists there the whole system of the Sodus Canal. We arrived in Boston on 4th, at my brother William's. I presented the plan to the bankers, Thayer and others, but they did not enter with any spirit into the subject.

February 1st, George W. Whistler and myself left Mount Vernon Place for New York. I had previously seen President Walker at Cambridge, and arranged with him for my son Foster, a graduate of Geneva College, to enter Harvard College as a junior. On my return to Brooklyn, met William G. McNeill, very ill, on his arrival from England, in the kind care of his mother-in-law, Mrs. Camman, where he died on 16th February. I wrote an obituary of this distinguished man, and sent it to the secretary of the Society of Civil Engineers in London, of which society General McNeill died an honorary member. He was a person of much talent, and commanding and winning manner, and was one of the principal pioneers of railroad improvements in the United States.

March 16th, I shipped to Wilmington, North Carolina, a marble slab that I had caused to be made in Brooklyn, and wrote my namesake, Swift Miller, a request to see this slab carefully erected at the grave of Mrs. Smith in "old Brunswick Cemetery, Cape Fear River." The inscription is thus: "In Memory of that Excellent Lady, Sarah Rhett Dry Smith, who died 21st November, 1821, aged 59 years. Also, of her Husband, Benjamin Smith of Belvedere, once Governor of North Carolina, who died January, 1826, aged 70." The slab was properly erected.

March 20th, wrote my son Foster at Harvard College, where he had entered as a junior, agreeably to the consent of the faculty; and sent him afterwards a memoir of my Grandfather Samuel Swift, a graduate of 1735, that was requested by some one at Harvard making memoirs of distinguished graduates of old times.

March 30th, gave Richard S. Tucker my opinion of forty years' duration in favor of supplying Brooklyn with the best of water, from the brooks east of the bridge that discharge themselves into the Jamaica Bay.

March 31st, wrote to Colonel Thayer upon the omission of due notice of Colonal Jonathan Williams, in the newly published register of West Point, by Captain Cullum, to promote a correction of that omission.

May. Early in this month essayed to retain Gold S. Silliman, Esq., as postmaster of Brooklyn; an excellent officer and worthy gentleman, with whom I had maintained friendly relations from the year 1800 at Newport, Rhode Island.

Met General Scott several times this month on the subject of recording his campaigns in Mexico. He read to me the first chapter. I deem it well done.

May 23d, kept the seventy-second birthday of my friend F. C. Tucker at No. 1 West Sixteenth Street. The age is a matter of doubt. He and General Scott, Major Robert Anderson, and Colonel James Monroe came to see Mr. and Mrs. Richards and Mrs. Swift at Brooklyn, on that day.

June 8th, Louisa and self visited our friends General Adams' family at Lyons, on the death of their daughter Jane in South America, and of their sons James and Sibley, all three very intelligent children. A sad bereavement.

June 16th, died our friend George R. Lewis at New London.

June 24th, to see my friend John Greig, Esq., Canandaigua; failing in health and strength.

In July I was confined some weeks by jaundice, and expected to depart, but by good nursing of my wife and daughter so far revived as to use horseback exercise, and to receive the children of my friend Charles A. Williamson, deceased, to wit., Wilhelmina and her husband Captain Wickham, of Thirty-third Regiment Infantry of the English Army, who was seeking a farm to retire upon in the United States.

August 1st I purchased a pony, and found benefit to my health by riding.

Ferdinand Hassler visited me to get my memoir of his father, the late superintendent of the United States coast survey. Rev. Dr. Judd read to me his reply to the high church doctrines about baptism; a well composed view of that subject, adverse to Romanism.

The month of September was noted for ague and fever at Geneva, especially in the lower parts of the village and the flats bordering the lake on the north, also several cases on the higher lands; my son Willy one of them. The treatment was quinine, and successful.

October 22d, died my friend John Delafield at Oaklands, on the opposite side of the lake, aged sixty-seven years, a great loss to the farming interests of Seneca County. I directed the interment on 25th in our Geneva cemetery.

1854. January 10th we celebrated Bell and Willy's marriage day, their twenty-first anniversary, at Willy's Geneva home.

January 30th, Mr. Robert Tillotson arrived, and we discoursed of our former days in the city. He described to me the mode of conversion of his son to Romanism, under the auspices of Cardinal Wiseman and Mr. Newman, and of that son's union with the Oratory at Birmingham, in England. So much for the Puseyism of Western New York.

February 2d, received from the singular William Wood, of Canandaigua, a present of a view of the Colosseum of Vespasian at Rome. He said that his life had been passed without being able to see it, and that as I had seen it he wished me to accept the engraving — an old Amsterdam production.

Sent to Colonel Thayer a memoir on West Point, and to Mr. Seaton of the *National Intelligencer*, a notice of the United States Military Academy, West Point.

February 10th, Mrs. Swift's nephew, James Walker Osborne of North Carolina, visited us, and also her cousin John Barrow, grandson of her aunt McLean.

Sent my application to government in favor of Mrs. Commodore Angus' claim for her late husband's back pay, etc., to Charles Abert, Esq., at Washington, to present to Congress. Wrote Mr. Barrow in London how to proceed to gain title to the lots in Dock Street, Wilmington, North Carolina, that belonged to Mr. Barrow's mother, Margaret Du Bois (McLean), and to Henry McLean, and to Mrs. Margaret McLean Hatfield.

March 15th, Major Tucker, Anna Beck and myself to R. S. Tucker's, at Gowanus, and revived some of "the club" music of other days.

March 20th, Colonel John Lind Smith, my useful and true friend, began to recover from a long confinement from a wound in the groin, received at the battle of Cerro Gordo in Mexico. A doubtful recovery. Dr. Buck.

April 10th, wrote Commodore Morris, United States Navy, advising to promote the use of the old ordnance upon Brown's statue of Washington, now in progress for Union Square, New York city.

April 22d, visited my friend Charles Hoyt and wife and children at

Norwalk, in Connecticut. He proposes going to Europe. Of doubtful benefit.

July 15th, my first report to the United States lighthouse board, through Colonel Abert, for a tripod iron light on South Shoal of Nantucket — my place of birth — probably the finale of my essays in civil engineering.

July 22d, my son Foster arrived at home. He had graduated at Harvard College respectably.

July 25th, David Williamson and wife, the daughter of the iron master of Tredegar, in Wales, made us a visit. The son of Charles A. Williamson.

A long drouth this summer, and on 8th and 9th September our first rain for three months. The leaves on the trees so dry as to rattle like wood in sound when shaken by wind.

On 12th I commenced writing the Secretary of Navy, General Scott and Commodore Charles Stewart on the difficulty of forming a retired list for the navy, unless the plan proposed be greatly modified, to do justice to faithful services performed.

On 22d November José's child, Margaret Weston, was born; named for Mrs. Cronkhite.

November 23d I attended a clerical party at Major Tucker's, of five bishops, fifty presbyters and deacons and twenty-five laymen.

1855. At the opening of this year I began a correspondence with several military friends on the condition of the country, and especially as to giving quiet to the South, where, under cover of opposing the tariff and abolition extravagancies their real object, I suppose to be, to perpetuate and extend slavery as a right of the South. As to the tariff, it is a question in which the Union has interests as well South as North, and should be equalized to meet those interests justly, and probably a direct tax may accomplish much toward quiet. As to abolition — an influence growing at the North — it is now about one voter to two hundred. But the South seems intent upon ruling or breaking up the Union. My letters reviewed Mr. Secretary-of-War Davis' plan to subvert the existing army organization under the guise of an imperfect staff. My chief correspondent being Colonel Abert. Sent some essays to the *National Intelligencer*.

January 6th, my application to Congress through Charles Abert succeeded, giving the widow of Captain Angus a pension. That lady sent me a goblet and ring of silver in token of her acknowledgements. I replied it was not my wish so to tax her income.

On 31st found the winter oppressively and unusually cold; the temperature was about as usual.

April 11th, fine weather. Mrs. Delafield (the widow of John of Oaklands) took leave of us, having sold their farm to Mr. Fuller.

April 25, gave my criticism of Major Douglass' memoirs, especially on the war of 1812 and Military Academy, to President Hale. Copy on my files.

May 23d, my brother and wife and Miss Eliza Howard arrived, and 29th, McRee consulted him about going to Iowa. On the same day I wrote Mrs. Gratiot on the death of her husband, the general.

June 1st, Sally designed a celebration of Louisa's and my fiftieth anniversary of our marriage 6th June, on which day twenty-six of the family had assembled at Geneva, and we kept up the season for some days. Louisa enjoyed this occasion and reunion exceedingly.

June 14th I was called to Lyons to the funeral of Mrs. Adams, the excellent wife of my friend General W. H. Adams. How close together our joys and sorrows.

June 30th, I replied to Daniel Huntington's inquiries as to the belief in General Washington's blasphemy, stating my total disbelief in such impressions; that I had conversed in my youth with General Alexander Hamilton, Lieutenant-Governor Cobb, Colonel Trumbull, Major Baylies and General Chief Justice Marshall as to the domestic and social character of Washington, all adverse to his having any habit of using oaths, etc.

July 4th, attended the exhibition of Dr. Reed's school as an examiner, at Walnut Hill.

July 20th, arrived my friends William Kemble and wife and Professor W. H. C. Bartlett and wife, from West Point, and on 30th Foster's friend Mr. ———, of Roxbury.

August 6th, Louisa, for the first time in our married life, made a visit abroad without me, going with Foster to see Hortense and family at Avon.

August 17th, wrote General Scott on the injurious tendency of Secretary Davis' plan to repeal the law of 1802 that limits the detail of a superintendent of the United States Military Academy to the corps of engineers; injurious in two material facts: extending executive power to defeat the purpose of the law of 1802, namely, by appointing an uneducated person, or a personal favorite to that office, making the office thereby a mere political or party agent, and annulling the only national institution in the Union, save the supreme court.

August 23d I commenced to execute a design long entertained, to visit my native place, Nantucket, and the residence also of my father, neither of which had I seen for sixty-three years. Arrived at Brooklyn on 29th, took the cars for Springfield and met my brother William and wife at Miss Howard's, and my sister and self visited the graves of my aunts Elizabeth and Mary Swift, (both had been wives of Colonel Burt of Longmeadow,) in which cemetery both with the colonel rest.

On 29th to Boston, and met at the depot my friend Colonel Thayer, and with him to Fort Warren on George's Island, where, in the year 1841, General H. A. S. Dearborn and myself had visited him in the early construction of that fort. I am much gratified at the scientific aspect of the colonel's work. We visited Fort Independence also, and Governor's Island, where thirty-eight years ago the colonel commenced his engineering career as a lieutenant.

September 4th Colonel Thayer accompanied me to Taunton, the scene of my school days, and on to New Bedford, where the Colonel had, in 1808, commenced a fort. We visited the scenes of those days, the residence of my grandmother Delano, Clark Cove, etc. The colonel was summoned back to Boston, and I explored the scenes of my childhood in Dartmouth, at Russell's Corners and Smith's Mills at the head of Pasquemonsett, where I lived at John Smith's, Esq., while at Master Hart's school, and the scene of rescuing a slave from the hands of William Anthony in 1791. I explored the old Hathaway house near Russell's corners, the residence of my father's family until we moved to Taunton, 1792. I took cuttings from the Talman sweeting apples that I enjoyed when a child. Returned in my "horse and chaise" to New Bedford and visited my cousins Betsy and Nancy, (Mrs. Bennett,) at Fair Haven, and on 6th September on board the steamer for Nantucket. My companions were Mrs. Brayton, an acquaintance of my mother's, a very aged Quaker lady, and Captain Matthew Crosby and his handsome wife, of Siasconset. I recognized Broat Point and Roach's old store on landing, and Delano Corner, Hammet's residence and "Wesco Hill." Met my schoolmate Timothy Hussy, and lodged at Captain Stephen Weet's, where his daughter, Mrs. Clasby, lived. The captain was in his eighty-fourth year, had been a friend of my grandfather Thomas Delano, who had lived at the opposite corner, my birthplace, and who died there 18th November, 1799, at the age of sixty-seven. At small cost entertained by Matthew Crosby with the old Nantucket dish, corn pudding. Met there Franklin Folger the chronologist, who gave me the lineage of the Delanos and Swains, and how they were the cousins of the Folgers and Coffins. I also met the Mitchells, especially Miss Maria the astronomer, and what with the excitement and consequent fatigue of examining every corner, I became ill, and was carefully nursed by Mrs. Clasby, and visited by Mr. Charles Folger and his sister of Geneva.

On 17th I left the beloved old island for home. My son James hearing of my illness had gone to Nantucket for me, so we passed each other in the steamers. He followed me to Brooklyn, where I was joined at Mr. Richards' by my daughter Sally. I came from New Bedford to Fall River, and thence by the steamer Metropolis to the city, finding Foster waiting my arrival.

On 6th October Mr. Richards accompanied me home, meeting the Kembles and Professor Bartlett at Peekskill and Garrisons. We two arrived at Geneva the next day, and found Louisa at her usual place at the window of the dining room watching our coming, and receiving us with her habitual cheerfulness. I had been at Brooklyn seized with gout, much to the surprise of Gouveneur Kemble, when we met at Peekskill.

November 4th, Louisa, Sally and I attended the communion. Louisa expressed great thankfulness for this reunion.

November 9th, Louisa had some indisposition from cold supposed to be taken in examining the corn in the stable, thought by her to be lumbago. On 10th she was languid and pale, though we played at domino in the evening.

November 11th, Louisa not well enough to go to church, but earnestly wished Sally and myself to go. On 13th McRee arrived, and on 14th Louisa growing more ill. In the morning she joined our hands and said she was to die, and at six A. M. 15th, this excellent wife and mother departed. · On the 16th it was deemed needful to inter the body. To the end of the year the loneliness of my bedroom, that had so recently been the scene of Louisa's early rising and industry, was essayed to be made tolerable by my children's attentions.

1856. January, occupied much of my time in replying to Mr. Birney's " Christians." See my letter book.

Middle of April, we left Geneva for Brooklyn, and found José with an excellent portrait of her mother suspended before her bed, the work of the artist, Daniel Huntington. This and photographs, and the family piece by the same Mr. Huntington, done by request of Alexander, (shades of a good wife, mother and friend,) were mournful relics.

July 19th, I had a unanimous call to preside at a meeting to approve the nomination of Colonel Fremont. On taking the chair I announced that I was thoroughly in favor of preventing the extension of slavery into the territories, but not in favor of meddling with slavery in the States where it existed; that under the constitution slaves were a species of property, not in the sense that horses and oxen were property; that slaves had a species of franchise through State action, and thus far had claims to personality adverse to chattelism.

July 25th, a letter from the widow of Alden Partridge, of West Point memory, to aid in getting his son a cadetship at the Military Academy. I wrote to the War Department and to Senator Foot in favor of the appointment.

1857. January 1st, Mr. Richards and myself, in pursuance of ancient usage, made new year's calls in Brooklyn.

January 12th, with General Scott in Twelfth Street conversing on the condition of slavery, and upon its influence in the relations of North and South, and also upon the Secretary of War's interference with the individual rights of army officers.

Mr. Edward Blunt explained to me the use of Trott's longitude chart ;— correct in principle, and useful to within four seconds of a degree. Also of the American telescope, that it was in all respects equal to the Munich glasses.

February 9th, Sally and I to Boston, and at Springfield called on the worthy Mrs. Carew, the friend of my mother and father. At Boston with my brother William and wife at No. 6 Mount Vernon Place. The families of the elder Quincy and his son very desirable visiting places, and I enjoyed them, and Dr. James Jackson, and Mr. Guile's and Mr. Elliot's (Samuel,) and Judge Warren's, where we met Colonel S. Thayer. The Athæneum a charming resort. At Mr. John Savage's, to converse on his forthcoming genealogical work ; also the families of Mills. Examined the Historical Society documents of Pemberton, Adams, Swift, etc., from 1720 to 1775. Had the pleasure to listen to Mrs. Kemble's readings of Shakspeare.

March 8th, visited my ancient maiden cousins, Sarah and Mary Swift, at Dorchester, the Baker house, and cousin Sally Delano Williams at Roxbury, and with Sally and sister Hannah to see our cousins on Milton Hill, and the cemetery, where are fifteen graves of the Swift family and a tomb. Went to see my cousin Fanny at Mrs. Harris', in Cambridge, and Roberdeau at Charlestown. Met Colonel Thomas Aspinwall at the Guiles', and Joseph Grafton.

March 16th, Sally and sister Hannah and myself to New York and Brooklyn. Visited several of the clubs there and in the city of New York. Useful establishments to promote intelligence and easy intercourse. Mr. Richards and Mr. Cronkhite members.

On 30th March Mr. Huntington commenced my portrait for a member of an historical picture.

April 6th, wrote Dr. Hawks on the promotion of quiet between the North and South by his contemplated efforts at the South, in speaking there on the anniversary of the Declaration of Independence at Mecklinburg, in May, 1776.

April 14th, wrote Mr. Howe, of Brooklyn, my opinion in favor of Mr. Kirkwood's location of the Nassau water works.

April 18th, wrote the venerable Quincy of Boston, and J. G. Wright of Wilmington, North Carolina, upon the troubles growing up between the North and South, and that non-extension of slavery was an essential element of any permanent settlement to quiet, and that Mr. Wright should urge this highly indispensable principle at the coming celebration in Mecklinburg County on 20th May, to promote quiet.

May 7th, wrote General Totten and Colonel Abert, United States Army, on the newly proposed organization — especially its staff. Commended G. B. Shaw to General Totten for an assistant engineer.

May 23d, died in Paraclepta, Arkansas, Eliza Younger Walker, the cousin of Mrs. Swift and wife of James W. Walker.

June 6th, heard of the death of my friend Thomas Biddle of Philadelphia, æ. eighty, and on this, my marriage day, found the turf on the grave of Louisa very fresh; José and Sally had placed many flowering plants there.

June 8th, the steamer "Loder" passed our house with thirty-eight canal boats " in tow," and a raft of lumber one-fourth of a mile in length.

June 17th, wrote the family of the late General J. De B. Walbach my readiness to promote adjustment of claims on the United States. Heard of the fate of the Ledyards in the steamer on the St. Lawrence.

September 6th, the worthy Henry Dwight died æ. seventy-six, at Geneva. My cousins Fanny and Elizabeth Swift of Milton visited us, and brought with them, for me, the family arms that had been brought from Rotherham in England, 1630, by our ancestor, Thomas Swift of Dorchester, son of Robert of Rotherham.

In October I wrote General Scott my impressions of the vulgar assault upon his Mexican services by General Pillow, and of the utter improbability of making any impression upon the public mind unfavorable to General Scott.

October 12th, wrote to the ordnance department upon a hemispherical empty shell opening by a hinge, being placed in the bore of a cannon or mortar before the cartridge, and opened by explosion, so as to prevent windage.

In November I wrote to the canal commissioners that great damage was occurring to the banks of Seneca Lake, by the obstructions placed in the outlet at Waterloo, in the process of what is commonly called "piling of water," *i. e.* back water, and referring them to the facts on Clyde River, near Lyons, for similar effects, and to experiments in France to sustain my opinion.

1858. In February wrote my cousin Fanny Swift, of Milton, for a transcript of the inscriptions on the grave stones of the fifteen graves there of our family.

February 18th, my cousin Henry Delano of New Hampshire with us. He informed me of the death of his mother, Elizabeth Hamet Delano, on 3d of this month, æ. seventy-eight years.

April 24th, my grandson Fitzhugh, failing to receive a cadetship, went to sea "before the mast" in the ship "Amaranth" for Australia, from New York.

April 12th, Joseph Fellows and myself attended the funeral of John Greig, Esq., of Canandaigua, who died on 9th April, æ. seventy-eight, leaving a fortune acquired in the United States to his relations in Scotland, after ten thousand dollars a year for life to his wife.

May 8th, a beautiful day. Sally aided me in surveying my forty-acre lot south of the town.

June 11th, my cousins, the Pattens, visited us. I gave them my certificate of my knowledge of a portrait of Washington by the elder Peale, after the "Battle of Princeton," painted by the consent of Washington for my uncle Jonathan Swift of Alexandria, where in 1804, and onward, I saw it, and my uncle gave me its history as above.

July 5th, wrote General Scott that the widow of his companion in imprisonment in Quebec, Major Van de Venter, wished his aid to secure a pension for her husband's just claims.

July 10th, received a present of charts of United States and South America from G. W. and Edward Blunt.

July 14th, in correspondence with the adjutant-general, Samuel Cooper, and sent him files of army memoir. 1800 to 1813.

August 5th, arrived the report of a successful laying of the cable from Newfoundland to Valencia in Ireland, one thousand seven hundred miles, greatest depth six thousand feet, and of a message between Victoria and the President of the United States going by that cable both ways.

September, the comet, of unusually brilliant aspect in the western sky. Query: Is it that which Professor Hassler and Colonel Williams, Mr. Garnett and the officers at West Point observed in this month in 1807?

September 26th, wrote General Webb of my purchasing, as United States agent, Sandy Hook in 1820, for twenty thousand dollars, and proposing that the dispute between New York and New Jersey be settled by the United States granting a site there for an hospital. Also sent Colonel Webb the facts of the Brooklyn water line in 1835; that my map and report had been secretly taken from the archives of the city of Brooklyn; of the line as adopted by the then common council, and of the infringements on that line by lot owners.

November 3d, visited Twilight Dell in Greenwood. Sally and I attended the singing of Picolomini at the Athæneum.

November 4th, Colonel J. L. Smith and Major W. H. Chase and wife, and adopted child, visited us. We had a conversation on the great question of slavery and its tendency. Chase a southern mind on that matter; Smith silent. He had made free his sixteen slaves, and sent them to Liberia.

On 8th November Colonel Smith, Mr. Cropsey and myself take the rail-cars at Green Point to Flushing, and thence by carriage to Willet's Point, examining the plan for the fort for that site, and then crossed over to the coöperating Fort Schuyler. The Colonel and I had some conversation on his making a will. He said he had no existing relative on earth to his knowledge. He and myself thence to Harlem, and thence by steamer to the city. The colonel though cheerful, and as ever, entertaining in his remarks, is much reduced in strength of body, and his appetite small.

November 9th, with J. P. Kirkwood and Captain Green inspecting the

Nassau water line on Long Island, and on 12th inspecting the beginnings of the Central Park of the city of New York, and the foundation of the large water reservoir therein.

November 19th, an interesting dinner party at B. D. Silliman's. Professsor Leiber, Dr. G. W. Bethune, Daniel Lord, Esq., Mr. Izard and Mr. Pringle from South Carolina, Mr. Pierrepont, Mr. G. S. Silliman, the father of B. D. Silliman. The constitutional aspects of slavery the subject of discourse, and the prospects of trouble between the South and the North sections. The fact that the North can never submit to an extension of slavery into the territories admitted, save by the gentlemen from South Carolina; and Mr. Lord, a very clever man, seemed to be of opinion that the constitution contemplated support to slavery.

November 27th, in reply to a letter from P. S. Sanger of Washington, on the subject of removing the dead from one cemetery to another, relied on him to advise me what had been done with those of my son James Foster Swift and the grave stones ; said son having been buried in the cemetery north of the President's mansion in March, 1830. Removed to a new cemetery.

December. Early in this month Major Chase and Captain Barnard advised me of the increasing illness of the best friend I ever had, Colonel John L. Smith. I wrote Colonel Thayer and General Gadsden of it.

December 13th, the colonel died very peacefully at Mrs. Ellen Robinson's boarding house, 64 Amity Street, New York City, at the age of about seventy years. A will could not be found, and the assets in the Leather Manufacturers' Bank went, with his library and other things at Fort Schuyler, into the hands of the city administrator. Buried at West Point on 16th. At Christmas we heard of the safe arrival of Mrs. De Lancy and the bishop in England.

1859. January 4th, wrote the chief engineer of the United States that a will of the late Colonel J. L. Smith might be found among the papers of the late General James Gadsden, of Charleston, South Carolina, an intimate friend of Colonel Smith's, and to whom I knew that Colonel Smith had sent money to aid a friend of his mother's.

In this month I commenced a correspondence with Colonel Delafield and Governor Morgan, to induce the Legislature to permit the property of Colonel Smith to be expended in constructing and endowing a school at West Point, in memory of Colonel Smith. The judiciary committee reported adversely.

January 14th came accounts of José's being very ill. Sally went to her. The dear child declined rapidly and died on 16th, and was interred in Twilight Dell at Greenwood.

April 19th, wrote Josiah Quincy my impression of his Life of John Quincy Adams, that Mr. Quincy had sent me; that it was an instructive volume, and remarkable for what had been omitted as to John Quincy Adams' early and long-continued Federalism, and abandonment of its principles; and also upon our prospects nationally; and that the growth of cotton in the East Indies, etc., would so depress the value of slaves as to convince the South that labor paid for would be more profitable than slave labor.

April 23d, the most severe snow storm of the year. It moderated soon after and swallows appeared 30th, and May opened most gently.

July 4th, sold my out-lots, about forty acres, to Dr. Reed for three thousand dollars.

July 15th, my brother William and wife passed a week with us, and we had pleasant conversations of our respective visits to Europe. William bought a fine picture in Italy, — a St. Cecilia.

September 18th, Mr. Richards and his brother, Dr. Wolcott Richards, go to South Hampton, England, in the Arago.

On 30th I requested the Secretary of the Interior to send me my land warrant. McRee had it located in Nebraska on the Rolling Fork of the Wolff River, by Mr. Everett.

October 14th, arrived our new bell for Trinity; gave twenty-five dollars on this birthday of Louisa.

At Christmas — Willy, Belle, Lizzy, James, Joseph G., Joseph S., Tony, Maggy, Sally and myself.

1860. As my family had not gone to Brooklyn in the past fall, and Mr. Richards was in Europe, leaving Tony and Maggy with Sally and myself to pass the winter in Geneva, it gave me plenty of time to reflect on the aspects of our country, that were growing in anxiety; and yet I have hopes that events may assuage the evils of meddling with the compromise line of 36° north latitude. The great object now being, as it appeared to me, to impress the South that an essay at secession would be ultimately defeated, and that, therefore, going out of the Union would be far more detrimental to southern interests than could be brought about by tariffs or abolition societies; and that the great desire of the South to maintain political rule must be defeated by the natural progress of northern population. In furtherance of these views I coöperated with my fellow citizens of Geneva of the Whig name, and presided at several of their meetings: commencing with a declaration of my creed, namely, not to countenance any interference with slavery in the States as protected by the constitution, but to oppose every species of extension of slavery into the United States Territories; because if such extension was tolerated slavery would become the basis of our government, and the consequence of such a government would be laziness of slave-owners and a descending scale of public and private morals, and thus a ruin to free institutions, for a free government can only be maintained by mental activity and bodily industry.

Early in the month of March, Mr. Richards' letters from Rome advised us of the death of Mr. J. P. Cronkhite in that city, and of his interment in the Protestant cemetery there. Mr. Richards and his brother, and the wife of Mr. Cronkhite were with her husband at his death.

On 6th November I voted for electors to elect Abraham Lincoln President, not that I deemed Mr. Lincoln to possess equal talents with Edward Everett, though Mr. Lincoln's speeches in Illinois adverse to the policy of Mr. Douglass evinced a strong common sense; and I deemed the Bell and Everett ticket favorable to too great a sacrifice of northern ability to prevent disunion. Immediately after voting I proceeded to the cars, and arrived the 7th at Brooklyn. On our arrival at the Delavan we received the first telegraph reports of Mr. Lincoln's success.

November 8th, called on General Scott, (with whom was Colonel Thomas, the assistant adjutant-general,) in Twelfth Street. Conversation at once commenced on the purposes of the South. The general had written to a host of acquaintance of his in *every Southern State* his views of the destructive consequences of secession. He expressed great fear that the earnest advice he had given in the past month of October to President Buchanan, to arm and furnish every fort at the South, *had been totally neglected.*

Before 20th November, South Carolina raised the palmetto flag, Virginia was summoned to an extra legislative session, and Major Anderson had been sent to relieve Colonel Gardner at Fort Moultrie.

At the meeting of Congress I was astonished by the tone of Mr. Buchanan's message, denying power in the executive to avert the action of secession.

On 14th December Governor Cass resigned the Department of State, a position he had filled during all the strange acts of the Secretary of War and Secretary of the Treasury, and must have seen some of the purposes of these men.

December 20th, South Carolina essays secession.

On 26th Major Anderson leaves Moultrie and occupies Sumter, with one hundred and eleven men.

I received several letters from Major W. H. Chase on the fine prospects of the South in forming a new confederacy. I replied in November that it would be better to know what they were doing at the South before going to extremes, and that he, Chase, being a Boston boy would find that the South would not trust him as "one to the manor born."

1861. January. After various consultations with Major J. G. Barnard and others, I selected a syenite from Mr. Edwards' marble factory, (it came from Aberdeen, in Scotland, and cost seven hundred and seventy-two dollars,) for a monument at West Point to the memory of Colonel John Lind Smith. This was done under the decree of the surrogate of New York, giving to my discretion one thousand dollars for the purpose, and on 7th May I had it at West Point set up in the cemetery there, and advised Mrs. Elizabeth Gray of Dundee, N. B., of my course in this matter. My grandsons Joseph S. and Huntington accompanied me. We were hospitably received by Professor W. H. C. Bartlett, and at Mr. Kemble's and Parrot's, at West Point foundry.

May 1st, I addressed a letter to Jefferson Davis on the strength of being his early commander, and urging on him my reasons why he could not succeed in breaking up the Union. I sent the letter for the perusal of President Lincoln, and to be forwarded by the Postmaster-General, so as to avoid the aspect of corresponding with traitors in an improper way. I also urged Mr. Davis to use the influence of his position to molify his coadjutors, and promote a quiet return to the Union. See my letter book.

While at West Point I wrote President Lincoln on the character of Thayer, Mansfield, Lee and others as capable general officers, especially W. H. C. Bartlett, and also upon the importance of having West Point under the superintendence of one as nearly like Thayer as might be found. See my letter book.

June 14. Digestion attended with nausea and vertigo.

In the past summer I met at Commodore Craven's in Geneva, Mrs. Farquhar of Pottsville, in Pennsylvania — quite a traveler. This lady said to me that she had met a cousin of mine at Aix-la-Chapelle who had been the conservator of the crown jewels in the tower of London, who gave to Mrs. Farquhar the circumstances of my meeting this gentleman, Sir Edmund Leuthal Swifte, and of the interview between myself and the yeoman of the guard who had mistaken me for Sir Edmund, and who had pointed out to me the residence of Sir Edmund in Ann Bolen's Tower, 1851–1852, as is mentioned in my journal of my travels in England, etc. Another of the curious coincidences of life in human affairs.

From the arrival of General Scott from France in December, 1861, I was with him frequently in conversation upon the passing events of our unhappy rebellion, until —

1862. April 15th, when he went to his home at Hampton, in Elizabeth-town, N. J., where I joined him on 17th, and remained most of the time until 1st of June, when he went to Cozzens' charming hotel below West Point, and I went to visit my friends at the Point and at West Point foundry, at Mr. Parrott's, enjoying theirs, and Gouverneur Kemble's and

William's hospitality, and at Mr. Parrott's had at dinner a warm discussion with the Russian ambassador on the condition of my country; he sorrowing for our downfall, and I denying the need of his sorrow.

In the course of the summer my son Foster and Miss Alida Fitzhugh had fixed on 29th October for their marriage at Geneseo, where both families assembled under the hospitality of Mrs. Bachus and Mrs. Brent, and Mr. Ayrault, with my late wife's cousin, Rev. John C. Du Bois of St. Croix. Both families met at the church, and the marriage was celebrated by the Rev. Mr. Ayrault, brother-in-law of the bride, and Rev. Mr. Du Bois, cousin of the groom.

In the year 1861 my son Foster, in the spring, volunteered as a surgeon in the 8th New York Regiment, and proceeded to Annapolis and Washington, and on 21st of July was in the battle of Bull Run in Virginia — a defeat of both armies. Foster deemed it his duty to remain with the wounded in the field and hospital, a prisoner; was sent for by Beauregard and parolled, and sent to Richmond, thence to Old Point Comfort and thence home, and has not been exchanged until the day of writing this, December, 1862.

1863. I had proposed to comment on the strategy of this war of rebellion in my diary, but the gazettes and the monthly journals so abound in knowledge of what should have been done, and what left undone, that I will refrain from remark save recording that I deem the yielding to party what belonged to the country (which has distinguished the States of New York and New Jersey) as lamentable evidences of want of patriotism. The anomalous interview between politicians and the English ambassador being among the most prominent of errors.

1864. We, after casting our votes on 8th November for Mr. Lincoln, took the cars on 9th, and arrived at No. 70 Eleventh Street on 10th.

On 30th December my brother William H. and myself attended the funeral of our cousin, Dr. William Swift, United States Navy, at the doctor's house No. 12 Carroll Place, Brooklyn. The doctor died of heart disease at the age of eighty-five years, a worthy man and a good officer. He had been while surgeon in the United States Navy our consul at Tunis,

Africa. He left a competence to his wife, an amiable and intelligent woman, and three nice young sons.

December 31. My son James Thomas gave me my birthday dinner; all my family there save Willy's, including two Misses Weston and General Scott and General Anderson. A nice party.

1865. January 4th, attended with General Scott, General Anderson, Mr. John Travers and others, as pall-bearers, the funeral of Mrs. Margaret C. Kemble, the wife of William Kemble, Esq. This excellent lady died at the age of sixty-eight years, forty-two of which she had been intimate in my family. Mrs. Kemble combined many qualities of heart and mind that made her dear to her family and to a long list of acquaintance.

January 7th, I wrote to Miss Susan M. Quincy, of Boston, on the death of her father, Josiah Quincy, at the age of ninety-three years—a useful and valuable citizen in many stations—as member of Congress and president of Harvard College, etc. I also mentioned to Miss Quincy that Mrs. Sigourney had sent to me, as a memorial, a letter to herself from Mr. Quincy.

On 24th January I wrote to the President of the United States on the miserable policy of retaliating upon the Confederate prisoners at Beaufort, South Carolina; and alluded to a substitute by confiscating rebel land and other rebel property, in favor of southern men who had not voluntarily aided the rebellion, and also in favor of aid to the slaves of such men; and that the whole subject might be embraced in a war proclamation, to meet the Confederate plan of arming their slaves to battle against the Union.

On 31st January I wrote again to President Lincoln on the subject of the treasonable talk in this city of New York in favor of southern independence, and expressing my hope that the subjects of treason, *habeas corpus,* State rights, tenure of civil office and executive power might be amended in the Constitution before the advent of peace.

THE writer of this journal died at Geneva, western New York, July 23d, 1865, and his remains rest in the family plot there, marked by a monument with the following inscription:

JOSEPH GARDNER SWIFT,

SON OF FOSTER AND DEBORAH SWIFT,

BORN NANTUCKET, MASS., DEC. 31, 1783.

DIED GENEVA, NEW YORK, JULY 23, 1865,

FIRST GRADUATE OF THE U. S. MILITARY ACADEMY,

WEST POINT.

CHIEF ENGINEER U. S. ARMY 1812.

BREVETTED BRIGADIER GENERAL 1814.

In the " Biographical Register of the Officers and Graduates of the United States Military Academy," by General Cullum, is the following record:

## "GRADUATES OF 1802.

" 1.   (Born, Mass.)    JOSEPH G. SWIFT.    (Apd. Mass.)

" *Military History*. — Cadet of the United States Military Academy from May 12, 1800 to October 12, 1802, when he was graduated and promoted in the army to Second Lieutenant Corps of Engineers, Oct. 12, 1802.

Served as superintending engineer of the construction of Fort Johnson, North Carolina, 1804–6; at the Military Academy, 1807; as superintending engineer in the erection of Governor's

(First Lieut. Corps of Engineer Jan. 11, 1805.)

(Capt. Corps of Engineers Oct. 30, 1806.)

Island batteries, Boston Harbor, Mass., and in general supervision of the defences of the northeastern coast, 1808–10;

(Major Corps of Engineers Feb. 23, 1808.)

as superintending engineer of the fortifications of the Carolina and Georgia harbors, 1810–12; in the war of 1812–15 with Great Britain, as aid-de-camp to Major-General Pinckney,

(Lieut.-Colonel Corps of Engineers July 6, 1812.)

(Colonel and Chief Engineer of the U. S. Army July 31, 1812.)

1812; as chief engineer of the army under command of Major-General Wilkinson in the campaign of 1813 on the St. Lawrence River, being engaged in the battle of Chrysler's Field, Upper Canada, Nov. 11, 1813; and of the forces for the defence of the city and harbor of New York (including Brooklyn and Harlem Heights,)

(Brev. Brig.-General Feb. 19, 1814, for meritorious services.)

1813–14; as superintending engineer of the construction of the fortifications of New York Harbor, 1814–17; in command of the corps of engineers July 31, 1812 to November 12, 1818, having charge of the Engineer Bureau at Washington, D. C., April 3 to Nov. 12, 1818; and *(ex-officio)* superintendent of the Military Academy July 31, 1812 to July 28, 1818; and its inspector April 7 to Nov. 12, 1818; and as member of board of engineers for the Atlantic coast of the United States April 21, 1817 to Nov. 12, 1818.

Resigned November 12, 1818."

*Civil History.* — Surveyor of the United States Revenue for the port of New York, 1818–27. Member of the board of visitors to the Military Academy 1822 and 1824. Chief Engineer of New Orleans and Lake Pontchartrain Railroad, (the first laid with **T** rail in the United States,) 1830–31. Civil engineer in the service of the United States, superintending harbor improvements on the lakes, 1829–45. Aided in suppressing Canada border disturbances 1839, and was appointed by the President in 1841 on a mission to the British Provinces with reference to a treaty with Great Britain. Member of several scientific and historical societies, and of "La Societe Française de Statique Universelle de Paris," 1839. Degree of LL. D. conferred by Kenyon College, Gambier, Ohio, 1843.

Died July 23, 1865, at Geneva, N. Y., aged eighty-two.

The superintendent of the Military Academy, General Cullum, directed honors to be paid to General Swift's memory in the following order:

"HEADQUARTERS U. S. MILITARY ACADEMY,<br>"West Point, N. Y., July 30, 1865.

" The first graduate of the U. S. Military Academy, General Joseph G. Swift, departed this life at his residence, Geneva, N. Y., on the 23d inst., at the advanced age of nearly eighty-two.

"General Swift was born Dec. 31, 1783, in Nantucket, Mass., was graduated at the Military Academy soon after its organization, and was promoted October 12,

1802, to be Second Lieutenant in the Corps of Engineers, in which branch of service he continued through all the successive grades, 'till he became Colonel and Chief Engineer of the Army, July 31, 1812 — during that period being chiefly engaged in the construction of fortifications on the Atlantic coast. In the war of 1812–15 with Great Britain, after serving as aid-de-camp to Major-General Pinkney, he became in 1813 the chief engineer in Wilkinson's campaign on the St. Lawrence, participating in the battle of Chrysler's Field, and was subsequently, in 1813–14, chief engineer of the forces for the defence of New York, receiving for his meritorious services the brevet of Brigadier-General Feb. 19, 1814. After the war he assumed the direct superintendency of the Military Academy, and was its inspector for a brief period preceding his resignation November 12, 1818. Upon leaving the army he, for nine years, was surveyor of the U. S. Revenue for the port of New York, and then became a distinguished civil engineer, employed by the government for a long period in directing harbor improvements on the northern lakes, and aiding in suppressing Canada border disturbances, being in 1841 honored by the President with a mission to the British Provinces with reference to a treaty of peace with Great Britain. 'Born at the close of the American Revolution, and dying at the termination of the American Rebellion, General Swift lived through the most momentous period of history, and was himself a prominent actor in the grand drama of our national existence. His military career began with that of the Military Academy, which he fostered in its feeble infancy, and he lived to see, in its developed maturity, the sons of his cherished *alma mater* directing the high destinies of his country on victorious fields in Canada, Florida, Mexico, and within the wide domain of our southern border. He now calmly sleeps, after a long and useful life of more than four score years, leaving this world in the blissful consciousness that he and his brother graduates of this institution have ably performed their allotted part in subduing the savage foe, in conquering foreign enemies, and crushing treason in our midst; and that he has left behind a regenerated fatherland of one people, with but one emblem of nationality, sacred to liberty, and the triumph of the best government on earth." The personal excellence of General Swift can be only appreciated by those who knew and loved him, and they were all whom he met on his long journey of life, for he had no enemies but his country's. Amiable and sincere, spotless in integrity, stanch in friendship, liberal in charity, General Swift was a model gentleman, a true patriot and Christian soldier, worthy of the imitation of all who, like him, would live honored and revered, and die universally regretted.

"As an appropriate tribute of respect from the Military Academy to his memory, there will be fired, under the direction of the commandant of cadets, eleven minute guns, commencing at meridian to-morrow, and the national flag will be displayed at half staff from the same hour until sunset."

SWIFT COAT OF ARMS AND OLD CHAIR.

# GENEALOGY.

## THE NAME.

The origin of family names, though obscured by time, has reference to the character, occupation or residence as also to parentage, and family devices or arms also indicate these names. Thus the device of "Deer at full speed," and that assumed by the Rector of Godrich of a dolphin round an anchor and the motto "*Festina Lente*," are in point, for in those days a dolphin was called a swift.—*Vide Scott's Swift*.

The name Swift, written by the Saxons Swiff or Swithen, as also Swyfte and Swifte, is found in the early annals of England. Sir Frs. Palgrave says in his *Rolls* that, anno eleven hundred and sixty-four (1164) lived Henry Swifte of Tavesham in Norfolk, and Walter Swifte of Metar in Berks, and John Swifte of Corford in Suffolk; and anno 1199 Gilbert and Albreda Swifte (his wife) of Riversdale, had lands allotted to them, and William Swift's daughters in Essex, to wit: Amecia and Matilda had lands devised to them, and Stephen Swift was a proprietor in Norfolk, and William in Essex, and anno 1275 Richard Swift of Cotax in Cambridge, and William of Customar and Adam Swift of Norfolk were proprietors, and Adam Swift lived in Wakefield in Yorkshire, and John at Corford.—*Vide 1164*. Anno 1280 Arnulph Swift was at Costisc in Tavesham in Norfolk (see 1164,) and Henry at Deniston, and Erwald Swift in the church, and Walter and Roger lived in North Hampshire, and the family in Lancaster held lands under Duke Henry. Anno 1300 Robert Swift and Margaret his wife lived at Canterbury on land granted by Edward I. In the *Parliamentary Writs* of Sir F. Palgrave, page 1483, Gilbert Swift of Devizes, in Shire of York, was a knight in Parliament 9th September, 1314. Anno 1317 Robert de Swyft, an honorable person, says Palgrave, a licentiate at Wineford in Essex. Anno 1321 John Swift of Leominster in Herts was a knight in Parliament.— *Palgrave, page 1483*. In 1356 Hugo Swift received a patent of land. Anno 1398, in Sir Harris Nicholas' *Proceedings of the King's Privy Council, page 80*, Mr. Swyft is secretary to the writ of summons of Richard II. Anno 1399 Roger Swift lived in Kent, and inherited a tenth of the lands of Hadels, and anno 1461 another Roger Swift also inherited a sixteenth of the same lands. Anno 1408 and 1420 John Swift was a land-holder in Norfolk.—*Vide 1164*. Anno 1508 Peter Swift was auditor of St. Pauls, London, and Richard, rector in Hereford. Anno 1530 Robert Swyft lived at Castle Ward in Notts, and his cousin lived in Lancaster. Anno 1531 John Swyft and Ann, his wife, had a lawsuit with Stanly of Mt. Eagle, for Hornby Castle and for Capton Manse, and other manors in Lancastershire. Anno 1535, in *26th Henry VIII.* Robert Swyft was prior of Shuldham in Norfolk, *(vide 1164,)* and William Swift was prior of Cateby in Lincoln, and anno 1535 Robert Swifte was rector of Rotherham in Yorkshire, and his sons Robert and William were auditors. Of this family was Thomas Swift our immediate ancestor, who migrated from Rotherham anno 1620 to 1629 to Massachusetts Bay, and brought with him the family arms, "Or, a Chevron vair Blue and White between Three Black Bucks in full Course." This Thomas became a "freeman" of Masssachusetts anno 1635. Of this Rotherham family Dugdale says, was the Dean of St. Patrick's, and also of the same was Robert Swift who, anno 1550, was proprietor of Wakefield manor in Yorkshire, *(vide anno 1280,)* and whose son Roger was seized of Rotherwell in the same shire, and another son, Robert, became sheriff of the county, and was knighted by Elizabeth 1599, and continued sheriff until 15th James I. Anno 1597 and '98 lived Garret and Jasper Swift of the same family. My uncle Jonathan Swift informed me they migrated to, and died bachelors in, Virginia. Anno 1658 Sir Edward Swift was in the army with Monk, and of the council that annoyed Monk in opposing Charles II.

The foregoing is written to show the location and condition of the name; but whether before anno 1535 any of them be ancestors of kin of ours I do not assert. Yet there must needs have been some consanguinity among so many persons of the same name, living at various times in contiguous counties. In the time of Alfred, mention is made, in the *Saxon Chronicle,* of the name as existing in repute and rank. When the Normans ruled prenomens became common; the conquered Saxon, probably for safety, adopted Norman christian names. I have not attempted, because I have not been in England, to accumulate later facts of the Yorkshire family, some of which may be seen in Walter Scott's *Life of Dean Jonathan Swift.* Anno 1802 I heard my father and his cousin John Swift, of Milton, conversing about the Rev. John Swift of Framingham as corresponding with the Dean, or with his cousin Dean Swift, and calling themselves cousins. When my uncle Jonathan Swift visited England, anno 1786, he visited Rotherham in Yorkshire, and found the family of respectable circle at Rotherham, and in other parts of the county, they having the tradition that a branch of that family had migrated to Boston in the previous century.

The foregoing account of the name was made by General Swift. Very interesting articles on the English family of Swift are contained in *Historic Notices of Rotherham,* by John Guest, F. S. A., and *South Yorkshire,* by Rev. Joseph Hunter. These works are in the Boston Public Library.

NOTE. — Burke's *General Armory* gives the arms of Robert Swift, Esq., of Rotherham, born 1448, the *rich mercer,* eldest son of Robert Swift, Esq., of that place, — or, a chevron vair between three bucks in full course proper. Crest, a sinister arm embowed, vested vert, cuffed ar., holding in hand a sheaf of five arrows, or feathered ppr., barbed az.: Viscount Carlingford, extinct 1634, grandson of William Swift, who was brother of Robert Swift, Esq., of Rotherham, bore the same arms and crest.

Godwin Swift, attorney-general to the Duke of Ormonde, and founder of the family in Ireland, son of the Rev. Thomas Swift of Goodrich and Briston Co., Hereford, bore the same arms: Crest a demi-buck ramp., ppr., in the mouth a honeysuckle, also ppr. stalked and leaved vert. Motto: *Festina Lente.* The use of the anchor entwined by a dolphin, Burke says, was an assumption of Godwin Swift as a parody on the name.

I.

# THOMAS SWIFT AND HIS DESCENDANTS.

𝕿𝖍𝖔𝖒𝖆𝖘 𝕾𝖜𝖎𝖋𝖙, one of the earliest settlers of Dorchester, Mass., according to Savage, was son of Robert Swift of Rotherham, Yorkshire, England. As he did not qualify this assertion, we may well believe that he derived his information from an authentic source.

He probably came with the first comers, but his name first appears, November 22, 1634, on the town records, as the grantee of five acres of land. Twenty more are recorded January 4, 1635, at the Great Hill between Roxbury and Dorchester; one acre of marsh February 18, 1635, near Goodman Munning's at the Point Neck, and March 18, of the same year, between three and four acres more. He also appears as grantee of four acres of meadow land beyond the Neponset River. Beside these grants he became the owner of other lots by purchase.*

He was admitted freeman of the colony May 6, 1635, was a member of the Rev. Mr. Wareham's church in 1636, as was his wife Elizabeth, and was occasionally called to serve the town in an official capacity. In 1658 he was a supervisor of the highway, from 1659 to 1662 was a fence viewer, and was further distinguished as quartermaster of a troop of horse.

In 1661–2 the commissioners for ending small causes met at his house, and the same year he received from the town one pound as part of the selectmen's expenses, and in 1665 three pounds. Probably they had met at his house to transact the affairs of the town. From all we can learn he appears to have been a man of enterprise, always ready for duty, and holding the respect of his fellow citizens. He was a malster by trade, which he seems to have combined with agriculture. His labors appear to have been well rewarded, for, beside rearing his family in a comfortable manner, giving his children a common education, and providing for his daughters at their marriage, he was enabled to leave to his family a goodly estate for that day, and was not unmindful of the church, and his dependents.

Among the household goods that he brought over was the ancient carved oak

---

*Henry Merifield æ. 66 yrs. and Margaret his wife æ. 65 yrs., Anthony Golifer æ. 64 yrs., Ann Spurr æ. 61 yrs., Thomas Tileston æ. 76 yrs., all of Dorchester, testifieth that Thomas Swift, late of Dorchester deceased, and Thomas Swift his son, of Milton, possessed by tillage and mowing a tract of upland and meadow in Dorchester 44 years; which is bounded southerly with meadow and upland formerly belonging to the worshipfull Mr. Israel Stoughton: the upland being bounded westerly with the highway, northerly with ——— Leads, his land, and easterly with the meadow formerly belonging to Mr. John Holman, and partly with the same meadow; and the meadow being bounded westerly with the same upland, and northerly with the meadow formerly belonging to Mr. John Holman, and easterly with a great salt creek or river.

Henry Merifield and wife also testifyeth that he, Swift, had two houses upon it and they were tenants. Ann Spurr also testifyeth there were two houses. Swift lived in one with his family, myself being one. William Sumner æ. 80 yrs., Richard Hall æ. 65 yrs., Thomas Holman æ. 45 yrs., Timothy Tileston æ. 49 yrs., testifyeth that he lived on it 36 years and upwards. — *Document dated Dec. 23, 1685. Suf. Deeds Lib. 13, Fol. 408.*

chair and the family coat-of-arms, painted in oil on canvas. These precious relics of the old Puritan are still in possession of his descendants; the former owned by Miss Elizabeth R. Swift of Milton, the latter by McKee Swift, Esq., of New Brunswick, N. J.

The old arm chair indicates by its style and workmanship that it belonged to the period of the emigration, and there is not the shadow of a doubt of the authenticity of its descent to the present day. It was inherited by Mr. Samuel Swift of the fifth generation from Thomas, whose house is still standing on Milton Hill. By some mistake, this valuable relic was sold by auction when Samuel Swift's estate was settled, for the paltry sum of eighteen cents. It was bought by Mr. Ezra Glover of Quincy, who could not be induced to give it up. At his decease it fell to his son, John J. Glover, who possessed a taste for antique furniture, and died leaving a fine collection. His furniture was sold by auction, and well advertised, which brought together many persons who were disposed to pay a large price for this interesting chair. Those desirous of getting it back into the family stated their case, and the parties wishing to purchase withdrew their claim, and the administrators, with the consent of the heirs, sold it to Miss Elizabeth R. Swift of Milton, in whose possession it now remains. Albertypes of the chair and the coat-of-arms have been successfully made for this work.

Savage says Elizabeth, wife of Thomas Swift, was probably daughter of Bernard Capen of Dorchester, which is doubtless correct, for Thomas Swift in his will calls John Capen his brother-in-law, and John Capen (who had a grant of an acre of land next to Goodman Swift to build a house on,) speaks of his sister Swift in a letter to Mary Bass, dated 1, 5 mo., 1647, printed in the *History of Dorchester, p. 45*. The Swift graves are also next to those of Capen.

Bernard Capen was from Dorchester, England. He was a very prominent citizen, serving as representative six times. He died Nov. 8, 1638, and his gravestone inscription is thought to be the earliest in New England. See *Hist. Gen. Register, Vol. xx., p. 246*, for an account of the family.

CHILDREN.

JOAN, perhaps b. in England, d. July 21, 1663; m. Nov. 5, 1657, (as Savage says, should be, without doubt, 1647,) John Baker of Boston, smith, by whom she had eight children, six of whom probably d. young, as only two, Thomas and Elizabeth, are named in their father's will, made March 26, 1666; proved July, 1666; invt. £798.19. Abstract of same in *Hist. Gen. Register, Vol. xv., p. 124*. He gave son Thomas land in Dorchester that had belonged to his grandfather Swift. He m. 2nd, 8, 11, 1663, Thankful, dau. of Lieut. Hopestill Foster of Dorchester, by whom he had John, and a posthumous dau. Silence, b. 28, 5, 1666. He was admitted townsman of Boston 1642, and his name appears in the Book of Possessions 1648; ar. co. 1644. His inventory shows he was a shipowner, and that he lived in good style.

2. **Thomas,** b. June 17, 1635.
3. **Obadiah,** b. July 16, 1638.
   ELIZABETH, b. Feb. 26, 1640; d. Jan. 9, 1641-2.

RUTH, b. Aug. 24, 1643; d. between 1677 and 1680; m. Oct. 10, 1660, Capt. Wm. Greenough, shipwright, of Boston, by whom she had seven children. He d. Aug. 6, 1693, æ. 53, (g. s. one of the most beautiful in Copp's Hill). Will made Aug. 1, 1693; proved Sept. 13, 1693; invt. £1245.9.4, showing large estate and house furnished in a superior manner. Had 2nd wife Elizabeth Rainsford; 3rd wife Sarah Shore of Chelmsford. See *N. E. Hist. Gen. Reg., Vol. xvii, pp. 167–9.*

MARY, b. Sept. 21, 1645; m. 11, 11, 1663, John White of Boston, joiner; bapt. in Dorchester 15th Dec., 1639; d. Aug. 6, 1690, æ. about 50; (g. s. Copp's Hill). Will made Apr. 26, 1690; proved Oct. 11, 1690; invt. £1077.7.8, consisting of dwelling houses and wharf, land at Dorchester, farm at Lynn, household effects showing he lived in the same style as his brother-in-laws. Names brother James White, of Dorchester, and son Edward. Was son of Edward White of Dorchester, 1635, who was b. 1593; m. Martha King in 1616 at St. Dunstan's church, Cranbrooke, Kent, Eng. John and Mary had, 1. Mary, b. 8, 8, 1663, m. John Robinson. 2. Martha, b. July 7, 1669, m. Samuel Warkman of R. I., housewright. 3. Sarah, b 16th Aug., 1671, m. Capt. Edward Martyn, merchant of Boston, son of Michael Martyn of Boston, mariner. In this line is descended Mrs. Harrison Ellery. 4. Elizabeth, m. John Welch, mariner. 5. Edward, m. Elizabeth —— ——; was cooper of Boston. 6. Susanna, d. June 18, 1678. 7. Thankful, b. Jan. 18, 1677, spinster in 1702. 8. John, b. Aug. 12, 1680.

ANNA, b. Nov. 16, 1647; d. Sept. 13, 1680, æ. 33, (g. s. Copp's Hill); m. Aug. 19, 1664, Obadiah Read of Boston, housewright, by whom she had several children. 1. Elizabeth, b. Mch. 29, 1669; m. July 6, 1691, Samuel Durham. 2. Anna, b. Feb. 3, 1672–3; m. Highinbottom. 3. James, b. Feb. 29, 1679–80. Others d. young. By his 2nd wife Elizabeth he had children. He d. Feb. 19, 1721–2, æ. 82, (g. s. Copp's Hill). Will made Jan. 3, 1718; invt. £875; names sons Thomas, James, and Obadiah to have 100 acres land in Kittery Co., York; grandson John Durram; daus. Sarah Hughes, Anna Highinbottom, Mary Miller, Elizabeth Durram, Elizabeth, dau. of Obadiah; sisters Hannah and Sarah Broughton.

JAMES, bapt. 10, 1, 1649; d. 4, 9, 1657.

SUSANNA, b. Feb. 11, 1651–2; d. Mch. 2, 1732, æ. 80; m. Apr. 18, 1672, Elder Hopestill Clapp of Dorchester. (See *Clapp's Genealogy*).

ELIZABETH,                         ; d. 6, 9, 1657.

The death of Goodman Swift is recorded May 4, 1675, but his grave-stone is inscribed May 30, 1675, and that of his wife January 26, 1677–8. These stones, still standing side by side in the western corner of the ancient graveyard of Dorchester, at Upham's corner, are of heavy slate well preserved, and bid fair to stand the storms and sunshine of two centuries more. The illustrations given, are directly from the stones. The inscriptions are also printed on page 166, Vol. iv. of the *N. E. Hist. and Gen. Register.*

The graves are covered with two large rough Roxbury pudding stones, placed there to protect the bodies from the wolves; a common custom with the early settlers, these rapacious animals being numerous at that period.

## WILL.

The last will and testam[t] of me Tho: Swift Sen[r] of dorchester, made the six and twentieth day of Aprill, sixteen hundred seveanty and five.

First. I Commit my soule to god that gave it, and my body to a decent buriall in the earth. And for this world's goods which god has gratiously given me, my will is that my just debts be paid and funerall discharged, and then my whole estate as now it is, I leave it with my wife for her comfortable livelyhood dureing her natural life, if she remaine a widow; but and if she Change her Condition by marrying with another man, then my will is that my wife shall have one hundred pounds out of my estate, either in land or goods, which she like best, and this hundred pounds shall be at her disposall when it shall please god to take her away by death. and for the rest of my estate, when this hundred pounds is taken away, my will is that my sonn Tho: shall have five pounds as a farther token of my love, beside what he have formerly had.

Also, I give and bequeath six pounds unto the towne of dorchester toward there maintaining of an able minestry in dorchester, and to be laid out by the selectmen & deacons in Something that may helpe the towne in there yearly maintenance. And twenty shillings I give unto Henry Merrifield, and twenty shillings unto Anne, the wife of Rob' Spurr, who were formerly my servants: the remainder of my estate I doe will and appointe that my sonn Obediah Swift shall have a double portion with any of his sisters, accounting what they have formerly had. and when my wife die or marry, if my sonn Obediah be able & willing, he may purchase the land and pay his sisters in other specie. further, my will is that Elizabeth, my deare and loving wife shall be Executrix of my whole estate, and my brother-in-Law W". Sumner, and my brother-in-Law John Capen I doe appointe to be Overseeres of my whole estate. In witness whereof I have hereunto set my hand and Seale y" day & yeare aforesaid.

the mark of W. Tho: Swift & a seale.

Signed, Sealed & Deliv<sup>d</sup> in presence of us, viz:

         JOHN CAPEN, Sen',
         Ric<sup>d</sup> SMITH.

         L.<sup>t</sup> Jn<sup>o</sup> Capen and Rich<sup>d</sup> Smith made oath in Court the 30 July, 1675, that they being present subscribed there names as witnesses to this Instrum', which Tho: Swift Signed, sealed and published to be his last will and testam', & y<sup>t</sup> when he soe did he was of a sound disposing minde to the best of there knowledge. this done as attests. *Lib. 6, Fol. 94, Suf. Wills.*

## INVENTORY.

An inventory of the estate of Tho: Swift of dorchester, who departed this life y" 4th of May, 1675, taken and appraised by us whose names are underwritten this 18th day of June, 1675:

| | £ | s. | d. |
|---|---|---|---|
| Imp<sup>rs</sup>. wearing apparrell of all Sorts, both linen and woolen, | 010 | 01 | 00 |
| It: some peses of new Cloath, viz: tecking, | 002 | 00 | 03 |
| It: 9 sheetes, 7 pillowbys, table cloath, one duz. and halfe of napkins, towells and a little flax, | 007 | 08 | 03 |
| It: one bed and bolster, blankets, pillows, curtaines, vallens, bedstead, | 010 | 13 | 06 |
| It: One Cupbord, Chests, truncke, table, Chaires, Cushins and forme, | 006 | 01 | 00 |
| In the Chamber. It: One featherbed, bolsters, Rugg, blanktis, | 005 | 01 | 06 |
| It: 3 p' Sheetes, one chest, Rugg and other small things, | 004 | 12 | 05 |
| Kitchen. It: 10 platters, 2 candlesticks, basons, fruttedishes, porengers, quart potts, bowles, &c., | 004 | 13 | 00 |
| It: 2 brass kittles, 1 Iron pot, 1 warming pan, 1 porsnet skillet, brase morter firepan and tongs, and other utinsells, | 007 | 14 | 06 |
| Malthouse. It: One skreene, hair cloth baggs, measures, and other utensels, | 003 | 10 | 06 |
| In the yard & field. It: 5 Cows, one horse, two oxen, two yung cattle, swine, Cart and wheeles, plow, chaine, sadle, pillion, bridle, and other utincells, | 033 | 10 | 04 |
| It: 22 acres and ½ of land on the north of Naponsett, | 011 | 05 | 00 |
| It: 20 acres land at the 20 acre lots, | 040 | 00 | 00 |
| It: 11 acres and ½ land in y" Cow walke, | 030 | 00 | 00 |
| It: the dwelling house, barne,     rooms, orchard, gardens, plowing land and pasture land on the hill neere the house, about 12 acres, | 160 | 00 | 00 |
| It: 4 acres of land called pops lott, and aboute two acres in the tounc feild, | 002 | 00 | 00 |
| It: 6 acres of meadow, | 000 | 00 | 00 |
| It: One muskit and p' of Sidar press, | 000 | 19 | 00 |
| the totall sume, errors excepted, is | 459 | 10 | 03 |

*Lib. 5, Fol. 259, Suf. Wills.*

JAMES HUMPSTREY,<br>WM. SUMNER,<br>JOHN CAPEN, Sen<sup>r</sup>.

Although Thomas Swift made his mark when signing his will, he could write, for a *fac-simile* of his autograph, with others, attached to a petition in 1641, is printed in Blake's *Annals of Dorchester.*

2

**Deacon Thomas, Swift,** *(Thomas¹)* of Milton, yeoman, b. in Dorchester, Mass.,
June 17, 1635; m. Dec. 9, 1657, Elizabeth, dau. of Robert Vose, of Milton. She
d. Jan. 26, 1676, and the 16th of the following October he m. Sarah Clapp. She
was dismissed from the church in Dorchester the 18, 7, 1681, and was admitted to
full communion at the Milton church Oct. 2, 1681. She may have been a daughter
of a brother of Roger Clapp. (See *Clapp Genealogy*, *p. 12*).

CHILDREN.

> THOMAS, b. July 30, 1659; dead in 1717, when his father, by will, gives a legacy to "Thomas
> Swift, the reputed Son of Son Thomas Swift, deceas'd."
> ELIZABETH, b. Aug. 21, 1662; m. ————— Pratt.
> EBENEZER, b. Oct. 21, 1667; d. Nov. 3, 1680.
> WILLIAM, b. May 5, 1670; killed in 1690 in the expedition against Quebec, Canada, being a mem-
> ber of John Withington's co. of Dorchester. His cousin James, member of same co., was also
> killed.
> 4. John, b. Mch, 14, 1678–9.
> 5. Samuel, b. Dec. 10, 1683.

Deacon Swift received from his father-in-law, in 1659, 19¾ acres of upland in
Milton, which was confirmed to him by deed dated Feb. 23, 1663.* This, with
other lots which he subsequently added by purchase, was the original homestead,
continued in the family until 1835, when it was sold by his great-grandson Samuel
Swift. This estate is now owned by Mr. Lewis W. Tappan, Jr., of Milton, a descendant
of Obadiah, brother of Dea. Thomas Swift.

He early showed a capacity for public affairs, and in 1662 was chosen to run a
line between Dorchester and Braintree, and was a supervisor of the highway. In
1661 he received a bounty of £1 for slaying a wolf.

He evidently settled in Milton about the time of his marriage, and became one of
the most prosperous and useful citizens, being constantly in office till within a few
years of his death.

The town was incorporated in 1662, but the records do not commence until 1669.
His name appears that year as one appointed to make the rate, and "get help for the
Sabbath." The same year he was on the grand jury, and also commenced his long
career of service as a selectman, which reached, almost without an intermission, to
the year 1700—a period of about thirty years. During this time he was also called
to serve in various other capacities; was clerk of the market; appointed in 1700–1
to oversee the building of the meeting house; was fence viewer, tything-man,
assessor, representative to General Court, and in 1714 moderator—probably the last
town office which he held.

---

*Mch. 18, 1727–8, Jonathan Gulliver æ. about 67 yrs., Stephen Crane about 70 yrs., John Wadsworth about
55 yrs., Peter White about 67 yrs., all testify that Dea. Thomas Swift of Milton, deceased, and Samuel Swift, his
son, for forty years have been in possession of a certain tract of land in Milton. — *Suf. Deeds, Lib. 42, Fol. 33.*

Beside these numerous offices he was made quartermaster of a troop of horse May 5, 1676, as had been his father, and bore the title of lieutenant. He was appointed by the General Court to take charge of the Neponset Indians at Brush Hill. Major Gookin, in his *Indian History* says that "Mr. Eliot and himself met every other week in the winter of 1676 among the Punkapoag Indians, who were brought up from Long Island, and placed near Brush Hill in Milton, under the charge of Quartermaster Swift. They came up late from the Island, yet they planted some ground procured for them by Major Swift, and they got some corn. Their wives and children were there with them."

The following orders and petitions, from the *Mass. Archives*, give us some idea of his valuable services.

29, 5, 1675. Coperall Thomas Swift was ordered by the council to take with him Indians, soldiers at Swanzy.

To the honorable Connsell now sitting in Boston:

Thes humbly sheweth that wheras I was ordered by the whorshipfull Mr. Danforth to aspect the Indians belonging to punckapoge the latter part of the last summer, and secondly of beinge ordered by the honnerd major Guggins, and so from the honnerd Counsell to tacke care of the aforesayd indians after that they came from the island. Thes humbly informeth that the last year I spent a grete deal of time about them, they being restraind from Commerse with the Inglish, and our English beinge so Redy, many of them, to tacke any advantage against them if that they were found out of tbar Limits, which necesitated me to doe much of ther business, beside all other ackomation conceringe them and the good of the Country, Considering how the case stood between us & the indian; which service I hop I did cheerfuly and in some mesure, I hop, to the utmost of my power, for which I have never reseved any alowance; but I humbly leve it to your honers Consideration. as to the ackompt of what time I spent, it was almost impossible for me to Kepe an ackompt of, considering how things have been with us. so I Rest, holding it my duty to pray for you honner.

your humbell servant in what I can or may,

THOMAS SWIFT.

5d. 8m., 76: }                                              *Mass. Archives, Lib. 30, Fol. 223.*

Ordered, that Lieu' Thomas Swift take Speedy care to provide Sixty or more of the Friend Indians, well furnish'd with arms & amunition, to be sent out under a Suitable Comander ag' the comon Enemy.

Past in the affirmative by the Magistrate.

Aug. 1690.                                                  Jo" ADDINGTON, Sec'y.
                                                           Neh. Jewet, p. ored.
          Consented to by the deputices.

These he furnished at an expense of £0.15.0. — *Mass. Archives.*

Not only in secular affairs was he prominent and useful, but the church found in him a ready supporter. He was one of the founders of the First Church in Milton, signing the covenant April 24, 1678, and Aug. 20, 1682, was ordained deacon. He and his wife Elizabeth had been members of the Dorchester church before the organization of the Milton church, and there their children were baptized. In 1686 he gave £2.5.0 to the support of the minister, being one of the largest subscribers.

The town records of Dorchester show that he and Ezra Clapp were granted, in 1681, liberty to catch fish at Neponset, below the mill, and to make a stage there.

Capt. Roger Clapp of Dorchester, Nov. 9, 1690, makes his *cousin* Thomas Swift one of the overseers of his will.

Deacon Swift lived to the good old age of 82 years, dying January 26, 1717–18. His wife died Feb. 4th, 1717–18, the day after her husband's funeral, as is recorded in the journal of her son, the Rev. John Swift of Framingham. Some accounts call the Rev. John the son of the first wife, Elizabeth, which is erroneous.

The gravestones of Mr. and Mrs. Swift—small, beautifully cut stones—are standing in the Milton cemetery among a number of stones, fifteen in all, of the family. That of Mr. Swift has been printed in the *N. E. H. G. Register*. They are reproduced for this work by the Albertype process.

## WILL.

In the Name of God. Amen. the Twenty-first day of September, Anno Domini One Thousand Seven Hundred and Seventeen. In the fourth Year of the Reign of our Sovereign Lord George over Great Brittain, &c., I, Thomas Swift of Milton, in the County of Suffolk within his Majesties province of the Massachusetts Bay, in New England, Yeoman, being in a Competent Measure of bodily health, and of sound mind & understanding, praised be almighty God for the same, Knowing the uncertainty of this present life, and being desireous to Settle that outward Estate the Lord hath lent me, Doe therefore make & Ordain this my Last will and Testament in manner and form following, (That is to say), First and principally I commend my Soul into the hands of God, my almighty Creator, hopeing to receive full pardon and remission of all my Sins, and Salvation through the alone Merits of Jesus Christ my Redeemer, And my Body to the Earth, to be decently Interred according to the discretion of my Ex^{rs}, herein after named, in hopes of a Glorious Resurrection into Eternall life. And as touching such worldly Estate as the Lord hath lent unto me, my will and meaning is, the same shall be Imploy'd and bestowed as hereafter in and by this my will is exprest. hereby revoking, renouncing & makeing null and void all wills and Testaments by me formerly made, declareing and appointing this to be my last will and Testament, wherein is contained the same.

Imp^{rs}. I will that all my just debts, and Funerall expences, bee well, truly and duely paid, by my son Samuel Swift of Milton afores^d, Husbandman, one of my Executors hereinafter named.

Item. I do give and bequeath unto my Loving wife Sarah Swift the use, benefit and improvement of the East End of my Dwelling House, from Bottom to top, with the liberty, use and privilidge of y^r Garden and well, and Three Milch Cows maintained Summer and winter, and Yearly the summe of Twelve Pounds Money, Quarterly (dureing the Terme of her naturall life,) or in what to her shall be Equivalent to money, and her Yearly firewood. I also give and bequeath unto my aforesaid wife Sarah Swift, her Heirs and Assigns forever, all my money and Moveable Estate within doors, And all Money, and debts owing or due to me by bill, Bond, or otherwise. I also give unto her my Negro Woman to be at her disposall, and the one-half of my Orchard dureing her natural life.

Item. I do hereby give, devise and bequeath unto my Son John Swift, and to his Heirs and Assigns forever. All that my whole Tract and parcell of upland, which I have lying in the Six Divisions (so called) within the township of Milton afores^d, bounded Easterly with the Land of Ephraim Newton, Westerly with Deacon Sumner's Land, Northerly with the Parralel Line, and Southerly with Brantry Line. Also all my Land Lying in the Twelve Divisions of Land (so called) in Dorchester afores^d, Containing between Three Score and Four score Acres. And also all that my Piece of Salt mairsh Meadow Lying in Dorchester afores^d, containing Estimation Seven Acres, be the same more or Less, which is bounded and Surrounded with Lands of the Late Ebenezer Clap, dec^d, John Daniel, Daniel Allen, and the River. And my mind and will is that my s^d Son John Swift, or his Heirs, shall possess all the afores^d uplands at my decease, and the Meadow at my s^d wife's decease or removeall by marriage, (I haveing given my s^d Son John Swift considerable before, beside his learning.) And if it happens that my s^d Son John Swift at any time hereafter he minded to sell and dispose of his aforesaid Lands and Meadow, it is my will and desire that his Brother Samuel Swift may have the first tender thereof, made to him for buying them on such reasonable Terms as any other person would give for the same. And if it happen that my s^d Son John, with his family, in his Mother's lifetime or afterwards Leaves Framingham, and is minded to come & Live in Milton, then in such case for the Accomodation of himself and Family while he shall remain in Milton, wether it be for term of his life or shorter, he shall have the Old East End of my dwelling House, up and downe from the Cellar to the Top, Liberty & use of the old Garden and well, with Ingress, Egress and Regress to and from the same for the aforesaid purpose freely, only having his Mother's Consent thereto. I give also to my S^d Son John Three Cows, to be delivered him at my decease.

Item. I give and bequeath unto my Daughter Elizabeth Pratt, and all her Children born of her body, One Hundred Pounds, to be equally divided between her and them, to be paid them within One Year after my decease, by my son Samuel Swift.

Item. I give and bequeath unto Thomas Swift, the reputed Son of Son Thomas Swift, deceas^d, Ten Shillings besides the Twenty Pounds I have given under my hand to pay him, and what is behind that I promised his Mother. And I do hereby Ordaine and appoint that the afors^d Thomas Swift, the reputed son of my s^d Son Tho: Swift, shall have no more of my said Estate.

Item. I do hereby give, devise, and bequeath unto my s^d Son Samuel Swift, and to his Heirs and Assignes forever, all my remaining upland and meadow Lying and being in Milton & Dorchester aforesaid, with all my Housing, Edifices, Buildings, Barnes, Yards, Gardens, Orchards appertaining thereto, and Fences Standing thereon, he paying my just Debts and Funerall Expences, and what I have herein before given Annually unto his Mother, and unto his Sister Elizabeth Pratt and her Children; and also supplying his Mother with Firewood at home at her doore at all time and times when she shall need it, as also an Horse to ride on at her pleasure; as also reserving out of the above given and bequeathed premises unto my Son John the privilige of his liveing in the Old East End of s⁴ Dwelling house in manner as afores⁴. I also give unto my son Samuel Swift all the rest of my whole Stock of Neat Cattle, and all my out door Implements & Utensills of Husbandry, as Carts, Wheels, Chains, Ploughs and the like. And I do appoint my Negro Man to be for the Equall use and Service of my Son Samuel and my wife while she Continues upon my place, and at her removeal thence by Death or otherwise the s⁴ Negro Man to be the Sole dispose of my s⁴ Son Samuel; and my Indian Boy Jehu to be at my Son Samuel's disposall for the remainder of his time at my decease. And it is my mind and will that my s⁴ Son Samuel Swift, out of that my Estate given unto him as above said, shall pay unto my aboves⁴ wife the summe of Twelve Pounds Pr. Annum dureing her naturall life, & all needfull firewood, and provide and maintaine for her Three Cows and a Horse dureing her abode in Milton as aboves⁴. And shall pay unto his Sister Pratt and her Children One Hundred Pounds as abovesaid, and unto Thomas Swift, the reputed Son of Thomas Swift, Ten Shillings as aboves⁴. And my will is that my wive's Three Cows afores⁴, and all the moveables before given unto her which remain at her my s⁴ wife's decease, be for my s⁴ Son John Swift and his Heirs.

Lastly. I do hereby constitute and appoint my Two before named Sons, John and Samuel Swift, to be the Executors of this my Last Will and Testament. In Testimony whereof I, the said Thomas Swift, have hereunto set my hand and Seal the day and Year first above written.

THOMAS SWIFT.        { SEAL }

> Signed, Sealed, Published & Declared by the s⁴ Thomas Swift, the Testator, as and for his Last will and Testament, in presence of us.
>
> EDWARD MILLS, JUN⁴,
> SAMUEL KNEELAND,
> EDWARD MILLS.

Suffolk, ss.                    By the Hon^ble SAMUEL SEWALL, Esq., Judge of Probate, &c.

The aforegoing Will being presented for Probate by John and Samuel Swift, Executors within Named, Edward Mills and Samuel Kneeland made Oath that they Saw Thomas Swift, the Subscriber to the aforegoing Instrument, Sign, Seal, and heard him publish and Declare the same to be his last Will and Testament. And that when he so did he was of Sound Disposing mind and memory according to these Depon^ts best Discerning. And that together with Edward Mills, Jun^r, (now at Marblehead,) set to their names as witnesses thereof in the presence of the said Testator.

SAMUEL SEWALL.

Boston, February 20^th, 1717.

> JOHN SWIFT of Framingham, Gent,
> SAMUEL SWIFT of Milton, Yeoman,
> THOMAS THATCHER of Boston, Brasier,
> JAMES TILESTONE of s⁴ Boston, Carpenter,

all of the county of Suffolk, gave bonds in the sum of Two thousand dollars for the fullfilment of the will Feb. 5, 1718. Lib. 20, Fol. 224.

------

4

**Rev. John³ Swift,** *(Thomas² Thomas¹.)* b. in Milton Mar. 14, 1678–9; d. Apr. 24, 1745; m. Dec. 16, 1701, Sarah, (b. Sept, 7, 1671; d. Feb. 1, 1747, æ. 73 yrs.) dau. of Timothy Tileston of Dorchester.

CHILDREN.

SARAH, b. Sept. 16, 1702; dead in 1745; adm. to Church Mar. 24, 1728; m. June 6, 1729, Eben Roby of Sudbury.

ELIZABETH, b. Mar. 26, 1704; d. Apr. 12, 1739; adm. to Church Mar. 24, 1728; m. Apr. 15, 1731, Rev. James Stone of Holliston.

ANNE, b. July 5, 1706; d. ——— ———; m. Dec. 5, 1733, Rev. Phillips Payson, H. C. 1724; settled at Walpole. Four of their sons were settled ministers: Rev. Phillips Payson, D. D., H. C. 1754; ord. at Chelsea 26 Oct., 1757. Rev. Samuel Payson, H. C. 1758; ord. at Lunenburg Sept., 1762. Rev. John Payson, H. C. 1764; ord. at Fitchburg 27 Jan., 1768. Rev. Seth Payson, D. D., H. C. 1777; ord. Rindge, N. H., 4 Dec., 1782, father of Rev. Edward Payson, D. D., of Portland, Me., H. C. 1803.

MARY, b. Nov. 16, 1708; unm. in 1745.

MARTHA, b. ——— ———; m. Oct. 13, 1740, Major John Farrar of Framingham. She died about 1749.

6.  John, b. Jan. 14, 1713–14.

Rev. John Swift was the senior minister of the Marlboro' Association of ministers at the time of its formation, although the name of Robert Breck stands first on the list of members. He graduated at Harvard College in 1697, and was ordained as the first minister of Framingham Oct. 8, 1701. His ministry was conducted with faithfulness and prudence; and not a notice occurs in all the transactions of the town in any degree qualifying the respect and estimation in which he was held. Of his ability as a preacher we have no means of judging. His printed sermons are marked with a pure and classical taste. He was free from all affectation of style as well as extravagance of zeal, or rashness of opinion. The subject of his ordinary discourses, as one may infer from his own diary, were often suggested by passing events. Some of these discourses bear marks of extemporaneous composition. Thus he notes on one occasion his preaching from the words "The voice of the Lord is upon the waters; the God of glory thundereth;" adding, "it being a day of thunder." A day of extreme severity suggested the text: "Who can stand before his cold?" And a few weeks later, doubtless while the snow drifted through the crevices of the ancient and dilapidated meeting-house, the motto of his sermon was "a covert from the storm." The halt of a detachment of soldiers in the village induced him to discourse from the word "a devout soldier." Mr. Swift preached the Election Sermon in 1732; also a discourse on the occasion of the death of the Rev. Robert Breck of Marlborough in 1731; both of which were printed.

He is spoken of as a wise counsellor and good man of a well cultivated mind, and held in great esteem in the churches. His salary was £70, equal to $233.33; to which, in the latter part of his ministry on account of the sickness of his wife, an additional grant of $10 was added. He is said to have been a correspondent of Dean Swift. He died April 24, 1745, in the 45th year of his ministry and the 67th year of his age. See *Hist. of Framingham, and Hist. of the Worcester Association.*

The following letter respecting the division of Framingham is interesting, as giving one some idea of the situation of a country minister at that period:

Framingham June 7, 1731.

Sir:—

    I hear that the Hon[ble] House of Representatives have granted a Division of the Town of Framingham (which upon 30 years' Experience or more of the capacity of the s[d] Town) I fear will prov. subversive to the best, especially religious, Interests of the Said Town.

    Such a Division, Sir, would be a great Ease to me in my Official performances were the Town capable of it; but by reason of the Town's deficiency in the payment of my dues, and trouble they have given me about my Settlement, I have been greatly impoverished, Spent a Considerable part of my paternal estate to Support the Ministry in Framingham, as I can easily make to appear.

    Settling in the year 1700, before there was any paper currency in the Governm[t]. (as I suppose), and having had but an inconsiderable allowance for the Change of the Species, I can't suppose my Loss to be much (if anything) short of 1000£. The Deficiency of the arrears since the Town had a discharge or receipt in full from me, which I know ought to be made good, and am well informed are recoverable in the Law, together with new charges which will accrue unavoidably, will be what one-half part of Framingham (notwithstanding their numbers) cannot accomplish without help, in my humble opinion, *verte Dominie.* In the year 1729 the Hon[ble] House of Representatives received it for good doctrine. I think, viz[t], that our Hon[ble] Legislature have it in their power to make reasonable allowance for the discount upon the paper currency whereby Minist[rs] small annuityes are much diminished, And I depend (under God) upon the Goodness & Justice of his Excellency & the Hon-

ourable Board that nothing shall be done to my hurt. If there should be any occasion, I pray, Sir, that you would communicate these lines, as in your wisdom you Shall See meet, and you will greatly oblige
Y' Obedient & humble Servant,

JOHN SWIFT.

To the Hon'<sup>ble</sup>
    JOHN WILLARD, Esq',
        Boston.
            Deliver
    Mass. Archives Lib. 114, fol. 56.

## OBITUARY.

[ From the *Boston Evening Post* of May 13th, 1745.]

Framingham, May 8. On the 24th of the last Month died here, after a long and tedious Indisposition, the Rev. Mr. John Swift, the first Pastor of the Church in this Place, in the 67th Year of his Age, and the 45th Year of his Ministry. As he was a Gentleman of considerable natural Powers, so he acquired a considerable Degree of human and useful Learning. He particularly excelled in Rhetoric, and Oratory, and as a Critic in the Greek Language. His Piety was sincere and eminent: His Preaching was sound and Evangelical. As a Pastor he was diligent, faithful and prudent; and in his Conversation he was sober, grave and profitable; yet affable, courteous and pleasant. He was a lover of Hospitality, and kept his Heart and his House open to all good People. When he received Injuries at any Time, he bore them with singular Discretion and Meekness; and the various Trials and Sorrows with which he was exercised, especially the latter part of his Life, gave Occasion for shewing forth his Wisdom, Humanity, Patience, and Resignation to the Divine Will. He was had in high Esteem by the Association to which he belonged, and respected by all who had any Acquaintance with his real Character and Merits.

The following inscription, from his monument in the Framingham graveyard, is printed in the history of that town :

HIC JACET
Qui obiit A. D. 1745, Aprilis 24<sup>to</sup>
Ætatisque anno 67<sup>mo</sup>
**VIR ILLE REVERENDUS D. JOHANNES SWIFT**
Dotibus et nativis et acquisitis ornatus ;
Docendi Artifex, Exemplar Vivendi,
Felix, dum vixit,
Mores exhibens secundum Divinas Regulas,
Episcopo necessarios
Commiscens Prudentiam Serpentis, Columbæque,
Innocentiam :
Commercium cum eo habentibus,
In vita Percharus,
Atque gratam sui, etsi mœstam, Memoriam
Post mortem, lis relinquens :
Qui per varios casus, variaque Rerum Discrimina
Atque usque ad mortem
Raram discretionem, Modestiam, Patientiam,
Voluntatique Supremi Numinis Submissionem
Spectandam prœbens ;
Jam tandam in Domino requievit
Adoptionem
Scilicet, Corporis obruti Redemtionem
Expectabundus.

Here lies the Reverend John Swift, who died in 1745, April 24th, in the 67th year of his age. Adorned with gifts both native and acquired; he was a master in the art of teaching; a model of living, conforming all his acts to the divine laws. To all those with whom he had to do he exhibited the wisdom of the serpent and the innocence of the dove. While living he was very much beloved, and he left at death a grateful though mournful memory to his friends. Through many scenes and trials, and even unto death, he manifested a rare discretion, modesty, patience and submisson to the Divine Will. He at length rests with the Lord, looking for the adoption that is the redemption of the body.

## WILL.

The following Will, dated September, 1743, commences with the usual formula:

Imp'. My Will is That my just Debts and funeral Charges be duly paid or discharged by my Executor.

Item. I give and bequeath unto Sarah, my Well beloved Wife (in lieu of Dower & Thirds) the use & Improvement of my House in Framingham, of late years used for my Study, as also of the Land and conveniences adjoining, & therewith used distinct from my former: and other improvements, & one Bed, and furniture, (of which my said wife to have her Choice,) and so much of my Other Household Goods as shall be Judged necessary and convenient in order to her keeping house there, as also the benefit of one Cow, to be kept for her use Winter and Summer, annually during her widowhood. and I further give & bequeath unto my said Wife one purse with Some Silver Money therein (Which may be found in the Till of my chest under Some writings); and further, my Will is That my Said Wife be Supplied (out of the Income of my Real Estate) with whatsoever shall be further needful for her comfortable & Decent Support & maintenance during her Widowhood as aforesaid, and for a Decent funeral after Death.

Item. I give and bequeath unto my Son John Swift (Minister of Acton,) whom I likewise Constitute Sole Executor of this my Will, my Whole Library, Books and Manuscript, also my Watch and my Negro-man named or called Francis. Also all my Right & Interest of Lands at a place called or known by the name of Dorchester, Canada; Which Right of Lands were Derived to me on acc' of my Brother William Swift, who (with many others) perished in the first Expedition against Canada; To him, my said son John, and To his heirs and assigns forever.

Item. I give & bequeath unto my Son-in-Law, Ebenezer Robye, Esq., & to his heirs and assigns, my Negro man named or called Nero, or such sum in Bills of Credit as he shall be valued at by a just appraizer.

Item. I give and bequeath unto my son-in-Law, M' Philips Payson. (minister of Walpole,) and to his heirs & assigns, my Negro Named or called Guy.

Item. My Will is that my other Two Negros, namely, Dido and Esther, serve with my aboves' Wife on her Order during her life, and after her Decease with my Daughter Farrar, her heirs or assigns.

Item. My Will is That all my Housing and Lands in Framingham, Stoughton and Elsewhere, with all my Personal Estate of what kind, nature or Denomination Soever (other than what is above mentioned & bequeathed) be Divided in five even & Equal parts or shares to and among the rest of my Children & Grand Children in Manner following: That is to say, one-fifth part thereof to my Daughter Anne Payson; one-fifth part thereof to my Daughter Mary Swift; one-fifth part thereof to my Daughter Martha Farrar; And one-fifth part thereof (to be Distributed part & part alike) to and among the Children of my Daughter Sarah Robye, Dec'd; and one-fifth part thereof in like manner to and among the Children of my Daughter Elizabeth Stone, Dec'd. To them, their heirs and assigns respectively forever.

Ult". My Will is That my Surviving Daughters, together with such as shall be appointed Guardian to my Grand Children, may (if they apprehend it needful or profitable) make Sale of Housing and Lands to them bequeathed as afores'', or any part thereof, during the minority of my Grand children, or any of them: and I accordingly authorize & Impower them so to do, by passing good and authentick Deed or Deeds of the same. And I do hereby utterly Revoke, Disannul & make void all other Wills, Bequests or Execut''

by me in any wise before Named, Willed or bequeathed; Ratifying and confirming this & none other to
be my last Will and Testament.  In Witness whereof I have hereunto set my hand & Seal the day & date
within written.

JOHN SWIFT.                    { SEAL }

> Signed, Sealed, published & declared by the within named John Swift, as his last
> Will & Testament, In the presence of us the Subscribers, who set to our
> names as Witnesses in the said Testator's presence.

> WILLIAM PIKE,
> STEPHEN BALLARD,
> MARY FARRAR.
> her X mark.

This Codicil or Schedule Witnesseth that I, the within Named John Swift, in addition to my Will bearing
date in the Month of September, 1745, Do hereby give and bequeath unto my Daughter Mary Swift, in consideration of her Trouble, and in requital of her Dutiful & tender care of me under my Weakness, my silver
Tankard, also my Horse & Shayes over & above what is expressed in my said Will; hereby Ratifying & Confirming the said Will, with Codicil, to be my last Will & Testament.  In witness whereof I have hereunto set my
hand & seal this 11th day of June, A. D. 1744.

JOHN SWIFT.                    { SEAL }

In the presence of

> JOSEPH BUCKMINSTER, JUN.,
> WILLIAM PIKE,
> STEPHEN BALLARD.

---

6

**Rev. John Swift,**[4] *(John,*[3] *Thomas,*[2] *Thomas,*[1]*)* born in Framingham Jan. 14,
1713–14; d. Nov. 7, 1776, æ. 61 yrs.; m. Nov. 19, 1740, Abigail, (b. July 20, 1717;
d. Mar. 18, 1782, in the 63d year of her age,) dau. of Jeremiah and Rebecca Adams,
of Medway.

CHILDREN.

7.      1.  **John,** b. Nov. 18, 1741.

Mr. Swift was graduated at Harvard College in 1733, and the same year was
schoolmaster in Framingham.  In May, 1738, he received an unanimous invitation
to settle in the ministry at Acton, and the following 8th of November was ordained
He first received £250 as a settlement, and £150 as an annual salary — to be made
of equal value should the currency depreciate.  This sum was altered several times,
and at last permanently fixed at £70 lawful money.

During the prevalence of the small pox in Acton, in 1775, he was severely
attacked by the disease, and never able to preach afterwards.

He was a little above the common height, rather slender, of pleasing address and
manners; opposed to excess and extravagance of every kind, and was a gentleman
of talent, learning and piety, though occasionally facetious, witty and eccentric.

His sermon, preached at the ordination of the Rev. Joseph Lee of Royalston,
was published.

## WILL.

His will, dated October 24, 1775, commences in the usual manner:

Imprimis. I will that all my just debts and funeral charges be well and truly paid in convenient time after my decease.

Item. I give unto my beloved Wife Abigail Swift my Horse and Chaise and Eighty pounds lawful money, together with two-thirds part of all the remainder of my personal estate, money, &c., to be at her disposal forever; and likewise the improvement of two-thirds part of all my Real Estate lying in Acton, so long as she remains my widow.

Item. I give unto my only Son, John Swift, all the remainder of my Real and personal Estate lying in Acton, not before disposed of. My will is that my said Son John shall come in possession of the whole of my Real Estate lying in Acton, after my wife's marriage or decease.

I give unto my Grand Children, Hollis and Luther, all my lands in Ashburnham in the County of Worcester, in the province aforesaid, to be equally divided between them in quality. My Will is that if either of my said Grand Children should die in minority, or when in a single state, the whole of said lands in Ashburnham I give to the other surviving grand son. Furthermore, I do hereby constitute and appoint my beloved wife Abigail and my son John Swift to be Executors to this my will and testament.

JOHN SWIFT. {SEAL}

Signed, sealed, and pronounced to be his last will and testament before

EDWARD SPRAGUE,
DANIEL ADAMS,
ABEL FISK.

---

### 7

**Dr. John[5] Swift,** *(John,[4] John,[3] Thomas,[2] Thomas,[1])* b. in Acton Nov. 18, 1741; H. C. 1762; physician of Acton; d. Dec. 23, 1781, in his 40th year. He m. Catharine Davis of Acton, b. May 6, 1748. She had a second husband, Dr. Whitman.

#### CHILDREN.

JOHN HOLLIS, b. ——————, 1768; d. Sept. 18, 1793, unm.
WILLIAM PITT, b. Mch. 3, 1771; d. Mch 26, 1774.
JEREMIAH ADAMS, b. ——————, 1772; d. Mch. 31, 1774.
8. **Luther,[6]** b. April 20, 1775;

---

### 8

**Luther Swift,[5]** *(John,[4] John,[3] Thomas,[2] Thomas,[1])* b. April 20, 1775; d. Dec. 6, 1857; m. —————— 1798, Hannah Brown, b. May 26, 1777; d. July 25, 1850.

#### CHILDREN.

JOHN HOLLIS, b. Dec. 12, 1799; d. s. p. Feb. 15, 1863; m. Jan. 11, 1822, Hannah H. Pulcifer; b. abt. 1799; d. Feb. 29, 1864.
CATHARINE, b. Jan. 23, 1802; d. Feb. 23, 1803.
CATHARINE ELIZA, b. Aug. 21, 1804; d. Apr. 9, 1807.
9. **William Pitt,** b. Apr. 30, 1806.
CAROLINE, b. June 3, 1809; d. May 22, 1882; unm.

## 9

**William⁷ Pitt Swift**, (*Luther,⁶ John,⁵ John,⁴ John,³ Thomas,² Thomas,¹*) b. April 30, 1806; d. Dec. 20, 1857; m. Mar. 30, 1835, Abigail, (b. Dec. 1813,) dau. of Asa and Mary (Leach) Shaw, of Norton, Mass. She m. a second husband —— French, who died in 1878. She resides in Malboro', Mass.

### CHILDREN.

WILLIAM PORTER, b. April 21, 1836; d. May 5, 1838.

JOHN, b. April 28, 1838; member of Co. D, 21st Reg't. Served 3 years in the Union Army. Residence, Sioux City; m. in 1866 Eliza A. Pratt, of Fitchburg.

LIZZIE F., b. Jan. 23, 1840; m. May 7, 1860, Luther F. Read of Westford, b. Feb. 1, 1838; killed at the battle of Antietam Sept. 17, 1862. She next m. Nov. 26, 1870, Wm. F. Hale of Acton, b. Nov. 7, 1840; served nine months in the Union army. Res. Stow. [I am indebted to Mrs. Hale for the information concerning the later generations of her branch of the family.]

ABBY, b. Aug. 16, 1841; d. Jan. 9, 1848.

GEO. LORING, b. Sept. 17, 1842; d. May 21, 1876. Served three years in the Union Army, Co. F, 13th Reg't; m. Sept. 27, 1864, Mary L. Watson of Fitchburg, b. June 3, 1838. They had two children, Sarah Abby and Willie.

JOSEPH ALBERT, b. Dec. 10, 1843. Served three years in the Union Army; reënlisted in 1864; wounded at the battle of Winchester, Va., Sept. 19, 1864; d. in hospital Oct. 12, 1864.*

SARAH, b. April 2, 1845.

LUCY W., b. July 28, 1846; m. Dec. 4, 1867, Joshua W. Carr of Stow, b. May 26, 1844; served three years in the Union Army. Residence, Stow, Mass.

NATHAN, b. Mar. 20, 1848. Residence, Marlboro, Mass.

ISAAC, b. Oct. 10, 1849; d. Sept. 28, 1874.

ANNIE, b. Sept. 22, 1851; m. Charles Sprinks of Albany, N. Y., Nov., 1871. He d. June 14, 1879. Residence, 93 Broad Street, Lynn.

EMMA S., b. June 6, 1853.

William Henry, b. Aug. 4, 1854; m. June 3, 1878, Mary E. Walcott of Stow. Residence, Marlboro, Mass. They had one child, Clarence L. Swift, who d. Oct. 8, 1881, at 9 mos. 21 ds.

---

*He wrote home from war as follows : —

In the Hospital at Winchester, Va., Sept. 26, '64.

DEAR MOTHER : —

I now write you a few more lines to let you know that I am getting along nicely, although the ball has not been found yet. I think it has struck some of the cords, but I hope not, for it may give me a stiff leg for life; then I should have to be discharged, and I don't want that you know, for I like soldiering too well. I like it as well as ever. Now do not worry about me for I have the best of spirits, and care too. This is what I enlisted for, and what I have got; and what I would do again if I were at home. I am glad that George did not reënlist, for two is enough. I wish that John had not, for he is so sick of it.

John Brown bore the colors. He did it well, too; he had his leg broken, but he will not lose it. He and I fell near together so we are in the same hospital. Our Acton captain has gone to Harper's Ferry and we shall go soon; then you can write to me.

Write to John and tell him we had a glorious victory. Bully for that!

I must close for the present; love to all and don't worry. This is from your loving son,

JOSEPH A. SWIFT.

He was but a boy when he enlisted, only about seventeen years old, and very small of his age. He was told that they would not take him. "Yes they will," he said, "for I have just made my heels three inches higher, and they will have to take me." When he reënlisted and came home his sister said to him she was sorry, and he replied, "I am not, for what is my life good for if we have not our freedom?"

The John Brown referred to was his schoolmate. They enlisted together, and he thought a great deal of him. Young Swift bled to death from his wounds, and was brought home and buried in Stow. His friend died in a few days after.

5

Col. Samuel³ Swift,* *(Thomas,² Thomas,¹)* of Milton, where he was b. Dec. 10, 1683; d. Oct. 13, 1747; m. Nov. 6, 1707, Ann, (d. May 19, 1769) dau. of Thomas Holman, a prominent citizen of Milton.

CHILDREN.

THOMAS, b. Feb. 16, 1709–10; m. Aug. 23, 1739, Elizabeth Crebore, who d. Aug. 23, 1782, æ. 71. Had a dau. Elizabeth, b. Jan. 9, 1741–2.
SARAH, b. Apr. 28, 1711; m. May 19, 1730, John Adams.
ANNA, b. Aug. 28, 1712; m. Aug. 28, 1739, Solomon Hersey, of Hingham.
PATIENCE, b. Mar. 19, 1714; d. Aug. 12, 1714.
10. Samuel, b. June 9, 1715.
EBENEZER, b. Dec. 6, 1716; d. Aug., 1717.
PATIENCE, b. Feb. 3, 1717–18; m. May 29, 1739, Ebenezer Wadsworth.
11. Nathaniel, b. Sept. 25, 1719.
JOHN, b. Jan. 23, 1720–1; housewright of Milton in 1748; probably d. unm.
ABIGAIL, bapt. Nov. 11, 1722.
12. Ebenezer, b. May 24, 1724.

Col. Swift was one of the wealthiest and most influential men of Milton. He inherited his father's capacity for public affairs, and we early find him filling such offices as constable, tythingman, surveyor of the highways, and so forth. He later became a judge of the court of common pleas, colonel of the militia, representative to the general court, moderator of the town-meetings, and filled the office of select-man almost constantly from 1725 to his death in 1747. In 1727 he was on the committee to build the meeting-house, and in 1729–30 one of four who paid the highest rate, and had his pew "first in the right hand going up the broad alley." He is designated in the town records by the various military titles from ensign to colonel.

The position he so many years sustained in the town tends to confirm the tradition that he was austere and of an arbitrary temper. Our imagination pictures him as a man of commanding aspect, with the dignified manner of his time — such a man as we see in the portraits of Smybert and Copley. The impress of his character is seen in many of his descendants, who have, in addition to ability, been distinguished by many of the social graces of life, a general elegance of bearing, and much personal beauty — those gifts which are seldom to be met with save through a goodly ancestry.

The gravestones of Mr. and Mrs. Swift are among the largest and finest in the Milton cemetery, and are illustrated in this work.

## WILL.

In the Name of God Amen, This Third day of May in the Year of our Lord one Thousand Seven Hundred Forty & Five. And in the Eighteenth Year of the Reign of our Sovereign Lord George the

---

* Continued from page seven. The line of Rev. John Swift, brother of Col. Samuel, being continued through three generations by only one son, in order to simplify matters I deemed it best to complete that branch before taking up the line of Col. Samuel.

Second, King of Great Britain, &c.—I Samuel Swift of Milton in the County of Suffolk, within His Majesties Province of the Massachusetts Bay in New-England, Esq'., being at present in a competent measure of bodily Health, and of perfect Mind and Memory, Thanks be given to God therefor: But calling to mind the mortality of my Body, and Knowing that it is appointed unto all men once to Dye, do make and ordain this my last Will and Testament; That is to say, Principally, and first of all, I Give and Recommend my Soul into the Hands of God that gave it; trusting alone for Salvation in Merits and Righteousness of Jesus Christ my only Saviour and Redeemer; And my Body I Recommend to the Earth, to be Buried in decent Christian Burial, at the discretion of my Executors hereafter named; not at all doubting but at the general Resurrection of the Dead I shall receive the same again by the mighty power of God. And as touching such worldly estate wherewith it has pleased God to bless me in this life, I Give and dispose of the same in the following manner and form. — —

Imprimis, I Give and Bequeath unto Ann my well beloved Wife, the use and Improvement of yᵉ old or Easterly end of my dwelling House, and the Cellar under it: Also the use and Improvement of all my Indoor Goods or Moveables Except my Clock, or such other particulars as I shall here after mention in any of my Childrens Portions: Also the use and Service of my Negro Woman Kate. And also I Give and order her Support and Subsistence in all respects, both in Meat & Drink, and also in Fuel and Medicine, and that in a plentiful and ample manner both in sickness and Health; to be found and provided by my Son Ebenezer Swift. And I also Give her the use of my old Garden. And I also order my sᵈ Son Ebenezer to provide her a Horse to Ride on when ever she shall have occasion, or think fit to use him. And all this above mentioned I give and provide for her so long as she shall remain my Widow and no longer. Also I Give and Bequeath unto her forever, all the Money or Cash that I shall leave at my decease, both Silver and Province or Colony Bills, and all the Debts that may be due to me at my decease, by Bill, Bond, Book debt, or any other ways whatsoever, and also all my Gold Buttons. And in Case she shall Marry again after my decease then I Give her yᵉ Sum of Fifty pounds in Province Bills of the old tenor; to be paid her by my Son Ebenezer within one year after her marriage.

Item, I Give and Bequeath unto my eldest Son Thomas Swift and to his Heirs and assigns forever, that part of my Lot of Land in Milton that lyeth upon the Southeasterly side of the Road leading to Stoughton between the Lands of John Newton & Benjamin Sumner, and being Bounded Northwesterly by yᵉ said Road, and Southeasterly by Braintree old line containing about Seventy Acres of Salt Marsh lying in Dorchester, being the piece he now improves, joyning to the marsh of Nathaniel and Ebenezer Houghton: Also my Cedar-swamp in Stoughton by Mashapoag Pond, containing about Six acres and one Quarter: And also the one half of my Stock of Cattle and Horses according to Quantity and Quality, after what I have herein particularly mentioned and disposed of are first taken out. And after the decease or Marriage of my Wife, I give him my Negro-woman Kate. And also give him the Iron Back that he now improveth.

Item, I give and Bequeath unto my second Son Samuel Swift, the Sum of Three Hundred pounds in Bills of Credit on this Province of the old tenor; to be paid him by my Son Ebenezer Swift, at Five equal yearly payments after my decease. And also I Give him my two Canes, that which he hath already in possession, and my other Cane which I now use; Also my Silver Hilted Sword; and my Horse-Colt now about Three Years old; and two Cows which he shall first choose.

Item, I Give and Bequeath unto my Third Son Nathanael Swift, and to his Heirs & assigns for ever The Ten acres of Land, be it more or less, where he now lives, with the House and Barn standing thereon And also my Eight acre piece of Salt-marsh lying in Dorchester, between yᵉ Marsh of Mr. Foye and Jeremiah Tucker; And also my Woodlot in Milton lying between the Parallel Line (so called), and the Road leading to Stoughton; and my Pasture within fence by the Meeting-house in Milton; He paying the Sum of Money hereafter mentioned.

Item, I Give and Bequeath unto my Fourth Son John Swift and to the Heirs of his own Body lawfully begotten, and to their Heirs for ever all my upland lying in Dorchester upon the Southeast side of the lower Road leading from Milton to Boston, containing about Twenty acres, be it more or less, and lyeth between Jeremiah Smiths orchard and the Land of Joseph Leeds: And Six acres of my piece of Saltmarsh joyning to the sᵈ upland and running from thence down to Neponsit River, the whole of the sᵈ piece of Marsh containing about Twenty acres; the sᵈ Six acres to be measured off and to ly next to the Ditch that parts between my sᵈ piece of Marsh, and the Marsh of Thomas Trott: Also Ten acres of my Wood-lot lying in Milton unfenced on the Easterly side of yᵉ Way leading to yᵉ Scotch-woods (so called) joyning to the land already mentioned in my Son Nathanaels Portion, and on the land of Colonel Miller, and the land of Ebenezer Wadsworth & Mr. Oxenbridge Thatcher; the sᵈ Ten acres to be measured off and to lye next to the sᵈ Way to Scotch-woods. And my Son Ebenezer is to have liberty to pass & repass across yᵉ said piece unto the other part of yᵉ sᵈ Lot. And in Case my sᵈ Son John should die without lawfull Issue of his Body, then what I have given him as aforesaid, to be equally divided among my Four Sons namely Thomas Swift, Samuel Swift, Nathanael Swift and Ebenezer Swift, or their Legal Representatives; them their Heirs and assigns for ever. I also give my sᵈ Son John all my Carpenter & Joyners Tools.

Item, I Give and Bequeath unto my Fifth Son Ebenezer Swift, my Clock, & *Coat of Arms, and my

---

* Now in possession of McKee Swift, Esq., of New Brunswick, New Jersey, and the same from which the Albertype in this work is taken.

Iron Back in the Kitchen; And also I Give him his Heirs and assigns for ever, all the Residue and Remainder of my Estate both Real and Personal wheresoever the same is or may be found, not heretofore or hereafter particularly mentioned and Disposed of in this my last Will: He paying the sums of Money heretofore & hereafter mentioned, and performing what I have enjoyned him to do for his mother as abovementioned.

Item, I Give and Bequeath unto my Daughter Sarah Adams the Sum of One Hundred Pounds in Bills of Credit on this Province of the old tenor, to be paid her by my s⁴ Son Nathanael Swift at Three Yearly equal payments after my decease. And I also give her my Molatto Girl Dinah.

Item, I Give and Bequeath unto my Daughter Anna Hearsay the wife of Solomon Hearsay the Sum of One Hundred pounds in Bills of Credit of this Province of the old tenor, to be paid at Three equal yearly payments next after my Decease, Fifty pounds part thereof to be paid by my s⁴ Son Nathanael Swift, and the remaining Fifty pounds to be paid by my s⁴ Son Ebenezer Swift and all to be Deposited in the Hands of my s⁴ Son Nathanael Swift and he to have power to demand and receive the same; and he is to Improve it for the Relief and benefit of my s⁴ Daughter Anna & her Children; and to distribute yᵉ same at such times and in such Quantity and Species as he shall judge to be most for her benefit. But in case the s⁴ Solomon Hearsay should decease before my s⁴ Daughter Anna then all the Remainder of the s⁴ Sum to be paid into her hands, having regard (if need be) to the times of payment above mentioned. And in case my s⁴ Son Nathanael should decease before the s⁴ Solomon Hearsay then all the Power care and trust hereby Reposed in my s⁴ Son Nathanael to devolve upon my Son Ebenezer Swift.

Item, I Give and Bequeath unto my Daughter Patience Wadsworth the Sum of one Hundred pounds old tenor, to be paid her by my s⁴ Son Ebenezer in Province Bills at Three equal yearly payments next after my decease.

Item, I Give and Bequeath unto my s⁴ three Daughters, Sarah Adams, Annah Hearsay & Patience Wadsworth, after the marriage or decease of my Wife, all my Indoor moveables, not before particularly mentioned and disposed of in this my last Will, to be Equally divided among them.

Item, My Will is that all my arms not before mentioned be distributed as follows, Viz. my long gun to my Son Thomas, my little Gun that I had of brother Pratt to my Son Ebenezer, and my Case of Pistols & Holsters to my Son Nathanael.

Item, My Will is, and I do hereby order that all my Just Debts and Funeral Expenses, be discharged and paid by my s⁴ Sons Thomas Nathanael and Ebenezer in Equal parts out of their own proper Portions; and to be delivered into yᵉ hands of my Executors hereafter mentioned for them to pay when they shall be due.

And I Exhort all my Children to live in love and peace among themselves, that the God of peace may dwell with them. And I desire them all to rest Satisfied and Contented with this my distribution of my Estate; wherein my Will is, that if any of my Children shall be discontented and give trouble to any other of my Children or Heirs mentioned, then he, she, or they, being so discontented and giving trouble as aforesaid, shall forfeit all I have herein bequeathed to them, and yᵉ same shall be equally divided among all those of my Children as shall rest Satisfied and Contented with this disposition of my Estate.

And I do hereby Constitute and appoint my two Sons Thomas Swift and Samuel Swift to be Co-Executors of this my last Will and Testament And I do hereby utterly disallow, revoke and disannul all other former Wills, Legacies and Bequests, and Executors, by me in any way before named, Willed and Bequeathed; Ratifying and Confirming this and no other to be my last Will and Testament.

In Witness whereof I the s⁴ Samuel Swift have hereunto set my Hand and Seal the Day and year first above written.

SAML. SWIFT.     { SEAL. }

Signed, Sealed, Published Pronounced and Declared by yᵉ
    Samuel Swift the Testator to be his last Will and
    Testament, in the presence of us the Subscribers,

       JAMES BLAKE
       SAMUEL BLAKE
       RUTH BLAKE

Suffolk ss :                  Lib. 40, fol. 360.

The will was proved January 12, 1747, but the following day Ann Swift appeared and renounced what was given her by her said husband, and claimed her dower. She made her will January 9, 1855; proved July 5, 1862; gives five shillings to her four sons, Thomas, Samuel, Nathaniel, Ebenezer, and the residue of her estate to her three daughters, Sarah Adams, Anna Hearsay and Patience Wadsworth.

10

Samuel⁴ Swift, Esq., *(Samuel,³ Thomas,² Thomas,¹)* of Boston, b. in Milton June 9, 1715; d. Aug. 30, 1775; m. in 1738 Eliphal, (b. Feb. 7, 1713,) dau. of Samuel and Eliphal Tilley. He m. second, Oct. 5, 1757, Ann, (b. Oct. 3, 1729; d. May 8, 1788,) dau. of Capt. Hopestill Foster,* of Boston.

### CHILDREN.

SARAH, m. Col. Putnam. Their dau., Mrs. Bryant, was living in New London, Ct., in 1828, with a son and a daughter.

ANN, died s. p.

ELIPHAL, died s. p.

ELIZABETH, b. June 23, 1758; m. (pub. Oct. 30, 1776,) John Newhall, of Belchertown, and had a son, Samuel S. Newhall. She next m. Col. Jed^h. Burt, of Longmeadow. No children.

13. Foster, b. Jan. 20, 1760.

MARY, b. ———, 1762; m. Col. Burt as his third wife.

14. Jonathan, b. Mar. 27, 1764.

LUCRETIA, b. July —, 1767; d. Dec., 1830; m. Sept. 23, 1787, John Lovering. "A worthy, exemplary wife, mother and kind friend."

PHILOMELA, b. ———, 1774; m. Elijah Stoddard, and had a son and daughter.

Mrs. Swift appears from her diary to have been a woman of more than ordinary intelligence, and of great piety.

She commenced to write before her marriage, and continued it, at intervals, for many years after. Her compositions, which are of a deeply religious character, are mostly in verse, commemorating the death of relatives and friends. She writes, May 6, 1758, that she was taken into Mr. Byles' church, and of her religious duties, etc. She was in the habit of writing out her thoughts on the sermons she heard preached, and she often wrote on passing events, as — on the frequenting the tavern Saturday nights; on Lisbon being shaken by an earthquake, Nov. 1, 1775; on the taking of Quebec, 1759; on the vanity of the world; on the safe delivery of a child; on the repeal of the cruel stamp act, May 20, 1766. She also wrote verses on the death of "the universally beloved Capt. Larrabee," and says "this worthy gentleman departed this life in the 75th year of his age, lamented by all who knew him." In June, 1775, she is at Springfield, and writes: "Here I am in the woods, Boston being so surrounded by armies that we could not enjoy our home: no school for the children,

---

* The Foster family, prominent in the history of Dorchester, commences with Hopestill¹ and Patience, whose son, Capt. Hopestill,² m. Mary, dau. of James Bate, and had, with other children, James,³ who m., Oct. 7, 1680, second wife, Anna, dau. of Job Lane. An engraving of the coat-of-arms on their gravestone may be seen on p. 26, vol. I, *Heraldic Journal.* Of their numerous children was Capt. Hopestill⁴ of Boston, housewright, (named in his father's Will and Suf. Deeds, L. 48, F. 76,) who m. Nov. 11, 1724, Sarah Allen, who d. Sept. 6, 1772, æ 70 yrs. 6 mos. He d. Dec. 26, 1772, æ 70 yrs. 10 mos. The family Bible of their son Hopestill⁵ (brother of Ann⁵ Swift), who m. Susannah Wood, is in possession of their grandson, James⁷ Foster, of Longwood, son of John Hancock⁶ Foster, who m. Elizabeth Allen. His brother, David W.⁷ Foster, of Boston, has the manuscript of Ann Swift. (For an account of the earlier generation, see *Hist. of Dor.,* p. 118, and *Savage Gen. Dict.*)

and the town forsaken by the ministers — the pillars of the land." About this time she wrote the following letter:

Capt. HANDFIELD, Sʳ.

Your kindness in undertaking to get a pass for me emboldens me to ask the like favor for my dear husband whom I hear is in a very weak state of health. The anxiety of my mind is great about him. A word from you would have more weight than all the arguments that he could make use of.

Could I come to him, this favor I would not ask. O, Sʳ I trust in your goodness that you will do what you can to forward Mʳ Swift to me and in doing so you will greatly oblige

Your distressed friend,

Should be glad if he would bring out two trunks which there is clothing in that I want very much for myself and children.      ANN SWIFT.

The appeal seems to have failed, for she writes under date Aug. 30, 1775: "Departed this life, in the 61st year of his age, my dear husband, Samuel Swift. He died in Boston, or in other words, murdered there. He was not allowed to come to see me and live with his wife and children in the country. There he gave up the ghost— his heart was broken; the cruel treatment he met with in being a friend to his country was more than he could bear, with six fatherless children (in the woods) and all my substance in Boston." Mrs. Swift was a woman of delicate health, but of much energy. She was living, Nov. 16, 1787, in her own house in Orange Street, Boston, when she deeded a small portion of her land to Ebenezer Pope, whose estate it joined.

Mr. Swift was graduated at Harvard College in 1735, studied law with Counsellor Gridley and became a barrister and fellow practitioner with John Adams, afterwards president of the United States.

Mr. Swift was a highly esteemed citizen of Boston, and was frequently invited by the selectmen to visit the schools with many other distinguished citizens.

He was one of those fearless and determined men who set the revolutionary ball in motion, and early gave up his life to the cause of freedom.

As a proof of his prominence and the esteem in which he was held, the town records of Boston attest. At a town meeting of the freeholders and other inhabitants of the town of Boston, legally warned, at Faneuil Hall, Monday, April 3, 1775, — an adjournment of the March meeting — Mr. Samuel Adams, moderator of the meeting, being at the Congress then sitting at Concord, Samuel Swift, Esq., was chosen moderator *pro tempore*. It was, indeed, no small honor to preside at one of the famous town meetings in those stirring times, and to take the place of such a patriot as Sam Adams.

Mr. Swift was a member of the Ancient and Honorable Artillery in 1746, and he is said by his friend, Colonel May, to have been one of those active in promoting the destruction of the tea in Boston Harbor.

However that may be, he is known to have been an active and influential patriot. President John Adams told his distinguished grandson, General Swift, while on a visit to his seat in Quincy in 1817 with President Monroe, that Samuel Swift was a good man and a generous lawyer, and was called the widows' friend; that he was a firm Whig whose memory the State ought to perpetuate. The same sentiments Mr. Adams expressed in a letter to William Wirt, of Virginia. Mr. Adams also said it was owing to the zeal and resolution of Samuel Swift that caused many Bostonians to secrete their arms when Gov. Gage offered the town freedom if arms were brought in to the arsenal; and that Mr. Swift presided at a freemason's meeting where it was covertly agreed to use the arms concealed, and, in addition, pitchforks and axes, if need be, to assail the soldiery on the common; which scheme was betrayed to Gage, causing the imprisonment of Swift and others. This imprisonment brought on disease from which he never recovered, and he died August 30, 1775, aged 60 years, as President Adams said, "a martyr to freedom's cause." His remains were interred in the tomb in the stone chapel ground that had belonged to Samuel Tylly, Esq., the father of his first wife.

He had acquired a competency by his profession, which, excepting a house in Boston and a few acres of land in Dorchester, was lost, including bonds, through the unfaithfulness of his agent, while Boston was garrisoned.

## WILL.

In the Name of God Amen   I Samuel Swift of Boston in the county of Suffolk in New England Esq' being sensible of what I am about make this my last Will & Testament First recommending my Soul to my merciful God hoping in his mercy and in the next place commiting my Body to the Earth to be buried by my Executrix hereafter named in the economical manner and as touching the small worldly estate (though enough) with which God has intrusted me after my just debts & funeral charges are paid and anything remains; I give & bequeath it as follows, viz' To my daughter Sarah Putnam I Give the sum of five shillings & no more and to my daughter Ann Swift I give her the like sum of five shillings and no more they and each of them having had already advanced to them their full equal part & proportion of my small estate   To my daughter Eliphal I give five shillings; to my daughter Elizabeth I give five shillings; to my son Foster Swift I give five shillings; to my daughter Mary Swift I give five shillings; to my son Jonathan Swift I give five shillings and to my daughter Lucretia Swift I give five shillings to be paid to each of them in three months after my decease   Then I Give all the remainder of my Estate as well real as personal to my well beloved wife Ann Swift viz'. the use and improvement of it during her natural life and with leave also to make ample Sale & disposal of all or any part of my personal Estate first used and then if need be of my real Estate for the support of herself and any of her children (always excepting my daughter Sarah Putnam and Ann Swift) and at her death she is hereby impowered by Will or otherwise to dispose of it to my children (not excepted as aforesaid) as she please or if she thinks proper to advance any thing to any one of them excepting as aforesaid she shall be at liberty so to do if they behave dutifully to her, of which she shall be the sole judge, being fully satisfied that she will do what is just & equitable but if my said wife should die without Willing or disposing of what I hereby give her for life & then my Will is that what she shall or may leave of my Estate whether real or personal, or both, be equally divided between my Children viz which is hereby given equally to them their heirs and assigns forever (excepting to Sarah Putnam and Ann Swift as aforesaid) and I hereby direct and order that no Inventory or Apprizement of any part of my Estate be had: In Witness whereof I have hereunto set my hand and Seal this twenty-third day of August, Anno Domini One Thousand seven hundred & seventy,

SAMUEL SWIFT.          { SEAL }

> Sign'd Seal'd publish'd pronounc'd & declared by the s'd Samuel Swift the Testator to be his Will & Testam'. in presence of us .......... ............ ............
> (first interlined in one place near the bottom)

JOHN PEIRCE
THOMAS BAYLEY Juner
JOSEPH FIELD                    Proved June 24, 1776.

II

Nathaniel[4] Swift, (*Samuel,[3] Thomas,[2] Thomas[1]*) of Milton, yeoman and gentleman, b. September 25, 1719; d. in 1767; m. (pub. Jan. 9, 1741-2) Rebecca Tucker, who d. Sept. 6, 1793. The town records show that he filled the offices of constable and fence-viewer. Adm. on his estate was granted to Rebecca Swift and Jeremiah Tucker, who presented the inventory Feb. 12, 1768; amt. £428, 9s., 6d. Josiah How appointed guardian of the children.

### CHILDREN.

REBECCA, b. Dec. 30. 1742; m. James Tucker (pub. Apr. 2, 1763).

SARAH, b. May 25, 1745; d. 1781; m. Samuel Henshaw (pub. May 30, 1777); son of Sam'l and Waitstill Henshaw, b. at Milton, 1744; grad. H. C. 1773; rem. to Northampton.

ELIPHAL, b. Oct. 11, 1747; m. John Baker, Jr., of Dorchester (pub. Aug. 15, 1777).

PATIENCE, bapt. Dec. 3, 1748; d. young.

PATIENCE, b. Nov. 14, 1749; m. Sept. 18, 1799, Daniel Newell, of Lynn.

MARY, b. Dec. 20, 1751; m. Joseph Bennett (pub. July 17, 1773).

15. Nathaniel, b. June 12, 1754.

ABIGAIL, b.                    ; m. Ruben Ferry, Sept. 13, 1781.

JONATHAN, b.                    ; m. Silence White. who d. in Boston, July 16, 1817, s. p. The adm. of her estate shows she was sister of John White, Esq., of Weymouth.

ELIZABETH, b. June 25, 1761; m. 1783, Samuel Babcock.

I 2

Ebenezer[4] Swift, (*Samuel,[3] Thomas,[2] Thomas[1]*), of Milton, gentleman, born March 24, 1724-5; d. Jan. 17, 1805, aged 80 yrs.; m. Judith [b. Jan. 30, 1728-9; d. Apr. 22, 1784, aged 55 yrs.], dau. of Dea. Nehemiah Clapp [pub. Jan. 17, 1746-7]. He served the town as surveyor of highways in 1758,'64,'71,'78.

### CHILDREN.

16. John, b. June 24, 1747.

17. Samuel, b. May 28, 1749.

18. Ebenezer, b. Jan. 15, 1752.

LYDIA, b. Feb. 14, 1754; d. July 10, 1758.

SUSANNAH, b. Dec. 31, 1756; m. Wm. Bartlett of Boston (pub. Sept. 9, 1780).

STEPHEN, b. Apr. 1, 1761.

LYDIA, b. Mar. 7, 1763; m. Wm. Pierce, (pub. Dec. 9, 1784).

ANN, b. Aug. 6, 1764; perhaps the same who was called Nancy; m. Samuel Berry of Brookline (pub May 20, 1786).

JUDITH, b. —————; m. Henry Crane, Jr. (pub. Mar. 20, 1784).

I 3

Dr. Foster[5] Swift, (*Samuel,[4] Samuel,[3] Thomas,[2] Thomas[1]*) b. Jan., 1760; d. Aug. 18, 1835; m. Feb. 18, 1783, Deborah [b. Sept. —— 1762; d. June 3, 1824], dau. of Capt. Thomas and Elizabeth Delano* of Nantucket. She was buried in the

*Here followeth some genealogical notes collected and made at Amsterdam in 1852 by Edward Delano, son of Warren:

Arnulph de Franchemont, proprietor of the estate of this name, took the oath of fealty to Conrad and was

Episcopal Cemetery of St. Ann's, Brooklyn, N. Y., June 5, 1824.   Their portraits, painted by Jarvis, in possession of their grandson, McRee Swift, Esq., are reproduced by the Albertype process for this work.

CHILDREN.

29. **Joseph Gardner,** b. Dec. 31, 1783.
    JONATHAN, b. ——————— 1785; d. young.
    SARAH DELANO, b. Feb. 24, 1788; d. May, 1839; m. December, 1810, Eli, son of James and Delia Adams, of Concord, Mass.   He d. July 18, 1822.   Besides children who died young, they had Col. Julius Walker Adams, b. Oct. 18, 1812; m. Dec. 2, 1835, Elizabeth Dennison, of Stonington, Conn.   He is a distinguished civil engineer, particularly devoted to sanitary science.   He was partially educated at West Point, and commanded a regiment from Brooklyn, N. Y., in the war of the Rebellion.   Delia Woodward Adams, b. Nov. 19, 1815; m. Col. Edward B. White, U. S. A., of Charleston, S. C.   Mary, b. Nov. 21, 1818; m. James P. Kirkwood, of Edinburgh, Scotland.
    DEBORAH ANN, b. ——————— 1790; d. Dec. —— 1805.   "A very beautiful woman."
20. **William Henry,** b. Nov. 6, 1800.
    MARY RODERDEAU, b. Aug. 8, 1804; d. Dec. —— 1827; m. Jan. 23, 1821, George W. Whistler,

---

created Count, A. D. 1139.   He married the daughter of the Seigneur Ivoy, and had Conrad the Count and Governor of Liege and Bouillon; he married Ermingarde Walcourt, 1166; their son Hugh married the heir of Bavaria.   Hallin, the successor to Franchemont, married Agnes, daughter of Guilbert of Ovras, 1225.   Walleron de Franchemont became Seigneur of de Launoy in 1310, between Selle and Tournay; their son, Hugh de Launoy, married Margarethe of Migneul, as appears on the tombstone.   Gilbert de Launoy of Wellnolle and Beaumont, married Catherine Molembix, and had three sons.   Baldwin de Launoy Michelle, Lady of Conray, and their descendant, Philip de Launoy, served Charles V, 12th Sept., 1543.   He married Margaret, daughter of Baldwin of Falaix, and died May 25, 1560.   The heir, Philip, died about 1594.   The arms of these de Launoys are a shield argent with three green lions and three red tongues.   On Dec. 7, 1603, was baptized in the Walloon church at Leyden, Philip, the son of John and Mary de Lonoye.   This Philip migrated to New Plymouth in November, 1621, and who, it is believed, was the same Philip who came to New Plymouth in the Fortune in 1621.   He married Dec. 19, 1634, and was about nineteen years of age, and it is thought is undoubtedly the same Philip de Lonoye.   They wrote their names de Lano, de la Noy and de Launoy.   One of them married at the Walloon church James de Lano, and is believed to be the brother of Philip, born 1603, and husband of Mary of Leyden, whom the record says went to New Spain or New Plymouth in 1621.   The first generation of the de Launoys, or de Lano, or Noy or Noye, known in America, was this Philip, who came to New Plymouth in the Fortune, in 1621, of 55 tons, the second vessel that reached the colony, and she was placed on the same footing with the Mayflower as to the distribution of land.   He married Hester Dewsbury of Duxbury; she had three sons, Samuel, Thomas and Jonathan, and a daughter.   Jonathan, the youngest son of Philip, was born 1648, and he married Mary Warren, daughter of Nathaniel Warren of Plymouth, on Feb. 26, 1677-78.   Their children were, Jonathan, married Ann Nash June 20th, 1704; Jabez, married his cousin, Mary Delano, 1710; Sarah; Mary; Nathan; Bethia; Nathaniel, married a Durfee, 1720; Esther; Jethro, married Elizabeth Pope Oct. 9, 1727; and Thomas, who married Jane Peckham, April, 1729.

The aforesaid Jonathan was lieutenant of the colony, military constable, and surveyor, as his father, Philip, had been also.   His farm was called Nonasketucket, in Dartmouth, now Fair Haven, and he died Dec. 28, 1720, and was buried at                         where the headstone was in 1850.

Thomas Delano, who married Jean Peckham in April, 1729, had children, Abishai, born July 9, 1731; Thomas, born in 1732 and died in November, 1799, married to Elizabeth Swain of Nantucket; Ephraim, born Aug. 14, 1733, married to Elizabeth Cushman Nov. 27th, 1760; Gideon, born Sept. 25, 1736, married Patience Tabor; Deborah, born June 14, 1739, married ——— Sherman; Jean, married Pierre Tobey.   J. G. Swift remembers great-uncle Abishai, who settled in Hampshire County, Mass., and also great-uncle Gideon, on board his very neat sloop that coasted between Boston and Carolina.   The aforesaid Thomas' wife was born in 1729, and was the granddaughter of Peter Folger, and daughter of Shubael Swain of Nantucket.   The aforesaid Ephraim, of whom I have heard my mother speak as of one she respected highly, married Elizabeth Cushman.   Their children were, Thomas, born Oct. 16, 1761, died February, 1782; Deborah, born July 16, 1773, died Feb. 9, 1851; Warren, born Oct. 28, 1779, married Deborah Church Nov. 6, 1808.   Their children, Warren, married Catherine Lyman; Franklin H. married Laura Acton; and Edward Delano, this last the collector of this memoir, except in reference to my grandfather, Thomas Delano.   The sons of the said Thomas were Ephraim, Henry, Thomas, Abishai and William, and daughters, Elizabeth Howland, Deborah Swift, my mother, and Sally Fitch.   My grandfather educated his first four sons in England.

U. S. A., son of Col. Wm. Whistler, U. S. A., b. in Indiana, cadet at the U. S. Military Academy from July 31, 1814, to July 1, 1819, when he was graduated and promoted to 2d lieutenant corp of artillery, July 1, 1819; 1st lieutenant 2d Artillery, Aug. 16, 1829; resigned, Dec. 31, 1833; civil engineer in U. S. from 1842-49; superintending engineer of the St. Petersburgh & Moscow R. R., Russia, in the employ of the emperor; died Apr. 7, 1849, aged 48 yrs.; children: 1, Geo. W. Whistler, b. ———; m. ——— dau. of Prof. Ducatel of Baltimore, by whom he had Geo. W., now living in Baltimore. His second wife, m. in 1854, was Julia, dau. of Ross W. Winans, of Baltimore; 2, Joseph Swift Whistler, d. young; 3, Deborah Delano Whistler, m. Seymour Hayden in England, the distinguished surgeon and artist of London, whose etchings have obtained such celebrity.

Dr. Swift was, at his father's death, preparing for college, but that affliction made other pursuits necessary. He commenced the study of medicine with Dr. Joseph Gardner in 1779, and about 1780 was appointed surgeon on board the Portsmouth, sloop-of-war, Capt. Daniel McNeill, and with a squadron destined for Holland, met a British fleet—Rodney's—and was captured by the Culloden, seventy-four, commanded by Lord Robert Manners, and sent to St. Lucie, where he was kept a prisoner thirteen months, escaping, with twelve others, in 1781. This escape was a remarkable event. Dr. Swift, who had prescribed successfully for the illness of the commander of the prison-ship, was allowed to visit the sick of the island, and was amply compensated by them—a guinea a visit. These fees gave him and his fellow-sufferers many comforts, but still they were prisoners. Twelve of them, officers and men, with Capt. McNeill at the head, had long been devising a plan of escape. They practiced swimming, and then waited for some trader to anchor near by. At last a brig partly laden with sugar lay at anchor. Now was their chance, which they hastened to improve. Selecting a night light enough to see the brig, the twelve lowered themselves quietly from a port into the water, and swam with a light bundle of clothes tied to their backs, to the cable of the vessel. One of their comrades on reaching the cable shinned up, and raising his body over the side bow, his indistinct form at that hour of the night struck the watch with terror, and they ran below. The others, following their leader, hastened to fasten the companion and hatches, cut the cable, and put to sea. In eleven days they reached Cape Cod with their prisoners, only eight, the remainder being on shore in St. Lucie at the time of the capture. The sale of the brig, a Hull trader, partly laden with sugar and rum, gave each of the twelve some hundreds of dollars, and much *éclat*, at the time " that truly tried men's souls."

Of this imprisonment his mother writes as follows:

Boston, Sept. 20, 1781.

*My Dear Sister:—*

I have heard from my son Foster, but oh, how can I tell, or how can you hear? He is on board a guard-ship at a place where they will not exchange prisoners, and he has written letters to Dr. Gardner and Deacon Davis, enough to break, or move a stone to speak, begging that some one would stir in the affair, and try to get the Americans released. Their number on board is two hundred and twenty, put down the hold at sunset—how can they live?

I have copied his letter to me and send you.  I fear nothing can be done, as I have not the least encouragement from either, and there he must lie and sicken and die.  My heart is too full.  Farewell.

Your sister,                    ANN SWIFT.

Your brother Foster tells me that your cousin Hearsey has seen the wharfs, and is quite of the notion of taking them, and Cunningham is going to quit them, and he would have you send him word if there is anything further you would have him do.

In November of 1782 Dr. Swift thought of settling professionally on the island of Nantucket, by the advice of Dr. Gardner, who gave him letters of introduction ; but not finding that place equal to his hopes, he went the next year to Virginia, by invitation of his only brother, Jonathan, where he received the friendly aid of Gen. Washington, to whom he had carried a package and introduction from Gen. Benjamin Lincoln, and succeeded, but lost his health and returned to Nantucket.  In 1786 he removed with his wife and son to Dartmouth, Mass., where he remained till July, 1792 ; then took up his residence and the practice of his profession in Taunton.  In 1809 he removed to Boston, and Feb. 18, 1814, was appointed garrison surgeon. He was post surgeon April 24, 1816, assistant surgeon May, 1821, and died at his post, New London, Conn.

## WILL.

Knowing the certainty of death I, Foster Swift, do make this my last Will and Testament.  In doing it I desire humbly to recommend my Soul to God, hoping for pardon and salvation through the mediation of a crucified Redeemer.  It is my wish to be buried in a plain pine coffin, simply stained, without any ornament, to have plain Gravestones with my name and profession, place of nativity and age, and time of death and no more.

After all my debts are paid I dispose of my estate as follows, viz:  One-half of my estate, real and personal, (excepting what is mentioned below,) I give to my daughter Sally D. Adams.  All the residue of my estate, real and personal, I give to my sons Joseph, William, and my grandchildren George, Joseph and Deborah Whistler, in equal parts, that is, George, Joseph and Deborah Whistler to have one-third of one-half.  If there should be any dividend from any source I give the same to my sons Joseph and William.  The Watch which I have worn belongs to my son Joseph.  To him I give my Silver Tankard, and the table spoons marked D. D. to Louisa Adams.  To my sisters Mary and Philomela I give Ten Dollars each, my Gold Seal and Watch Chain I give to Julius W. Adams.  To my early friend Lyman Law, Esq., I give my Gold Ring.

I hereby appoint my sons Joseph and William executors, and my daughter Sally executrix of this will.

In testimony of which I have hereunto set my hand and seal this thirteenth day of February, A. D. 1834.

FOSTER SWIFT.          { SEAL }

Signed, sealed, and declared by the Testator }
  as his last Will and Testament, in the }
  presence of us : }

     JONATHAN COIT,
     JOSEPH SMITH, JR.,
     E. F. DUTTON.

**FOSTER SWIFT, M. D.,**

Surgeon in the

U. S. Army,

Born in Boston

20th Jan<sup>y</sup>, 1760,

Died in New London

18 Aug., 1835.

MRS. FOSTER SWIFT.

14

Jonathan⁵ Swift, (*Foster,⁴ Samuel,³ Thomas,² Thomas¹*), b. in Boston, March 22, 1764; d. Aug. 22, 1824; m. Sept. 24, 1785, Ann (b. Dec. 3, 1767; d. Jan. 16, 1833), dau. of Gen. Daniel Roberdeau of the Revolutionary War and the Congress of 1778. (See *Roberdeau Genealogy*).

Mrs. Swift was present at the inauguration ball in honor of Gen. Washington, and during the evening was led out to dance by him. A life-like miniature of her on ivory at the age of twenty-two is in possession of her daughter, Mrs. Patten, who has also an oil painting at the age of sixty.

### CHILDREN.

A son still born Oct. 10, 1786.

WILLIAM ROBERDEAU, b. Aug. 29, 1787; d. Oct., 1833; m. Aug. 1, 1815, Mary Donaldson (d. Apr. 30, 1870, aged 83), dau. of Edward Harper, of Alexandria; early was in the counting-room of Wm. Taylor, and made voyages for this house as supercargo with great success; was afterwards established as a merchant in Baltimore with Eli Adams; finally moved to Washington, N. C., where he died, s. p. Oct. 1833.

A son, b. Nov. 12, 1789; d. Nov. 13, 1789.

DANIEL ROBERDEAU, b. Nov. 9, 1790; d. unm. Aug., 1825.

JONATHAN, b. Dec. 2, 1792; d. July 1, 1793.

ISAAC BOSTWICK, b. Feb. 2, 1795.

ANN SELINA, b. Feb. 18, 1797; d. July 18, 1798.

GEO. WASHINGTON, b. Feb. 11, 1800; d. unm. Sept. 19, 1819.

ANN FOSTER, b. Oct. 11, 1802; m. Jan. 13, 1829, Jonathan T. Patten, a prosperous wholesale merchant of New York, where they still reside. For their children, see *Roberdeau Genealogy*.

MARY SELINA, b. Jan. 18, 1805; m. Aug. 8, 1826, Henry Allison, b. in Va. Dec. 23, 1793; d. Dec. 26, 1871; settled in Missouri, where, at Brownsville, Mrs. A. lives. For children, see *Roberdeau Genealogy*.

WM. TAYLOR, b. Sept. 20, 1808; d. next day.

FOSTER, b. May 20, 1810; d. unm. Sept., 1825.

Mr. Swift was for forty years a prominent citizen of Alexandria, Va. He was bred to mercantile life by Mr. May of Boston, and early (before 1785), established himself in commerce at Alexandria, where he met with success, accumulating a fortune. His fine place bore the unique name of Grasshopper Hall, since known as Kolros, where he frequently entertained Gen. Washington, with whom he was on intimate terms. He had a fine portrait of him painted by Peale, now in possession of Jonathan Patten, Esq., of New York.

Mr. Swift was a Mason, and received his degree in the Washington Lodge, Alexandria; initiated and passed Feb. 25, 1785, and raised to a Master Mason Feb. 24, 1786.

As a brother Mason Mr. Swift attended the funeral of Gen. Washington, and was the one who sprinkled the earth over the body during the services. He was also buried with Masonic honors by the lodge. A gentleman of dignified and elegant manners, tall, of commanding aspect; his eyes were blue, and his complexion dark.

He was an intelligent traveler, visiting England and Ireland in 1786-7, when he improved the opportunity of a visit to Rotherham, in Yorkshire, the home of his ancestors.  Here and elsewhere in the county he found the name respectably represented; some having the tradition that a branch of the family had migrated to Boston in the previous century.  On visiting Dublin some members of St. Patrick's Society thought they traced a resemblance between him and the Dean, and with the characteristic poetry of Irish feeling, they gave him a dinner and presented him with a portrait of the Dean, with the arms of the Yorkshire family.  His valuable papers, among which were many letters from Gen. Washington, were all lost at sea soon after the death of his son, while being sent to New York.  His portrait, which was painted abroad, was so injured on the voyage home that he destroyed it.

---

### 15

Nathaniel,⁵ (*Nathaniel,⁴ Samuel,³ Thomas,² Thomas¹,*) of Dorchester, b. in Milton, June 12, 1754; d. Nov. 16, 1831; m. Sept. 25, 1777, Mary Baker, b. Feb. 7, 1754.

CHILDREN.

21. Nathaniel, b. July 15, 1778.
22. William, b. Sept. 11, 1779.
    MARY, b. Mar. 18, 1781; d. unm. in 1877.
    SARAH, b. Dec. 23, 1782; d. unm. in 1877.
23. Samuel, b. Dec. 2, 1784.

The daughters, Mary and Sarah, were charming ladies of great intelligence, residing till their death in Dorchester.  The family tomb is situated in the old Dorchester graveyard.

---

### 16

John⁵ Swift, Esq. (*Ebenezer,⁴ Samuel,³ Thomas,² Thomas,¹*) b. in Milton on the ancestral farm, June 24, 1747; d. Jan. 14, 1819; m. May 17, 1772, Elizabeth (born Jan. 14, 1754; d. Dec. 13, 1825), dau. of William and Hannah (Blake) Babcock of Milton.

CHILDREN.

BETSEY, b. Apr. 27, 1773; d. 1774.
24. John, b. Mar. 12, 1775.
    WILLIAM, b. June 13, 1777; merchant of Milton; adm. to John Swift, Esq., Feb. 7, 1808, d. s. p.
    ELIZABETH, b. Jan. 4, 1779; d. June 10, 1805; m. Capt. P. B. Rogers; children: 1, Charles; 2, Elizabeth; 3, Judith, m. E. P. Porter of Boston, d. s. p.; 4, John Swift, m. and left four children; 5, George B., d. leaving a widow and three children; 6, Fanny, m. J. A. Veazie of Boston, has three children; 7, Penuel, dead.

> FANNY, b. Dec. 30, 1780; d. unm. Mar. 2, 1868. A lady much beloved. She owned the ancient
> coat of arms before mentioned, which she gave in 1860 to Gen. Swift, now in possession of
> his son, McKee.
> CHARLES, b. May 2, 1783; d. single.
> EDWARD, b. Aug. 15, 1788; d. single.

Capt. John Swift, as he is frequently called on the Milton record, was one of the leading men of the town. He built the house now standing on Adams Street near Canton Avenue, Milton Hill, from which the following picture was made, about one hundred years ago, on land his wife inherited from her ancestors.

In business he was a successful manufacturer of gentlemen's and ladies' beaver hats, in which he rivalled those imported from the mother country.

The Milton records during the Revolutionary period of its history, show that he was an active and ardent patriot, filling the most important offices with signal ability. Before the memorable year of 1776, when he was chosen as one of the committee of safety and correspondence, he had filled numerous minor offices, as clerk of the market, surveyor, and so forth; and in 1781 he was appointed with his brother Samuel to raise men for the Continental army, and was also chosen to examine the treasurer's accounts and to regulate the schools. No committee during these exciting times seemed complete unless his name was attached to it, and all we can learn of him stamps him as a determined and resolute man, greatly respected by his townsmen.  In 1817 he was a second lieutenant in a company which went to assist in quelling Shay's rebellion.

The following incident, giving us some insight into his character, was given by the Rev. Frederick Frothingham, in his two hundredth anniversary discourse: "June 19, 1796, the church of Milton called the Rev. John Pierce, afterwards the famous Dr. Pierce, of Brookline, but the town would not concur.  Dr. Pierce used to say in his jovial fashion that Mr. John Swift was the cause of his not coming to Milton. Being a man of influence, he made such a fuss in the town that the town refused to ratify the vote of the church in favor of inviting Mr. Pierce.  And the weighty ground of Mr. Swift's opposition was, that he did not like Mr. Pierce's step-mother."

A note to a sermon by John H. Morrison, D. D., of Milton, says: "About sixty years ago, I have been told that at a town meeting in Milton, no public measure could be carried which was opposed by John Swift, the energetic head of an important family which is now represented by only one male member."

Squire Swift was a politician of the old Jeffersonian school, and made his influence felt both in his town and county.  He is said to have been tendered the nomination for Congress, but declined.  In writing his political squibs, as he called them, he signed himself "The Man of Fur."

Mr. E. J. Baker of Dorchester writes: "His was no negative character.  He loved his friends and hated his enemies, while he rendered to Cæsar the things that are Cæsar's, and to God the things that are God's.  In the days of my boyhood I met him frequently, when he was at the age of threescore years and ten, and my remembrance of him is that he was tall and portly, dignified in his person and in his gait, and elastic in his step.  His hair was very white, with the queue of the former generation.  He was always social and pleasant in his conversation, and a constant attendant at church.  His hospitality was bounteous, and shared alike by his neighbors and transient visitors."

Administration on his estate was granted to his son John, February 2, 1819. The inventory, amounting to three thousand, seven hundred and forty-six dollars and four cents, showed two pews in the Milton meeting house, and about one hundred books in the library.  His family tomb is near by the graves of his ancestors in the Milton cemetery.

---

17

Samuel⁴ Swift, (*Ebenezer,*¹ *Samuel,*² *Thomas,*² *Thomas*¹), b. at the paternal mansion, Milton Hill, May 28, 1749; d. February 1, 1830, aged 81; m. (pub. October 4, 1782), Abigail (b. May 15, 1759; d. August 16, 1834, aged 76), dau. of William and Eunice (Bent) Pierce.

CHILDREN.

23. Samuel, b. Sept. 22, 1783.
Judith, b. July 17, 1785; d. unm. Oct. 23, 1857.
Lewis, b. Aug. 5, 1787; d. young.
Andrew, b. Aug. 20, 1789; d. unm. Feb. 19, 1851.
William, b. July 27, 1791; d. s. p. June 8, 1865.
Ebenezer, b. June 19, 1793; d. June 16, 1827.
Abigail, b. Dec. 25, 1795; d. unm. July 22, 1838.
Eunice, b. June 6, 1798; m. Nov. 20, 1823, Josiah Wadsworth.
George, b. Nov. 29, 1800; d. unm.
Thomas Oliver, b. Apr. 12, 1803; d. unm. June 6, 1837.

Mr. Swift, like his brother John, was an ardent patriot of the Revolution, and we find his name on many of the important committees of those stirring times. In 1781 he was on the committee of safety and correspondence, also to raise men for the Continental army. Besides various other committees to which his name was attached, he was surveyor of the highways, constable, and overseer of the poor. Mr. Swift by occupation was a farmer, tilling the acres that had been cultivated by his ancestors. By his will, dated Sept. 24, 1827, he disposed of an estate of nearly six thousand dollars among his children, who, Aug. 25, 1835, sold the property to Mr. Thomas Hollis, of Milton. Singular to say, the estate has got back again into Swift blood, having been bought by Lewis W. Tappan, Jr., a descendant of Obadiah, son of the first Thomas. Mr. Tappan has remodeled the old mansion and occupies it as a residence. Mr. Swift was the owner of the Swift chair, previously mentioned.

---

## 18

**Ebenezer[5] Swift**, *(Ebenezer,[4] Samuel,[3] Thomas,[2] Thomas,[1])* born in Milton Jan. 15, 1752; d. in Framingham Sept. 3, 1775, æ. 23, (g. s.); m. ————, 1775, Martha Rice of Natick. Had one son, Ebenezer[6], b. ————, d. ————; m. Sept. 7, 1800, Sally Greenwood, by whom he had the following children:

CHILDREN.

Martha, b. Nov. 3, 1800.
Mary, b. May 1, 1803.
George, b. May 20, 1805.
Hiram, b. Feb. 5, 1814.

---

## 19*

**General Joseph[6] Gardner Swift, LL. D.**, *(Foster,[5] Samuel,[4] Samuel,[3] Thomas,[2] Thomas,[1])* b. at Nantucket Dec. 31, 1783; d. July 23, 1865; m. June 6, 1805,

---

*By a typographical error the number to which this refers is 29 instead of 19, as it should be.

Louisa Margaret (b. Oct. 14, 1788; d. Nov. 15, 1855,) dau. of Capt. James Walker,* a rice planter of Wilmington, N. C.

CHILDREN.

JAMES FOSTER, b. May 15, 1806; d. March 18, 1830; m. Jan. 2, 1830, Mary F. Jephson of New York. Partially educated at West Point; U. S. assistant engineer when he died.

26. Jonathan Williams, b. March 30, 1808.

ALEXANDER JOSEPH, b. March 4, 1810; Cadet at the U. S. Military Academy from July 1, 1826, to July 1, 1830, when he was graduated and promoted in the army to Bvt. Second Lieut. Corps of Engineers, July 1, 1830. Served: as Asst. Engineer in the construction of Ft. Caswell, N. C., and improvement of Cape Fear River, N. C., 1830–32, and in the erection of Ft. Adams, Newport Harbor, R. I., 1832–35; as Superintending Engineer of the opening of Ocracock Inlet, N. C., 1835–39; of the improvement of Cape Fear River of Pamlico Sound, N. C., (First Lieut. Corps of Engineers Oct. 31, 1836,) 1836–39; of the construction of Ft. Caswell, N. C., 1836–39, and of improvement of Cose Sound and of New River, N. C., 1838–39; on professional duty in Europe at the School of Application (Capt. Corps of Engineers July 7, 1838,) for the Artillery and Engineers at Metz, France, 1840–41; at the Military Academy as Instructor of practical military engineering June 30, 1841, to Sept. 12, 1846; Treasurer Dec. 19, 1845, to Sept. 12, 1846; Superintending Engineer of the construction of cadets' barracks 1844–46; and in the war with Mexico 1856–7, in command of Sappers and Miners and Pontoniers, being engaged in the siege of Vera Cruz March 9–18, 1847. Died April 24, 1847, at New Orleans.

THOMAS DELANO, b. March 23, 1812; d. Sept 2, 1829.

JULIUS HENRY, b. Sept. 1, 1814; d. Feb. 6, 1850.

SARAH DELANO, b. March 30, 1816; d. March 22, 1876; m. Oct. 18, 1861, Peter Richards of New York.

27. McKee, b. April 15, 1819.

LOUISA JOSEPHINE, b. April 30, 1821; d. Jan. 16, 1859; m. June 22, 1843, Peter Richards of New York.

HARRIET WALKER, b. Feb. 3, 1824; d. Dec. 7, 1826.

CHARLOTTE FARQUHAR, b. April 5, 1826; d. Dec. 31, 1840.

JAMES THOMAS, b. Aug. 30, 1829; m. Nov. 14, 1861, Margaret Weston, only dau. of Judge Weston of Sandy Hill, N. Y. Is a successful merchant of New York, and member of the Chamber of Commerce. He has made admirable use of his surplus income in charities, particularly in founding the Home for Old People of Geneva, N. Y., in memory of his brother Foster.

28. Foster, b. Oct. 31, 1833.

---

*Robert Walker, a kinsman probably of the Rev. George Walker, the hero of Londonderry and resident of Portaferry, Ireland, m. Ann Shearer, a dau. of the family of Montgomery of Mt. Alexander, and migrated in 1738 with many of his retainers, among them the Owens and Kenons, to Wilmington, N. C., where were born, Ann, (Quince) 1740; James, 1742; d. Feb. 1808, æ. 66 yrs.; m. Jan. 1770, Magdalene Margaret Dubois, who d. Dec. 1827, æ. 72; and had James W., b. Dec. 25, 1770, who, with his family and son Henry migrated to Ashtourne, thence to southwest part of Arkansas; Harriet, b. Dec. 10, 1784; Louisa Margaret, b. Oct. 14, 1788; m. J. G. Swift. Julius Henry, b. Oct. 26, 1793; d. 1827 in Pendleton, S. C.

Domine Petrus Dubois of Amsterdam, of a refugee Huguenot family from Rochelle in France, about the time of the massacre of St. Bartholomew, was the father of the Rev. Walter Dubois, pastor of the Reformed Dutch Church in Garden Street, New York, who married Helena Van Baal. He d. Oct. 1751, æ. 80. Of their children, John, b. 1707, by his second wife Gabriella De Rosset of Wilmington, N. C., had Magdalene Margaret, b. Feb. 19, 1765, wife of James Walker.

I have a copper plate portraiture of Dom. Petrus Dubois of Amsterdam in my library, and I have placed in the consistory of the early Dutch Church of New York, whose pastor is the Rev. Mr. De Witt, a full-sized and excellent work of art in oil portrait of the aforesaid Dom. Gualthemus Dubois.

The De Rossets were a Huguenot family of long existence in France. Two sons, Louis and John, emigrated to Wilmington, N. C. Louis was of the King's Council, and with his brother, and William Montgomery Walker, brother of James Walker, were the founders of St. James Episcopal Church in Wilmington. — *From J. G. Swift's Notes.*

A Memoir of General Swift having been already published, it is unnecessary here to give more than a brief reference to his character.

From his ancestors, who were of the best Puritan type, he inherited a rare combination of qualities, that formed a noble manhood. He was not only a brave soldier, but a man whose character and influence would have gained him distinction in any position of life. He was a staunch supporter of the Episcopal Church. He took much interest in agricultural pursuits, was possessed of much musical talent, which displayed itself in early childhood, and had a great deal of love for the fine arts. Although not what would be called a student, he was well read, possessed a decided literary taste, and had a remarkable memory. He was particularly interested in historical matters, and gave considerable attention to the genealogy of his own family and kindred. He was a careful observer, wrote tersely and with much force. He was a staunch supporter of the government during the late civil war, and threw the whole weight of his influence against secession. His last recorded utterance was for the safe delivery, and future prosperity of his country, just emerging from the horrors of a four years civil war.

He was particularly happy in his domestic relations, and the most charming and interesting of companions, pouring out the hoarded stores of long years' close observation, silent thought and clear analysis of striking events.

His dignity and simplicity, courtly politeness and lively sympathies, always secured for him the warm regard of old and young. For the latter, he felt a paternal interest, and was ever a wise counsellor and faithful friend.

General Swift's portrait was painted several times. Once by Jarvis, by order of the city government of New York, to be hung in the City Hall. The Corps of Engineers, to show their respect and affection for their chief, requested him to sit to Tully, which picture now hangs in the library of the Military Academy at West Point — a fit depository of the portrait of its first graduate, second Superintendent, and subsequent Inspector. Later in life his portrait was painted by Huntington, and from this admirable likeness, and valuable work of art, the plates are furnished for this book.

"A man he seemed of cheerful yesterdays and confident to-morrows; with a face not worldly minded, for it bore so much of nature's impress, gayety and health, freedom and hope, but keen withal, and shrewd."

At the age of eighty-two he passed away, surrounded by his family, full of years and honors, with faculties bright, and affections warm to the last; much lamented by the public, and sincerely mourned by a wide circle of friends.

For the above we are chiefly indebted to a *Biogaphical Sketch of Gen. Swift* by Gen. G. W. Cullum, U. S. A., printed in 1877.

## WILL.

I give to my daughter, Sarah D. Swift Richards, all my Lot and House and Furniture at Mill Point, in fee simple. I give to my executors, McKee Swift and Peter Richards, all the remainder of my property of every kind in trust to be conveyed to them in five equal shares, to the five following named of my children, to wit: Jonathan W. Swift or heirs, to McRee Swift or heirs, to my son-in-law, Peter Richards (Josie's share,) to James Tho⁵. Swift, and to Foster Swift. I give to Maria Jephson, widow of my son James Foster, Five Hundred Dollars, and I give to our faithful family servant Mary Simpson, Five Hundred Dollars, to buy an annuity.

Done in the City of New York this 20th day of March, Eighteen Hundred and Sixty-five, in presence of us witnesses, and in presence of each other, and at the request of the Testator. He declaring this to be his last will.

J. G. SWIFT.    { SEAL }

WINFIELD SCOTT, U. S. Army, City of New York.
JOHN HAMILTON, 17 W. 20th St., New York.


MEM⁰. To my Brother the Family Bible and my Mother's and Father's Portraits for life, and then to my oldest male Heir. The Urn belongs to Sally, the Statuette of Napoleon to my son McRee. The Silver Tea Pot and Sugar Dish and Basin from the Canteen to Sally. The City Plate and Library divided among my Children within two years after my demise. Nearly all the rest of the Pictures belong to Mr. Richards. The Arms to the eldest male. Math'l Instruments to McRee.

J. G. SWIFT.

---

20

**Capt. William Henry Swift, A. M., U. S. A.,** (*Foster,⁵ Samuel,⁴ Samuel,³ Thomas,² Thomas,¹*) b. at Taunton Nov. 6, 1800; d. Apr. 7, 1879; m. ———— ———— 1825, Mary, dau. of Charles Stuart, British Consul at New London, Ct. She died in Nov. 1837, leaving two children. His second wife, to whom he was m. Apr. ——, 1844, was Hannah W., dau. of John Howard of Springfield, Mass. She died at her residence, No. 11 West 16th St., New York, Jan. 6, 1884, æ. 63.

CHILDREN.

29. **Charles W.**, b. ——, 1828.
     MARY, b. ——, 1826; m. George Ironside, merchant, born in England.

Gen. Geo. W. Cullum, U. S. Army, printed a biographical account of Capt Swift, from which the following abstracts are made:

"It is difficult in fitting phrase to do justice to the beloved memory of such a nobleman of nature as Captain Swift, and to portray his gentle, cheerful and buoyant spirit: his refined courtesy and vivacity of manner; his sweet serenity of temper, abounding humor and genial conversation; his conscientious candor and ingenuous frankness; his lofty honor, without soil or blemish; his devotion to duty as to a shrine of worship; his fulfillment of pledges and fidelity to every trust; his judgment in meeting and energy in overcoming obstacles; his patient and tireless industry in all pursuits; his modesty in measuring his achievements; his probity and justice under every temptation; his cheerful confidence and tranquil courage amid difficulties; his love of home and affection for kindred and friends; and, in fine, render due honor to all the varied virtues harmoniously fused together to form this upright officer, who

"bore, without abuse<br>
The grand old name of gentleman."

"In his official relations, one who had known Swift intimately for forty years, says in a letter: 'He carried into business the same qualities that distinguished him elsewhere — the instinct of a thorough gentleman, and the training of a soldier: sound sense, and a delicacy of feeling that made it impossible for him to look on the right or left of the path of duty and honor. I never thought of him as a trader, but always as a trustee; and trustworthiness, in every act, thought or opinion, is the word above all others to characterize him. He was naturally conservative and added to these qualities a sense of order, both natural and acquired, which maintained every piece of work at all times in as great completeness as it could be. He was tenacious of his opinions, and they became a part of himself; and if he once set a black mark against a man, it was not easy to induce him to erase it, but his instincts were so true that he rarely had occasion to change his judgments of men.'

But Swift's daily contact with the outside crafty world never blunted his sensibilities nor dwarfed his intellect. Nature had imbued him with a simplicity of heart, a refined unconsciousness of excellence which had not the slightest taint of vanity or tarnish of self-complacency. This gentle, childlike simplicity was one of the great charms of his character, and gave a placid repose to his entire life. He had a sensibility feelingly responsive to every fine impulse; a kindness, like golden threads running through the tissue of his whole being; and a modesty, which was reflected in all his acts, which colored all his surroundings, and heightened all his virtues. His modesty forbade his ever dwelling upon his own great achievements or daily acts of benevolence, though from others he keenly appreciated generous commendations that were deserved. His heart was always open, his counsel ever ready, and his sympathy warmly alive to all modest merit struggling with adversity. This tender compassion for the unfortunate was so strong that even his stern moral sense would soften to the evil-doer led astray by alluring temptation, his considerate reply to relentless Pharisees being always: "put yourself in the poor fellow's place, that is the only way to judge a man." Though his melting charity of thought commiserated wrong, he never swerved a tittle from an open expression and earnest advocacy of right. His candour courted the light; rectitude was the pole-star of his intellectual as of his moral nature; and honor his sacred tie of humanity, 'the noble mind's distinguishing perfection.' His sense of justice was so strong and so unselfish that, even in matters involving his own interest, no one hesitated to abide by his decisions, for they were strictly impartial and based on truth. In his crystal conscience truth entered as a beam of pure white light, without the tinge of one deviated ray of duplicity, directing him in the path of duty. Thus duty was not the mere routine of business, but a great moral obligation, the mainspring of his transactions. Whatever he did was well done and done systematically, for to him order was ' heaven's first law ' in conducting the smallest detail as the greatest undertaking; and untiring industry was the prodigious lever of his success. Work, to attain a worthy and useful purpose, sweetened his every moment with profit, seasoned all hours with joy, and idle days were canker-worms of his happiness. In all his acts practical common sense was conspicuous, and his views were plainly presented without the slightest garniture of show, or veiled with any gossamer of conventional phraseology. Ever ready at the opportune moment, he struck while the iron was hot, never, however, disdaining through perseverance to make the iron hot by striking. He prudently looked well to the past and forward to the future, but his habitual caution, which weighed in nice balance truth against error, was not the ' leaden servitor of dull delay.' He rarely lost his admirable equipoise amid all the disturbing elements of a jarring world; and his sound judgment, though so promptly rendered as to appear an intuition, was always based on ascertained facts, sagacious arguments, and mature reflection. His capacity for affairs was incontestable, and such confidence was reposed in his skilful management and well-tried fidelity that, till a few years before he died, he held, besides his public, no less than twenty-eight private trusts; was the safe custodian of many secrets of sorrow, trial and misfortune; and gave as careful and minute supervision to the interests of his family, relatives, and intimates, as to his own. Yet, while accomplishing so much, he never seemed busy. His study, in which most of his work was done, was at all hours open to his friends, and no matter how troublesome or complicated his work in hand might be, he was always ready to turn from it to offer his hearty, genial welcome to a visitor, or to patiently listen to any domestic or business affair brought to him for advice or consideration. But, when his day's work was done, his task was over, and he enjoyed his quiet evenings, his friends and his books, when their turn came, without a trace of preoccupation. Books he read for recreation as well as for knowledge; but the chief joys of his life were his family and friends, particularly his army associates, for whom his heart ever yearned. He was especially fond of the Military Academy and its traditions, and toward its graduates he grew more and more kindly and sympathetic with every waning year of life. This affection was warmly reciprocated, for he had a magnetic influence over all his intimates, and even the casual acquaintance was won by his sincerity, fidelity, manly virtues, and capacity of brotherhood. He inspired love and confidence also in those, whatever their stations, transiently employed on the various works under his supervision, for their interests became his; their claims upon his sympathy or consideration met with a prompt response; and no worthy subordinate, however necessary to him, failed of his influence to be advanced to a more lucrative position. It is therefore not strange that Swift was beloved and honored by the whole community with which he associated. For every one he had a gentle and kind word, a hearty, cordial greeting, and put all at ease by that urbanity of manner, or high breed-

ing which comes from the heart, and is refined into an inexpressible charm by the constant mingling with
polished society. With the world, both at home and abroad, he had had much intercourse which gave him an
affable, yet dignified demeanor, not as a garment put on for court occasion, but which was the habitual, graceful
drapery of life. They who knew him slightly perhaps thought him reserved, but no intimate could approach
him without catching the merry twinkle of his speaking eyes. His mirth and cheerfulness were the fountain-
springs, sparkling and bright, of his social life, which diffused refreshing dews of gladness upon all others, and
to himself gave that happy temperament, rarely clouded by care, which, like the dial, mark only the hours that
shine.

"Swift was indeed the light and strength of his immediate circle, and at his own fireside was most truly
appreciated, for he was the most devoted of husbands and the tenderest of parents; to the friends he had, and
their adoption tried, his heart was faithful to the last hour of life; he was the incorruptible citizen whom neither
power nor pay could swerve; the firm patriot whose whole country was holy ground; the efficient officer ever
at his post of duty; the able agent punctiliously faithful in the administration of every trust; the soul of honor
with the courage to execute the commands of conscience; and in his manly bosom lofty sentiments were em-
bellished by the softer refinements of a most noble nature, which

> "like gold, the more 'tis tried
> The more shall its intrinsic worth proclaim."

Capt. Swift was appointed a cadet at the U. S. Military Academy April 15,
1813, when but thirteen years old, entering Aug. 13, 1813, and there was distinguished for a love of fun rather than a devotion to study. In December, 1818, he·
was ordered on Major Long's expedition to the Rocky Mountains, which somewhat
tamed his playfulness. Once, while on a buffalo hunt, he was captured by Pawnee
Indians, who detained him some months, being kindly treated, and learning their
habits of life.

On the return of the expedition in February, 1821, although his class had been
graduated, he was attached to the end of the class roll, and promoted from July 1,
1819, as Second Lieutenant Corps of Artillery.

After the completion of Major Long's map of the expedition he was, till 1826,
under Colonel Abert of the topographical engineers, on surveys for military
defenses on the Atlantic coast, and was detailed from 1828–29, on the improvement
of railroads.

From 1830 to 1832 he was engaged in the United States Post Office department, in compiling, almost entirely with his own hands, an elaborate post-route map
of the United States, with books of distance, which were so complete that they have
been the basis of all since used. During these two years he also assisted in the
survey of several railroads.

In the meantime, August 5, 1824, he had been promoted First Lieutenant, 1st
Artillery, and August 1, 1832, was attached to the general staff of the army as Brevet
Captain of Topographical Engineers, and full captain July 7, 1838.

Captain Swift's attainments were considered so high that, at the request of
Professor Hassler, he was detailed from 1833 to 1843 on the great geodetic survey
of the Atlantic coast, and at various times had charge of fifteen river and harbor
improvements along the Atlantic coast, from Portland, Me., to Westport, Ct. From

1836 to 1840 was resident superintending engineer of the Massachusetts Western Railroad.

In 1840–41 was in Europe, and after his return, in 1843, was a member of the board of visitors to the Military Academy. From 1843 till July 31, 1849, when he resigned from the army, he was the principal assistant to Colonel Abert, during which time he was often detailed on important duties. The principal of these was as a commissioner of the Illinois and Michigan Canal, of which, from June 26, 1845, to August 16, 1871, he was president of the board of trustees. His was the organizing brain and directing hand of the board, of this great work from its inception, and during which $10,913,765 passed through its hands, faithfully accounting for every dollar. The success of the negotiation to secure the loan from Baring Bros., to carry on this work was greatly due to the business tact, engineering experience, and upright character of Captain Swift; and they communicated their high appreciation of the services he had rendered, and their personal regards, and asked him to accept an extra year's salary.

In 1843 he erected the iron beacon still standing at the entrance of Black Rock Harbor, Ct., and in 1848 Minot Ledge lighthouse.

Shortly after resigning his commission he was appointed president of the Philadelphia, Wilmington and Baltimore Railroad, which position he filled with great acceptance. On his resignation he accepted the presidency of the Massachusetts Western railroad, acquitting himself to the entire satisfaction of the company. In 1853 Harvard College conferred on him the honorary degree of A. M. He became prominently identified with other great railroads, and in 1874 went to England for the purpose of making favorable financial arrangements with Messrs. Baring & Co.

Captain Swift, from his first acquaintance with these bankers possessed their entire confidence, and to the day of his death was their confidential adviser relating to American railroads.

Captain Swift lived to see nearly four-score years, passing away with love, honor and troops of friends.

-----

21

**Dr. Nathaniel**[6] **Swift,** (*Nathaniel,*[5] *Nathaniel,*[4] *Samuel,*[3] *Thomas,*[2] *Thomas,*[1]) of Andover, Mass., physician; b. in Dorchester July 15, 1778; d. Dec. 7, 1840; m. Nov. 27, 1803, Sarah, (b. May 22, 1783; d. Sept. 11, 1858, æ. 75,) dau. of Timothy Abbott of Andover.

CHILDREN.

30.  Nathaniel, b. May 12, 1805.
31.  George Baker, b. July 30, 1806.
     SARAH FRANCIS, b. Nov. 15, 1807; m. June 19, 1833, Rev. Jeffries Hall. Children:  1, Caroline, b. May 26, 1834; m. Moses Foster of Andover.  2, Edward Percival, b. April 3, 1836.  3, Henry Kirke White, b. July 24, 18—.  4, SARAH FRANCES, b. Jan. 23, 1841; m. Dr. J. C. W. Moore, Concord, N. H.  5, Helen Maria, b. Oct. 23, 1847, res., Chesterfield, N. H.
     WILLIAM, b. Dec. 17, 1809; d. Nov. 20, 1833.

CATHARINE, b. July 6, 1813; m. Aug. 12, 1834, John F. (b. Jan 29, 1810) son of Capt. John and Martha (Swan) Trow, of North Andover, Mass. Children: 1, Sarah F. Trow, b. Aug. 22, 1835; m. Oct. 1, 1856, A. Carter, Jr., manufacturing jeweler, res., Orange, N. J. 2, George W. Trow, b. June 21, 1827; d. Oct. 8, 1872. 3, Catharine S. Trow, b. Aug. 28, 1842; m. Aug. 12, 1863, Dr. James B. Cutter. 4. Martha Elizabeth Trow, b. Sept. 20, 1844; m. Oct. 10, 1887, Hugo Peipers, merchant of New York. 5, John Fowler Trow, Jr., b. May 19, 1850; m. April 14, 1880, Cora Munn.

JOHN F. TROW commenced life as a printer, and at the age of twenty-two established and published the *Nashua Herald*, at Nashua, N. H. He sold out his interest to the editor, and in 1833 left for New York, where, in May of that year he engaged in business under the firm name of West & Trow. From 1840 to 1848 he was of the firm of Leavitt, Trow & Co., publishers and booksellers, and John F. Trow, printers. In 1848 he commenced the publication of Wilson's Business Directory, and in 1852 of Trow's New York City Directory, which publications are still continued. He is president and treasurer of Trow's Printing and Bookbinding Company, and treasurer of the National Needle Company. Mr. Trow has been an elder in the Presbyterian church for thirty-five years.

32.  Samuel, b. Feb. 21, 1815.

    CHARLES, } b. July 25, 1816; lives in Boston.
33.  Jonathan, } b. July 25, 1816.


## OBITUARY.


Died at Andover, on the 7th instant, after a short illness, Dr. Nathaniel Swift, in the sixty-third year of his age. By this providence an affectionate family have been bereft of a kind and tender father, the community of a strictly honest and upright citizen, and the church of a sincere and devoted member.

Dr. Swift was affectionate and kind in his disposition, cheerful and friendly in his social intercourse, and prompt to every professional call, without regard to the unseasonableness of the hour, the inclemency of the weather, or the poverty of the applicant.

The poor and the aged have lost in him a friend indeed. It was his special delight to minister to their comfort. They experienced his care and attention in sickness, and his counsel and charity in health. At his death, those who had experienced the value of his services and kindness gathered around his remains, to shed the silent tear, and to speak of his many virtues, and his self-denial for their good.

He held several important public offices: those of Justice of the Peace and Postmaster, for nearly twenty years, and those of Coroner, Notary Public, and Director in the Essex Bank for many years. The duties of each he continued to discharge until his decease.

He had been a member of the church about forty years. His religion was of the heart and not in word only. His favorite books were his Bible, with Orton's Exposition, and Bunyan's Pilgrim's Progress, with Scott's Notes; the latter of which he read through in course not less than twenty times. It had been his habit for years to rise between four and five o'clock and spend a season in religious reading. The blessing of his paternal care and instruction will long be cherished in grateful recollection, and be felt, we trust, when time shall be no more. His numerous family of children all became at an early age members of the Church of Christ. One most devout and heavenly minded, some years since, entered, we cannot doubt, in his eternal rest. May the bereaved widow and children, and the sisters and brothers in this hour of deep affliction find the consolation which flows alone from the Christian's life; and be trained, under the discipline of heaven, for a union with the departed dead where tears and parting shall be unknown.

DECEMBER 26, 1840.


22


Dr. William⁶ Swift, U. S. N., (*Nathaniel,⁵ Nathaniel,⁴ Samuel,³ Thomas,² Thomas,¹*) b. in Dorchester Sept. 11, 1779; d. Dec. 27, 1864; m. Dec. 31, 1850, Martha Elizabeth, dau. of Luke and Mary (Montague) Phelps, of Westhampton, Mass.

### CHILDREN.

WILLIAM JONATHAN, b. March 10, 1852; grad. at Amherst College 1873; College of Physicians and Surgeons, N. Y., 1878; Bellevue Hospital, N. Y., 1880; m. June, 13, 1882, Marie Aborn, dau. of S. J. Jacobs, of New York. Residence New York. They have Lawrence, b. June 8, 1883.

JOHN BAKER, b. Sept. 30, 1853; grad. Amherst College 1873; Harvard Medical School 1877; m. Oct 11, 1882, Hettie, dau. of Andrew H. Potter, of New Bedford, Mass. Residence, Boston. They have John Baker, b. Aug. 12, 1883.

GEORGE MONTAGUE, b. Sept. 2, 1856; grad. Amherst College 1876; College of Physicians and Surgeons, N. Y., 1879; Bellevue Hospital, N. Y., 1881; residence, New York.

Dr. Swift was graduated from Harvard College in 1809, and from the Harvard Medical School in 1812. The same year he entered the United States navy as a volunteer, and sailed to the coast of Africa on board the "Chesapeake." On her return he received from President Madison his commission as a surgeon in the navy. He was on board the "Chesapeake" during her engagement in Boston Harbor with the British man-o'-war "Shannon," was made prisoner, and with others was sent to Halifax, Nova Scotia, from which place he was sent home with the wounded. Dr. Swift was with Lawrence when he died, and was presented by him with his belt. In 1813 he was on the brig "Syren," was again taken prisoner and sent to the Cape of Good Hope, where he was kept six months. In 1820 Dr. Swift was on the "Ontario," from which vessel he was detached and sent to Tunis as acting United States consul, where he remained sixteen months. In 1827 he was on the frigate "Erie;" 1829 on the "Constellation," cruising to England, France, and in the Mediterranean. From about 1833 to 1836 Dr. Swift was stationed at the Naval Hospital in New York. This service was during the cholera epidemic. In 1836 he was on the "North Carolina;" was fleet surgeon of the Pacific squadron, and on his return in 1839 was stationed at New York, Boston and Newport, for different periods. In 1862, at his own request, he was placed on the retired list, having spent fifty-one years in the service of his country. His residence for several years was Brooklyn, N. Y., where he died in 1864. Dr. Swift was a gentleman of polished manners, extremely methodical, and always avoiding anything like display. He was a great reader, very fond of books, and collected a large library.

---

23

Capt. Samuel⁶ Swift, *(Nathaniel,⁵ Nathaniel,⁴ Samuel,³ Thomas,² Thomas,¹)* b. in Dorchester Dec. 2, 1785; d. March 15, 1862; m. Nov. 3, 1819, Eliza Hester, (b. Oct. 15, 1800; d. May 1, 1866,) dau. of John Willkings of Wilmington, N. C.

### CHILDREN.

MARY WYATT, b. May 1, 1823; drowned May 1, 1841.

ELIZA HESTER, b. Feb. 1, 1825; m. Feb. 4, 1845, Thomas M. Woodruff of Trenton, N. J., who died in Chicago Jan. 28, 1880. Children: George, b. Jan. 30, 1846; William Swift, b. March 4, 1849; m. in Dixon, Ill., July 19, 1879, Ruth Frances Wood.

GEORGE BAKER, b. Nov. 21, 1826; d. March 28, 1827.

34.   Samuel, b. May 22, 1828.

ISABELLA SARAH, b. April 11, 1832; m. Oct. 28, 1852, Robert J. Woodruff, M. D., of Trenton, N. J. Children: Mary Jean, b. Aug. 28, 1835; m. Jan. 24, 1880, A. B. Charbonnel of Chicago; Isabella Louisa, b. Aug. 6, 1855; d. May 28, 1859; Susan Hester, b. June 16, 1858.

HARRIET, b. Aug. 19, 1834; died Sept. 22, 1835.

HARRIET, b. July 4, 1836; died Feb. 5, 1880; m. Sept. — 1866, Henry O. Nichols of Dorchester. Children: Grace Swift, b. Nov. 3, 1867; Arthur Topliff, b. July 7, 1869; Carrie Frances, b. Oct. 3, 1877.

35.   William, b. July 22, 1839.

MARY, b. Sept. 4, 1841; m. at Springfield, Ill., Feb. 14, 1871, Professor Orestes H. St. John of Topeka, Kansas. He is a geologist and paleontologist. No children.

CHARLOTTE, b. May 27, 1843; m. at Princeton February 22, 1866, to Charles F. Little, M. D. Practiced a number of years in Princeton, then removed to Manhattan, Kansas. Children: Eliza Ada, b. June 22, 1867; Nellie Perkins, b. Dec. 15, 1868; Blanche Alpine, b. Dec. 18, 1869; d. Nov. 27, 1878. Jennie Belle, b. Oct. 8, 1871; Frederick Swift, b. June 25, 1873.

Capt. Swift chose as his profession a seafaring life, and in 1806 made his first voyage, following the sea as a shipmaster twenty-four years.

He commanded, with success, the ships of Stephen Girard of Philadelphia, and those of Goodhue & Co., and is said to have been the first American to make a voyage to the north-west coast.

He was a man of commanding presence, and possessed much personal beauty. A portrait painted in Antwerp is in the possession of his son-in-law, Mr. Nichols, of Dorchester. His daughter, Mrs. E. H. Woodruff of Princeton, Ill., has a miniature of him taken in early life, and his daughter, Mrs. Charlotte Little, has one of her mother.

In 1836 Capt. Swift left the sea, and removed from Dorchester to Geneva, N. Y., and in 1838 he removed to Princeton, Ill., where he died.


## OBITUARY. ·

Died in Princeton, on Saturday morning the 15th, of Paralysis, Capt. Samuel Swift, in the 78th year of his age.

[ COMMUNICATED.]

He was born in Dorchester, Massachusetts, and having early in life manifested a predilection for the sea, he entered into the service of the Boston and London Shipping Company. He subsequently commanded some of the best merchant ships of New York and Philadelphia, and made in them many long and perilous voyages. He five times circumnavigated the globe, and from long and active service acquired a high character for professional skill. He was a man of marked individuality of character; he possessed great determination and courage, and displayed a rare and admirable coolness in the presence of danger. Though a great part of his life had been spent on the sea in active employment, which does not afford much for the acquisition of knowledge unconnected with nautical pursuits, the fund of general information he possessed was large. He was well read in the English classics, and had an especial admiration of the works of Pope, Addison, Goldsmith and Johnson.

In all his long and eventful life his probity and honor were never questioned, and it might with truth be said of him that he was that "noblest work of God, an honest man."

MARCH 15, 1862.

24

**John⁶ Swift**, (*John,⁵ Ebenezer,⁴ Samuel,³ Thomas,² Thomas,¹*) b. March 12, 1775; d. Sept. 26, 1838; m. Elizabeth Parker, b.                ; d. Aug. 27, 1863, daughter of Capt. Gideon and Elizabeth Hovey Parker, of Ipswich, a meritorious officer of the Revolution and correspondent of Washington.

CHILDREN.

JOHN MCLEAN, b. Nov. 23, 1818; went to sea; never heard from.
ELIZABETH ROGERS, b. Jan. 19, 1820.
WILLIAM PARKER, b. Dec. 27, 1821; d. June 3, 1875.
DEAN MANNING, b. Oct. 23, 1824; d. Aug. 26, 1859; m. April 30, 1850, Mary Sumner, b. Aug. 20, 1827, dau. of Lemuel Sumner. She m. 2d, Moses C. Chapman. Had two children who died young, Mary Frances and Dean Manning.
MARY FRANCES, b. Oct. 12, 1828.

Mr. Swift followed his father's business, and occupied the family mansion on Milton Hill, in which all his children were born. He was a man of standing in the community; universally esteemed for his integrity, and filled several important offices. His only surviving children, Misses Elizabeth R. and Mary F. Swift, ladies of refinement and culture, live near by the old homestead. Their charming home contains many interesting and valuable relics of the olden time, chief among which is the old oak chair before mentioned. They also have a rare and curious Venetian mirror of large size, and a fine old book-case which is thought to have belonged to Gov. Hutchinson. These ladies are the last of a family prominent in Milton's history for two centuries, though representatives still sustain the character of the family in other towns.  ·

---

25

**Samuel⁶ Swift**, (*Samuel,⁵ Ebenezer,⁴ Samuel,³ Thomas,² Thomas,¹*) b. Sept. 22, 1783; d. Jan. 11, 1826; m. Nov. 2, 1806, Polly Cheney, b. in Roxbury                ; d. May 5, 1828, æ. 42: dau. of Lieut. Thomas and Jane (Foster) Cheney of Roxbury.

CHILDREN.

SAMUEL FOSTER, b. Oct. 6, 1807; a drummer in the U. S. Army; died in service at Old Point Comfort.
Child died in infancy.
36. **William Augustus**, b. Oct. 18, 1811.
37. **Lewis**, b. Jan. 16, 1815.
ANDREW,                        ; d. in Philadelphia Mar. 22, 1841.
EBENEZER,
THOMAS,                        ; d. young in Roxbury.

Mr. Swift was a hatter of Roxbury; a man of great humor, of whom many anecdotes are told.

### 26

Commodore Jonathan **Williams**[7] **Swift**, U. S. N., (*Joseph Gardner*[8], *Foster*[5], *Samuel*[4], *Samuel*[3], *Thomas*[2], *Thomas*[1],) b. March 30, 1808, at Taunton, Mass.; d. July 30, 1877; m. Jan. 10, 1833, Isabella Fitzhugh, youngest child of Col. William Fitzhugh of Hampton. Mrs. Swift resides at Geneva, N. Y.

#### CHILDREN.

FITZHUGH, b. March 12, 1841; d. Dec. 31, 1860, at sea.

JOSEPH GARDNER, b. Feb. 4, 1844; d. March 2, 1871; cadet at the U. S. Military Academy from Sept. 1862 to June 18, 1866, when he was graduated and promoted in the army to 2d Artillery. Served in garrison at Richmond, Va., Sept. 30, 1866.

ANN ELIZABETH, b. Oct. 31, 1846; m. Sept. 3, 1872, Lieut. John Williams Martin, 4th U. S. Cavalry. They have William Swift Martin, b. Feb. 4, 1874; John Throop Martin, b. Jan. 20th, 1884, d. Jan. 22, 1885.

Commodore Swift was appointed from North Carolina August 25, 1823; went to the Mediterranean in 1824; returned in 1826; went to the Pacific in frigate "Brandywine" in 1826; returned in 1829; examined in 1820 and promoted in 1831; went to the Mediterranean in 1831; returned in 1832; steamship "Fulton" Atlantic coast 1840; special service 1850–5. Commissioned Lieutenant March 3, 1861; commissioned a Commodore July 16, 1862.

---

### 27

**McRee**[7] **Swift**, (*Joseph Gardner*[6], *Foster*[5], *Samuel*[4], *Samuel*[3], *Thomas*[2], *Thomas*[1],) b. April 15, 1819, in New York; m. Sept. 15, 1842, Abby Hortense Chew, daughter of Thomas John Chew, U. S. N. For her ancestry see *Pedigree of Chew* by Rev. L. B. Thomas, p. 33.

#### CHILDREN.

HORTENSE HALLAM, b. Aug. 22, 1843; d. April 28, 1848.

LOUISA WALKER, b. Aug. 23, 1845.

ELIZABETH CHEW, b. July 29, 1847; m. June 11, 1879, George Henry Janeway of New Brunswick, N. J.

ALEXANDER JOSEPH, b. Aug. 20, 1849; grad. Rutgers College 1868; Polytechnic Institute, Troy, 1872.

LAWRENCE CHEW, b. Feb. 24, 1852; grad. College of Physicians and Surgeons, N. Y., 1878, Charity Hospital, N. Y., 1880; m. April 16, 1884, Mabel Bruce, dau. of Col. Joseph M. Griffith of Des Moines, Iowa. They have ———— Swift, b. March 16, 1885.

THOMAS DELANO, b. Feb. 10, 1854; grad. Rutgers College 1875; College of Physicians and Surgeons, N. Y., 1879; Bellevue Hospital 1881.

JONATHAN WILLIAMS, b. March 30, 1856; d. May 2, 1862.

JOSEPHINE RICHARDS, b. Jan. 10, 1859.

ROBERT HALLAM, b. June 16, 1863; d. March 4, 1865.

MARY LEWIS, b. May 11, 1865.

Mr. Swift, now retired from active business life, resides at New Brunswick, New Jersey. He has been a successful civil engineer, engaged in the construction and management of railroads in various States, and later in manufacturing enterprises. He inherits much of his father's literary tastes and high-bred courtesy; and the warm interest he has shown in the progress of this work has been of material assistance to the compiler. From the family Bible, which belonged to his father, the late General Joseph Gardner Swift, he has furnished much data; and by his kind permission the Journal of General Swift has been printed from the original copy in his possession. Besides this valuable document, Mr. Swift has inherited the ancient oil painting of the family coat-of-arms, and the portraits of his grandparents, Dr. and Mrs. Foster Swift, by Jarvis, and has had them photographed for this work.

In 1852, when Mr. Swift was traveling abroad with his father, General Joseph Gardner Swift, and while walking in the grounds of the Tower of London, his father was accosted by one of the guards, who expressed surprise at seeing Mr. Swift out so early in the day.

"How do you know me, my man?" said General Swift.

"Why, sir, I see you constantly."

The man had mistaken the General for Mr. Swift, the keeper of the crown jewels. They found Mr. Swift lived in the enclosure and went to his house, and to their astonishment were met by a gentleman of advanced years, the counterpart almost of Mr. Swift's grandfather, Dr. Foster Swift — Edmund Lenthal Swift, barrister, K. C. J. They lunched and spent several hours with him, and found he was of the Rotherham family of Swifts. This interview is mentioned in *Notes and Queries* by E. L. Swift.

---

28

Dr. **Foster**[7] **Swift**, *( Joseph Gardner,*[6] *Foster,*[5] *Samuel,*[4] *Samuel,*[3] *Thomas,*[2] *Thomas,*[1] *)* b. at Geneva, N. Y., Oct. 31, 1833; d. May 10, 1875; m. Oct. 29, 1862, Alida Carroll, daughter of Dr. D. H. Fitzhugh, and had

SARAH DELANO, b. Feb. 5, 1864.

## MEMORIAL.

Dr. Swift, who is said to have resembled his father more than any of his sons, was graduated at Hobart College, Geneva, in 1852. During the last year of his college course he attended lectures in the Medical College in Geneva, but was dissuaded from continuing his medical studies after graduation, by his father, who thought him too delicate, physically, to endure the arduous labors of a doctor's life. To gratify his father he read law reluctantly for eight months, in the office of Judge Kent, in this city, and then, feeling the need of a more liberal classical and literary culture than he had obtained at Hobart College, he entered the Junior class at Harvard University, and graduated at that institution in the class of 1854, the subject of his inaugural thesis being "The Influence of Shakspeare's Plays on the Popular Estimation of Historical Characters." Thus furnished with the broad foundation of a liberal education and a fine literary taste, he resolved to gratify his early inclination to study medicine. In the fall of 1854 he became a favorite pupil of Dr. Willard Parker, and from that time until the summer of 1870, when he was prostrated by the disease which finally destroyed him, he gave himself with untiring energy and self-sacrificing devotion to the study and practice of his profession. He graduated at the College of Physicians and Surgeons, in the class of 1857. He immediately entered Bellevue Hospital, and served during two years on the same staff with his attached friend, Dr. Edward B. Dalton. In the spring of 1859 he established himself in private practice in this city. He had already passed the precarious period in the young doctor's course, and had begun to lay the foundation of a brilliant career as a teacher and practitioner, when the war broke out, in the spring of 1861, and animated by a loyalty which, with him, was something more than the contagious enthusiasm which pervaded the country at that time, he forsook his practice and went as surgeon to the 8th regiment of New York State Militia, in response to the first call for troops to defend the capitol. At the battle of Bull Run he and his staff were captured while in the performance of their duty, and being almost the only prisoners who were not taken in the act of hasty retreat, they were released on parole in the city of Richmond, by Gen. Beauregard, and, after a brief detention, returned on parole to their homes. Thus debarred from the privilege of further service in the army, Dr. Swift resumed the practice of his profession. In 1862 he married the daughter of Dr. Fitzhugh, of Livingston County, who with one child, a daughter, survives him. His success from this time was rapid and exceptionally brilliant. He was successively appointed physician to St. Luke's, and the Children's Hospital; Assistant Professor of Obstetrics in the College of Physicians and Surgeons, and afterwards Clinical Professor of skin diseases in the Bellevue Hospital College, and Professor of Obstetrics in the Long Island Medical College. He had thus obtained within the brief period of ten years, by his scholarly acquirements, by his ability as a teacher, and by his skill as a practitioner, a claim to the first rank in his profession. He had scarcely begun to enjoy the honor and rewards of his well-earned position, when, in the summer of 1870, after a season of untiring labor and peculiarly trying experiences, he began to exhibit the signs of the pulmonary disease to which he finally succumbed. Conscious as he was of the threatening nature of his malady, he worked on for some time, regardless of the affectionate warnings of his friends and medical advisers, and only reluctantly yielded to their counsels when he fainted in the Theatre at the Bellevue College, in the effort to fulfil an engagement to lecture in the opening session of that institution in the fall of 1870. He soon afterwards went to Europe, but returned in the spring of 1871, without material improvement in health. The winter of 1871–72 he passed on the Pacific Coast, in the congenial companionship of his friend, Dr. Dalton, whose brief but brilliant career he there saw closed. The following winter he passed in the south of France, where, having procured an authorization from the French government, he hoped to practice his profession. He returned to this country, however, in the spring of 1873, to visit his family, and his disease having made considerable progress, he was induced to remain at home, instead of returning to France as he had intended. His experience of the effects of a warm climate upon his disease not having been entirely satisfactory, he resolved to try the experiment of spending a winter in the northern part of this State, at Morrisville, in Madison County. He was so encouraged by the promising effects of a cold climate, that he purchased a house at Morrisville, and determined to abandon, for a time, all hopes of resuming his practice, and devote himself to the recovery of his health. In the summer of 1874, however, it became evident to him and to his friends that he was fast losing ground in the conflict with his disease, and last fall he decided to try again the effect of a warm climate. He went to the Island of Santa Cruz, where he passed a lonely winter, separated from his wife and child, and sustained only by the hope, which grew fainter day by day, of arresting the progress of his disease. The last weeks of his life were cheered by the presence of a sister who, with her husband and a nephew, went to him in the hope of bringing him back to his home to die. This hope was not abandoned until a few days before his death, when he began to fail so rapidly that he realized the near approach of death, and met it with cheerful resignation, and in the complete assurance of a Christian faith. He died on the 10th of May. His remains were brought home, and now rest in the family ground at Geneva. Such is the brief record of a life of which we all knew the promise and now lament the untimely end. Dr. Swift's professional career, though too brief to be marked by any work which will perpetuate his name on the scroll of fame, was one that will leave a lasting and enviable impression on the memory of all who enjoyed his friendship, or had the privilege of intercourse with him as a teacher or physician. He possessed in a high degree the intellectual and moral qualities which fit a man for the responsible office of a physician. Love of nature and loyalty to the truth were his pre-eminent characteristics. He was imbued with the true scientific spirit, and his professional acquirements, in all departments, as far as they went, were free from the chaff of speculation and hypothesis. He hated sham wherever he found it, whether it lay in the conceit of those who deceived themselves, or in the dishonest practices of those who sought to deceive others. He had all the qualities of a successful teacher, thorough honesty, large experience, liberal acquirements, and literary attainments, and there can be no doubt that the cause of sound medical education lost one of its ablest and most promising exponents in his early death. As a physician, it may be truly said, that few men in our profession possessed or deserved in a larger degree than Dr. Swift the confidence and affection of his patients. His gentle and winning address, his sagacity and skill as a clinical observer, his fertility of resources, and above all, his fidelity, commanded the affection, respect and absolute trust of all to whom he ministered. His work was always thorough, and he gave to his cases a thoughtful and laborious study, which distinguished him from the routine practitioner. His sense of professional duty was so high that he never counted the cost to his health in fulfilling it, and there is little question in the minds of his friends that he finally fell a victim to his untiring and self-sacrificing labors. This sense of professional duty in Dr. Swift was not dictated simply by a sympathetic nature, or by a desire to please or win the confidence of his patients, but mainly by a profound conviction of the responsibility he assumed, whenever he was called to the bedside of those who trusted themselves to his care. But to all who enjoyed the privilege of Dr. Swift's companionship, his remarkable social qualities gave a charm to his character which your memory of him will recall better than any words of mine. Who of us can forget his refined and genial presence; his humor, that would illumine tears, and the wit whose shafts were never poisoned with malice, but always gleamed with mirth? Cultivated beyond most men in our profession in general literature, and devoted to all that was pure and elevating in art, his conversation was always entertaining and often brilliant in the originality and keenness of his criticism. He was never commonplace, because he never borrowed his convictions from other men unless they accorded with his own observation, or had been first subjected to his own enlightened reflection. But with all his intellectual gifts and accomplishments, Dr. Swift possessed a kindly and sympathetic nature that was quick to share the sorrows as well as the joys of his friends. As in his professional relations there was no self sacrifice too great for him to make in the discharge of what he recognized as his duty, so in his closer relations to his family and his friends there was a love and a loyalty that knew no bounds. The keenness with which he sometimes suffered from his sense of his professional responsibility was only exceeded by the painful sympathy with which he realized the trials of his friends. To the severe strain which he suffered from both of these causes in the last year of his practice, his illness, as I have before suggested, was doubtless largely due, and while we cannot but grieve that a man of so great promise is lost so early to our profession, and a friend of such genial and noble nature is gone from us in the fullness of his manhood, we have reason to rejoice that we were permitted for even a brief period to enjoy the privilege of his friendship, and the precious example of his character. — *From a sketch by Wm. H. Draper, M. D., printed in 1875.*

---

## 29

**Charles[7] W. Swift,** *( William Henry,[6] Foster,[5] Samuel,[4] Samuel,[3] Thomas,[2] Thomas,[1] )* b. ———, 1828; m. ———, Margaret, dau. of John Howard of Springfield, Mass., sister of his stepmother. Summer residence Pequot Avenue, New London, Ct.

CHILDREN.

Mary H.
Louisa Josephine.

---

## 30

**Nathaniel[7] Swift,** *(Nathaniel,[6] Nathaniel,[5] Nathaniel,[4] Samuel,[3] Thomas,[2] Thomas,[1] )* of Andover, merchant; b. May 12, 1805; d. Sept. 6, 1878; m. Oct. 10, 1832,

Martha Jane, dau. of Francis Kidder of Andover. She died Nov. 28, 1843, aged 30 years. He next married Oct. 13, 1847, Almena Jacobs.

### CHILDREN.

George Francis, b. Dec. 10, 1833.
Martha Elizabeth, b. Feb. 15, 1836.
Charlotte Harris, b. July 26, 1839.
Anna Hartwell, b. Sept. 18, 1842.

---

## OBITUARY.

[From the *Boston Daily Advertiser* of Sept. 20, 1878.]

One by one our older citizens and fellow townsmen are passing away. To those who are following next in file, the ranks must appear to be rapidly thinning out. But two weeks ago we cast a last sorrowful glance upon the bier of our honored and esteemed townsman, Captain Oliver Hazard Perry.

One week later, to a day, the funeral obsequies were held over the mortal remains of Mr. Swift, a native and life-long resident of Andover. The light of a pure and unblemished life has gone out. A kind-hearted, generous, useful and esteemed citizen has passed away from our sight. One more is added to the great majority on the other side of the chasm between the present life. But the memory of the just is blessed. In this thought is the consolation which remains to those nearest and dearest in the relations of life to our departed friend.

Mr. Swift was born in Danvers May 12, 1805, and was the eldest son of the late Dr. Nathaniel and Sarah Abbot Swift. Early in life — almost in his boyhood — he engaged in mercantile pursuits, and upon attaining his majority he became a partner in a mercantile firm in Andover. A business tact and shrewdness was manifested from the earliest stage of his business career. Promptness, straightforwardness and honesty, three sterling qualities of the business man, were prominent in his character, and promised from the outset assurance of success. And success came readily and naturally; gradually, but not spasmodically — a healthy success. By a prudent, sagacious and careful management of his business affairs, he was enabled to retire therefrom with a competency for his family before he was fifty years of age. But these qualities, which were so prominently manifested in the duties pertaining to his business, were by no means unnoticed or overlooked. His correct judgment and capacity for usefulness were very soon called into active exercise in positions which, while benefitting society, the cause of education, the interest of his native town, and the general welfare of his fellow-men, reflected a lasting honor upon his good name and reputation. He proved himself to be more than a successful business man. His instinctive honesty, his unswerving integrity, his forecast, his sound judgment and his correct and exquisite taste, were all brought together and made to subserve and round out happily a very useful and honorable life of official duties. For twenty-eight years a working director in the Andover Bank (State and National,) for thirty-six years a trustee of the Andover Savings Bank, and its president for eighteen years—to the date of his decease, and for twenty-eight years a trustee of the Abbot Academy for young ladies, his advice and counsel always commanded the attention and respect of his associates. In 1852 he was elected treasurer of the Abbot Academy, and to the permanent life and success of this institution he devoted himself with unwonted ardor, and with a strength and vigor indicative of his earnest and unstinted love for the work he had undertaken. From the very first he manifested a determination to render the surroundings of the Academy pleasing and attractive, to enlarge the area of its domain, to beautify and adorn the same, and all his ardent aspirations to this end appear to have been crowned with admirable and wonderful success.

---

### 31

Dr. George Baker⁷ Swift, (*Nathaniel,⁶ Nathaniel,⁵ Nathaniel,⁴ Samuel,³ Thomas², Thomas,¹*) b. July 30, 1806; d.     1872; m. Nov. 8, 1831, Mary Bennett Warren, of Framingham, Mass. Dr. Swift was graduated at the Harvard Medical School in 1830, and practiced in Manchester, N. H., Lawrence, Mass., and New York.

CHILDREN.

Mary.
George Warren.
Catherine.
Frank.

---

32

**Samuel[7] Swift,** *(Nathaniel,[6] Nathaniel,[5] Nathaniel,[4] Samuel,[3] Thomas,[2] Thomas,[1])* merchant, b. Feb. 21, 1815; d. Dec. 5, 1851, in Brooklyn, N. Y.;  m. Nov. 16, 1842, Mary Phelps, b. in Westhampton, Mass., Dec. 8, 1818.

CHILDREN.

Mary, b. July 5, 1844; d. July 31, 1846.
Martha Elizabeth, b. Sept. 16, 1847; m. Feb. 18, 1869, W. B. Dickerman, banker, of 66 Broadway, N. Y.
38. Samuel, b. Aug. 5, 1849.

---

33

**Jonathan[7] Swift,** *(Nathaniel,[6] Nathaniel,[5] Nathaniel,[4] Samuel,[3] Thomas,[2] Thomas,[1])* of Andover, b. July 25, 1816; m. Oct. 30, 1850, Almena Jacobs of Cherryfield, Maine; b. Jan. 6, 1831, Columbia, Me.

CHILDREN.

Elizabeth Florence, b. Oct. 25, 1860; grad. 1881 at the Andover Female Academy.
Kate Adams, b. March 4, 1869.

---

34

**Samuel[7] Swift,** *(Samuel,[6] Nathaniel,[5] Nathaniel,[4] Samuel,[3] Thomas,[2] Thomas,[1])* of San Francisco, California; b. May 22, 1828; m. Nov. 24, 18—, Emma Newberry.

CHILDREN.

Mary Hester, b. June —, 1866.

Mr. Swift was brought up on a farm near Princeton, Illinois.   His father's intention was to give him a collegiate education, but losing his fortune, he moved to Illinois at an early day, so that he had no opportunity for an education except what he got himself.   In 1852 he went to California, crossing the plains with a party of nine young men from Princeton with two ox teams; the one with which he was connected, however, had three yoke of oxen and one yoke of cows, which afforded them milk most of the way.   They were five months in making the trip from Princeton, Ill., to Downsville, Simon Co., Cal. On reaching the sink of the Humboldt River their team was so diminished, having lost two oxen and one cow, that they could not attempt to cross the fifty-mile desert that there was open before them, with their wagon, as the rest of their team was insufficient to make the trip over the desert, and then over the Sierra Nevada range of mountains, so they sold what was left of the team, and used the wagon for camp-fires for the party, and having given and thrown away everything else that was portable, except what provisions they could carry and were necessary to last them for the remainder of the journey, they started next morning early, with their provisons and one quart of water to each man, for which they paid one dollar per quart. After some severe hardships they reached California, not having seen a house or other habitation of any white man, after leaving the Missouri river, except Fort Laramie and Fort Hall, where some United States troops were stationed. In 1857 he made a trip up Frazier river into British Columbia, navigating that river in a small boat a distance of two hundred and fifty miles, with an Indian for a guide, adding another chapter to his frontier life, which for roughness of experience surpassed anything he had previously gone through, being constantly surrounded by dangers to life in various ways. In 1859 he returned to California and received a letter from his father, requesting him to return home, as he was quite old and decrepit. He did so, and remained in Princeton, Ill., until 1866, during which time his father and mother both died, and he then returned again to California, and has resided the most of the time in San Francisco. He joined the Order of F. and A. Masons in California in 1855, in Forest Lodge, No. 66, Sierra County; afterwards joined Bureau Lodge, No. 112, in Princeton, then was a member of two different Lodges in San Francisco. Is now a member of Portland Lodge, No. 55, Portland, Oregon. While in Princeton the last time he joined Princeton Chapter, No. 28, of Royal Arch Masons, also Orion Council, No. 8, Royal and Select Masters and Temple Commandery, No. 20, Knights Templar. He is now a member of San Francisco Chapter, No. 1, Royal Arch Masons, California Council, No. 1, Royal and Select Masters and Golden Gate Commandery, No. 16, Knights Templar, San Francisco. When leaving San Francisco in 1881 to go to Montana, he was Secretary of San Francisco Chapter, and Recorder of Golden Gate Commandery, Knights Templar, and was also President of the Masonic Veteran Association of the Pacific Coast. Mr. Swift's present address is 1112 East Sixteenth Street, Oakland, California.

--- --- ---

### 35

**William**[7] **Swift**, (*Samuel*,[6] *Nathaniel*,[5] *Nathaniel*,[4] *Samuel*,[3] *Thomas*,[2] *Thomas*,[1]) of Princeton, Illinois, b. July 22, 1839; m. Nov. 6, 1865, at Fiskeleva, Ill., to Maria King.

CHILDREN.

Ida Wyatt, b. Feb. 7, 1867.
Minnie Belle, b. Sept. 22, 1868.
Samuel Jackson, b. Oct. 15, 1870.
William Sherman, b. Jan. 28, 1872.

Mr. Swift was a volunteer during the late civil war in the 93d Illinois Regiment.

---

## 36

**William Augustus**[7] **Swift**, (*Samuel,*[6] *Samuel,*[5] *Ebenezer,*[4] *Samuel,*[3] *Thomas,*[2] *Thomas,*[1]) b. in Roxbury Oct. 18, 1811; m. June 15, 1836, Anna Young, daughter of Abigail and Barnabas Atwood, of Brewster, Mass. She was b. Aug. 12, 1811; d. without issue January 3d, 1744. Mr. Swift married her sister, Mrs. Thankful Maker, April 10th, 1845. She was b. Sept. 11, 1815. Mr. Swift is a builder now residing in Roxbury.

CHILDREN.

Anna Augusta, b. June 1, 1846.
William, b. Oct. 31, 1849; book-keeper in the Maverick National Bank, Boston; m. Feb. 22, 1882, Addie W. Jacobs.

---

## 37

**Lewis**[7] **Swift**, (*Samuel,*[6] *Samuel,*[5] *Ebenezer,*[4] *Samuel,*[3] *Thomas,*[2] *Thomas,*[1]) a pianoforte maker residing at 255 Lybrand Street, Philadelphia; b. in Roxbury Jan. 16, 1815; m. Nov. 6, 1844, Maria A. Engelman, b. in Philadelphia Feb. 29, 1824.

CHILDREN.

Samuel,[8] b. Aug. 9, 1845; d. Aug. 7, 1858.
Andrew,[8] b. Aug. 4, 1848; d. May 6, 1850.
William,[8] b. May 29, 1852; m. Sept. 15, 1875, Fanny M. Umsted; have Lewis,[9] b. Feb. 13, 1879.

---

## 38

**Dr. Samuel**[7] **Swift**, (*Samuel,*[6] *Nathaniel,*[5] *Nathaniel,*[4] *Samuel,*[3] *Thomas,*[2] *Thomas,*[1]) b. Aug. 5, 1849; m. April 21, 1875, Lucy, dau. of Judge H. E. Davies of New York, by his wife Rebecca Waldo Tappan of Boston. Dr. Swift is a physician of Yonkers. He was graduated at the Yale Scientific School in 1868; also at the College of Physicians and Surgeons, medical department, Columbia College, New York, class of 1872. Was mayor of Yonkers, April 1882, to April 1884.

CHILDREN.

Martha, b. July 27, 1878.

NOTE.—Up to this point in the genealogy, the descendants of Lieut. Thomas[2] Swift, son of the first Thomas[1], have been followed out. The descendants of his brother Obadiah[2] will now be continued from page 4, and numbered consecutively after the posterity of Thomas[2].

---

### 3

**Obadiah,[2]** *(Thomas)* b. in Dorchester, July 16, 1638; d. Dec. 27, 1690; m. March 15, 1660, Rest, (b. ———, 1639) dau. of Maj. Gen. Humphrey Atherton. In a deed dated July 1, 1664, conveying one hundred and forty acres of land to Gyles and Edward Payson, he and Timothy Mather call themselves administrators of their father in-law, Maj. Gen. Humphrey Atherton. He was a blacksmith by trade, and in 1672 "Rece an hundred of Iron, for which he made axes and bows for Endian gratuetie by Capt. Foster's order." He was fence viewer in 1664, and several times afterwards; was constable in 1662, and supervisor in 1674. Savage gives him a second wife, Abigail, but I think he is in error, and that she was the wife of his son, Obadiah, Jr. Rest Swift and Obadiah Swift returned the inventory of Obadiah's estate March 24, 1691-2. A Rest Swift died Nov. 3, 1708, who was probably his widow.

#### CHILDREN.

REMEMBER, b. 5, 10 mo., 1661; d. 5, 12 mo., 1661.
REST, b. 13, 10 mo., 1662.
JAMES, b.
39.   **Obadiah**, b. 28, 11 mo., 1670.
HOPESTILL, b. March 11, 1674.
ELIZABETH, b. Sept. 7, 1675; d. Sept. 17, 1675.
ABIGAIL, b. Jan. 4, 1676; m. ——— Apply. June 12, 1734, James Apply of Norwich, Conn., in a deed, calls Sarah Swift, of Dorchester, spinster, his cousin or kinswoman, he being the youngest of the two sons, and only heir of Abigail Apply, of Preston County, New London, deceased, daughter of Obadiah Swift of Dorchester, blacksmith. He deeds to said Sarah all his rights in lands in Dorchester and Stoughton which belonged to their grandfather, Obadiah Swift, deceased, and great-grandfather, Maj. Humphrey Atherton.
ELIZABETH, b. Jan. 4, 1679; d. Nov. 2, 1683.

---

### 39

**Obadiah,[3]** *(Obadiah,[2] Thomas,[1])* b. in Dorchester, 28, 11 mo., 1670; d. Jan. 20, 1747; m. Abigail Blake, last day of December, 1695. She was admitted to full communion at the Dorchester church, Nov. 7, 1702-3, and d. March 19, 1737-8. He was admitted to the church in November, 1696. He was a blacksmith.

CHILDREN.

40.  James, b. Nov. 1, 1696.
     SUSANNA, b. July 14, 1701; m. Henry Newell of Boston, shipwright, Nov. 22, 1722.
     JANE, b. Dec. 9, 1703; m. James Young Dec. 7, 1727.
     PRISCILLA. b. Oct. 3, 1706; m. Henry Ledbetter March 30, 1732, eldest son of Increase Ledbetter.
     SARAH, b.                ; m. James Leeds June 23, 1737.

He was one of the grantees in 1737-8 of a right in the new township of Dorchester, Canada, incorporated in 1765 as Ashburnham, derived from the services of his brother James, who was killed while a member of Capt. Withington's company of Dorchester, in the expedition against Quebec, Canada, in 1690.

---

## 40

James,[4] *(Obadiah,[3] Obadiah,[2] Thomas,[1])* b. in Dorchester, Nov. 1, 1696; m. Silence, dau. of Sherebiah and Silence Butt, April 9, 1718.  He was a yeoman of Dorchester.

CHILDREN.

41.  James, b. June 21, 1719.
     SUSANNA, b. March 6, 1720-1; m. Joseph Whiston of Boston, Nov. 24, 1738.
     OBADIAH, b. Jan. 31, 1723-4.
     EZRA, b. Oct. 23, 1726; d. Feb. 9, 1726-7 (grave stone).
     SILENCE, b. Oct. 21, 1728; m. Desire Hawes, Oct. 6, 1748.
42.  Elijah, b. March 9, 1730-31.
     JOAB, b. March 29, 1733; d. May 16, 1745.
     SHEREBIAH, b. July 2, 1735.
     ABIGAIL, b. Oct. 29, 1738; m. John Purpoon, Oct. 31, 1759.
     EZRA, b. Nov. 15, 1740.

April 25, 1737, James Swift and wife Silence; Hopestill and Hannah Blake; Abigail, widow of John Woodward, husbandman; Mary Butt, spinster, all of Dorchester; Hannah, Silence, Abigail and Mary, being children of Silence Butt, deceased, late wife of Sherebiah Butt, also deceased; said Silence Butt was one of the grandchildren of Henry Merrifield, of Dorchester, deceased.  They sell land to Benj. Bird of Dorchester, gentleman, in Dorchester and Stoughton, which belonged to their great-grandfather, Henry Merrifield.

---

## 41

James,[5] *(James,[4] Obadiah,[3] Obadiah,[2] Thomas[1],)* b. June 21, 1719; m. Mary Mayer June 11, 1741.  He was admitted to the New North Church, Boston, Feb. 14, 1741-2.  He was a shipwright.

CHILDREN.

43.  **James,** bapt. July 10, 1743.
44.  **Henry,** bapt. June 22, 1746.
      WILLIAM, bapt. Nov. 20, 1748; probably d. young.
      WILLIAM, bapt. Aug. 12, 1750.
      MARY, bapt. Sept. 30, 1753; d. April 9, 1764 (grave stone).
      SILENCE, bapt. Nov. 30, 1755; probably same pub. to Paul Ingerfield, Dec. 29, 1773.
      SUSANNAH, bapt. Dec. 24, 1758; probably same pub. to Robert Jones, Aug. 28, 1785.
      ABIGAIL, bapt. June 7, 1761.

42

**Elijah,**[5] *(James,*[4] *Obadiah,*[3] *Obadiah,*[2] *Thomas,*[1]*)* b. in Dorchester, March 9, 1730-31; m. Edee Seward, pub. Nov. 24, 1757.   She owned the covenant July 2, 1758; d. Oct. 12, 1795, æ. 64 years.   He was a shipwright, living in Henchman's Lane in 1789. He died May 9, 1803, æ. 73 years.   Administration on his estate was granted to Jacob Rhodes of Boston, shipwright, May 30, 1803.   Ebenezer Rhodes, printer, and James White Burditt, bookseller, gave bond.   Their gravestones are still standing in Copp's Hill burying ground, with those of some of their children.   The inventory of the estate amounted to $2053, of which $2000 was house and land in Henchman's Lane.

CHILDREN.

45.  **Elijah,** bapt. Aug. 27, 1758.
      ELIZABETH, bapt. Aug. 31, 1760; m. July 14, 1779, Capt. James Hutchinson, by whom she had Hannah.  He died, and she next married David Oliver, a mast and spar maker on Oliver's Dock, now Battery March Street and Liberty Square.  They had four children: 1, David Oliver, m. Susan Parkman, both dead; 2, Sally Oliver, m. Wm. Parkman, who d. 1809; 3, Harriet, spinster; 4, Edee, spinster.
      SARAH, bapt. Dec. 12, 1762; m. May 23, 1779, Capt. Samuel Makin, of Philadelphia, who d. long since.  She lived to be 94 years old, a remarkable woman, in the full enjoyment of all her faculties.  Capt. Makin was sailing master of the Queen of France, a government vessel in the war of 1812.  He had his leg broken in the service off Boston harbor, was landed in Boston, and cared for till well.  In 1836 or '40 Mrs. Makin obtained a pension, with back pay, from the government.  They had five children, now dead, whose children are wealthy citizens of Philadelphia, filling honorable positions.
      WILLIAM, bapt. Sept. 16, 1764; d. April 1, 1765 (grave stone).
      MARY, bapt. May 31, 1767; d. young.
      MARY, bapt. Sept. 4, 1768, m. first, March 3, 1793, Francis Sloan; had one son, now dead; m. second, —— Avery, had one dau., dead; m. third, John French, had three children, now dead.   She d. about 1846, in Boston.
46.  **Benjamin,** bapt. Aug. 19, 1770.

43

**James,**[6] *(James,*[5] *James,*[4] *Obadiah,*[3] *Obadiah,*[2] *Thomas,*[1]*)* baptized in Boston,

July 10, 1743; m. Winifred Davis of Charlestown, Nov. 29, 1764. She owned the covenant at the New North Church, Oct. 20, 1765.

CHILDREN.

WILLIAM, b. Oct. 8, 1767.
SARAH BRIGDEN, b. Sept. 11, 1769.
ELIZABETH GILLAM, b. Feb. 28, 1771.
JAMES, bapt. Mar. 14, 1773.
WINNIFRED, bapt. Dec. 15, 1776.
JOHN, bapt Nov. 7, 1779.

Mrs. Swift, daughter of Barnabas and Winifred (Brigden) Davis, of Charlestown, was born June 17, 1743. For ancestry see Wyman, p. 281.

44

**Henry,**[6] (*James,*[5] *James,*[4] *Obadiah,*[3] *Obadiah,*[2] *Thomas,*[1]) b. in Boston, June 22, 1746; m. June 14, 1768, Mary Richardson. She owned the covenant at the New North Church Nov. 6, 1767. He was a shipwright, and lived in Hull Street.

CHILDREN.

47. **Henry,** } Twins, bapt. Nov. 6, 1768.
 MARY, }
SARAH, bapt. Dec. 16, 1770.
PEGGY RICHARDSON, bapt. March 21, 1773; m. Thomas Adan, Nov. 1, 1791, and had John R., Esq.; Catherine E. R. m. Henry S. Waldo, merchant.

Perhaps he is the same Henry Swift who died November, 1789, æ. 44.

45

**Elijah,**[6] (*Elijah,*[5] *James,*[4] *Obadiah,*[3] *Obadiah,*[2] *Thomas,*[1]) b. in Boston, Aug. 27, 1758; m. April 22, 1781, Nancy Brown. She owned the covenant at the New North Church Dec. 30, 1781. They lived in Lynn Street. He was a shipwright and died before Feb. 13, 1804, when Henry Swift, baker, of Boston, was chosen guardian of his children, viz: Elijah and Benjamin, more than 14; Elizabeth George, Thomas, Catherine, under 14. Children baptized at the New North Church.

CHILDREN.

NANCY LAPIS, bapt. Jan. 27, 1782; probably d. young.
ELIJAH, bapt. Nov. 30, 1783.
WILLIAM, bapt. Sept. 25, 1785; probably d. young.
BENJAMIN, bapt. Sept. 2, 1787.
ELIZABETH HUDSON, bapt. Oct. 25, 1789.

George W., bapt. Feb. 12, 1792; in 1813 a baker, and same year sells property in Lynn Street, that belonged to his father.

Katy Richardson, bapt. Nov. 9, 1794; schoolmistress in 1821, when she sells her right in her father's estate.

Thomas,        ; was of Hancock, N. H., Feb. 4, 1823, when he sells his right in his father's estate.

---

## 46

Benjamin,[6] (*Elijah,*[5] *James,*[4] *Obadiah,*[3] *Obadiah,*[2] *Thomas,*[1]) shipmaster of Boston; commanded the ship Hazard in 1805, owned by Thomas H. Perkins. With wife Hannah was living in Charlestown in 1827. He was b. in Boston, Aug. 19, 1770; m. Hannah Rhoades, Aug. 6, 1796; merchant in 1831. She was b. Nov. 17, 1777; dau. of Jacob Rhoades; d. Nov. 28, 1831. He d. March 15, 1858. He removed to Pepperill. Children baptized in Boston in 1811.

### CHILDREN.

Eliza Rhoades, b. April 14, 1797; d. Oct. 2, 1829; m. April 30, 1821, Abraham Andrews.

Benjamin, b. March 31, 1800; d. Oct. 2, 1801.

Hannah, b. Jan. 26, 1803; d. Aug. 27, 1852; m. Oct. 17, 1826, Thomas M. Thompson of Charlestown, d. June 27, 1836. Hardware dealer of Boston.

Caroline, b. April 26, 1806; d. June 8, 1806.

Caroline, b. March 29, 1807; m. Nov. 14, 1830, Abraham Andrews, of Charlestown. He d. March 7, 1869.

Benjamin, b. July 11, 1810; d. Aug. 10, 1883.

Sarah Stevens, b. Sept 9, 1812; d. Nov. 16, 1866.

Mary Burdett, b. June 21, 1814; m John Farrar, Oct. 20, 1841. He d. Feb. 6, 1849.

Susan, b. March 27, 1816.

Abby, b. Jan. 30, 1818; d. Aug. 24, 1862.

Ellen Louisa, b. Oct. 13, 1820.

William Henry, b. July 25, 1822.

Capt. Swift was an active and prominent member of the Harvard Church, Charlestown, and furnished the lower row of windows in the auditory with "India blinds" at his own charge. His pew was No. 33, and he owned pew No. 14.

---

## 47

Henry,[7] (*Henry,*[6] *James,*[5] *James,*[4] *Obadiah,*[3] *Obadiah,*[2] *Thomas,*[1]) b. in Boston, Sept. 7, 1768; m. Nov. 18, 1790, Sarah Brown, b. May 2, 1766; d. July 28, 1799. He next m. May 4, 1800, Agnes, dau. of William McKean, sister of Prof. Joseph McKean of Harvard College. She was b. Jan. 13, 1766.

He was engaged in the bakery business, corner of Charter and Unity Streets, at the north end. He d. April 3, 1808. The inventory of his estate amounted to upwards of ten thousand dollars, but it proved insolvent.  His widow possessed property in her own right, and bought in the estate, corner of Charter and Unity Streets, which is still owned by his descendants.

### CHILDREN.

HENRY, b. Jan 1, 1792; d. Oct. 11, 1793.
48.  Henry, b. July 5, 1793.
WILLIAM, b. Sept. 3, 1797; d. Oct 14, 1798.
SARAH, b. Feb. 7, 1801.
WILLIAM JOSEPH, b. Jan. 29, 1804; d. Oct 11, 1807.
49.  John James, b. April 16, 1805.
WILLIAM JOSEPH, b. Oct. 19, 1807; drowned March 16, 1824, on his passage from Göttenburg, as second mate of ship Galena.

---

## 48

Henry,[8] (*Henry,[7] Henry,[6] James,[5] James,[4] Obadiah,[3] Obadiah,[2] Thomas,[1]*) b. July 5, 1793, in Boston; d. March 13, 1862.  He removed early in life to Nantucket, where he was established in the hardware business.  He was one of the original members of the New England Guards.  He m. June 5, 1817, Mary, dau. of Zenas and Abial Coffin, one of the wealthiest merchants and largest ship-owners of that place.  Mrs. Swift was b. Feb. 15, 1799; d. July 2, 1827.  He m. second, Elizabeth dau. of Benjamin and Judith Glover.  She d. Feb. 22, 1872.

### CHILDREN.

SARAH BROWN, b. March 25, 1820; d. July 11, 1825.
MARY COFFIN, b. March 24, 1822; m. Dec. 5, 1838, Lewis W. Tappan, son of John Tappan, of Boston.  Their son, Lewis Wm., Jr., b. Feb. 16, 1840, m. Olivia Buckminster, dau. of the Rev. Samuel K. Lothrop of Boston.  She d. 1878, leaving one daughter, b. Sept. 1, 1876.
CHILD, b. and d. Sept. 1, 1824.
SARAH BROWN, b. Feb. 23, 1826; lives with Mrs. Tappan.
HENRY, b. Dec. 11, 1832; m. Emma Potter of Concord, N. H., and has Harry, Frank, Maud.  Residence, Durham Park, Marion Co., Kansas.
WILLIAM JOSEPH, b. May 27, 1835, in Nantucket; m. Oct. 20, 1858, Anna C. Stearns, dau. of Marshall Stearns of Brookline, Mass., and has Susan Stearns, b. Jan. 12, 1867; Henry Marshall, b. Feb. 16, 1872.
MARGARET, b. March 10, 1838; d. March 18, 1869; m. Oct.    1858, William Stearns, of Brookline, Mass.

---

## 49

John James,[8] (*Henry,[7] Henry,[6] James,[5] James,[4] Obadiah,[3] Obadiah,[2] Thomas,[1]*) b. April 16, 1805; m. Mary, dau. of Samuel Hitchborn of Boston.  Mr. Swift was a merchant of Boston.  He was a clerk in 1823 with Bradshaw & Parker, on Long

Wharf; from 1829 to 1840 was of the firm of Parker & Swift; then from 1840 to 1844, J. J. Swift & Co.   He was successful, and accumulated a fortune.

CHILDREN.

AGNES McKEAN.
ELIZA T.
MARY, b.                 ; m. J. H. Lombard.
AMY.
W. II.
FRANCES, b.              ; m. Edward Holbrook.
LILLIAN ALICE.

Mr. Swift early manifested a lively interest in the extension of the railway system of the country, and upon retiring from active mercantile pursuits in 1854, was elected a director in the Fitchburg Railroad Company, and on Feb. 8, 1855, was chosen its President, which office he held till August 17, 1864, when he voluntarily retired from the board, but continued to be consulted by the management upon all matters of importance during the remainder of his life.

Having now no active business to occupy his mind, and being an energetic and public-spirited man, he must needs turn his attention to some beneficent enterprise. In 1865 and 1866 he took a leading interest in the establishment of the National Steamship Company, in the interest of Boston, and for which company the Erie and Ontario were built, but from lack of adequate support, and from the unstable conditon of the times, the scheme was abandoned, and the pioneer vessels sold and taken from that port.

In 1869 he took an active interest in the Caughnawaga Ship Canal, a project for uniting the St. Lawrence River with Lake Champlain, thereby uniting the commerce of the great lakes with New England, and with others secured a charter from the Dominion Parliament, and kept it alive by subsequent legislation for several years, but from the lack of general interest in Boston, which was mainly relied upon for the means of construction, this great internal improvement was given up.

# APPENDIX.

## ENGLISH ANCESTRY.

Since that portion of the genealogy was printed which relates to Thomas Swift and his wife Elizabeth, the founders of the Dorchester family in America, some investigations have been made in England with a certain degree of success. Their marriage has been found on the parish register of the Church of the Holy Trinity, Dorchester, England; but nothing there indicates that Thomas Swift was born in Dorchester, or that the name existed there previous to the date of his marriage. It is possible that he was born in an adjoining parish or county, and that, being imbued with the religious fervor of the time, had gathered there with others, preparatory to embarking for the New World.

Savage says, that Thomas Swift of Dorchester was the son of Robert of Rotherham, Yorkshire. I am inclined to think that this statement is not based on any more substantial evidence than family tradition. Such a tradition has existed in the family. It is well-known that the handing down of christian names common to families was very strictly followed, but in no instance do we find the name of Robert, among the children or grandchildren of Thomas, and in fact, I think the name has never been borne by any of his descendants.

But Savage's conjectures as to the parentage of Elizabeth, wife of Thomas Swift, have proved to be right. He says, she was probably the daughter of Bernard Capen, who was from Dorchester, England. Thomas Swift, in his will, calls John Capen, who was son of Bernard, his brother-in-law, and John Capen in a letter to Mary Bass, printed in the History of Dorchester, Mass., p. 45, speaks of his sister Swift and sister Upsall.

With this clew, it seemed to me that an examination of the parish registers of Dorchester, England, might disclose something in relation to Thomas and Elizabeth Swift. Accordingly a search was made, and on the parish register of Holy

Trinity was found the entry, that "Thomas Swifte and Elizabeth Capen were married 18 Oct., 1630," and "20 Nov., 1631, Joane, daughter of Thomas Swifte, was baptized." These two are the only instances of the appearance of the name on the register.

The next child we find to them recorded is on the Dorchester records in America, when, June 17, 1635, the birth of their son Thomas appears. It is possible that other children were born, between these two periods, who died young.

The same parish register, records the marriage of Nicholas Upsale and Dorothie Capen, 17 Jan., 1629. Nicholas Upsale is well known, as one of those who was persecuted as a Quaker. An account of him has been printed in the *New England Historical and Genealogical Register*, vol. XXXIV., p. 21.

A William Rockwell and Susan Capen, were married 14 April, 1624, doubtless the same person, who with his wife Susanna, appear in Dorchester, Mass., in 1630, when he was made freeman. He was one of the first deacons of the Dorchester Church and the history of that town, p. 79, gives the name of his wife as Susanna Chapin, doubtless mistaken for Capen. Probably she was another daughter of Bernard Capen, for according to the family Bible, he had a child of this name.

There are four parish churches at Dorchester, England, all of about the same date, but none possess registers earlier than about 1663–4, except Holy Trinity, whose register commences as early as 1559. Its covers are gone, but the entries are perfectly legible. A great many Capens appear on it between 1559 and 1652, some of which are here appended. The name on the registers seems to have finally resolved itself into Galpin. For an account of the Capen family, see vol. II., p. 80, and vol. XX., p. 246, of the *New England Historical and Genealogical Register*.

# DORCHESTER.

*Extracts from the Church Registers of Holy Trinity,*

### COMMENCING 1559.

| 14 | April, | 1624. | Wm. Rockwell and Susan Capon, | Married |
|---|---|---|---|---|
| 4 | Aug., | 1629. | Robert Gifford and Hannah Capon, | " |
| 17 | Jan., | 1629. | Nicholas Upsale and Dorothie Capen, | " |
| 18 | Oct., | 1630. | Thomas Swifte and Elizabeth Capen, | " |

| 23 | Feb., | 1633. | Elizabeth, daughter of Thomas Capen, | Baptized |
|---|---|---|---|---|
| 29 | April, | 1632. | Ruth, daughter of Bernard Capen, | " |
| 12 | July, | 1635. | Barnard, son of Bernard Capen, | " |
| 5 | Nov., | 1637. | William, son of Bernard Capen, | " |
| 8 | Nov., | 1640. | Mary, daughter of Bernard Capen, | " |
| 1 | Jan., | 1642. | John, son of Bernard Capen, | " |

| 8 | Sept., | 1628. | James Capen, | Buried |
|---|---|---|---|---|
| 28 | May, | 1632. | Margaret, wife of Thomas Capen, | " |
| 3 | March, | 1633. | Elizabeth, daughter of Thomas Capen, | " |
| 6 | Jan., | 1642. | John, son of Barnard Gapen, | " |
| 22 | April, | 1643. | William, son of Thomas Gapen, | " |
| 26 | March, | 1646. | Ruth, daughter of Barnard Galpen, | " |
| 10 | April, | 1646. | Elizabeth, daughter of Barnard Galpen, | " |
| 20 | April, | 1646. | Barnard, son of Barnard Galpen, | " |
| 27 | April, | 1646. | Mary, daughter of Barnard Galpen, | " |
| 6 | May, | 1646. | William, son of Barnard Galpen, | " |

To 1652.